THE LOST GIRL IN PARIS

JINA BACARR

Boldwood

First published in Great Britain in 2021 by Boldwood Books Ltd.

This paperback edition first published in 2023.

1

A CIP catalogue record for this book is available from the British Library.

Paperback ISBN: 978-1-83751-991-0

Ebook ISBN: 978-1-83889-382-8

Kindle ISBN: 978-1-83889-383-5

Audio CD ISBN: 978-1-83889-379-8

Digital audio download ISBN: 978-1-83889-380-4

Large Print ISBN: 978-1-80280-851-3

Boldwood Books Ltd.

23 Bowerdean Street, London, SW6 3TN

www.boldwoodbooks.com

To the brave Jewish and Roma souls who died in the Holocaust and to all those who survived.
You will never be forgotten.

1

NEW YORK CITY, 2003

Emma

Perfume:
Mystère D'Amour
Tuscan mandarin, mimosa, ambrette.

I tilt my head as Madame de Cadieux, the grande dame of French perfume, makes her entrance into the Waldorf Grand Ballroom. Pausing under a crystal chandelier, her wisps of fiery color frame her beautiful face, as flawless as a queen's pearl. I bet she made a bargain with the devil to have skin that smooth at her age. God, she must be eighty.

I keep my distance, observing this woman in detail, making notes in my reporter's notebook. She's taller than I expected, slender like a single rose with that *je ne sais quoi* quality Frenchwomen have that makes you feel as plain as a church mouse. Uplifted chin, straight back, elegant hand gestures say she doesn't give a damn what anyone thinks. Angéline de Cadieux commands attention even when she doesn't speak. Her lips are Paris red, eyelids smudged with a smoky haze. No jewelry.

I move in closer and get a whiff of the scent trailing behind her, subtle but unforgettable: *rose absolute, pepper, lavender.*

Her signature perfume.

Naomie's Dream.

Created in Paris in 1941 for the House of Doujan.

I grin with the memory of a summer night when I was sixteen and my date gave me a bottle of *Naomie's Dream*. I was obsessed with impressing him with my uncanny 'nose talent', rattling off the ingredients. Then, in college, I peddled fragrances in department stores but regret not going to Paris to learn the art of perfume. What I wouldn't give to study under Madame de Cadieux. Watch the legend herself blending essences.

Wearing a white silk georgette gown with long Juliet sleeves, she never cracks a smile. As if she's posing for a Renoir painting. I'm dying to know what makes this woman tick. Grab an interview with her to see if she can take the lid off this strange addiction I have to unraveling the secrets of scent. By knowing what drives *her*, I can figure myself out.

And help my mom find her roots.

My grandmother was a political prisoner, a Polish woman who died in Dachau at the end of the war... *Madame* was a prisoner there from 1944–1945. Did they know each other? What a story that would make.

When Mom was diagnosed with lung cancer last year, she tried getting more info about her biological family on those 'find your relatives' websites but didn't get anywhere. I know she was disappointed, and I'd love to see her smile if I uncovered info about her mom. Which is why I've always had a soft spot for seeking out survivor stories like *madame*'s.

Her eyes move in every direction, scrutinizing the crowd with precision, her nose twitching as if the collective scent is distasteful to her. I can only imagine what she's smelled in her lifetime. Love, hate... war. There's an aura of danger about her, a life filled with close calls, hardship and excitement, according to what I dug up from the TV station's archives. She's known in the perfume business as a *premier nez* – nose. Hard to believe this woman survived two Nazi concentration camps –

Auschwitz and Dachau – and rose to the top of the fragrance business during a time when female creators were ignored if not outright banned.

My boss, Theodore Granger, hit the roof when I stomped into his office and told him I wanted to do a piece on the legendary perfume goddess when I heard she'd flown in from Paris to accept a tribute from an esteemed Long Island charity for her work with the 'forgotten children of war'. I snagged an invite to cover the event for WJJR-TV Channel 6 News by promising Granger I'd take any boring assignment he threw my way for the next six months if he let me follow my hunch.

I had to cover it.

Two years ago, when I became involved with a Holocaust project covering human interest stories with nursing home residents, I heard about a German woman who survived Dachau. I went to interview her, but the staff told me the thin, lonely woman wasn't 'all there'; that she refused to cut her long gray braid wrapped around her head, and referred to herself as Luise, though her name was Gretchen. When I asked her if she knew a Polish political prisoner who had a baby in the camp in 1944, she started twitching, hunching her shoulders, turning her head at awkward angles. No, she insisted, then she kept jabbering about a secret baby born to a *French* prisoner in a camp near Dachau. A woman from Paris, a fair-haired *mademoiselle* who made perfume.

I believe *madame* is that Frenchwoman.

Call it a reporter's hunch, but I've been a fan girl of Madame de Cadieux since I was fifteen and got my first whiff of *Angéline*, the perfume named after her. Spanish mimosa, tuberose, and musk. I've loved the art of perfume since I was a kid and doused myself in my grandmother's sweet jasmine scent until I reeked. She bought gallons of the stuff from the PX. I drove my mother crazy, collecting vials of sample perfume from the cosmetic counter and trying to figure out the floral and spicy ingredients. I moved on when I discovered I have a nose for news, but I still get excited when I sniff an exotic perfume that tickles my brain to unravel its fragrant mystery.

But it's nowhere as intriguing as *madame* herself.

What happened to her baby? I want to know. *Who was the father?* I'm not leaving the Waldorf until I make my pitch to Madame de Cadieux.

Satisfied she's captured every eye, *madame* glides across the room, her long white silk gown trailing after her like a cloud, a slender woman with eternal grace in every movement, traits I envy. Ever since I was a kid, I've jumped into situations headfirst and asked questions afterwards. That crazy streak makes me a damned good reporter.

I set my sights on *her*, my cameraman hot on my heels as I push in to grab a quick interview with the famous *parfumier* for the eleven o'clock news. She moves fast for a woman her age, skirting past admirers trying to grab her attention. I step it up a notch, zigzagging between chatty glammed up attendees, working up a sweat.

'Get a shot of Madame de Cadieux in the background, Hank,' I call out, 'when I do my tease.'

'You got it, babe.'

I roll my eyes. 'I'm not your babe. *Got it?*'

'Yes, ma'am.' He snickers, but does as I ask. Where did Granger get this guy? Wouldn't you know he'd stick me with a jerk to remind me to get the story in the can and get back to covering *real* news.

I shrug off his comment and go into my spiel, 'This is Emma Keane coming to you from the famed Waldorf Astoria...' hoping Hank is getting the shot while I do my intro, then I'm off to get the interview and show my boss I'm not crazy. I push through the crowd gawking at *madame* when—

Hold on, is that Brooke Hansen from the *NYC Sun*?

What's she doing here?

She did an interview with *madame* regarding synthetics in perfume about two years ago. What she was really after was a tell-all about the war.

When Madame de Cadieux refused to talk about her wartime experiences, Brooke splashed the story on the front page of the scandal sheet with the headline: 'Fake Perfumes by a Fake Nose'. She accused Madame de Cadieux of making up her story about being in Auschwitz because the Frenchwoman refused to show her a prisoner number tattooed on her arm. Brooke wrote she never had one.

She also hinted *madame* collaborated with the Germans during the war.

I never believed a word of it and the story got buried. I imagine the New York investors who bought into the House of Doujan had something to do with it. I'm surprised the blonde reporter had the audacity to show up here. She lost her job and didn't work until a third-rate tabloid specializing in sleaze picked her up.

I study her moves. She's cagey... trying to fit in with the giggling groupies crowding around the French *parfumier*. I get my speed on to nail the interview when—

Yikes... I almost drop my mike as a tall, gorgeous man in a gray silk suit rushes by me, cell phone to his ear, and heads toward the starstruck women.

I shake my head. I know the type. He can never have too many phone numbers in his black book. Or he's an out of work actor eager to get on Brooke's good side – if she has one – and get his picture in the papers. Whatever. He's not going to screw up my interview.

'Hey, you, Mr Gray Suit. I'm working here.'

He shoots around and I lock eyes with a dark, handsome stranger with pure Bond masculinity.

'You were addressing *me*?' he quips in a disapproving tone with a sexy Irish accent, his arms crossed, his distaste of anyone getting in his way so obvious I feel my cheeks tint.

'You nearly ran me over.'

'You ran into *me*,' he insists, though not a wrinkle mars his elegant silk suit. 'Then again, you *are* a member of the press,' he says, reading my badge, 'and tend to engage in rash, irresponsible behavior.'

'I don't know how they do things in Dublin,' I shoot back, well aware his overwhelming maleness would make any other woman swoon, 'but here in New York, a gentleman says *excuse me*.'

'Who says I'm a gentleman?' he fires back, brushing me off as if I'm the bad guy here.

Why do I always come up against the brooding playboys? Not that I have time for men on my insane schedule. On occasion, I take the plunge, but it never ends well.

When I look over my shoulder, the Irish stud is gone. And so are the groupies.

Just as well. This interview means more to me than giving Mr Gray Suit a piece of my mind. When I first pitched the story to Granger about Madame de Cadieux's secret baby, he said I needed conclusive proof for such a far-fetched tale. The rumor is the Frenchwoman abandoned her child and escaped the camp. Writing a story about her was near to impossible since I've never been to Paris and I don't run in the same social circles as the famous French *parfumier*. Instead, I wrote a nice piece for the local newspaper about the courageous woman in the nursing home who survived the war and escaped to America, giving her closure before she died.

I spin around. Damn, those few moments sparring with the Irish heartbreaker cost me. Madame de Cadieux is getting away from me... oh, no, not when I've come this far.

'According to what I read in old Paris newspapers from after the war,' I begin, pushing in front of the other reporters and putting on my best 'on camera smile', 'you're a woman with secrets, Madame de Cadieux.'

She ignores my question. 'You speak French, *mademoiselle*?'

'I speak Google translation.'

Laughter from the crowd of onlookers, eager to see where this is going. Madame de Cadieux is scowling. My quip didn't go over well. She marches off. I gather she's not turned on by camera interviews, so I send Hank off to grab a coffee and try another approach.

I appeal to her ego.

'You created an amazing perfume during the war, *madame*,' I begin, talking to her quietly away from the crowd, 'that hasn't been produced since.'

'What do you know of this perfume, *mademoiselle*?' she asks, impressed.

'You called it *Le Courage.*'

Her eyes blaze. 'You speak of a dark moment in the history of France, *mademoiselle.*'

'Which is why your perfume was such a sensation. You gave women hope when no one else could.'

Her eyelids flutter. Yes, she's listening... remembering.

Now for the kicker. I quote from a story about the perfume I memorized, each word having the effect I want.

'A perfume with heart, Madame de Cadieux, that evoked apple blossom mornings when the world was at peace. Spicy, exotic nights when the green fairy danced around lovers in intoxicating rhythms, wrapping the wearer up in a slow, burning passion...' I take a beat to imagine Paris at war and the madness of never knowing if this day was your last. 'And the fervent purity of the French lily, undaunted by the presence of the occupiers, a symbol of hope for every woman waiting for her man to return.'

'I'm impressed, *mademoiselle.*' She looks at me wide-eyed, as if I've brought her the Holy Grail of perfume. '*Bien.* I shall grant you the interview... the next time I'm in New York.'

She never comes to America.

'Your brand is hot right now, *madame*, what with the publicity you've gotten with this award.' I check out the crowded ballroom. I need to keep my conversation with her on the down low, so I maneuver her over to a dark corner. To my surprise, she doesn't protest. 'Do the interview with me about a topic you've never discussed – the war years at the House of Doujan and how you became the diva of scent.' I toss off the words in a heartbeat before I lose my courage. 'I guarantee you, sales will soar for your perfume line.'

She gives me 'that' look. 'I'll have my publicist send you a press kit. It has everything you need to write a story.'

'Really, *madame*?' I challenge her. 'How can I write about Madame de Cadieux if I don't know you? Get into your head?'

'And why would you want to do that?' she asks, curious.

'Because I wasn't there, *madame*. I didn't live with rationing; shiver every time I heard a knock on the door, wondering if it was the Gestapo; smell the stench of the dead in the camps; weep with the living... fear I'd be shot for stealing a crumb of bread. But you were. And by *getting into your head*,' I repeat with emphasis, 'I can create an amazing experience for my viewers as powerful as any memory.'

'I'm not the only woman who survived the camps, *mademoiselle*, there are hundreds, *thousands* of us. Why would anyone care about me?'

'Because you have to tell *your* story, *madame*, all of it. You lived through an amazing time in history and no one has any idea what part you played.'

'No one wants to read about an old woman's heartbreak and pain, *mademoiselle*,' she insists. 'Torture and degradation at the hands of the Nazis is not, how do you say, *cool*.'

'You're wrong. My readers are hungry for honest, heartfelt emotions, not silly laugh tracks.'

'*Pardon*?' She looks baffled.

'It's not important, what *is* important is that you stop hiding behind that mask of glamor you've created and let your hair down. You owe it to yourself... and them.' Why I said that, I don't know, but a residing sadness in her eyes alerts me I'm onto something.

'Who would believe me if I told the truth?'

'I would.'

She gives me a grim smile. 'You don't give up, do you?'

'No,' I say, not embarrassed.

She thinks for a moment, then nods. 'Agreed.'

I let out the breath I'd been holding. 'When can we start?'

She waves her gloved hand and I expect to see fairy dust sprinkle the air. 'Tomorrow.'

'Here at the hotel?' I ask, praying Granger will okay my expense account for the fancy meals it'll cost me to impress *madame*.

'No... we're going on an adventure.'

I blow out my breath. 'We can head out to City Island. I know a great fish place on the water—'

She raises her hand to stop me. 'You will join me on my return flight to Paris, *mademoiselle*. We leave at 8 a.m. sharp.'

I smile weakly. 'You're kidding, right?'

A big grin. 'On the Concorde, of course.'

I let out a low whistle. This is *so* not what I expected. A round trip to Paris on the supersonic jet costs more than three months' salary. She's got to be making a joke at my expense.

'I can't go to Paris, *madame*. I have a job here, deadlines to meet—'

I have several big stories in the hopper, but they pale compared to this opportunity to get to know this woman, find out if the rumor about a secret baby is true, as well as follow my perfume dream... but most of all, help my mom find out what *her* mom went through in the camps to bring her into the world.

Madame de Cadieux wrinkles her brow. 'Do you have a valid passport?'

'Yes.'

I got it for work, never used it.

'Then you can go.'

'I have to okay it with my boss,' I admit, hoping I can convince him to say *yes* and hang the consequences. I'll ask Granger for an advance on my salary. 'He's picky about sending his reporters on trips to the EU.'

Especially when he pooh-poohed my original story about Madame de Cadieux.

'You'll be my guest. I'll take care of your expenses.'

Did she say *her guest*? I look around, wondering if her generous offer is a publicity stunt, but the crowd has thinned out and no one's paying attention to us. They're too busy gulping down the 'last call' for free champagne. I'm ready to cough out a resounding 'yes' to her offer, but my skeptical-reporter antennae go up.

She takes my hesitation as a weakness. 'I see. You don't have the courage to walk in my shoes... see what horrors I've seen... suffer the pain of loss... unbearable loss, yet believing so hard in yourself you don't give up because you can't. You'll do anything to live another day.'

I grit my teeth. 'I'm more like you than you know, *madame*.'

She stares me down. Something in my eyes must have told her I have secrets of my own and it intrigues her.

She asks, 'Do you wish the interview or not?'

'Yes, *yes*, I want the interview.'

Who cares if I lose my job if I can't make my deadlines? The clock is ticking. I'll never get this chance again.

'*Bon*. What is your name, *mademoiselle*?'

'Emma. Emma Keane.'

'Now we'll see what you're made of, *mademoiselle*.' She looks me up and down and her nose twitches. 'Though I have little faith in what we'll find.'

* * *

Angéline

I blow out a breath and bobs of false hair flutter around my face as I stare into the oval mirror. I couldn't wait to get back to my hotel room, kick off my shoes. Damn hair extensions are pulling at my scalp, itching... how does anyone put up with these things? My assistant, Henri-Justin, insisted glamor impresses the American media so Marie spent hours making me up (since when did my lips look so thin when she applied red lipstick?). Frustrated, I wipe it off. I've been out of touch since I found myself alone. For years, I've lived an isolated existence, presenting a mystique worthy of the perfumes I create, but it's become both a suit of armor and a way of life.

And I'm *not* about to change.

After tonight it's back to my Paris château, my garden, books. My perfumes. I can hardly wait. My feet are killing me. Red and swollen after being stuffed into a pair of white satin heels, but I didn't let the pain slow me down, *anything* to keep up the pretense of a successful businesswoman with the energy of a woman half her age.

Hard to remember I once outran the Gestapo.

And now I've foolishly agreed to do an interview about that time in my life. I seethe with anger, reminding myself why I never speak about those days. Why bring it up now? I have no one left, no family. Rather than feel brave I survived, I suffer a thorny irritation because so many others didn't. How I cheated death using my wits.

I trust no one.

You can't help it when you've walked through hell in your bare feet. I felt like an imposter earlier, prancing through the famous hotel like a film star when I'm anything but that. I'm a brazen girl of Roma blood who dared to dream in a world that put us down then tried to destroy us. I never backed down from adversity – I was bred on it. I was young and filled with fire and I built a perfume empire. It's that success that brought me here to New York to pay tribute to the forgotten children from all wars and add the Doujan name to this important cause.

My way of paying tribute to those I lost during the war. No one knows more about that loss than I do.

I sit up straighter, but the woman staring back at me in the vanity mirror is so far removed from the headstrong girl I was during the war, a girl who fought the Nazis and created *Le Courage*.

Guess what, you damn Boches, I'm still here.

And *merde*, I won't apologize for who I am.

Why does everyone have such a fascination with that time in my life? I turned down numerous requests tonight for interviews from reporters digging for dirt.

Until that pushy American reporter blindsided me.

What was I thinking when I agreed to give Emma Keane an interview? She can't be more than twenty-something, maybe thirty. Streaked blonde hair and such fair skin, but it's her eyes that drew me to her. A strange mix of blue and hazel.

Like Maman's.

A lovely softness revisits me when I think of my mother, but I'm afraid to embrace it. I chalk it up to the musings of an old woman indulging in memories I keep hidden in my heart and imbibing in too much champagne.

For thirty years I couldn't talk about it, even with those close to me.

I shudder. A feeling of resolve not to let Mademoiselle Keane get too nosy during our interview settles in me, reminding me why I take reporters in stride, never getting personal with them after my encounter with that newspaper woman... Brooke Hansen. My head pounds thinking about her. When that nasty reporter conned me into giving her an interview, I expected sympathy, compassion, but her bizarre curiosity to see the prisoner tattoo on my left forearm struck a different chord in me. That I was a freak in a sideshow and she wanted to gawk at me. It made me feel cheap, used, so I pretended not to understand when she asked me to show her the series of numbers.

I never shall. That would be exposing my soul. *And* my past.

The number tattooed on my left arm begins with a Z for *Zigeuner*.

Gypsy.

I never forgot her crushing questions about my time in the camps.

I had déjà vu when I thought I saw her in the crowd earlier, but I must have been mistaken. I jumped quickly to speak to the closest reporter at hand to avert her, but I ended up in deeper trouble.

Mademoiselle Keane hit me way down in the gut by bringing up *Le Courage* perfume, stinging my memory with the words I wrote when we launched the perfume in a manner never done before.

Weren't you that young and brash when you were climbing up the ladder?

Does she remind you of yourself?

Ah, mais oui, she does. Tall, slim figure with that funny tilt of the head, long fingers like my own, even that quirky lopsided smile. It's been a long time since I visited those early days when my soul burned with romance and passion for France... when I wanted to help Parisians keep their heads up and be proud to be Frenchwomen no matter what the Germans did to us. We must never forget.

So, make sure they don't. Tell your story to the girl.

No, I can't. I'm too old to go through the pain, the heartache of the war years. I'll call the TV station, tell her I've changed my mind—

Then what? You sit in that old château feeling sorry for yourself?

She's a reporter. I can't trust her.

Better her than that Hansen woman.

Alors, what to do? I thought about writing a memoir and focusing on the war years... put everything down, from the joy of loving a good, strong man to the ugly, sadistic moments I experienced at the hands of the occupiers during the war that keep me up at nights.

I couldn't face writing it alone.

Do I dare take a chance on this girl?

Do I have a choice? I can either spend the rest of my life wishing I'd taken the plunge and opened up old wounds... or do it.

Deep in my heart, I've always believed *someday* I will find the baby daughter taken from me before it's too late. A whimsical thought, but one I cling to. It's my secret. Everyone, even the man I loved for nearly fifty years, accepted my story that the child died in Dachau. I never found any trace of her, though I secretly tried. Perhaps by writing down the truth about my life with this inquisitive reporter, someone will see it and give me the answers I seek.

Feeling better about my impulsive decision, I call Henri-Justin and give him instructions that Mademoiselle Emma Keane will accompany us back to Paris. I hear him chuckle. He thinks I've lost my mind, but something about this girl pricks at my heart, reminding me I have unfinished business with my past.

Years ago, I tucked that past away in a glass box I've yet to shatter by speaking about it.

Now I shall.

Until then, I've learned to embrace who I am, a woman of an age when it's more about the illusion you create with makeup and hair than the reality of a life well lived. Beginning tomorrow, I shall put aside the redheaded *madame* known as Angéline de Cadieux and reconcile with the girl I was back then.

A girl with long fair hair and a fiery temper.
A Roma girl named Tiena.
I hope I don't regret it.

2

CHAMBOISE-SUR-MARLY, FRANCE, AUGUST 1940

Tiena

Perfume:
Un Bel Jour
Sweet rose, lilac, citrus, woodsy moss

A strange man is following us. Maman and me. His smell *and* his attire tell me he's not French. Black trench coat with a tight leather belt. Hat pulled down over his clean-shaven face. A pungent, bleach-like odor and strong tobacco scent drift to my nostrils and get stronger the closer he gets to us.

He gives me the chills.

I've heard stories about such men around the blazing campfire at night, my stepfather Zegul spewing jargon in both French and Romani about these hated creatures who stop our people and ask for their papers. Anthropometric booklets we're forced to carry on our persons with pages and pages of physical characteristics and visas stamped with blue ink intended to keep tabs on us.

We are what they call 'gypsies'.

Zigeuner.

When these men snap their fingers, someone disappears. That's what frightens me. I pray that's not his agenda on this hot, unbearable summer day. A day when the heat seems to make everything smell, even the nun-gray cobblestones digging into the thin soles of my riding boots. I rustle my multi-layered skirts and the scent of jasmine and rose tempts my mood to brighten, but life isn't the same since the Boches raped the land my clan has called home for hundreds of years.

La belle France.

We are nomads, travelers from the *Litaro* clan, and find ourselves the target of the Nazi bastards who ravaged the country. I shall never forget the long line of people, young and old, clamoring along the road leading south from Paris as they fled the city on foot pushing handcarts piled high with their belongings, in motorcars and riding bicycles, while we hitched up our wagons and horses and stayed behind to fight. We love France even if we're banned from moving about at will and setting up camp, forcing us into hiding. We fight the Germans even if the French police chase us, their white gloves soiled with defeat like wounded cats with bloodied paws, blaming us for the occupiers.

Us? We're a small caravan... five, six wagons... four, five families depending on the season... though there are those who proclaim we don't belong anywhere.

They raise their fists and call us gypsies.

I toss my waist-long hair over my shoulder and refuse to allow their insults to bother me. My small clan is a proud people of musicians and horse traders. Maman taught me that we are descended from the Romani people who worked on the restoration of châteaux and manor houses and the estate of a French king – a scandal back then. How my ancestors broke the bloodline and were cast into exile because we found passion among the royals. We're often shunned by other clans with pure gypsy blood like the Sinti when they see my fair hair and Maman's blue eyes. She says we must be proud, that we have a special gift of healing and a compassionate heart and that's the most important medicine of all.

Something I learned over a pot of rose petals. I was eight, round-cheeked, hair the color of white gardenia... and so curious. Sniffing the petals floating in the warm water, I was mesmerized by the bubbling pink, red, and orange flowers emitting the most delicious smells.

Sweet rose, fruity, even clove.

Maman said she never knew anyone who could smell scents like I do except *her* mother. Made me so proud, I spent three days scooping up rose petals on the château grounds.

'Let them simmer in the pot, Tiena,' Maman told me, 'to give your curious nose the treat you seek, my child.'

Standing on tiptoe, I stirred the petals in the pot. I was a big girl now... Papa put me on his black horse and let me hold the bridle even if my feet didn't reach the stirrups.

Maman told Papa I wasn't old enough to ride by myself. He laughed and said I could do anything I put my mind to because I was Roma.

I lifted the pot filled with petals and steamy, warm water off the stove in our *vardo*, wagon, with both hands. Oh, it was heavy... oops, my boot slid off the stool.

'Maman, come quickly, *vite*!' I called out, wobbling back and forth.

I couldn't hold onto the pot handle—

Crash!

Down it went... rose petals and water splashing everywhere. On me. On Maman's clean floor.

'Tiena!'

Maman came rushing into the wagon, her blue eyes dark as midnight. She scooped me up in her arms, checking my face, hands. 'My baby... are you hurt?'

I shook my head. 'My rose water, Maman... it's gone!'

I stared at the petals scattered on the stove, the floor. All glistening wet and soggy.

'We shall gather more petals, Tiena, I promise.' Then she hugged me and laughed.

I've never forgotten that day... the love I found wrapped up in my mother's arms... tears running down her cheeks that I wasn't hurt. She didn't yell at me, but showed compassion for my dream. Of course, she made me clean up the mess. Our wagon smelled of lovely roses for days.

Now those memories are threatened.

I cast a wary eye over my shoulder.

He's still there.

Writing on what appears to be a newspaper.

I have a bad feeling. I'm not afraid of the curious lads who peek down my low-cut white blouse, then try to squeeze my waist laced in tight with a black velvet bodice when I dance in the street for *francs* while Maman sings and plays the fiddle. I *know* what's on their minds, but this man following us sends shivers through me. He's up to no good.

What does he want from us?

Two Roma women going about our business on a hot day in this country village with its cobbled streets and sloping rooftops. Maman with her black braids streaked with silver-gray hanging down her back, a red and gold scarf tied around her head, her golden earrings and bracelet made from old bronze coins jangling, fingers adorned with ancient rings, including her favorite. A garnet and sapphire crest ring Papa gave her.

And me with my long fair hair catching the sunlight like a lost halo.

My hair is wild and curly and always getting in my eyes, so I pull it back and fasten it with a silver-plated bodkin passed down from my grandmother to my mother to me. An ornamental hairpin Maman says once belonged to a 'French queen', then winks. She loves to tease me about us being descended from aristocrats, but I happen to know my *grand-mère* traded two chickens for it from a peddler and who knows where *he* got it. I'm never without it since I don't wear a scarf. Only married women do.

Alors, I usually find such curious looks amusing and use them to my advantage to engage the town folk, dabbing scent on my cotton handkerchief and waving it at them, enticing them to try a dab on their wrists... and then buy a tiny bottle of perfume from me.

Not this man.

I sense danger, its smell as real to me as the pungent odor of dead flowers. Maman also knows something's up. She turns her head left then right, her blue eyes flashing with a hint of hazel darkening in their depths.

She shakes the bracelet on her wrist as she's wont to do when she's nervous. A habit. She believes the clinking sound of the funny old bronze coins repels negative energy.

Did a handsome gentleman catch my eye? her eyes ask. No. My heart is not for sale, nor my body. I have no time for romance. I have ambitions. Big ambitions to study the art of perfume in Paris, but I'd never leave Maman. I'd rather die than do that.

Though the question of me marrying comes up often these days. Maman married the wild, impetuous 'traveler' from England she loved at fifteen, a tall, fair-haired ex-soldier who stole her heart with his stories about how the Great War took his soul and how my *maman* gave it back to him. By the time she was eighteen, she'd lost two babies and was pregnant with me.

And here I am not even close to finding love. Unlike my friend Hannah. Since she kissed the eldest son of the Simms family, she acts like she's special. I have better things to do than tie myself down with a boy I don't love because I get queasy feelings in the pit of my stomach.

Feelings Maman told me are special when I meet the right man. 'How will I know?' I ask her. She smiles and jangles her bracelet. 'You'll know when your heart races like you're dancing on a cloud. And when it happens,' she's fond of adding, '*la vie est bon...* life is good, *n'est-ce pas?*'

Still, the elders lecture me that it's bad luck for me not to be joined with a man and bless the tribe with a child soon after. I want to use this nose God gave me and make lovely perfumes and give hope to the women I see trudging through life with soiled aprons and mussed-up hair with babies on their hips and coal smudges on their cheeks. Give them hope they *are* pretty and should know their worth to their families... like Maman. She loves the fragrance I created for her with rose, hyacinth, lavender... ginger and... it needs more notes, spices I don't have yet, but I will. I have plenty of time.

I'm only seventeen... a virgin by choice. I shan't discuss it again.

Though it's not uncommon for Roma menfolk from other tribes to kidnap a girl while she's sleeping, which is why Maman showed me the hidden door behind the storage box at the rear of our wagon, a door *she* used to sneak out to meet up with my papa before they were married.

I take no chances. I carry a sharp-pointed, Celtic pocket-knife Papa gave me tucked inside a sheath and fastened onto my brassiere next to my strap, making it easy for me to grab it with my other hand should I need to defend myself. Maman says not to worry, that my nose tells me when there's trouble about, that I have a rare gift.

I can detect *hundreds* of smells.

Blend essences into lovely, aromatic perfumes. I have no formal training which, I admit, limits me in defining the technical aspect of what I do. Maman says I make up for that in my raw ability to create floral and fruit scents purely by smell.

Somehow, some day, I *will* become a *parfumier*.

I attempt to put aside my fears of the man following us and breathe in the uniqueness of this small village in the Loire Valley, a place where pigeons coo of a glorious past not forgotten, their white and gray chests puffed out and proud in spite of the ugly green uniforms that kick them aside when they land to grab the spare crumbs. A place where we've come to sell our oils, our essences, and perfumes I created to the shopkeepers, making *les madames* swoon and take orders for bottles of the lovely scents. Since Papa died three years ago, Maman and I support ourselves with our healing oils, like rose petal oil to rub on the soles of your feet to help a bad headache.

Unlike my lazy stepfather, who plays cards when he's not trading horseflesh. From his morning cognac to his evening brandy, his blood-shot black eyes lust after my *maman*. She's only too happy to see him fall into his cot drunk, pulling her shawl tight around her bosom, covering the bruises on her arms, her mind at peace for the night.

When I ask her why she puts up with him, she insists she had to follow Litaro tradition and marry him after my father was killed.

'A woman alone with a child is not the way of our people, Tiena,' she tells me every time I ask, avoiding my eyes.

I know my stepfather beats her, but she refuses to give him up. *We'd do fine without him*, I insist, *make enough money with my perfumes*. I implore Maman to run away from this terrible life with a man as cruel as any Boche, but she won't listen.

I pick up my pace, in fear of the heavy footsteps gaining on us, the man making no attempt to silence his pursuit. Every nerve in my feet burns as my boots hit the cobblestones hard. His overt display of purpose and arrogance leaves no doubt the man is Gestapo. He must have followed us into the village while I, foolish girl that I am, had my mind on selling perfume and not taking care of Maman.

He's everywhere.

Behind us, smoking. Then watching us from a doorway... writing again on his newspaper, then skirting around the corner and waiting for us on the other side. Maman notices him, too, her lovely blue eyes telling me not to stop, that we must not show fear.

Maman and I tramp along the road arm in arm, looking over my shoulder as we sing a ditty she taught me. The summer sun burns my cheeks scarlet, my white blouse sticking to my skin.

We arrived at the flower market around noon in the medieval town after we quartered our horses – Zeus, my spirited black stallion and Maman's bay mare, Faithful Mary – at a fancy stable on the manor house grounds down the road. Maman has known Monsieur du Monde, the stable groom, for years after she saved his wife with her healing skills and herbs when the woman fell ill. He's a good friend to my people, trading and buying horses with us, and he's never without a smile for her, though this time he told us not to dally in the village... it's too dangerous with 'them Nazis' about, which is why I convinced Maman to take the shortcut to the stable, a tunnel leading under the outhouses to the road and into the woods.

I pray our horses are rested and ready to ride.

My clan comes through here every few months, camping on the outskirts of the estate while Maman and I go into the village alone. Everyone else is too scared they'll be blamed for something they didn't do.

I turn slightly. The Gestapo man is gaining on us, pulling down his hat and huffing and puffing like he's tired of the game. *Run* is my immediate instinct, but it's not easy for Maman, what with her back acting up from bending over last night fixing vials of essence to sell today.

Now it's too late.

The German is at my side and in a remarkably smooth but inquisitive tone he says, 'You're gypsies, *mademoiselle*?'

The secret policeman looks me up and down with curiosity. I smile in spite of myself. No matter how many times the Boches go through this drill of questioning me, it amuses me how they pretend not to know the answers before I give them.

'We are Roma, *monsieur*,' I answer, head high. 'I am Tiena Cordova and this is my mother, Naomie.' I grab Maman's hand and squeeze it. I make no move to remove my identity booklet nestled in my bodice along with my Celtic pocket-knife fastened to my brassiere strap. I pray my answer is enough for him.

I'm wrong, so terribly wrong.

'Come with me, *mademoiselle*. Both of you,' he says with the arrogance of a man who can't imagine anyone rebuking his order.

'We've done nothing, *monsieur*,' I protest. 'We're perfume traders.' He grabs my left arm and, for a beat, he stares at the jagged scar on my forearm. Red, the flesh tender. I wince but I refuse to show weakness in front of him. I'm not ashamed to admit I fought back when my stepfather cut me with a broken bottle a fortnight ago when I tried to save Maman from his drunken rage. 'Where are you taking us?'

'You'll find out.' His face tightens, his eyes unnaturally dark and sinister. 'Now shut up or I'll close that pretty mouth of yours with my fist.'

He grabs us by the hair, first me then Maman, and drags us back to the main square where a boxy black motorcar is parked, then pushes us into the backseat. Maman and I hold onto each other, too shocked to speak. Escape is impossible as he settles in on the passenger side. The driver guns the engine and takes off while the Gestapo man pulls out his newspaper and hums a jaunty tune. I see him smile then scribble letters on a crossword puzzle, his upbeat humming at finding the right word ringing in my ears louder than a death knell.

I am truly afraid of him.

* * *

'Zeus is not for sale, *monsieur.*'

I stand my ground against the German officer sneering at me and inspecting me like I'm a slave on the auction block. A slightly boned man filling out his Nazi uniform with more pomp than girth, his padded square shoulders make him look like an upside-down triangle. Pepper-pricked blond hair, reddened cheeks from the sun with a dribble of sweat when he removes his cap and wipes his face with the back of his gloved hand. He takes his time with his 'inspection', grumbling in German to the Gestapo man when he dumped us off outside the stable and then sped off, most likely to harass someone else who doesn't fit his Aryan profile.

Forget him. A bigger problem presents itself.

The Nazi major was waiting for us, his right foot leaning on the big fender of his Mercedes touring car, tapping his baton in his gloved hand. A grim smile in my direction, then he forced us inside the stable, pacing up and down the straw-covered floor. Mumbling about how Herr Reichsmarschall Göring will be pleased with his latest appropriation of French culture. I know his type. He fills himself with importance by associating with men in power. Like my stepfather, Zegul. A big man known to cavort with the local authorities wherever we set up camp, bribing them with a bottle of cognac and a spiel to let us be. This man uses the swastika band on his arm to evoke fear. He doesn't impress me. A sharp beam of sunlight from the overhead window high in the hayloft casts a theatrical spotlight on his sorry figure. Hot, sticky air permeates the stable, the smell of horseflesh overpowering. He kicks a pitchfork out of his way with his hobnail boot, then gags.

His words come fast, bleak and unsettling.

'I intend to purchase your horses.' The officer points to Zeus, snorting and tossing his head in his stall. 'The black stallion to race...' He waves his hand about, barely acknowledging Faithful Mary munching on oats. 'And the sagging bay mare to the horsemeat factory.'

'No... you can't... *please*,' Maman gasps, her hand going to her throat. An unforgiveable act in her eyes. She helped birth the gentle horse... the mare is a holy sign of life to this woman who buried two babies before I was born and can no longer conceive.

I, on the other hand, answer back in an inexplicable show of courage more foolish than wise since I've not yet felt the sting of the Boche bee in my bonnet.

'Our horses aren't for sale, *monsieur*. We board them here while we go about our errands in the village.'

'While you go about pickpocketing,' he sneers.

'You insult me, *monsieur*.' I regard him with contempt and show it by jutting out my chin. 'We're God-fearing folk, not thieves.'

'You *are* gypsies?'

'Yes...'

He sneers. 'It's against the law, *mademoiselle*, for gypsies to own horses.'

I raise my chest. 'I know of no such law, *monsieur*.'

'You and your kind should make merry while you can. The Führer has plans. Soon we will rid this country of filth like your gypsy friends. Jews, too.' He spits on the floor to emphasize his threat.

'I don't believe you.'

'No?' His gaze wanders over my body with that superior look in his eyes that turns my stomach. 'If you cooperate, *mademoiselle*, I can arrange to spare you such unpleasantry.'

'I'd rather die—' I take a step forward. Brave words, believing that good triumphs over Nazi evil.

'Please, *monsieur*,' Maman interrupts, keeping calm, knowing better than to question the power of a German officer. 'I beg you to allow us to keep Faithful Mary so we can return to camp.'

'No, Maman, we can't let him take Zeus or we've lost everything.' I've learned men like him talk big, but show them you're not a helpless female and you stand a better chance. I turn to the Nazi. 'I repeat, *monsieur*, my horse is *not* for sale. We'll be on our way.'

I turn, but the major grabs me by the arm, squeezing so tight it hurts. I wince.

'Too bad *mademoiselle* is so stubborn.' He grins and his nose twitches as my scent overpowers the awful stink in here. 'I haven't seen a better piece of horseflesh since I arrived from Berlin.' He breathes in my ear and I shiver. The duality of his words is not lost on me. Or Maman. She jangles her bracelets, bites her lip. She'd claw his eyes out if reason didn't keep her from making the same mistake I did.

'Let me go, *monsieur*,' I say, 'you're hurting me.'

'Don't be so hasty, *mademoiselle*, I will pay you for the stallion.'

'I don't want your money.'

He cocks a brow. 'It's not money I'm offering you, but the honor of serving an officer of the Reich.' He lets me go and clicks his heels. 'Major Ernst von Risinger at your service.'

'Of course, how stupid of me,' I rattle on, hands on my hips. 'The Reich doesn't bargain with anyone, it *takes* what it wants no matter who gets hurt.'

'I prefer to call it a cultural exchange.' He circles me, tapping his baton on his thigh. 'Monsieur du Monde didn't mention the owner of the stallion was such a spirited filly, or I would have sent Herr Geller after you sooner.'

'You wouldn't *dare* touch my daughter.' Maman rushes to my defense. She can't hold back her rising emotions any longer. 'She's pure and too good for the likes of you.'

'She's a gypsy *and* a virgin, *madame*?' He leans closer and I want to gag. He smells like warm beer and the sweat of a whore. 'I didn't believe such a mythical creature existed.'

I choke back a nasty retort, but the moment costs me. He advances toward me, licking his lips. 'It's my duty to examine you to safeguard the morals of the French people.'

'*Don't touch me*, you dirty Nazi swine.' I pull my knife from inside my white blouse and go after the German with a broad swipe at his face. The bastard is wily like a fox. He ducks and knocks the knife out of my hand, but not before I draw blood when I strike his high cheekbone with the sharp blade. He curses at me in German, the oozing red streak dribbling down to his clean-shaven chin. He wipes it off with the back of his hand and stares at his blood-soiled glove as if he can't believe he'd actually bleed, the look in his eye as savage as a wild boar incapable of stopping once it charges its victim.

I've gone too far.

'You shall pay for your insolence, *mademoiselle*.' He pulls his Luger from his holster and points it straight at my heart, his hand steady, his aim sure. 'With your life. First, I shall make you beg. On your knees.'

'No.'

I can't let him shoot me.

I never imagined I'd face a Nazi aiming a gun at me, but instinct tells me his feeling of superiority comes from wearing that Nazi uniform, not his inner core. He's an errand boy for some German bigwig out to prove himself. If I show weakness, he won't hesitate to pull the trigger. He wants to play games, show his power over me. Then brag about how he took me down.

Then let's play.

I cross my arms over my chest, chin up.

'I'll give you one more chance, *mademoiselle*.' He cocks the hammer.

'I won't bow to you or any Nazi.'

He's breathing hard, getting excited. *Bon*. If I can get him to let his lust override his ego, I can take him down with a swift kick to his groin. I do it with my stepfather when he sneaks up on me and grabs my breast then plants a wet kiss on my lips.

I didn't count on Maman.

'Please, *monsieur*, have mercy. She's an innocent child,' Maman yells, clasping her hands together and praying.

'Go, Maman, run!'

'*No*, Tiena, let me help the major.' She rips off her scarf and tries to tend to his wound, but he kicks her with his black boot. She stumbles, clutching her stomach.

'How *dare* you hurt my *maman*!'

Anger this man dared to touch my mother overrides my fear. I've got to grab something, *anything* to throw at him. A lost iron horseshoe. Pitchfork. Even the damn straw.

'Time is up, *mademoiselle*.'

He takes aim at me. Maman panics. '*No*, not my Tiena... you wretched bastard!'

Her sharp words startle him and he turns, stares at her, and it happens so fast I can't grasp how the next few seconds set into motion the most horrible thing imaginable in my world.

Yelling at the top of his lungs in German, the major fires his weapon—

But not before Maman throws herself in front of the Nazi.

And takes the bullet meant for me.

3

CONCORDE, 2003

Emma

Perfume:
Naomie's Dream
Rose absolute, pepper, lavender

I sit in my seat in the back of the jet, mouth open, heart pumping. Gasping for air, waiting for Madame de Cadieux to tell me what happened after the Nazi major shot her mom.

Instead, she stares straight ahead. Silent.

I've read her bio and her Roma roots were never mentioned. Now I know why.

It's too painful for her.

I can't stand it. I'm hanging by a thread, *dying* to hear what comes next without giving away she's the key to me understanding my talent with scent and learning more about my Polish grandmother. The suspense is killing me. This is uncharted territory for me, with a woman with an obsession for privacy and a deeper perspective on life than I could ever hope of having, a clash of generations that challenges my skills to find common ground with her.

Finally, she says in a calm voice, 'I shall continue my story after we've enjoyed a special blend of *café, mademoiselle.*' She leans back in the plush seat.

'Please, *madame*,' I urge her, the shock of what she told me rattling my bones and making me shake, my entire body in panic mode. 'You can't leave me hanging like you're going to a commercial break.'

She smiles. 'I find your American sense of humor refreshing, *mademoiselle*, but first, *du café, then* you shall have your answer.'

She rings for the flight attendant, who shows up pronto with a silver pot of hot, steaming coffee and the most delicate white china cups with the airline's logo engraved in gold leaf. I swear *madame* breathes in the alluring coffee smell as if to assuage her pain. I study her stiff expression, her pursed lips, her eyes closed. I'm sitting next to her, close enough to feel the shift in her mood, as if willing herself not to cry, something I get the feeling she sees as a weakness.

I know a forced grin when I see one. Her red lips are cracked like dried clay and a horribly sad darkness resides in her eyes where flecks of green and brown dazzled earlier. She's in pain, suffering through that day. Sure, she talks big, but she was a teenager. Not even kissed yet. At seventeen, I was stylin' through cheerleading camp and writing snarky op-eds for my high school newspaper *and* dating the good-looking captain of the swim team with the body of a bronze god (we girls never forget our first kiss).

I get a delicious whiff of the coffee, my brain detecting each ingredient... cinnamon, mint and anise... *hmm*... I also smell a dark roasted bean from the island of Bali.

I keep mum. Why give away my secret?

Meanwhile, I can't stand the tension sitting between us like cold tea, so I ramble on about stories I've covered to break the ice. Film stars behaving badly... politicians behaving worse. 'So I'm interviewing this A-list actor putting the moves on me at an Italian restaurant when his ex-girlfriend shows up and dumps a bowl of spaghetti on his head.'

'*Mais non!*' She cracks a genuine smile, finally.

'*Mais* yes,' I shoot back. 'With meatballs.'

She laughs as I feed her more gossip about egotistical celebs to take her mind off her sadness. She likes to laugh. She strikes me as a woman who doesn't do much of it these days and that makes me want to keep telling her funny stories.

'So then I snagged this big interview with a rock star,' I continue with enthusiasm, 'who'd only meet me in a fast food place.'

She gives me that 'look'. '*Mademoiselle*?'

'You know... burgers and French fries.'

'*Pommes frites.*'

'Okay, *pommes frites*... he kept stuffing them in his mouth when I asked him questions so I made him write down his answers on cheesy napkins. His fingers were too greasy to text me.'

'Text you?'

'Write a message on your cell phone... like this.' I type, *Bonjour, Madame de Cadieux* on the screen of my boxy phone then show her.

She wriggles her nose. 'Aargh... it's like opening a lovely bottle of perfume and not smelling anything. It has no heart.'

I nod. She has a point.

We go on for several minutes, bantering back and forth about everything from whose fries are crispier... Paris or New York... to the downfall of modern civilization if texting keeps gaining in popularity. All the while, I swear I hear a zippy soundtrack of vintage pop songs bouncing around in my head. Then it hits me. I'm talking fries and text messaging with the grande dame of scent like we're best buds.

Am I nuts?

She must think me brash and bourgeois. Which I am or I wouldn't have made it this far. It's tough to be a 'girl' in the news biz and I can tell you, without the courageous women who came before me back in the seventies and eighties, I wouldn't be here. I still have to fight the 'sweetie' syndrome ('Bring me a latte, sweetie, I'm on deadline.' As if I'm not), but my boss Granger is one of the good guys. Tough but fair. He brought me on board as a field reporter to WJJR News here in New York after I interned for him, then got a job at a small station in New Jersey.

Over the next four years I learned the mechanics of reporting the news, how 'no' doesn't exist in a reporter's vocabulary, and how *not* to run in high heels after an elusive congressman (I wear sneakers or ballet flats now). The rest was easy: be on time for your on-air story, notes prepared, lipstick not smeared on your teeth, and *always* rely on your gut.

I work hard at my job, bagging several big-time interviews and covering the crime beat, including the special victims unit. What convinced him to bring me to New York was a series of on-air human-interest stories I created about how the average Joe was coping after 9/11. *Emma's Heartbeats*. I interviewed survivors, their families, and the guy on the street.

Going into battle is in my blood. My mom's dad was a US Army captain who served in Europe during World War II – he and my grandma enjoyed fifty-three beautiful years of marriage before she suffered a fall and died from complications. Grandpop meanders a lot these days, trying my mom's soul. Judy Elizabeth Keane, née O'Fla-herty, was a US Army nurse and met my dad, Terence 'Captain Terry' Keane when he was wounded in Vietnam. He works with wounded warriors after a career as a math professor.

No one can figure out where I got the 'nose' for news. Or perfume.

I bite my lip. About my mom... she's the reason I ran after this story like Alice on a mission, but I'm living in no wonderland. I try not to dwell on what she's going through every day since she got the lung cancer diagnosis. The treatments... the personal loss of dignity... *damn*, I want so bad to make her happy. She says how proud she is of me, what I've accomplished. My journalism prof said I write 'deep from the heart while most reporters punch out headlines', which is where the title of my series comes from. I strive to get my facts right, but I'm more interested in the human condition and its connection to the story, no matter how painful.

And this one is a goody.

A sick, twisted Nazi major... an exotic gypsy mom who sacrificed her life for her daughter... and a beautiful, fair-haired sniffer of scents.

I let this idea mull over in my head while *madame* closes her eyes with a smile on her face and I sip my coffee, hot and delicious. I indulge in the raspberry cream and croissants while waiting for her to continue her story. We've been in the air for over two hours on the three-and-a-half-hour flight, cruising at thirty thousand feet over the Atlantic and heading for Charles de Gaulle Airport. Madame de Cadieux insisted we sit in the rear of the plane to have as much privacy as possible.

I note her tapping her clear polished nails on her tray, humming to herself. She seems more in tune with me now, though earlier she insisted, 'No tape recorder, no pounding on a keyboard.'

When I asked her why, she refused to answer.

I've been scribbling madly on a yellow-lined notebook since we left JFK on the 8 a.m. flight to Paris. I barely had time to call Granger (I never gave him a chance to say 'no'), grab my go-bag, along with an envelope filled with 'Angéline de Cadieux research' and get to the airport. I pray I can read my handwriting later to transcribe my notes on my laptop.

I see that gypsy girl so clearly in my mind... proud, defiant... brave. No, I mean *Roma* as she's quick to correct me, but I think *madame* enjoys the notoriety of the word. That it denotes a strong, mysterious female. A rebel. Soul sister. A dreamer... leaving a potent, long-lasting mark on anyone she touches with her magic.

Including me.

Which is why I have major guilt for not mentioning my real motive for pushing for an interview with her. Would I be here if I had? I doubt it. Which leaves me in a quandary. Here I am, barely a day since I first set eyes on Angéline de Cadieux, trying to figure out how I'm going to tell her my real agenda. How much it means to me to help my mom find out more about what her *own* mother went through in the camps... and for me to learn more about this uncanny talent I have for identifying scents.

The simple answer is, I can't.

If I tell her I want to pick her brain about whether or not a perfumer is born not made, that I've got this inkling I'm a nose, she'll think I'm crazy. I'm also sensitive about bringing up what happened to her in the camps before she's ready to talk about it. It could turn her off completely. Then I'm stuck with no story, no nose, and no closure for Mom.

Madame has wrapped herself in glamor, but I get the feeling she's been reluctant to allow anyone to peel back the layers to see what's underneath.

Until now.

I don't know why she first agreed to this interview, but we've got this vibe going between us that's working. Chatting like two French hens. I'm surprised she opened up to me – did my funny stories get to her? Or something else? Like no one ever took the time to really *listen* to her. Be *simpatico*. I work in a fast-paced world where everyone chases after the *breaking story* over doing an in-depth interview that can take weeks and even then you have to find the 'hook'.

I'm not looking for a hook. I want to see into the soul of this woman.

So whatever we've got between us, I can't jeopardize it. Not when her backstory is coming into focus. *Madame*'s honest account of her early life is not only fascinating but heart-breaking. I can't imagine living through the degrading prejudice directed toward the Roma.

A clearing of her throat alerts me to her insistent gaze. How long has she been watching me?

'I've been living in the past for too long behind closed doors, *mademoiselle*. It's time I come out into the sunshine.' She smiles wide. 'Maybe I'll even learn how to text message.'

Wow... who would have thought?

'I shall continue with my story,' she says, 'but I warn you, I shall not hold anything back. The torture, the ugliness of what the Nazis did to us in the camps. Humiliation, filth, sleeping with the nearly-dead, their cold bodies drawing warmth from your own, mud seeping through the soles of your shoes and squishing between your toes... the pungent, burning smell from the crematoriums.'

She sips her coffee, waiting.

'I can handle it, *madame*. I've covered ugly crime scenes.' Why I said that, I don't know, but I feel an urgent need to let her know I'm no softie.

'*Bon*. But you've never covered a crime against humanity, *mademoiselle*. It's important you know the pain I suffered, the joys. I will take you to a place where the unthinkable happens *because* you're a woman. It's the only way you'll understand the choices I made, the humiliation I suffered at the hands of the Boches.'

She closes her eyes and a hint of a tear escapes from her right eye, but she makes no move to wipe it away.

I have no doubt it's the first of many tears to fall before we're done.

4

CHAMBOISE-SUR-MARLY, AUGUST 1940

Tiena

Perfume:
Lady Pink
Pink tangerine, rose, Indonesian patchouli

I race over to my mother, fall to my knees and check her pulse. Rapid. Dilated pupils. Sweaty, hot skin. A sheer look of terror makes her eyes shine like angels' swords clashing as she struggles to breathe.

'*Ti-e-na...*' she breathes my name in a whisper, the pain in her eyes punching me in the gut. I lose it then... rambling dumb, stupid meanderings. Nothing in my life prepared me for this heartless atrocity. Not the jeers and taunts of bullies, the assault of a drunken sod. And it crushes my soul.

My dear, sweet mother, lost if I don't work fast.

Yet I can't ignore the enraged Nazi cursing at me in German as he checks his gun, counting how many bullets he has left. I expect to feel the burn of a 9mm rip through my flesh.

Then he does something I never expect.

He takes a step back and snorts.

'I should kill you, *mademoiselle*, but I haven't passed such an interesting afternoon since we shot Jews for amusement at General Dunkel-
fuhr's birthday party in Warsaw.'

'*You're inhuman*, how can you be so cruel?'

'It's a matter of order, *mademoiselle*. Only the fittest survive in the
Reich and I regret to say, this woman will not.'

'She's my mother. I won't let her die!'

'You can't save her, *mademoiselle*, though I enjoy watching you try.'

He begins whistling an irritating tune as I whip off the bandana
around my waist and stuff it into the gaping wound on Maman's shoulder, my heart knocking so hard, as though this is a bad dream.

It isn't.

Slumped down on top of the dirty straw, her chest barely moving, I
lean on the wound hard to stop the bleeding. Maman cries out in pain
when I press down, her face contorting with anguish, hands shaking,
head wobbling. Her eyes dart from left to right as if she's trying to stop
the darkness edging inward into her brain. She's struggling for breath,
but I can't let up on the wound, the hot, stifling barn turning into a
ghostly chill. The jangle of her bracelet rings in my ears as she groans
and I swear I see the trail of her scent appear like a wisp of smoke
before my eyes, making me dizzy.

Merde, the bleeding won't stop.

I lean on the wound with my knee, praying the blood will clot. It
slows finally and I tear off the bottom of my petticoat as a dressing.

Meanwhile, the horrible Boche won't stop his insults, kicking me with
his hobnail boot. I hold my ribs, swearing the pain won't stop me from
giving aid to Maman. I look up at him, the depravity of the man defined in
the way he enjoys using words as much as bullets to wound me. The more
he spews, the more my chest hurts. My brain whirls at a frenetic speed as I
process the gut-wrenching scene. It's not the insults that anger me, I've
heard worse, but this Boche *enjoys* inflicting pain and *that* makes him a
dangerous foe. I can't predict what he'll do next and that frightens me.

He checks the bullet chamber in his weapon... again... to sort out what to do next... *Fire again without warning*? I can't stop shaking and my stomach rolls over. Bile fills my throat.

God, no, please.

'Isn't she dead yet?' he blurts out, agitated. He wants to finish the game and my poor *maman* is complicating his pleasure. He taps his boot on the dirt floor, bits of straw marring its shine, then in disgust he rushes out of the barn, muttering in German. He's insufferable, the situation spiraling downward, rage at his complacency ripping me apart. That intense anger fuels my resolve. I have a job to do. She's my mother and I'd do anything for her.

I must get her out of here before the Nazi returns.

She's all I've got.

'Tiena... *go to Paris*,' Maman mumbles, scratching at her face, her arms.

I grab her hand and hold it tight. The blood loss is making her delusional.

'Stay with me, Maman. *Stay with me.*'

Moaning, she clutches her chest, rambling nonsense, alerting me she's in pain and has difficulty breathing. Somewhere in the deep recesses of her mind, she's telling me to go, *run*.

'No, Maman, I won't leave you!'

I see a wildness in her eyes that frightens me. She knows she's dying.

An endless groan erupts from my throat. I always said Maman had the brightest blue eyes. Now those eyes darken with fear. It's my fault because I couldn't swallow my pride, lower my head, and not balk when people called us names. Maman always said my streak of wildness would get me in trouble, then she'd smile and say she wouldn't have me any other way, that I was a throwback to the strong Roma female healers revered by the community for our nursing skills with herbs, and that someday I'd be famous. That I'd do what she couldn't because I had the gift of extraordinary smell.

Now she'll never see it happen. Because of that Nazi bastard.

She reaches for my hand, the hot stickiness burning against my cold flesh, then she closes her eyes and her fingers let go of mine.

I pick up her hand and check her pulse. *Still.*

She's gone.

A heaving pain cuts through my chest, digging so deep it feels like knives piercing my flesh. I can't change what happened here. The day is gray and tarnished with lost hope, shattered dreams, my thoughts tangled up in the straw matted with Maman's blood. Her mouth open. Lips tinged blue. Her slender body losing its softness as her spirit hovers unseen, waiting to leave the earth.

She can't.

It's not the Roma way. I must return her to camp, do her sendoff proper. I've never felt so low, my earthly soul seized by the Nazi demon that took her from me.

Then he's back. I smell him. Sour like vinegar.

'*Gut.* She's dead. It's your turn, *Fräulein.*'

I turn. His cut cheek is wiped clean, his gloves changed... *his Luger reloaded?*

I must fight back, distract him.

God, help me, please.

Out of the corner of my eye, I see Zeus pacing in his stall, instinct fueling my mount's response that something's wrong. My voice catches in my throat, 'You won't get away with cold blooded murder, *monsieur.* The law will find you.'

The major laughs. 'I *am* the law, *mademoiselle.*' He raises his Luger in a slow, deliberate manner, jeering at me in triumph. He enjoys taunting me. 'You and your kind will find that out when we destroy you.'

'My people are strong and we love France. You will *never* destroy us.'

He hesitates, his eyes fixed on my body. 'You tempt me to prolong our game... I've never seen a more beautiful gypsy, not even in the cabarets of Paris... the curves of your body... your earthy passion... stir a man's loins to a hardness that aches for release—'

He sickens me.

I use his Aryan arrogance to my advantage. 'You'll never touch me... *never*, you Nazi bastard!'

His face reddens. 'I've had enough of your insults, *mademoiselle*—'

'Go to hell!' I give out a loud whistle and the great stallion snorts and causes a ruckus in his stall, trying to break free, startling the Nazi. He turns away from me and aims his weapon at Zeus—

My heart slams into my throat. Cold fear jolts my instincts and I grab a large handful of sharp, spindly straw off the floor with both hands. 'Coward!' I yell and when he turns around, I toss the straw into the Nazi's face. Big, heaving bunches, catching him off guard.

'Damn gypsy whore!'

Yelling, cursing, he fires his weapon with a wild unpredictability as prickly straw stings his eyes. Rubbing them, he groans in agony.

Now's my chance.

I pick up the pitchfork lying nearby and whack him across the shoulders with it. Hard. He stumbles then spins around, looking for me. I spy my knife and grab it. I'm tempted to slash his throat with its sharp blade, but what if he gets the upper hand? Then I can't do right by Maman. Instead, I pick up my skirts and run... run... *run*... out of the stable... through the woods... into the thick bramble.

I tremble and shake, every nerve taut, teeth clenched. *Why am I running away? Have I no spine?* My gut tells me I'm doomed if I don't, that I'm no match for an angry Nazi with a gun. A monster so depraved even the devil turned his back on his ugly deed. I must leave Maman behind, then return when the stink of the Boche is gone to retrieve her body.

It's that thought that drives me to gamble on God's grace to give this Roma girl a chance to live so I can do right for *ma maman*. Give her the respect she deserves. There will be time to cry later. *Oh, God, will there be*... I shall never be the same girl again.

I hide in the crumbling old tunnel near the outhouses, hunched over, shaking, crying, bathed in blackness until I hear the rumble of a truck pass over my head, then what I imagine is a horse trailer, then a loud motorcar, its driver racing the engine.

The major.

I sink down to my knees, hold my head in my hands, but I can't stop shaking. Somehow, I must burn what happened here today in my brain, what the Nazi looks like, his voice, his disgusting odor that reeks of mold and sweet yeast and burnt tobacco. Every aspect of this degenerate, so when the day comes and I face him again, I will have no doubt *this* is the man.

As for my heart remembering the anguish of losing Maman... does the Damask rose ever forget the anguish when it's pulled from its roots?

I will *never* forget what the Nazi did to me. *Never*.

With clenched fists raised high, I vow to seek revenge against the whole damn Third Reich.

5

CONCORDE, 2003

Emma

Perfume:
Séduction de Noir
Casablanca jasmine, tuberose, patchouli

I head toward the front of the aircraft, so wrapped up in *madame's* story I run smack into a man coming down the narrow aisle. *Wow*... it's like hitting a punching bag.

'*Pardon, monsieur,*' I say, trying to sound French. A whiff of gray silk, the scent of citrus, musk... and is that licorice I smell? I look up. In an instant, my whole world flips. *Oh, no, not him. It can't be.* Mr Gray Suit. *Here* on this aircraft. Tormenting me with his rudeness. *And* his good looks. How did he get on board without me seeing him? Then again, I was so involved with *not* messing up with *madame*, he must have sneaked past me.

I don't need this. I don't want this.

Our gazes lock across the open aisle.

'*Mademoiselle,*' he sneers.

'What twisted piece of bad luck put you on this flight?'

'I could ask you the same question,' he smirks. I won't give him the satisfaction of letting him use those baby blues giving me a penetrating stare to put me in my place. His princely arrogance annoys me even at this altitude.

I lift my chin. 'Only one reason why you're here. You're stalking Madame de Cadieux.'

'I could say the same about you.' He gives me that smile again, but with questions etched on his face. I take my time, assess him. Unlike most Concorde passengers opting for a casual look, he's dressed to impress in a fitted suit with pristine white shirt molded to his tall frame, dark gray tie tied in a perfect Windsor knot. The effect is quite attractive considering his handsome face is tanned, making his light blue eyes beam like ice lasers.

'I know. You're an international playboy with too much time on your hands.'

'I'm not,' he states flatly. 'I'm going to Paris on business.'

'What kind of business?' I bite, curious.

'You might say I'm an entrepreneur.'

I smirk. 'Which is another way of saying you stalk wealthy female celebrities. You could be a jewel thief.'

'No.'

'Art forger?'

'No.'

'Then you're on the hunt for a wealthy woman to marry.'

A sad light comes into his eyes, but he quickly recovers. 'No.'

'You're not off the hook, *monsieur*. I saw you at the Waldorf and whatever phony story you come up with for being on this flight, it won't fly.'

'Really?' He gives me a bemused look after my dumb pun.

'Yes. I'm turning you in to the flight attendant.' I sigh. Just my luck. A single man with shoulders to die for and I have to turn him in for stalking *madame*.

His eyes narrow. 'I wouldn't do that if I were you.'

'Don't threaten me. I'm on this flight to protect Madame de Cadieux from stalkers like you.'

'You are?' He seems genuinely surprised.

'Yes. I'm acting as her personal bodyguard.'

'Moonlighting, *mademoiselle*?'

'Yes. My TV station offers protection services to important interviewees like *madame*,' I lie. 'So don't get any ideas or you'll have to answer to me. I'm tougher than I look.' I straighten my shoulders, push out my chest, which doesn't go unnoticed. He smiles his approval. Being tall has its advantages, but even standing up to my full height, he's three to four inches taller than I am.

'I have no doubt you can hold your own in a sticky situation, *mademoiselle*. Good day,' he says finally. 'Unfortunately, I'm sure we'll meet again.'

His tone is cool.

Before I can spit out a sassy retort, he returns to his aisle seat next to an older woman wearing a blue and yellow sunhat and knitting. She looks up at him and smiles. Naturally he smiles back and two dimples appear in his cheeks. Is there no end to the man's charm arsenal? What's bothering me is that he didn't seem surprised to see me, though I don't know if he bought my story about being *madame's* bodyguard. I feel a need to protect her even if I just met her.

I have this romantic notion the French diva and I were destined to meet. Like I drew a Tarot card with her face on it and I have to see how this plays out... in spite of Mr Gray Suit, a man I swear has ice in his veins.

'Ah, Mademoiselle Keane,' I hear behind me. 'I assume *madame* asked you to fetch me to go over last-minute instructions before we land in Paris.'

I turn around and *madame's* personal assistant Henri-Justin greets me with a kiss to my hand and a slight bow. He's a perfect gentleman, with a cultured smile and inquisitive eyes, about forty with boyish blonde hair that touches his collar. We met earlier in the exclusive First Class lounge for the airline in New York, the lively Frenchman making sure we boarded first as *madame* wished, then sped off, cell phone to his ear, jabbering in French.

We chat about this being my first trip to Paris and the weather, and he tells me I'm not to worry about a thing. I'm only half listening as we return to the back of the aircraft. That's when I see Mr Gray Suit poke his head into the aisle and give me a 'V' for victory sign and then disappear.

It isn't till I return to my seat that it hits me.

What did he mean, 'We'll meet again'?

6

A ROMA CAMP OUTSIDE PARIS, 1940

Tiena

Perfume:
Blue Rose
Desert blue rose, violet, vanilla

Today I went against Romani tradition on the journey from life to death. Under skies fat with dark clouds ready to burst, I lay Maman in her final resting place. Without wailing and ceremony, procession and pomp. I pray her *mulo*, ghost, will understand my decision. I was forced into the situation by the cruelest of fates. I shall never forget Monsieur du Monde's words when I returned to the stable to retrieve Maman's body after the Nazi scum had left.

'You must go, *mademoiselle*, and never return,' he cried out in horror when he jammed through the back door of the stable and went about calming the horses. 'You've made a dangerous enemy in Major von Risinger, a man who doesn't forget a face, especially one as beautiful as yours.'

From what I gather, the Nazi stomped off in disgust after I ran out, dismissing the incident as trivial as my mother lay dead in her own pool of blood. In the eyes of the German, my people, my *maman*, damn him, are no more important than a dead flea. What makes me look over my shoulder is knowing the major is out there, my face cataloged in that prissy mind of his for extermination.

Monsieur du Monde helped me wrap Maman in a warm blanket, tucking in her long braids and laying her hands across her chest. Her white blouse ran red with her blood, which heightened the cool pallor of her face and made her look so young. As we laid her on the back of Faithful Mary, I gave thanks to God the major left the bay mare behind.

Ironic.

The animal wasn't worth his trouble.

Now, as the first drops of a crying heaven wet my cheeks, I have to accept we're at war with the most inhuman regime our people have ever faced. Rumor is the French police boast they've handled the 'gypsy problem' by putting our people in internment camps in the Unoccupied Zone. *What about here in the North?* If what the major says is true and Nazi death squads are roaming the French countryside seeking Roma, my life hangs on a silver thread. A thread so fragile that if word reaches the French authorities about a 'gypsy caravan' traveling openly along the roads to bury a Roma woman, they'll be upon us. Fortune favors us since the local gendarmes are slow to round up offenders, but I wouldn't put it past the Nazi major to sniff us out and arrest the whole lot if we show ourselves.

Then send us to the labor camps we've heard about.

Maman would never find peace.

I let out a long sigh. How quiet it is here in the *forêt de Chouffard*, barely a breeze to whisper *adieu*. It's near sundown and I'm struck by the seasoned scent of summer flora reaching its peak. I'm surrounded by yellow and purple and white petals under a canopy of lime-green trees shielding us from discovery. I'm attended to in the burial only by my friend Hannah and her two older brothers. My stepfather Zegul left yesterday for a horse fair south of Paris, though it's dangerous for any Roma to travel. He barely blinked when I went over my story, how Maman was shot by an unknown hunter mistaking her for wild game.

An honorable death in the eyes of Roma, since 'gypsies' are often vilified in the annals of the law after finding themselves on the wrong end of a hangman's noose. Being shot by a Nazi would bring more pain to the clan and wouldn't bring Maman back.

I'm not saddened by his absence. Maman's ghost is keeping him away from me. I never did trust him. His hands lingering on the small of my back, his hot whispers in my ear. He sickens me. For now, I lament we can't give my mother a proper Romani burial. A loving tribute to send the departed off with their memories and a few possessions celebrating her life well lived, her colorful dresses, captivating jewelry. Tradition dictates I cover the oval mirror in our wagon and empty the clay pottery filled with water, wear black taffeta skirts and a black blouse (I added a red lacy petticoat. Maman loved red). I don't wash or comb my hair; I eat nothing. Drink only coffee and brandy, though I shy away from liquor. I need to keep my wits about me.

The heavens hold back the rain long enough for us to bury her as we settle Maman on a hillside filled with rich soil, wild root violets, and flowers. Lay her to rest in a tangled wood of fallen branches with so many falling leaves they cover the spot with a mantle of green velvet.

No one will look for her here.

But I'll always know where she is.

* * *

My time to grieve for Maman is short-lived.

A week later, when the arrogant sun singes the earth with unbearable heat, I hear my stepfather's heavy boots climbing up the peeling wooden steps of my wagon. The door slams open and he stands there, a bottle of cognac in one hand and a coarse rope in the other.

'I've waited two years for you, Tiena. I can't wait any longer.'

'I don't know what you're talking about,' I lie. But I do. I was fifteen when the brash wanderer joined our caravan, big and strong with a roving eye for horses *and* women.

'No? I should have taken you to bed then, but your Maman offered herself to me instead, got me drunk and convinced me to marry her.' He snorts. 'Now the situation has changed and I want you—'

'What kind of a fiend are you?' I cry out, turning my back, fighting back anger. 'Maman's dead and all you think about is sex?'

Ignoring my plea, he creeps up behind me and blows on the back of my neck. In spite of the hot day, I shiver.

'You're more beautiful than your mother, Tiena.' He sniffs me and a slimy feeling makes me scratch at my arms as though maggots have come to feast. 'And you smell like heaven.'

I never expected my stepfather would force my hand.

'And *you* smell like hell,' I shoot back. 'Cognac and clove tobacco.'

I move away, but he pulls me back to him, his hands rough and hurting, running up and down my body, lingering on my breasts.

I bring down my elbows on his arms. Hard.

'If you touch me again, Zegul' – I draw my knife – 'I'll cut a hole in your heart.'

He laughs. 'You don't have the nerve, Tiena.'

'Try me.' I snarl like a she-wolf defending her brood.

'Put down the knife.' He advances on me. I back away and lower my knife, taking my threat down a notch, praying I can reason with him instead. I want to scream that he's no better than that Nazi major, a man with the arrogance of a hissing snake crawling through a herd of sheep, but I keep quiet. I'm not reassured the German officer won't alert the Gestapo man and he'll come looking for me, no doubt to put me in a neat square on his crossword puzzle as a four-letter word for 'dead'.

I don't take my eyes off my stepfather, seeing in his dark, bloodshot eyes how he's savoring the anticipation of having me writhing beneath him, an act I *swear* will never happen. I should break away from the caravan, go out on my own. The wagon doesn't belong to my stepfather, it's mine, but I have no doubt he'll claim it since both my parents have passed. Unlike most Romani, he's heartless and doesn't believe in their ghosts hovering close, watching me and judging him.

In his mind, he's asking, *Who will know*?

No one is aware our caravan traveled south toward Paris after escaping from the latest roundup by the French police. Fortunately for us, the gendarmerie have been too busy with placating their Nazi bosses to enforce the spring decree to intern all 'nomads' – including Roma – and we made camp near the abandoned château overgrown with weeds and history, a forgotten place.

I reel from a new dilemma when he whispers, 'We shall be married, Tiena, as per your mother's wishes.'

'Maman would *never* want that for me.'

'It's your word against mine.' He snickers. 'Now put away that knife.'

'I will, but I expect you to mourn for her in the Roma way.' I return my knife to its nesting place inside my blouse, desperate to avoid anything physical with him. I'm not a fool. He's moody and strong. I don't trust him. I rustle my ruffled black taffeta skirt to make my point. 'Custom dictates we wear black, tend to her grave, and receive mourners.' I list everything I can think of – except selling her possessions to a non-Roma to sever material ties so she can rest in peace. No doubt my stepfather would pocket the money. I've secured her garnet and sapphire ring with the crest along with her bracelet of old bronze coins in a hidden pocket in my red petticoat. I know a man in Paris where I can sell it... *a keeper of dreams*, Papa called him when he took me to the pawnshop, *a man I can trust*, but I must bide my time. It's too risky for Roma to venture into the city with Germans everywhere.

'No time for your silly rituals.' My stomach clenches tight as he wipes his mouth with the back of his hand. I turn away, but it doesn't stop him from licking the nape of my neck with his slimy tongue, smelling not only of cloves and cognac but a sickening absinthe.

I keep talking, praying to buy time so I can think, *act*. 'You must leave, Zegul, *now*. It's against our spiritual teachings for a male not related by blood to remain alone with me in my wagon.'

'Fear not, Tiena, I *will* marry you, but I won't wait for a damned priest from the village to give me permission to take what is already mine.'

I huddle in the corner with an unsettling shiver in my bones. I get it. He wants possession of my parents' wagon and to secure his place with the council by wedding me.

'I'll not be married off to a brute like you.' I spit at his feet. 'You disgust me.'

I raise my chin, making me an easier target when he raises his hand and slaps me. Hard. I flinch, feel my cheeks burning.

'Watch your mouth, *ma fille*, or you'll feel the sting of my rope on your bare back.' He snaps the thick rope through the air with a loud *crack*. I shudder. He knew I'd never bed him willingly so he thought to intimidate me with the rope.

I refuse to let him bully me. Yes, I'm afraid of him. He wields the whip hard, easy for a man with powerfully built shoulders from breaking horses.

I hate him.

'I demand you leave my wagon, Zegul... *now*!'

'*Your* wagon?' He laughs and his belly shakes. 'You and the *vardo* belong to me. You shall lie with me tonight, *ma belle*.'

Before I can think about the consequences, before I can stop myself, I blurt out the frustration that's been building up in me since the moment the German pointed his Luger at me, the pain of everything I've suffered taking its terrible toll. I have trouble focusing on anything but wanting to lash out at my stepfather, do *anything* to keep him from raping me. Yet it's a fool's errand I embark on.

'*You bastard...* you're no better than the Nazi major who killed Maman.'

His dark brows cross. He looks genuinely shocked. 'What the hell are you talking about?'

'He couldn't have me and neither can you.'

'You told me her death was an accident.'

Nausea hits me. I wring my hands on my mourning skirt. *What have I done?*

He takes a slug from the bottle of cognac. 'Goddamn, *stupid* bitch. We're done for if the Nazis come looking for you. I saw what happened on the streets of Paris to anyone who gets in their way, anyone who even *breathes* their dislike of the Germans. We'll be shot.'

I clasp my hands together in prayer. 'You can't tell anyone... *please.*'

A weak plea, but I'm desperate.

He grins. 'I should toss you to the dogs, but that insane story of yours makes me want you more. Take what the Nazi couldn't.' He puffs out his chest. 'Strip off your clothes or I'll do it for you.'

No, I won't. Once he beds me, he'll never let me go. Yet how to stop him? Fighting with him only excites him... pleading with him gets me nowhere. No, I have to appeal to his Roma masculinity, something he's so proud of.

'You're a strong, virile man, Zegul, capable of taking any woman you want even after a few drinks.' I move toward the box of vials holding Maman's special herbs. 'Why don't we have a brandy together?'

'You'd drink with me?'

'Why not?' I smile, praying he's so filled with an urgent need for sexual release, he won't notice – or care – about my compliant sweetness. 'You'll have your way with me no matter what I say. I may as well kill the pain.'

He laughs. 'Love is hate, *ma belle*... once you get over the first pain, you'll beg me not to stop.'

I shiver. No, making love isn't like that... is it?

With my back turned to him, I pour laudanum from a vial into a tall glass, my hands shaking. How long can I keep him from touching me? Violating my body with his ugly lust.

I must escape—

Before I can pour the brandy, he knocks the glass off the counter and it crashes to the wagon floor, breaking into large, jagged pieces.

'Did you think I was fool enough to fall for your game, Tiena?'

'I won't let you touch me, Zegul, *I won't!*'

'You have no choice. I want you and I shall have you *now*.' He grabs me from behind as I struggle against him, then he pins my arms to my sides, grappling with the strong rope and wrapping it around my wrists to bind them together behind me. It cuts into the bare flesh of my arms, my wrists, rendering me helpless. Then he pulls my knife from its sheath inside my blouse and stuffs it into his waistband. Secure I can't cut him, he squeezes my breasts, moaning, 'You're so soft, Tiena... I can't wait to—'

I rail against him with my body, but he's too strong for me. He throws me down on the floor, the wagon rocking back and forth under us like a cradle.

I can't use my hands, but I can spit right in his eye when he tries to kiss me, startling him. That gives me the opportunity to bring my knee up and kick him in the groin hard, his hefty paunch putting him off balance... his manly pride swelling with violent pain, not desire.

'You dirty whore,' he screams, his voice catching in his throat, his powerful body curling up into a ball. 'You think you're too good for me, like your mother. You're not. I have my pick of girls eager to share my bed. *Begging* for it.' He grunts, breathing heavily, the fire raging in his eyes, sending me a clear signal he's not done with me. 'You'll be sorry you didn't behave, Tiena. *Real* sorry. But first, I have business to attend to.'

Aggravated by my defiance, he snarls at me, then embeds my knife into the wooden door out of my reach.

The bastard.

I struggle to free my arms from the knotted rope. 'You can't keep me here.'

He laughs, then ties the end of the rope to the black kerosene stove. 'Even if you get free, you won't escape your fate, *ma fille*. That I promise you.'

Then he bolts the door from the outside, leaving me in fear of what the coming dawn will bring.

7

PARIS, 2003

Angéline

Perfume:
Paris Starry Night
White rose, deep lavender, patchouli

Bringing that reporter Emma Keane to Paris was a mistake.

Yes, I let my hair down and she didn't let up the entire flight, cajoling me with her smile, flattering me and, *mon Dieu*, listening to every word I said, writing it down in flamboyant handwriting. Still, I'm tempted to put her back on the next flight to New York after we land. It's one thing to give her an interview, rattle off dates and places best left to old black and white films, but her charming and peculiar style of asking questions has left me unsettled, like a wobbly bowl of cold consommé. I've told her things about my Roma life I've never told anyone. *Damn her*. That girl has an uncanny knack of drawing things out of me with her peculiar directness, asking questions with that 'wide-eyed look' as if we're turning back the pages of a fairytale book together and she's overjoyed to go along for the ride. She's either a damned good reporter or...

Or what?

I don't know what it is, but I feel a certain comfort with her, making me feel at ease with spilling my guts as she sits next to me, grabbing onto every word.

As if it means more to her than another tale of war and sacrifice during France's darkest hour. That she's more than a reporter, that she's a woman on a quest.

I'd give anything to know her real reason for taking me up on my offer. I imagine she expects I'll lead her to a bigger story, a 'perfume tell-all' book, but if that's what she's after, she'll be disappointed. What dirty laundry the House of Doujan is hiding in the shadows shall remain there. I'm ashamed of how I've closed my eyes these past years to the running of the business because I couldn't get over a broken heart. You'd think after all I've been through – the despicable Nazis were the worst of it – I'd not let down my defenses. But the charmed life I enjoyed after the war came crashing down like an avalanche several years ago, and I was content to lie buried beneath it all.

Until the big thaw. And I had to face reality.

That I'm alone... again... and I'm going to spend the rest of my life alone.

Do you know how depressing that is for a woman in her eighth decade? No one knows, cares. I could be gone next week and the press would say, *Angéline de Cadieux lived a long and lovely life.* Full stop. Nothing about the pain, the suffering. Or God help me, I could last till a hundred and four and spend every damned day of it alone.

I straighten my shoulders when the aircraft hits the tarmac with a few bumps and a massive wind blast. My story is just beginning. We move through the exit tunnel of the aircraft and into the passenger arrival terminal. With a bright, red-lipped smile, I assume my 'place in the world' as Maman would say. Talking about her on the flight over brought up wonderful memories I'd let fade, memories as refreshing as spraying a lovely lemon fragrance with a top note of succulent zest. Speaking about her to Mademoiselle Keane was as if I was telling someone else's life.

You have yet to face life without Maman... life on the run with Nazis hunting you... Auschwitz... Dachau.

Oh, God... I can't go through that again. I can't.

I stumble on the rubber matting, blaming my wobbly high heels. Emma comes to my rescue, insisting on carrying the round blue hatbox I've had since the fifties when I made my mark in the perfume business. It's not heavy, but I carry it with me because it speaks of another era when travel was more like a royal adventure.

I always get photographed by the press when I carry that hatbox.

Now Emma has it and I'm not disturbed by that. Strange. She smiles at me and goes on ahead, looking for Henri-Justin. I breathe out, putting off my decision to send her back.

She *does* make me laugh.

We've arrived at the terminal bustling with drivers in black or gray uniforms, black gloves, wearing chauffeur caps and holding those ubiquitous white placards announcing the name of the party they're picking up. I have my usual driver, Marcel, meeting me. He tips his hat and tells me he'll collect our baggage and I'm to wait here, and where is Monsieur Henri-Justin?

Knowing my assistant, he's already standing sentry at the familiar black Citroen town car parked outside at the curb. *But where did Emma run off to?* filters through my mind.

Then I hear her saying, 'You've got your nerve, *monsieur*, trying to steal *madame's* bag.'

Mon Dieu... what's this?

I turn and see Emma struggling over possession of my large, round hatbox with a tall man hidden by passengers blocking my view.

'I beg to differ, *mademoiselle*—'

'I put it down for one second... *one second*... to check my phone and you grab it.'

'You don't know who you're speaking to.'

'Oh, I know your type,' Emma says. 'Cozy up to the sweet young thing traveling with the famous grande dame then steal her jewelry.'

'How do I know *you're* not a jewel thief *posing* as a reporter?'

'Because I wouldn't be stupid enough to grab it in front of witnesses.' Emma huffs and puffs. 'Now let go of her bag before I deck you.'

'That would be amusing.'

'If you don't think I can take on a guy your size... try me.'

'Don't... tempt... me.' The man comes out of the shadows and I chuckle. Ryker, of course. A broken soldier, a lonely man, what the Americans call a 'heartbreaker'. Flashing a gorgeous Irish smile at Emma that undermines her best intentions whether she'll admit it not. I have to give it to her. She doesn't back down or fall apart when my audacious and handsome private bodyguard advances on her, getting closer... closer... *mais oui,* she's weakening. She got a sniff of that scent I created for him.

Licorice... cypress and buttery leather.

A wide grin pulls at my red lips. It warms my soul to see them banter back and forth, their bodies becoming heated, their voices husky and low... their eye contact intense. His eyes glow like black amber, challenging her, his lips curling into a sexy snarl. She lifts her chin, defiant.

Neither backs down.

The scent of the chase is in the air with a feminine splash of lush rose tempting him, though I wonder, *who's chasing whom?*

Emma has no idea she's dealing with a skilled martial artist, former spy, and an officer in the Irish Defence Forces and Ryker is enjoying every moment of the charade. It's the closest I've seen to a smile from him since he came into my employ eight years ago.

I send a silent thanks to my Roma ancestors for bringing me this man, broken in spirit, but tougher and smarter than other security team I've ever had. We clicked when Ryker saved me from an assault outside a posh London boutique when a thug ripped a diamond necklace off my neck in broad daylight. I momentarily blacked out, the incident bringing back a moment of terror when back in 1944 an SS guard at Auschwitz ripped off my brassiere during inspection and I stood up to him, defiant.

After that day in London, I never wore jewelry in public again.

Fool that I was, I'd refused a security detail for an appearance at a fragrance event, citing I wasn't that important. The reality is, I can't stand being followed by *anyone*, a by-product of the war when the Gestapo were more often than not peeking over my shoulder. However, the insurance company insisted I have protection, so without my knowledge they contacted a security firm and put Ryker on my tail. Even with his handsome looks, I never saw him.

He's not only good at his job, but he speaks French.

Why? He never talks about it... the pain is too great.

I lured him away to work for me as my personal bodyguard and never regretted it. If anything, we're soulmates.

We both have demons in our past we've yet to conquer.

Settling in, I ease up on my reluctance to continue the interview with Mademoiselle Keane. I can't keep tottering about on a seesaw. I'm not a quitter. I won't send her home. Besides, I haven't seen two people more attracted to each other since I met *mon amour*. I wouldn't miss this for anything, to relive the joy of youth, discovering and falling in love, for I shall need a pleasant diversion as I embark on the next part of my story. I have to dredge up a sordid and ugly encounter that rattles my nerves, wondering where I got the courage to forsake everything about my old Roma life and head to Paris.

I say nothing when Mademoiselle Keane and I get into the black Citroen with Henri-Justin sitting across from us. I chuckle. Now to watch the fireworks when Ryker climbs into the front seat and sits down next to Marcel.

'*Madame*,' Emma squeals, 'that man in your front seat is a stalker!'

'Mademoiselle Keane,' I say without missing a beat, 'I would like to introduce Ryker... my personal bodyguard.'

'Your bodyguard?' She folds her arms across her chest, then leans forward to make sure Ryker hears what she has to say. 'You never said a word and let me make a complete fool of myself.'

'I'm sure it's not the first time you spouted off like a wild banshee when you didn't get your way.'

His direct stare toward Emma speaks of stormy interludes to come.

Oh, my. This is a side of the man I've never seen before... raw emotion where I thought there was none.

'I wouldn't talk if I were you, Mr Ryker. You're no angel. I saw how you corralled those women at the Waldorf like they were dairy cows.'

'The name is Ryker... nothing more.'

'Whatever you call yourself, I'm no weak female you can charm and disarm with that smile. I'm a New York City reporter and where I come from, that means war. *Got it*?'

I see Ryker's defenses double up. He clenches his fists, his knight in shining armor sliding in place, though more to shield *him* from pain. I was right. The young American girl is getting under his skin. *La vie est bon.* Life is good.

'If that's how you want it, Mademoiselle Keane.' He turns around and gives instructions to Marcel in French, who can't keep a straight face.

I smile. Ah, to be young again when you embark on a romantic adventure, that fluttering in your belly that won't stop and your whole being is on fire. I feel better than I have in years. Not so alone... if only for a while.

This is going to be fun. Look at them, doing their best to ignore each other, but I see Ryker peeking over his shoulders when he thinks she isn't looking. It's a romance in the making even if they don't know it yet... I do. Because I was once young and equally at odds with a man I thought to be the most pompous, arrogant... dangerous man I'd ever met, and then I fell in love with him in the late summer of 1940 when—

I draw in my breath and pull back my emotions before I get teary-eyed and act like an old fool... I have business to attend to.

I lean back in the plush seat of the town car to prepare myself to tell Emma the next part of my story, distance myself emotionally from the sequence of dastardly events that occurred after my stepfather Zegul tried to rape me. His dirty mind and foul smell plunging me into deep despair when a stranger showed up in our camp the next afternoon.

The man in the black trench coat.

8

CHAMBOISE-SUR-MARLY, FRANCE, AUGUST 1940

Tiena

Perfume:
Chocolat Noir
Moroccan chocolate, sweet orange, vanilla

'I demand, in the name of the Third Reich, you hand over the gypsy girl called Tiena Cordova.'

Blood thunders through my veins when I recognize that voice.

The Gestapo man.

His boasting tone commanding compliance is loud and clear to me. *What now?* I'm trapped inside my wagon. My only escape is to slip through the hidden trapdoor under the storage box.

I don't have much time. My heart is racing, I'm sweaty and hot... the skin on my wrists red and raw from struggling to free myself. Scuffling along the floor, I find a large, sharp piece of glass and begin cutting away at the long rope binding my wrists together and tying me to the rounded leg of the stove.

Then *he* shows up.

And I'm not free yet.

I pull the rope taut, stretching it to its full length so I can peek out the side window. I feel the sting of recognition as I confirm my worst suspicion. *Yes, it's him.* The Gestapo man with the crossword puzzle. Somehow, that awful man found me. *How?*

'Who are you, *monsieur*?' I hear my stepfather's voice in a tone bolder than I would have expected facing the German secret police.

Why this show of bravado? What's his game?

'Herr Avicus Geller, *monsieur*, from the Gestapo.'

Zegul smiles. '*Bon.* The French police assured me I'd receive recompense for my actions. I believe we have business to conduct.'

'I don't do business with gypsies,' Herr Geller bellows.

'That wasn't the deal, *monsieur*.' He clenches his fists, a bold move. 'I was told I'd be rewarded for aiding in the capture of the girl.'

What? He brought the German here?

I hear the frustration in Zegul's voice as I keep sawing the rope with the broken glass... *back and forth* across the wiry strands wrapped around my wrists cutting into my bare flesh and binding me to the stove. I have only minutes... *seconds*... before Herr Geller finds me and brings down the wrath of the whole Nazi army on my head. I blink back tears of frustration, the salty drippings on my lips leaving a foul taste in my mouth.

I must set myself free... escape.

'*Reward?*' Herr Geller laughs. 'She's wanted for assaulting an officer of the Third Reich. I suggest you give her up quickly,' demands the Gestapo man. 'Or I shall arrest everyone in your filthy nomad camp.'

'What guarantee do I have we'll be left in peace?' my stepfather insists. He backs down. He's more practical than I expected. Then again, it's no secret the French police put our people under house arrest to keep us off the roads so we don't impede the movement of German forces.

'It's up to the local *Préfet* to round up Zigeunerin, gypsies, and I assure you, *monsieur*, *they* take orders from *me*. I suggest you move your camp once our business is concluded. Get me the girl.'

'You'll find her tied up in my *vardo*, the blue wagon with the stars on it.'

He nods. 'I need to be certain it's her. The girl I'm looking for,' the Gestapo man says in a nonchalant voice, 'has a scar on her left forearm.'

'Yes.'

You gave me that scar when I tried to protect Maman and you cut me.

'Otherwise, she's unsoiled, as you promised?'

I hear a loud grunt, then my stepfather says, 'You have my word on it.'

Herr Geller sneers. 'The word of a gypsy? You jest.'

'I swear on my life, I didn't touch her.'

'*Gut.*'

I move away from the window, working fast, my heart racing as I continue jabbing at the damn rope, trying to slice through it with the cut glass... praying I have a fighting chance... waiting for the door to burst open—

I feel the touch of my mother's hand on my cheek and refuse to believe it's the breeze coming through the window cooling my skin. *Maman's ghost*... her whispering urging me to keep working the rope so I can escape through the hidden trapdoor. Giving me courage.

Not too soon.

Outside I hear the two men's heated voices haggling over the reward for turning me in. Zegul is undeniably a bastard, but I never thought he'd stoop this low. Selling me to fill his belly and buy his whores. He must be drunk, why else is he arguing with the Gestapo? Lucky for me, it gives me more time. I hear no sound of heavy boots approaching. No one else has dared leave their wagon, waiting, wondering... *what will happen to them*?

Zegul continues playing games, demanding he be paid.

The fool. He'll be shot dead if he doesn't shut up.

I use his greed to my advantage, taking the time the gods have granted me, remembering his cruel, lustful look stripping me of my dignity, giving me the strength to pull hard on the wiry rope strands fraying ever so slowly, twisting them until—

The rope snaps.

Setting me free.

I shudder with relief. *Merci, Maman.*

The next few moments are a blur as I pull my knife free from the wood, stuff it into the sheath fastened to my brassiere and grab a fringed green shawl. I refuse to become a victim of this man. I open the hidden trapdoor under the storage box, praying I'm slim enough to get through it. I'm taller, broader than my mother and I pray my womanly curves won't be the end of me, that I can slide through the narrow space.

I drop my shawl through the opening and it lands on the dirt. I suck in a breath. I dangle my boots through the hole when—

I hear footsteps crunching on the grass coming closer... *closer.*

I suck in my gut so tight I nearly black out, then I slip off my ruffled black taffeta skirt and red petticoat and drop them through the hole then push... *push* myself through wearing my drawers. I tune out the angry male voices echoing in my ears, imagining my stepfather stalling before he unhinges the lock on the door, demanding that reward, thinking he can outwit the Gestapo... it's his foolishness that saves me when I hear—

The sharp sound of a pistol firing and the yelp of a man. Then Herr Geller's dead cold order to open the door *now*. I can't wait another second. I give a final big push, scraping my arms raw on the wood and landing on my behind on the hard dirt. I grab my skirt, petticoat, shawl, then turn and run, racing deeper into the woods to the hidden spot by the stream where we tether our horses. There I find Faithful Mary grazing on a pile of hay as if waiting for me.

'*Whoa, girl, steady,*' I coo in her ear as I attach the bridle hanging from the tree, then mount her bareback and shift my weight to keep my balance as we take off through the forest toward Paris like a mythical creature racing on the wind.

I never look back.

9

HÔTEL DE VENDÔME, PARIS, 2003

Angéline

Perfume:
Paris Débutante
Lavender, Hungarian rose, oakmoss

I stare into the hand mirror at the face of a woman scrubbed clean of makeup and see that frightened gypsy girl betrayed to the Gestapo by her own stepfather.

Have you ever met a soulless man? I voiced years later to my therapist, a quiet, bespectacled *monsieur* who always wore a bow tie. *No? I have.*

I spent hours counting the polka dots on his tie while he made notes in a neat hand. I'd talk about Zegul, a despicable creature never to be forgiven. He'd sooner slit my throat like a squawking hen then let me go. Which is why my stepfather warrants the purest of hate I keep in a secret place in my mind (not in my heart... that's a precious abode where Maman and Papa and *mon amour* reside), swearing I shall never forget what he did to me, to Maman, praying he burns hot in hell.

My intense anger toward him festers, equal to how I feel about the major with the prissy manners and the Gestapo man who, even God will agree, was a black devil in human form.

I hold my hand up to the mirror, surprised at what I see.

I'm not shaking. My hand is steady, my heartbeat humming along in a comfortable rhythm. *Why? What's happened?* Usually when I reside in the past, open that door if only a crack, I become wildly emotional, sweat, and shake.

Not today. I find a certain freedom, a solace I've not felt before as I peel back the years with each swipe of the cotton pad, removing the façade I crafted for the public.

Then Emma drops the 'G' word.

'Tell me more about your gypsy life, *madame.*'

'*Eh, bien, mademoiselle?*' I shoot her a disapproving look. To her, it's an innocent question. To me, it goes deeper.

She senses my discomfort. 'Oh, my God, *madame*, I didn't mean any disrespect.' Her voice is laced with apology. 'It's just that there's so much fascination with gypsies and golden earrings. Pretty, ruffled bohemian skirts and big, chunky jewelry, and dancing barefoot to fiery music. *Ta da.*'

She snaps her fingers.

'You want *me* to dance barefoot?' I raise a brow. 'At my age?'

'Why not, *madame*?' She grins. 'You're not old. You never could be.'

'*Alors, mademoiselle*, like this?'

I kick off my soft slippers, jump up and dance around my dressing table, humming a ditty Maman taught me. Why not have a little fun? It feels good to let go. I give it my all, twirling round and round till I'm out of breath and I plop back down on the stool.

'What do you think now about this *gypsy* girl?' I ask.

Emma claps her hands. 'That you're braver than anyone I ever knew because you refused to become a victim, a woman abused by a horrible stepfather.'

I glance at her in the mirror's reflection, trying to compose herself, squeezing lemon into her tea, yellow pad on her lap, pencil down, but I have no doubt she'll pick it up in a snap when I resume speaking. She looks up, holds my gaze for a moment, smiles when she sees the amusement in my eyes, then goes back to her soggy lemon. I smile back, enjoying this new camaraderie between us, but inside I'm shuffling back and forth in my approach to this woman interviewing me. Against my better judgment, I've formed a warm connection to her I can't shake. Her probing voice sounding so much like Maman's as she urged me not to leave out a single detail, then the way she sniffed the lotions and creams I instructed Marie to give her for her stay in Paris, her nose wiggling, sniffing, eyebrows furrowing, as if she was deciphering the formula of each blend. Peach, milky tuberose, vanilla.

No. Impossible. Must be my imagination.

Wiping the sweat off my face, I gaze into the hand mirror. Oh, my, youth is prized by society, even during the war in the concentration camps where I was imprisoned. I remember how older women would smudge coal from the stove on their roots to appear younger so they could work and live another day. I'm fortunate. Serums and creams have kept my face smooth. Not bad for a woman in her eighth decade, though I pout as I run my hand over my neck, which refuses to do the bidding of the most expensive creams. I can't escape the pull of time, but I've learned to accept that God in His infinite knowledge has blessed women of an indeterminate age with something more valuable than wisdom.

Good lighting. It erases all sins.

Which makes me smile. It doesn't matter how rich, how famous a woman becomes, she never escapes scrutiny from the gossips, the critics… as if women are no longer viable once we've lost that lilac bloom.

Emma has no idea what's roaming in my head as she delights in everything she sees in this seventeenth-century hotel once the family residence of a royal architect to the Sun King. I pointed out to her the burnished gold accents adorning the walls, the handsome door levers, and how every time I travel up and down the winding stairway, I swear I smell the pungent odor of rosewood or a fruity tobacco scent from the snuff lingering there.

I insisted we stay at the small business hotel on the Place Vendôme for more than its history. I love the intimacy here. The Hôtel de Vendôme is a classic establishment and though not as expensive as the nearby Hôtel Ritz, it has a charm I find appealing.

I shift my weight on the silk brocade stool. Melancholy is not on the agenda today. I put down the hand mirror, look over at Emma sipping tea. Waiting for me to continue. I noticed her peeking around the corner earlier, down the hall, over her shoulder when she thought I wasn't looking. Her cheeks tinted when I asked her if she was looking for someone.

Of course she was, but she denied it with an embarrassed smile.

I have no doubt she was hoping a certain Irish bodyguard would find an excuse to check in on us. He didn't. Men and their pride. He's probably dying to get another look at her, but stewing like they do when a woman challenges them.

Ryker is a good man, but he's also a man with a deep secret.

He knows firsthand the pain of loss. Having lived with such pain, I know what it can do to you. For Ryker, he started drinking, becoming a loner, drifting from job to job in the security business, trying to forget, until that day in London when he rescued me. It's the only time I ever felt safe again since I lost my wild adventurer, a dashing man who captured my heart so many years ago. They're cut from the same cloth... or should I say, sheet of steel, nearly impossible for any woman to penetrate.

La belle Emma has her work cut out for her as I did. *If* she's woman enough to rip through his covert façade of disinterest toward the female sex. The man is lonely for the warmth of a woman, but he'd rather dive into the flames of hell than admit it. I know. It took daring on my part to win *mon amour*, make him see me as a woman, not a teenage runaway, as we'd say today. And when I did, our life was glorious together. Filled with laughter and joy and nights of passion when we prayed we'd conceive another child after the SS took my baby... have two, three. We wanted babies to share our love with, our fortune, our future... but it wasn't to be.

I never planned on being alone.

I'm not as lonely with Emma here, but I'm not getting any younger. I've provided for Ryker and Henri-Justin when I'm gone, Marie and her brood, along with the rest of my staff, making sure they're well taken care of. It makes me happy. I have no one else, no family, something once so important to this Roma girl.

I chuckle. I have no doubt the next time Emma and Ryker meet, it will be a delight to watch. What also amuses me is since I started this interview, I enjoy gossip again, indulging in raspberry jam and croissants, and talking about – God help me – sex. For the first time in years, I have a female presence in my life that tempts me to let down my guard.

I look forward to walking the streets of Paris with Emma so she can understand the rich tapestry of events woven into 'Tiena' becoming 'Angéline'. I admit, I've been remiss with cultivating relationships over the years since I suffered such terrible losses of comrades during the war. But I feel drawn to Emma... she makes me laugh. I don't laugh any more since *mon amour* passed. And she listens to me with an intensity I haven't felt since Maman used to hold flowers and spices under my nose while I rattled off what they were with my eyes closed. I imagine it's because I've invited her into my past. Introduced her to Maman.

Because you see a resemblance in the eyes?

A risky move for a woman as vulnerable as I am, but I don't want to give it up either.

So I don't.

'What happened next, Madame de Cadieux,' Emma asks, waving her pencil in the air, 'when you escaped that horrible Herr Geller and your stepfather?'

I relax, grin. 'Call me Angéline.'

'*Seriously*?' Her eyes widen.

'Seriously,' I repeat, smiling. So with a new rapport established between us, I venture back in my story, speaking slowly in English, to that hot August day in 1940, when I again escaped the Gestapo. I wouldn't always be so lucky... as I will recall later. For now, I recount my wild bareback ride on Faithful Mary along the road toward Paris, expecting to hear the loud roar of a German motorcar at my heels and the sting of bullets grazing my cheeks.

My newfound confidence in our relationship hits a bump along the way when I peek at her notes and read: *find a way to tell her the truth... and play up her gypsy roots.*

What does that mean?

I feel queasy recounting every detail to her. There's still a part of the old me that's been hurt deeply in the past by a member of the press, but Emma has drawn me out of my cave with her intense curiosity and induced me to reveal a painful truth... about how I attacked the major and sought revenge. *Will she use it against me?* I pray not, but I don't forget easily. Not when you've learned to survive in the camps by suspecting everyone of spying, cheating... lying.

I scratch at that old wound out of habit, though I hate myself for doing it. I want terribly to continue riding high on the crest of this wave with this charming young woman, but what if I'm wrong about her? What if she's writing a story that will make a fool out of me? I don't think I could bear it.

To quiet my fears, I'll have Henri-Justin dig into her background, find out what this American girl is about. Where she comes from. Any skeletons that influence her writing. My assistant has connections in high places that can dig deep and give me more than the usual birth-date, schools attended, and census stats.

I ponder what the results will be.

I pray Emma doesn't disappoint me.

* * *

Emma

We're at a critical point in the interview. This amazing piece of theater, watching *madame* at her vanity table, is something so extraordinary even my attraction to her handsome bodyguard takes a backseat. She asked me to call her 'Angéline'. I can't. I respect her too much to get that personal.

While I wait for her to gather her thoughts, I observe her.

Why am I not surprised *madame* reminds me of the fairytale queen with her mirror? But unlike the wicked royal, she's the most charming, honest, and fascinating woman I've ever interviewed. I expect the mirror to answer back when she stares into it.

What does she see? An old woman? Or that gypsy girl who had guts?

I hover in the shadows, watching her, learning more about her by the way she applies cream on her face. There's an acceptance of her age in her brisk movements, plumping, pulling her skin to get the desired effect, as if she's proud of every line.

It's how she got those lines that interests me.

Finally, she says, 'You were watching me.'

'Yes.' I don't deny it. I've spent my life poking into other people's business, trying to read between the talking points during an interview, find out what they're trying to hide. And this star in her own right is showing me her soul by exposing her naked face. It takes a lot of guts to reveal every pore and wrinkle, every dark spot and skimpy lash. She's bringing me into her fold.

An initiation into her secret world.

10

ON THE ROAD TO PARIS, 1940

Tiena

Perfume:
Her Escapade
Dutch hyacinth, pink carnation, sandalwood

With the wind at my back, I race Faithful Mary as fast as the mare can go through the thick forest, shifting my weight high then low to give her commands, turning my head to make sure I'm not followed. I struggle to keep astride her, sweat covering the bay's bare hide like sheer bronze Oriental silk. The faster I ride, the harder it is to breathe, knowing my freedom could be but a waking dream and not last.

I come alive when I ride... I miss Zeus, his power to race over the green land under the cover of darkness when everyone in camp is asleep, running on strong legs faster than the ancient gods. Nothing can stop me. *Nothing.* In my fantasy, I'm Queen of the Gypsies like in the pictures. Bold, daring, beautiful. *Mais oui*, I find the cinematic term romantic and daring, unlike my fellow Roma. But that's in my past. I must concentrate on now. Fleeing from my stepfather, I'm free from the yoke imposed upon me by my bloodline. Yet I'm proud of my heritage and it pains me to leave it behind.

Forgive me, Maman... Papa... I love you both, but I can no longer be Roma if I'm to survive this war.

The wind is at my back as I near Paris, a gentle wind I pray doesn't carry my scent to the Gestapo man. I have no doubt he's searching for me so I can't dawdle when I come to a rambling makeshift camp of battered *vardos*, wagons, in Saint-Denis in the northern outskirts of Paris. I bring the bay mare to a canter, taking my time to assess the situation the best way I know how.

Smell.

I surmise how many travelers I'll find by the stench of human waste that singes my nostrils. The strong odor of frying oil and garlic. I estimate a small caravan with no more than a dozen Romani. They're not French. I can tell by the designs painted on their wagons.

I dismount and let my mare cool down as I approach the makeshift Sinto camp, no doubt they're fleeing from their home in Germany. I keep my head down and, with deep respect, ask to speak to their tribe leader.

A stout man with long whiskers and blue and gold striped trousers.

'You're alone, *mademoiselle*?' he asks in broken French, noting my torn black skirt and red petticoat peeking from underneath. I keep my shawl wrapped close around me so he can't see my ripped blouse.

'*Oui, monsieur*,' I speak French rather than Romani. We Litaro aren't always welcomed by those who believe our bloodline isn't pure. 'I'm running away to meet my lover... *please*, take my mare and see she has food and water.' I clear my throat. 'I'll not be needing her and wish to sell her.'

I run my hand down her neck, wiping her down with the hanging end of my shawl. Faithful Mary shakes her head in denial, as if the sensitive creature doesn't approve. That moment crushes me, the finality of Maman's passing made more painful by selling her precious mare. I can't take the chance of someone seeing me with the mount, especially that despicable Gestapo man. With luck, the caravan is headed south, away from Paris toward the Unoccupied Zone where no one will question them about a fair-haired gypsy girl with a bay mare. I have no choice. I can't ride her through the streets. I heard in the villages motorcars are banned and only horse-drawn wagons and bicycles are allowed. Paris is an occupied city with German soldiers everywhere. I'd be spotted and hauled away to a labor camp.

The caravan leader shakes his head, pulls on his large round earring, thinking. 'She's not much in the way of horseflesh, *mademoiselle*. I wouldn't even steal her... *if* I was a thief.' He winks, then looks me up and down, my body shivering from tension. 'You can't fool me, girl, you're Roma.'

'No, *monsieur*,' I blurt out, but like when someone accuses you of stealing their watch, I keep denying it. 'I ran away from the convent at St Mimosa de Bernadette.' I make up the first name I can think of using a fragrant root.

'Wearing a red petticoat?' he gloats.

Chin up, I don't back down. 'I come from the Loire Valley.'

'Whatever your story, *mademoiselle*, I've not seen such fear in a girl's eyes.' He digs into his pocket and pulls out folded-up notes. 'I'll give you five *francs*.'

'That's robbery,' I cry out. 'I've seen common breeding mares go for ten times that.'

'Have you now? And where would that be? At the *Atelier* horse sales?' he baits me. 'Is that where I can find your kin?'

I clam up.

'*Merci, monsieur*, I'll take it.'

With a gleeful laugh, he slaps the money into my palm. I close my fist around the notes. A late afternoon sky threatens rain, misty drops tickling my nose. I have to find shelter. I won't get far with five *francs*. I have a plan, thanks to Papa and the trips we took here when I was a young girl.

Then, with a long look at Faithful Mary and a grand tug of my heart that nearly spills over into tears, I turn and head for the heart of

Paris on foot. Maman's garnet and sapphire crest ring hidden in the secret pocket of my red petticoat along with her bracelet.

I shake my skirts and the jangle of the bronze coins plays a sorrowful tune in my ears.

Telling me I can never go back.

11

PARIS, 1940

Tiena

Perfume:
Je suis une femme dangereuse
Plum, orchid, incense

The early evening storm rages with such intensity, I'm not certain if God is granting His approval or disdain for my insane plan.

I race down the tree-lined street on the Left Bank toward the pawn-shop near Rue Saint-Jacques, holding newssheets over my head to keep dry, dodging the rain puddles. I found a stack of pamphlets protesting the occupiers and urging the people of France to rise up against them dropped in haste in an alley and grabbed them. My eyes widened when I read the seditious words against the Reich on the mimeograph papers with runny blue ink.

I no longer feel alone.

I turn my head left then right, looking everywhere, praying I'm not being followed, that no one saw me grab the newssheets. People jostle about like nervous rabbits trying to avoid the hunter's snare. Skirting around official looking motorcars with small Nazi flags waving, their horns honking, then jumping out of the way when a mini car commandeered by a German soldier comes out of nowhere. He gives me such a fright when he looks at me I clamp my legs together and cover my face with the newssheet, but he keeps going.

I pick up the pace. It's getting dark... there's a curfew... nine o'clock, is it? The coming night seduces the light of the day into a deep, black velvet pocket and puts a button on it. The street is dark and forbidding. The flash of someone lighting a cigarette pops on then sputters in the rain.

A sudden chill makes me shudder.

I don't have a good feeling. The atmosphere has a dangerous, rough feel about it.

Rumor has it the Nazi military police operate in a hotel in this part of Paris. A place once filled with artists and writers. Hotel Letitia. No respectable girl would be out this close to curfew.

I walk quickly down a narrow passageway away from the Nazi-occupied hotel where shabby shopfronts and secondhand businesses abound with what looks like junk spilling out into the street. The few passers-by walk briskly with their collars up and shoulders stooped, hiding their faces, but I find what I'm looking for. The pawnshop.

My pulse races.

More than one curious gawker stares at me. A strange tingling makes me shake inside, as if Maman's ghost warns me there's danger ahead. The damp night makes me wiggle my toes in my boots. My cotton stockings are wet. I've caught a chill. Nothing more.

I see a white enamel plaque proclaiming the pawnshop has stood on this spot since 1779. I don't remember seeing that when Papa and I came here.

You will find Monsieur Bémet an honest man, ma belle *Tiena... sound of heart and a friend to Roma.*

Standing under the overhang, I fold up the wet newssheets and wipe the raindrops off my shawl. The last time Papa took me here, the cold rain poured down on our heads with the same intensity and Monsieur Bémet gave us shelter for the night. I was fourteen and in awe of the treasures I saw here. A trumpet, gold watches, exquisite jewelry, a round silver plate.

And perfume bottles.

Who pawns perfume? I wondered.

Monsieur Bémet told me about the beautiful *madame* with the silky voice who pawned her jewels and furs to pay for her husband's illness until all she had left were three bottles filled with expensive perfume. He took them as a loan because she was such a kind *madame*, but she never returned. I coveted the story in my soul and the love she had for her husband, wondering if she couldn't bear to retrieve the perfumes because each scent reminded her of a moment in his arms.

I want to create perfumes that evoke such emotion, such heart.

Beautiful memories that linger long after the heat, the dripping passion between a man and a woman, cools. I smile, remembering how amazed Monsieur Bémet was that I could name the floral and spicy ingredients when he let me sniff from the bottles. I never forgot the joy of inhaling the beautiful fragrances from Mandel, Ici, and the House of Doujan.

I squeeze my eyes tight and slip my hand into the secret pocket of my petticoat and squeeze Maman's bracelet in my fist for luck. I pray Monsieur Bémet will shelter this Roma girl until I can find a room.

I try the front door. Panic strikes my brain, unhinging my pleasant memories. *It's locked. No...* it can't be. I have no place to go, no money, save the five *francs* I got for Faithful Mary. That won't take me far and I've yet to figure out how I'm going to rent a room with my papers identifying me as Roma. I pray Monsieur Bémet will take pity on me and refer me to a concierge who's not a Nazi stooge and will look the other way. A shiver down my spine tells me Maman's ghost hasn't forgiven me for selling her mare, but I can't think about that now. I peek through the beveled glass pane, bang on the glass, but it's dark inside the shop. What am I to do? Hover in the alcove until morning, beating off the rain? Something isn't right... different somehow. Yes, Monsieur Bémet let us use the secret entrance accessible only by sneaking into the nearby convent behind the church and then following the old passageway. It was once used by aristocrats escaping during the Revolution. He told Papa it was bad for business if 'gypsies' were seen entering and leaving his shop.

I chuckle. The dubious reputation of my people saves me.

I go around to the back of the church and find the trellis suffocated by purple blooms twisting their vines around the decaying wood. The old convent entrance. I pull it toward me to reveal a plain wooden door as dark and foreboding as the gates to hell, push down on the lever, my heart racing... *Mon Dieu*, it's stuck.

In anger, I kick the door and *voilà*, it opens. I heave out a breath, then make my way along the dimly lit passageway with careful steps, grateful for the warmth of shelter embracing me until I come to a locked door.

I shake off the rain and toss down the soggy newssheets, then draw my knife from the sheath pinned to my brassiere. With a light touch, I place my knife in between the door and the frame, then slide the knife in as far as it will go, grip the knife handle and push downward, pressing my body against the door. It won't budge.

I refuse to give up. I grab the bodkin from my hair. Papa taught me how to pick a lock, a circus trick he learned when he was bound in chains as part of his act. I insert the silver-plated hairpin into the simple lock until I feel the tip hit the back, then turn it like a key, wiggling it in and out of the lock... until it turns.

I'm in.

I lay my wet shawl over a rickety chair and look around. The evocative smell of cinnamon and a fragrant wine tickles my nose. I breathe in the pleasing scent, relieved. Nothing's changed. A mysterious amenity overwhelms me. Warm and comforting in a night of cold and rain and dampness.

What is it about this shop that welcomes me? Has Maman's spirit followed me here? I miss her terribly. My breath snags when I remember how she'd brush my long hair, telling me stories about strong Roma women, how there was always a Roma spirit there to guide me if I asked. Now that spirit is her. I don't move, letting her nearness wash over me, hearing her telling me she'd do it again to save me. That warm thought allows me to drift a moment in the past to give me courage. A strange word. *Courage.*

It's up to me to make her proud.

I won't let you down, Maman.

I let go of my self-pity. I have to change my appearance and for that I need funds. Major von Risinger won't forget how I humiliated him. I have no doubt he's already engaged that Gestapo man to put me in that awful notebook of his.

I look around. No one's here in the back room. Quiet, dark except for a lit kerosene lamp someone left by the door to guide them on their way out.

I'm not alone... Monsieur Bémet must be in the shop, working on his accounts, but wouldn't he be here at the back desk?

'Monsieur Bémet, are you here?' I whisper. 'It's Tiena... Tony Cordova's daughter. The Roma girl.'

Nothing. Then I hear scraping noises... men's voices. Monsieur Bémet *must* be here, but where? And who is with him? The shop is closed... has he found himself on the wrong side of the Boches? Are they interrogating him? No, they'd drag him away. I dare not allow myself to believe he's a Nazi sympathizer and I've walked into a trap with a bombastic German officer ready to pounce upon me, asking me questions I won't answer.

I pull back, cautious, planning. Again, my girlish curiosity does well by me because I remember poking my nose everywhere when I was here and I discovered the irascible shopkeeper's secret.

Peepholes.

Cleverly concealed on the other side of the wall. Raised velvet rose wallpaper. Monsieur Bémet monitored the pulse of Paris by spying on who came and went in his pawnshop. I remember running my fingers over the plush velvet, then giggling as I looked through to the other side.

I put my eye against a peephole now, allowing me to see into the shop. A smattering of moonlight reflects off the beveled glass door, casting a glowy aura over everything. I look around, curious. A blue silk wingback chair stands next to the cabinet, its lone pillow plump and full as if no one ever sits on it. Polished brass fixtures hang from the ceiling and Persian carpets cover the floors.

Where is Monsieur Bémet? I see no one.

I glance at the tall standing grandfather clock in the corner, its fancy curly-Q numbers inching their way toward nine o'clock, and the items sitting in cases waiting to be reclaimed. Like lost souls in purgatory. It's their owners who are lost. Like me. I must make my case to the shop owner. The idea of sleeping in a rainy doorway chills me.

The second peephole proves more interesting.

It opens to reveal a private room.

There I see men hovering over a long table... and is that a map spread out? Three men speaking in heated voices. I don't see Monsieur Bémet. Two men are laborers... berets, dark shirts, cigarettes hanging out of their mouths. Then I see a hunchback with long, greasy hair, an unseemly creature with pointy ears, his eyes glancing toward the peephole. I swear he knows I'm here... did he see me come in, hear me breathing hard?

What if he gives me away? I ponder that question when—

'*Messieurs*, our mission is of utmost importance.'

Rich, masculine voice, a restless energy giving urgency to his words... a fourth man, his face hidden from me. I suck in my breath. Never before have I witnessed anything like the dark, elusive man dressed in black taking his place at the table, his low gravelly voice speaking about railway lines and explosives and timetables. How he's seen partisans in Poland destroy the German supply lines. The two laborers shake their heads, not convinced, but he doesn't let up. He cuts an avenging figure, like the gypsy bandits Maman told me about... rogue characters who roamed France a century ago robbing from the rich to give to the poor.

I see this man also as arrogant, a man who enjoys the game of resisting the Nazis.

He circles the table, turning his back to me, but never has a man caused such feverish agitation in my soul that I can't speak, move or think. I know in my heart he's handsome and the girlish part of me swoons over his broad shoulders, but something about the way he draws the attention of the other men unsettles my defenses. He's commanding... sharp in his tone as he says that 'printing pamphlets spreads the word, gives the people hope, but it's not enough. We must hit them in their supply lines... we have the edge over the enemy, but not for long... the Nazis have their spies everywhere... don't trust anyone.'

Which leads me to accept what my pounding heart couldn't imagine a minute ago – these men are fighting the Nazis like me... *can it be true*? That I'm not alone in my brashness to stand up to the Boches?

Are they the brave souls printing the pamphlets I found?

I consider this possibility, my body tingling with raw energy. I can't take my eye off the man in black. I study him closer when he turns. His face is in partial shadow, but I can make out his profile in silhouette. Strong, steel-cut jaw, Roman nose that reminds me of the warriors on the bronze coins on Maman's bracelet. Longish hair that hugs his neck like a stallion's mane. His muscular build rivals any Roma handler of horses I've known and that blazing voice is enough to sting my skin with a strange heat. I must not let down my guard but keep to myself... I owe it to Maman. She gave her life for me, and the ache for revenge residing in my heart overflows with the need to avenge her.

No man must tempt me to veer from that path, not now, *not ever.*

I should run, forget what I've seen, but the clap of thunder over-head and the pounding rain outside leave me in a dubious situation.

Explain what I'm doing here to a gang of spies.

Or end up dying in the streets.

I choose to remain and not because I find the man in black to my liking. It's my own hide I aim to save.

I try to focus, squinting through the peephole as I squirm with the awful realization my sacred nose is about to give me away. I hold back a sneeze. Barely. My clothes are soaking wet and I can't help but shiver. I ignore the chill overtaking me, my senses tuned into this man. I can't place his accent... which surprises me because in my travels I'm well aware of the nuances of French. He's a man not to be ignored. Giving orders in that distinct baritone dripping with velvety tones, then listening intently when another man gives his opinion: 'we must get weapons or we'll be crushed' and 'we need brave men not sympathetic to the Vichy government to carry out what you ask, Count.'

Count?

I press my eye harder against the peephole, desperate to see him better. Odd place to find an aristocrat in a pawnshop, though these days anything is possible with the Boches everywhere, demanding we French act as if everything is normal when it isn't. Because of their ruthless behavior, good people like Maman died. I wait to hear more, eager to glean what information I can. I fear what monstrous deeds the occupiers will invoke on us, not just Roma but all Frenchwomen.

'So it's weapons you want, Alain?' the Count shoots back. 'We have shotguns, hunting rifles, pistols, *messieurs, and* we have what the Germans don't.' The man in black takes a beat, rolls up the map and stuffs it into the large side pocket of his overcoat. 'Courage.'

I suck in a breath. Again that word, *courage.*

I strain to hear what he's saying... about weeding out the professional agitators, *Communists,* he calls them, a term I'm vaguely familiar with. Then he gives the men encouragement, promising them the Nazis will be defeated. 'I'll meet up with you and the others at the appointed rendezvous at...'

Ooh, I can't hear what he's saying when he drops his voice. I'm aching to know more about him, his plans, but the meeting has ended. I flatten myself against the wall, holding my breath, my pulse racing when the two laborers pass by me but don't see me in the dark, then exit the shop through the secret entrance. *Thank God.* I make a sharp turn on my heel and stumble against a large wooden box, losing my balance when the hem of my skirt catches on a nail. I go sprawling on the floor, banging my knee before I land on my back.

I hear heavy footsteps and I'm aware of a strong smell. Incense? My nostrils burn like I'm inhaling fire. I *have* to escape.

I crawl into a dark corner and press my rear against the wall while I slowly pull myself up into a standing position. Before I can take a breath, a bright light hits me in the eye and that commanding tone I've come to know chills me when I hear—

'You were right about the Peeping Tom, Jarnak,' he says in a voice as smooth as black silk. 'She heard everything. I have no choice but to shoot her.'

12

PARIS, 1940

Tiena

Perfume:
Sunday's Rose
China rose, white carnation, musk

I hear the sound of a hammer being cocked. I put my hand up to block the light shining in my eyes. I can't see anything, but the smell of gunpowder residue tells me he's a man of his word.

'She's too pretty to shoot, Count.'

It's the hunchback Jarnak.

'Then what shall I do with her?' He keeps the light trained on me, keeping me from seeing his face or the weapon. I stand tall, refuse to back down. 'She's seen and heard too much for me to allow her to leave.'

'She could be a thief come to steal from you, Count,' Jarnak offers.

'I have no doubt the beautiful *mademoiselle* steals many men's hearts.'

'Or she could be a German spy.'

'Then I *will* have to shoot her.'

I hold my tongue, barely. I can't see him, but I can smell him. Maleness rich and deep, mixed with the pungent odor of tobacco filling the room and a damp musky raw aroma that reminds me of an animalic scent.

'She could be a Nazi collaborator,' the Count continues, 'a beautiful *mademoiselle* who sleeps with the enemy.'

That does it. I've taken enough insults.

I spit on the floor.

'How *dare* you, *monsieur*, accuse me of allowing those slimy Nazis to touch me.' I cross my arms over my chest. I can't remain quiet any longer, shaking in my boots and wondering what happens next. 'I hate *them* even more than I hate you for accusing me of such depravity.'

'So the *mademoiselle* has spirit.' He laughs. 'Intriguing, but why should I trust you? I don't even know your name.'

'Tiena Cordova.'

'How do I know you're telling me the truth? Show me your identity card.'

I clench my fists. I can't show him my booklet identifying me as *Zigeunerin*, Roma.

'I lost my card, *monsieur*.'

'Very convenient, *mademoiselle*,' he says. 'Who sent you here? I need a name.'

'No one, *monsieur*. I came to Paris to sell my mother's ring and her bracelet.' I take them from the hidden pocket in my petticoat, hold them up to the light. 'I have need of funds.'

'Ah, so you're running away from someone, which means they'll be looking for you. And that makes you a danger to my operation, *mademoiselle*. Why did you choose my shop?'

'*Your* shop?' I take a step back. 'Where is Monsieur Bémet?'

'The shopkeeper had no stomach for the Germans and fled Paris, leaving the shop to me.'

Do I believe him? Or is he hiding something?

'I'm even more curious about how you got in here,' he says. 'The front door is locked.'

'I sneaked in through the passageway near the church, the secret entrance hidden behind the trellis overgrown with flowers.' I grin, pride popping up in my smile. I put one over on this enigmatic Count. 'You should get a better lock.'

'No one knows about that entrance.'

'Papa and I came here often to sell our goods and Monsieur Bémet didn't want anyone to see us because...'

He throws his head back and laughs. 'You're a gypsy... that's why you won't show me your papers... you wish to sell your mother's jewelry to a *gadje*, non-gypsy, which tells me she died recently.'

How does he know our ways?

'I prefer Roma, *monsieur*. My papa was an honorable tradesman. He sold trinkets and coins to Monsieur Bémet that he found near an old, abandoned château.'

'I can't let you go. You've seen too much. What am I to do with you?'

I don't speak. I'm hurting inside, everything coming to the surface as I struggle not to show weakness and let the tears fall. Then I start shivering, shuddering from the grave chill invading my body. I hear him whisper to the hunchback who disappears.

'You're clever, *mademoiselle*, which could be useful to me... unless you're lying and you followed me here after I left the cabaret.'

Indignant, I say, 'Why would I follow you?'

'It wouldn't be the first time a woman couldn't resist my charm.'

I shrug. 'You're not my type, Count.' *Liar*. 'I *swear* I came to the pawnshop often with Papa before the Nazis occupied Paris.'

'Prove it.'

'How else would I know about the secret entrance?'

'Tradecraft.'

'*Monsieur*?' I ask, not understanding.

'You've been watching my men... seen them use the passageway... and now you're trying to convince me you're an innocent girl so you can infiltrate my organization.'

'I'm a true daughter of France, *monsieur*.'

'I'd like to believe you, *mademoiselle*, but too many lives depend on what you saw here tonight. If word about our plans leaks to the Nazis... men will die.'

I hear a rustle behind me and Jarnak returns with a tattered, deep burgundy velvet cloak. He scowls.

'You could dispose of her in Père Lachaise, Count.' The hunchback chuckles.

'Dump her in the cemetery? And such a pretty corpse for the maggots to feast on.'

They are joking... *non*?

I shiver when he throws the cloak over my shoulders, pinning my arms to my side, its velvety softness hugging me with a warmth I can't resist in spite of my fear. Frantic, I shake my brain, trying to talk my way of this mess, pull up something that will prove my story.

'Wait, *monsieur*, please... when I was here with Papa, I became fascinated with three perfume bottles Monsieur Bémet had for sale. *Mandel*, *Ici*, and *Bel Amour 27* from the House of Doujan.'

'Perfume? How will that prove your story?'

'Monsieur Bémet challenged me to name the oils and essences in each one if I wanted extra raspberry jam.'

'Merely another trick to keep me from disposing of a German spy.'

'I'm no spy, *monsieur*. I'm a nose,' I exaggerate. 'I can recognize *hundreds* of scents... blend the most beautiful perfumes that will take your breath away. That's why I came to Paris. I want to work for the best perfume house in the city.'

'Dressed in those clothes?'

'I'm in mourning, *monsieur*.'

'Wearing a red petticoat?' He snickers.

'It was Maman's favorite. I wear it to honor her spirit. I beg you, *monsieur*, let me show you how I broke down every formula for the shopkeeper, from the top note to the heart to the base. I'll take you on a melodic journey from the first whiff of sweet tangerine to shaffali jasmine to the passionate depth of *Evernia prunastri*.'

'Mademoiselle...?'

I smile. 'Oakmoss. *Please*. Let me sniff the perfumes and then you'll know I'm telling the truth about being a *parfumier*. I know exactly where Monsieur Bémet hid the perfume so customers wouldn't sample their contents behind his back.'

He thinks a moment. 'Shall we give the *mademoiselle* a chance to prove herself, Jarnak?'

The hunchback wrinkles his face. 'I have no gumption to go out in this rain, Count.'

'*Alors, mademoiselle*,' says the Count, 'how do I know I can trust you not to make up a fabrication of perfume essences and deceive me? That you're both a perfumer *and* a spy... though I'm told Hitler hates perfume.'

'You have my word, *monsieur*.'

'The word of a gypsy?' he asks, teasing.

'You insult me, *monsieur*. You're no better than the Boches, trying to round us up like cattle.' I shiver. I remember the Nazi major's boast to rid France of gypsies. 'I dread what this war will bring to my people. I must fight the enemy, bring courage to Frenchwomen *not* to let them win, take everything from us until we're puppets on a string controlled by the Reich.'

'Brave words, *mademoiselle*. *Alors*, I'll put you to the test. I know a connoisseur of perfumes who can assess your knowledge. Yvette Pacquet.'

Smug, I say, 'How do you know you can trust *her*?'

'Yvette is Alain's sister, one of my best men. She works for the House of Doujan in their perfume shop on the Rue Saint-Honoré.'

'Is she a nose, *monsieur*?' I ask, curious.

'No, but she's well acquainted with their perfumes and her knowledge makes her popular with their German clientele.' He leans closer, whispers in my ear, 'She keeps her eyes and ears open for me, reporting gossip useful in our work. Her background makes her a valuable asset in working to defeat the Nazis. Of course, if you breathe a word of this to anyone, they'll find you floating in the Seine.'

'Tell me more about her, *monsieur*.' I refuse to let him scare me. A different emotion rips through me. Could I also join the fight?

'She was a ballerina until a sandbag fell from the rafters during a performance and struck her. It ended her career on the stage, but not her ability to attract men.'

'Men like you, *monsieur*?'

A sharp intake of breath tells me I hit a nerve. He plays his hand like a man who knows his attraction to women and makes no excuses for it. 'Jealous, *mademoiselle*?'

I scoff at his notion. 'I have no time for men or romance, *monsieur*. Perfume and fighting Nazis is my life... *and* seeking revenge against the Boches.'

He doesn't question me further and for that I'm glad. I'm shaking from the chill... my wet clothes sticking to me like a sea siren's skin.

'I'll send for Yvette in the morning. Meanwhile, you shall stay here tonight.' He clears his throat. 'Bring appropriate clothing for the *mamselle*, Jarnak, then lock her in Monsieur Bémet's old room. I don't want her escaping.'

I panic. 'You can't keep me prisoner here.'

'Can't I?' Even hidden in the shadows, I feel his piercing eyes upon me. 'You leave me no choice.'

I lean closer, a daring move. 'And why should I trust *you*? You hide in darkness.'

'*Mademoiselle* is afraid of the dark?'

'I'm afraid of no one.'

'You're afraid of love.'

Say something. Don't let him get away with that even if it is true.

'Why won't you tell me who you are? Show me your face in the light?' I go on the attack. 'Unless you're trying to trap me and you wear a Nazi uniform under your coat.'

He feels the sting of my words and comes back at me hard with: 'I hate the Boches as much as you do, *mademoiselle*, but who I am doesn't concern you.' He shines the light up and down over my body, stopping on where the wiry rope hugged my wrists, cutting deep red marks onto my skin. I try to hide my scar from him, but he sees it and scowls. 'Did the Nazis torture you? Was it the Gestapo? They have unspeakable methods that turn even the bravest woman into a shattered human being no one can save.'

Did he know such a woman? Is she dead?

'My stepfather did this to me, *monsieur*.' I refuse to tell him about the Nazi major. If he knows the Gestapo has me in their sights, he'll turn me away.

'Now I understand.' He lowers his voice to a loud whisper. 'If you're telling the truth, Mademoiselle Cordova, then I shall help you, and if you're not—'

'Then you shall shoot me.'

He laughs, a sexy, liberating laugh that warms my soul. 'I pray I shall *not* have to shoot you.' He sucks in a sharp breath. 'You fascinate me, *mademoiselle*,' he says, a blend of romance and drama reverberating in his tone that makes something catch in my throat and tears well up behind my eyes.

I fancy a daring remark to divert his attention from my moment of weakness. 'Then you won't leave me to the maggots?'

'A man would be a fool not to want you for himself.' He groans, the meaning of his words sensual and deliberate.

We're alone, but I don't resist when he pulls me into the shadows with him and holds me tight, kissing my forehead.

'How *dare* you, *monsieur*—'

He brushes my lips with his, teasing the back of my neck ever so lightly with airy kisses that betray a wicked playfulness both intimate and frightening. I moan... sigh... his feverish touch hitting me low in the belly, his hands moving over me, then I'm immediately ashamed for responding to him.

Then—

'Forgive me for my boldness, *mademoiselle*,' he whispers in my ear, 'but I had to disarm you for your own protection. And mine.'

'What—?' My hand goes to my blouse, my fingers searching for the sheath attached to my brassiere. *My knife is gone*. 'You thief!'

'*Mademoiselle* isn't the first Roma girl I've kissed... a sharp blade often accompanies a sharp tongue.'

I hear him suck in a breath as he lets me go and the luxurious scent of his manliness disappears on a cool breeze. Woodsy... cedar... cinnamon. I hear a door close.

And he's gone.

And my pride with him.

He's outwitted you, ma petite. I hear Maman's voice in my head. *And he's dangerous... but exciting. A challenge for you.*

'He won't get the better of me again, Maman, I *swear*,' I scold her ghost. Something wicked gets hold of me then, a desperate need to prove to him I'm not a wild gypsy girl and that I can be an elegant *Parisienne.*

Someone coughs behind me.

'Follow me, *mademoiselle, s'il vous plaît.*'

I turn to see Jarnak holding a box filled with women's clothes... a deep blue dress with a round white collar, underwear, nude-colored slip, black shoes with straps, cotton stockings, garters, even a fancy lace white brassiere like I've seen in the shop window on Rue Cambon.

I don't protest when the hunchback locks me in the backroom. *Where else have I to go?* It's a cozy room with a tiny high window, rain beating down on the glass pane, a cot and empty garderobe, even a chamber pot.

And a cup of hot, lemony tea sitting on the cot.

'I'll bring you food in the morning. *Bonne nuit, mademoiselle...* sweet dreams.' He chuckles and then locks the door behind him.

I toss the cloak into the garderobe and in a slow dance, remove my clothes, as if shedding my Roma roots. I have no choice but to accept the fate the gods dealt me like a lucky Tarot card played on this stormy night. But a new sadness for the girl I was settles in me as rain beats down against the window, echoing my beating heart. I put on the underwear and the slip... thinking... *a man kissed me tonight*. And awakened something in me I've never felt before. I should be frightened and angry with him, but I'm not.

He's hiding something... a great hurt and more. I intend to find out what it is. But I can't fall in love with him. I've got a war to fight and I don't need him messing with my head... and my heart. His sleight of hand in finding my hidden knife makes me know he's no pushover.

Damn him.

I collapse on the cot and cry. My emotions spill over, my heartache catches in my chest as I confess to Maman's ghost I will never stop blaming myself for her death. Yet I'm left wondering how I, Tiena Cordova... Roma girl... can defeat the Nazis?

I pick up the hot tea and sip it. Its sweetness coats my tongue, but my nose detects a sleeping herb swimming down my throat in the tea, *a way to subdue the wild gypsy girl.* I don't fight it. I'm grateful to the Count for not tossing me out even if he *did* steal my knife. I feel my cheeks color in spite of the chill. Then again, he's right. I know too much about his operation. He can't turn me in to the Gestapo.

I snicker.

My snoopiness paid off.

13

PARIS, 2003

Angéline

Perfume:
Raspberry Cream
Bergamot orange, French raspberry, tonka absolute

'*Ooh,* I love how the Count stole your heart, *madame,*' Emma says. 'How romantic.'

'He was both clever and a rogue. I knew it that first night when he found me hiding in the pawnshop. His voice, his scent, everything about him snared my senses and turned them round and round into a whirling dervish.'

I savor hot mocha coffee as I speak, enjoying recalling that night with the New York reporter in the privacy of my hotel room. A room vibrating with seventeenth-century gold gilding co-existing with a light, floral pastoral scene worthy of Marie Antoinette. A royal setting to engage in the memory of a man who was anything but royal. Of course, I shan't reveal that to Emma. I'll let her discover his true identity as I did. Sparring with him... challenging him to let me join his secret underground organization in a time where an anti-Nazi pamphlet could get you shot... while falling in love with him.

I smile at Emma and her eyes drip with questions, dying for the next part of my story.

And so she shall have it.

'I never met a man so strong and sure of himself, *mademoiselle,*' I continue. 'Yet he didn't take advantage of me as some men would, finding a young girl shivering in wet clothes with an aching heart. Filled with a furious anger over the killing of my mother coursing through my veins.'

'He *did* kiss you, *madame,*' Emma giggles.

'Ah, that kiss.' I sigh. 'It's taken on a life of its own over the years with each retelling, becoming more and more passionate to my lonely heart. *Alors...*' I lean closer to the young reporter and whisper in a breathy, schoolgirl tone, 'You must remember, I'm no longer that naïve Roma girl blossoming under a man's touch. I've since enjoyed the fruits of the Count's passion and so I embellish that first moment as I wish to experience it now, the passion that ruled the man and his ability to please a woman in ways I never imagined.'

Her eyes widen. '*Madame...* you... surprise me.'

I chuckle. 'Do you think a woman my age loses her ability to remember a man's hands upon her? Passion endures, *ma chère* Emma, if the bond lovers share is strong and solid like a knotted golden cord. They only cool if that bond is forged from straw fibers woven together with falsehoods and lies.'

I see Emma writing furiously in her notebook, doing her best to capture my words. Words I feel so strongly about because I still miss him. His voice, his laughter... *his arms around me.*

I put down my coffee cup. I don't pour another from the silver Baroque pot with the swanlike handle. Instead, I continue my story. 'As the years passed, I refused to let my emotions simmer in a pot too long left on the stove, the grinds becoming bitter, the taste crude, the smell ugly and burnt. I adored the Count, though at the time I wouldn't admit I was falling in love with him. I wanted revenge for my mother's death and wouldn't let anything stand in my way. I believed if I could get a job in the perfume industry, I could fight the war on my terms, walk among the enemy and seduce them with scent while helping the slowly forming Underground gather intelligence, feed vital information to the Allies that in the end won the war.'

'What about the fighting in the streets of Paris... arming the ramparts near Notre-Dame?' Emma asks, remembering the glory scenes depicted in black and white newsreels.

I shake my head. 'In the summer of 1940, the Resistance was barely more than printing pamphlets criticizing the Vichy government for working with the Nazis and angry protests against the Reich. The armed resistance came later.' I lower my eyes, staring into my empty cup. I'm embarrassed to admit so many Parisians 'went along' with the occupiers, weary of war and grateful Paris hadn't been destroyed by German bombs.

'I saw Paris with different eyes after that night in the pawnshop when I entered French society with a new identity, thanks to the Count and the charming Yvette, whom I will never forget. She was one of many Frenchwomen at odds with how to deal with the occupiers. *Collaborate or resist?* For many, it was far easier to do nothing.'

'But not you, *madame*... you fought back.'

I smile. 'I wish I could say I was as brave and strong as the fearless women who joined the Underground, many of whom were tortured and died in the concentration camps. *Mais non*, I didn't lead downed evaders – airmen – to freedom over the mountains. I didn't operate a wireless, nor was my name entered in the annals of the SOE – the British operation of spies in France. I, *ma chère* Emma, created exquisite perfumes that—'

A sudden rush of emotion forces me to stop.

Long after the war, I felt guilty I didn't do more to help Frenchwomen escape the Nazis, that I followed my dream to create fragrances. Then I'd hear Maman's voice – would Emma understand I speak to her ghost or think me an old fool? – telling me what I gave to France no one else could. *Courage*. Freeing me to embrace what I did and not be ashamed. I shall never forget those years and the amazing success I found as a *parfumier*, rising in the ranks fast and quick because of the unusual circumstances war brings and the final outcome that led me to Dachau.

And the loss of my daughter.

I heave out a heavy sigh and ask Emma to pour me a glass of brandy. I can't continue until I get over the deep imprint of pain that squeezes my heart every time I remember that day in the concentration camp during the winter of 1945... cold snowflakes frosted my baby's long, dark lashes like white daisies the last time I hugged her. I stifle a cry... *you can't break down, not Angéline de Cadieux... never*. I look up to see Emma hasn't taken her eyes off me, her writing stopped, whatever notes she took forgotten.

I close my eyes. 'I shall speak next about what happened after that rainy night, how I sniffed a bottle of *Bel Amour 27* to save my sorry gypsy arse,' I joke, 'and the twist of fate that led me to the House of Doujan. Where I began my career as a nose and created a perfume some say changed the course of the war. Do I exaggerate my claim?' I smile. 'I'll let you decide, Emma.'

14

PARIS, 2003

Emma

Perfume:
Mamselle after Midnight
Cascarilla, Florentine iris, amber

I ignore the bustle of tourists in the lobby of the Hôtel de Vendôme as I gush into the Art Deco ivory phone in the lobby, giving Granger amazing details of my interview with Madame de Cadieux. My face is flushed, my heart pounding.

I've never felt so excited in my life.

'The perfume diva is spilling her secrets,' I say into the public phone since the TV station is too cheap to give me an international calling card and the hotel maid is cleaning my room. 'She revealed things to me she's never told anyone.' I scout around the area with a reporter's eye. Nothing out of the ordinary, then I tell my boss about *madame*'s Roma roots, how her *maman* was murdered by a crazed Nazi major... and the night she met the elusive Resistance fighter known as the Count.

Am I talking too much? I scope out the lobby. No one's paying attention to me. Two businessmen arguing in French, a brunette wearing big sunglasses reading a tourist guide, the desk clerk munching on cheese squares when he thinks no one is looking.

'I'm telling you, Granger,' I continue, 'this is a story that will knock your socks off and I've got the exclusive.' I ramble on about my amazing flight on the Concorde and the crazy supersonic boom that freaked me out... though I leave out my run-in with Mr Gray Suit. He's my private nightmare. A sense of guilt gnaws at me. We're supposed to be on the same team, but he's insufferable. Not accepting me... why? Because I'm not 'posh' enough to interview *madame*? Or is he hiding something he doesn't want me to uncover... something that will jeopardize his position with the perfume diva.

I opt for both.

'Yes, we're continuing the interview after lunch,' I say into the phone, '*Madame* wants to fill me in on how she became Angéline de Cadieux, then show me the pawnshop where she met this seriously hot Resistance fighter... it's located on Rue Saint-Jacques or it was. God knows what's there now. Probably a laundromat... and yes, I'm tying it in with my personal story about my Polish grandmother who died in the Holocaust. I'm glad you like that angle. I'll keep in touch... and thanks, Granger, for believing in me.'

I hang up the phone, grateful to end the call. He's anxious for me to wrap this up and get back to New York. He ran the idea by the segment producer for *Sunday Travel Tales* and they're talking about expanding my interview into an hour-long special. I write the story, they decide what they want to use, then they'll send a film crew for background shots, as well as do an *on-camera* interview with her. Talk about pressure... I have to get *madame* to agree to a film crew following her around Paris.

Jeez, I haven't even finished the interview yet.

Which means I have to bring up my personal story with *madame* at some point... but when? The awful truth is, I'm afraid if I lay on her,

'Hey, my grandmother died in Dachau and by some chance did you run into her, *madame*?' she'll send me back to New York. She's so into honesty and truth from the press. Right now, I can't lay claim to either.

'Planning to run off on a secret rendezvous, *mademoiselle*?'

Ryker pops out of the corner like he's waiting for me. Spying on me is more like it. A rumble goes through me. I do my best to avoid the eye candy, him in his fabulous gray silk suit that hugs his broad shoulders, but I can't ignore the growing tension between us. What's his game?

'If I were dashing off to Monte Carlo with the *real* James Bond and not an Irish lookalike,' I snap back, 'I wouldn't tell you.'

'I'd find out anyway.' A snarky 007 smirk crosses his lips.

'Why would you care?' I toss back.

'I don't.'

Ooh... that hurt. He doesn't have to be so honest about how he feels about me.

Damn him.

'Contrary to the cool persona Madame de Cadieux portrays, Mademoiselle Keane, she's under a lot of stress and quite vulnerable after she experienced a recent stalking incident.'

'Who.... *why*?' I demand, feeling protective of her.

'I'm not at liberty to say, but I advise you to be aware of your surroundings... and *don't* talk to strangers.'

'I'm not a child, Monsieur Ryker.'

'Ryker.'

'I can handle myself and if anyone tries to hurt Madame de Cadieux, they'll have *me* to answer to. Now, if you'll excuse me, I have luncheon plans with *madame*.'

I hustle up the winding stairway, taking two steps at a time. Why does this guy unnerve me like this? We don't get along, we never will... we're two individualists who never let *anyone* interfere with our work. And we make no bones about it. We're not even oil and water. We're an ongoing storm with no sign of stopping. Yet my gut tells me he's a man of his word and he's genuinely worried about *madame's* safety. I give him credit for filling me in, but this conversation puts a new spin on the interview.

What isn't *madame* telling me?

15

Tiena

Perfume:
Heavenly Lace
Violet leaves, French jonquil, honey

Perfume bottles.

Standing tall and perfectly aligned on the narrow shelf behind the cash register like elegant, feminine soldiers with a touch of class. Placed there by Jarnak after I told him where to find the perfumes stashed under the counter in a carved ivory box.

I'm beside myself with excitement when the bright morning sunshine flashes its sparkle on the bottles like diamonds. I can't wait to embrace their lovely scents.

But no Count in sight.

Why doesn't that surprise me?

Sadness shimmies through me, a provocative emotion I dismiss and focus instead on the here and now. I awoke earlier to the overwhelming smell of hot coffee and fresh croissants. And raspberry jam infused with a pinch of lemon.

Jarnak brought me a tray then disappeared while I dressed. Strange not to hear wood creaking under the weight of my body as I slept... or the vibration of the wagon as I fell into a deep, dark sleep, no doubt from the sleeping powder in the tea. I had a moment of sadness when I awoke and accepted the fact I'd never again sleep in a *vardo*. The cozy space filled with memories of Maman and Papa, but I soon put it behind me.

I have yet to earn my freedom.

I embrace the perfume bottles to my chest, hugging them like old friends. Mandel and Ici and the House of Doujan. Perfumes I've smelled in the *Galeries Lafayette* or wandering among the mahogany cases in *Aux Trois Quartiers* department stores. The salesclerks gave us dirty looks and told us to hurry along, but Maman charmed them with her wit and wise woman sayings... and reading their palms so they'd give me a sample perfume to dab on my wrist. Then I'd dazzle them by naming the florals and spices in each fragrance. Grand, wonderful days I shall never know again.

Pain swells up in me, so painful my chest hurts.

I can barely hold back the tears as I run my fingers over the labels on the bottles embossed with gold lettering, dull and dusty when—

'*Bonjour, mademoiselle, comment ça va?*'

A woman's voice, silky and theatrical. I don't have to turn around to know it's the ex-ballerina. Slim, lithe, wearing a tight-fitting plaid dress with big pockets, buttoned up at the front, black pumps, light brown hair tucked into a snood, her pale face dotted with a bow mouth polished with a red lipstick so dark it vibrates. The young woman walks around me slowly in a circle, giving me the once-over. No doubt at the Count's request.

'*Bonjour*, Mademoiselle Pacquet.'

'So you're the gypsy girl.'

'Roma.'

'*Pardon.* I meant no offense, *mademoiselle*. I was remembering the time I danced the role of a gypsy princess in the ballet, a wonderful role filled with fire and romance and tambourines beating out a savage rhythm. I never thought I'd meet a *real* gypsy.' Her stare is disconcerting, but her smile is warm. 'Ah, *oui*, you're more beautiful than the Count said you were.'

'*Me, beautiful*? He said that?' I hover in the innocence of the girlish notion he likes me, only to find out he's more of a rogue than I thought.

She laughs. 'Whatever you're thinking, *mademoiselle*, don't go there. The Count will break your heart.'

'Did he break yours?' I ask to cover my embarrassment.

'I admit I fell in love with him. So tall and handsome, his voice as rich and deep as red wine, his eyes glowing with a secret fire, hot and liquid. His touch cold yet burning...' She shivers, her pale face blushing for a moment, then it's gone. 'You can *never* escape him once he looks at you with those gorgeous dark eyes.' She sighs. 'But he never notices me, *mademoiselle*. He has a one-track mind.'

'Oh?'

'All he cares about is beating the Nazis and driving them out of France.' She pauses. 'I don't know what dark force pushes him with such passion.' She grins. 'Maybe you can find out.'

I avert her curious look and arrange the three old bottles of perfume on the counter. 'When I was here with Papa, I remember thinking how these perfume bottles reminded me of lonely souls with no one to tell their stories. Scandals about vain ladies on the Rue de Rivoli. Cabaret dancers at the Moulin Rouge. Young girls in love.'

'Like you, *mademoiselle*?' Yvette asks, pulling off the glass stopper of a perfume bottle and wrinkling her nose. '*Ooh*, it's strong.'

'Let me sniff.' She puts the open bottle under my nose and I take a whiff. '*Whew*... it's spicy, smells like curry. I'd say this perfume must be from the late twenties.'

'Why is it so strong? It makes my head spin.'

'It smells that way because the chemical structure of the scent broke down over the years.'

I try the other bottle, then the next. One smells like alcohol... the other has a faint smell. I'm disappointed... how can I prove I'm a nose?

'Can you name the composition of *this* perfume, *mademoiselle*?'

Yvette pulls a turquoise crystal bottle out of her large skirt pocket, a square bottle embossed with a gold label from the House of Doujan.

I sniff the crook of my elbow to 'reset' my nose, a trick I learned from Maman who learned it from her *maman*. Then I pull off the stopper and inhale the luxurious scent while Yvette checks my accuracy against a folded-up piece of paper she draws from her pocket.

'Blackcurrant, Chinese plum, raspberry... very fruity,' I begin. 'Then a heavenly floral note. Italian, *no*, shaffali jasmine and succulent June rose... and a sensual, lasting base note... amber, iris, and incense.'

She claps her hands. '*Bravo, mademoiselle!* Perfect.'

'How did you get the formula?' I ask, curious.

'I conned Professor Zunz into giving it to me over the telephone.' She giggles. 'He's the head of our laboratory in Argenteuil and a stickler for the rules, but he's such a darling. Kind. And insistent on perfection in his blends. When I told him a customer complained about breaking out into a rash and wanted to know if there was oakmoss in the formula, the professor became so upset, he rattled off the ingredients so fast I could hardly write them down quick enough.'

'What if someone in the shop finds out about your deception?'

'They won't.'

'How can you be sure, Yvette?'

'Because I'm good at what I do, *mademoiselle*, what we *all* must do to help free France from the occupiers.' An unhappy look crosses her face. 'We lie.'

16

PARIS, 2003

Angéline

Perfume:
Doujan Glamor Girl
Hungarian rose, Casablanca jasmine, civet

'Passing the "nose test" with Yvonne was the first step of going from Roma girl to Resistance fighter. I went through a complete transformation – hair, clothes, how I walked, talked... but could I fool the Nazis? That, *mademoiselle*, was the unknown factor, which brings us here to the Hôtel Ritz.'

'Cool,' Emma says, smiling. 'It's showtime.'

I shake my head. She never ceases to amuse me with her Americanisms.

We cross the courtyard from our hotel to the Ritz, dodging taxicabs and luxury motorcars. A small crowd of American tourists are taking photos of the famed hotel with its elegant canopies and tall, multi-paned windows where Göring once stood peering down at the square, never knowing refugees were hidden in secret rooms. A French guide rambles on about the hotel's history and the rich and famous who stayed here, but he mentions nothing about the war years, as if they never happened. That saddens me. So many lives sacrificed and they're brushed over like dead leaves trampled by time.

'What better place to try out my new identity,' I continue, gearing up for an emotional interlude and linking arms with Emma – to give me courage? 'Than here in the most famous place in Paris to hobnob with the hierarchy of the Third Reich and snobby Parisians.'

'Amazing, *madame*, you could pull it off.'

'I was too naïve to know how dangerous it was,' I admit, walking at a slow pace... stalling, actually.

'You were so young and, if I may say, brash?'

'Like you, *mademoiselle*?' I stop, turn to look at her. She's smiling.

'Guilty as charged. That's why you like me.'

'Who says I like you?'

'You do... or you wouldn't put up with me.'

I let that last comment pass as we head for the hotel entrance. Of course, she's right. Linking arms with someone I barely know isn't in my perfumer's playbook, but it seems natural to share my feelings with her. I didn't think twice about it. Of all the reporters who have interviewed me, Emma is the most engaging with curious blue eyes and blonde hair squished back in a messy ponytail.

I stop, stare at the infamous revolving doors of the Ritz. 'Back in 1940, when I entered the lobby, the glitzy establishment was swarming with Nazis and French sympathizers, a place where German officers surrendered their weapons upon entering the hotel to an attendant who placed them in a kiosk.'

'You're joking?' Emma asks, then smirks. 'No wonder the chandeliers lasted through the war. The Nazis couldn't use them for target practice.'

I smile. 'And the intrigue... from the owner's widow, Madame Ritz, feuding with the hotel director's wife, to the secret Resistance group run from the hotel kitchen. Then you had the Nazi sympathizers... aristocrats, film stars, fashion leaders. It was a fascinating moment in time when glamor and silk rubbed elbows with Boche gray-green, praying they could wash off the stink later. I can tell you this, *mademoiselle*, the smell of collaboration reminded me of powdery incense and burnt, dark red roses.'

Suddenly, admitting what went through my mind then, I feel the same sickening nausea overcome me. I can't take that final step and get on the carousel whirl of revolving doors that will sweep us inside the hotel. Back then the elegant establishment reminded me of an aristocrat on her way to the guillotine. Haughty, proud... but reduced to wearing last year's gown. Soiled, dirty. Her perfumed, powdered wig reeked of death.

How many of these SS officers have blood on their hands? I wondered. *How many Frenchmen are also guilty?*

I feel out of sorts, standing outside the hotel entrance, steeped in my past. I can't go in. My hands are cold. My memories hot. I do not so much as blink. I need to get past the anger because I didn't know then my instincts were right. There were battles yet to be fought, but on that day when I strolled through the Ritz, I feared I'd be recognized by one arrogant major and hauled off to a concentration camp. I glance at Emma. She's chewing on her pencil eraser, biting her lip, and her eyes speak of an avid curiosity she's too polite to spell out.

She takes my silence as a game, waiting for me to say something provocative. When I don't, she does it for me.

'Were you on a secret mission for the Count, *madame*?'

Her wide-eyed look makes me smile, diffusing my anger like a puff of smoke. She has a way of taking my moments of angst and seeing deeper into me, as if she knows I'm squirming inwardly and wants to make it easier for me to talk about the past. *A reporter's trick?* No, I don't think so. The girl possesses the one thing that often makes her job impossible.

She has a soul.

'*Ah, mais oui, mademoiselle*, a mission of sorts. Dangerous... and *very* hush hush,' I tease her back. 'I kept thinking, *Is my wig on straight?*'

'And was it?'

'No. I kept peeking in the fancy hotel mirrors, straightening it, scratching my head, fixing a hairpin digging into my scalp and *dying* to take the damn thing off. I didn't dare,' I confess and we both laugh. I give her my best *perfume diva* smile in spite of the uncomfortable feeling settling in my gut like a sticky brown resin. 'It's good to have a moment to see the lighter side of a dark time, Mademoiselle Emma. Which reminds me, we've spoken about so much heartache I've yet to tell you how I went from gypsy girl to *parfumier*.'

She smiles when I use the phrase *gypsy girl* to refer to my rambunctious personality when I was known as Tiena. It seems more fitting between us. An affectionate shorthand that makes us both nostalgic for that girl. A freedom to speak freely about my feelings, sexual or romantic, something that wasn't possible in those times, but the world has changed and I can enjoy the pleasure of sharing 'girl talk' as Emma calls it. Though part of me is hoping for a deeper connection, that she won't abandon me as I turn a corner in my life, letting go of a past that has haunted me. I believe, when my story is told, I'll need a friend to hold my hand through the jabs and scrutiny that are certain to come.

I hope it's her.

Feeling energized, I step through the hotel's revolving door and marvel at how the clientele has changed. Society grande dames rub elbows with rock divas and women of industry.

'Yvette was so impressed with my knowledge of scents,' I begin, nodding to several women acknowledging me with pleasant smiles, 'she wanted to make certain I'd get a job at the House of Doujan. She insisted on giving me a complete makeover, then we tried out my new persona at the Ritz to see if I could fool the Germans into believing I was a charming *Parisienne*.'

'Oh, how fun, *madame*.' Emma giggles. Her head moves left then right, taking in the luxury hotel, but it's the long gallery I lead her toward, the mirrors reminding me of liquid glass we can slide through and into the past as I tell my story.

'Yvette used a chemical colorant on my hair later, but for now I wore a wig of rich, black tresses that set off my pale skin and hazel eyes.'

'*Ooh la la*, I can see you as a classic 1940s brunette with a pompadour and victory rolls.' She sighs. 'I bet you were gorgeous.'

'*Merci, mademoiselle*, but gorgeous isn't how I see myself. More like a traveler in disguise to keep me safe from the Nazi wolves.'

'I like that. I'll use it in my piece.' She keeps writing.

'Yvette reshaped my brows with high, dark arches, applied so much face powder my poor nose temporarily lost its sense of smell, then she smoothed dusky pink rouge and highlights on my cheekbones and drew a bow on my mouth with a bright scarlet-red lipstick. I couldn't believe the girl in the mirror was me, Tiena Cordova. Dark hair, tight black and white striped dress... black ankle-strap pumps and long black gloves to cover the scar on my arm. Finally, she placed a saucy hat on my head with a feather tipped at an angle. The only thing I kept from my gypsy life was Maman's bracelet jangling on my wrist.'

I eye the change in the fashion displayed in the gallery, but the mirrors haven't changed. Only what I see in them. An elegant woman in soft mauve silk passing for someone much younger.

But I can't erase the scars.

On my skin or in my heart. I smooth the silk sleeve over my arm, feeling the jagged scar with my fingers as raw in my mind as the day my stepfather cut me, along with the number tattooed on the outer side of my left forearm. Some former prisoners show it as a badge of honor and I understand that; others have it removed.

I keep it to remind me how precious life is.

'I'm proud to say I received many admiring stares from the Nazi officers that day, our walk through the Hôtel Ritz in late 1940 accomplishing what Yvette hoped it would do. Especially when we walked by a German officer I *swear* was the Nazi major who killed my mother. Laughing, flirting with a sultry woman smoking a cigarette in an ivory holder. He never recognized me and it took every ounce of my resolve not to call him a murderer.'

I know my emotional outburst catches her off guard and shocks her. Of course, there's more wishful thinking than truth in my words, but I dreamed of it happening so many times, I wanted to believe it.

Suspicious, Emma lifts a brow. 'A terrific hook, *madame*, but seriously? You *accidentally* bumping into that creepy major makes a lovely "tag" to the story, but how believable is it?' she challenges me.

I argue back, 'Is it not the prerogative of a woman of my age to anoint my past with a bit of fabrication?'

'No.'

She shakes her head and that's the end of it.

That's what I like about her. She humors me, but she'll only go so far. She has her own code of ethics and, even if I throw a fit, that last part won't make it into her story.

Instead, she says, 'New clothes, makeup... even a new hair color to change your looks. Did it work, *madame*?'

'Yes. I was convinced I could get a job at the House of Doujan with my new look *and* Yvonne's coaching. She taught me how a perfume had to evoke a fantasy. The bottles, the packaging, the salesclerks' uniforms, the advertising – such as it was during the war – even the name of the perfume must evoke a pleasurable emotion or a daring desire. A forbidden tryst.'

I look into the mirror behind a window case spotlighting jewelry so delicate, as if the tiny hands of pixie fairies forged them. I don't see a woman of eight decades who hasn't slept since we arrived back in Paris staring back at me. I see that Roma girl not believing *she* was the ultrasophisticate staring back at her with big, wide eyes with lashes lathered with black crystal shoe polish, what Yvette called 'mascara'.

What I didn't know then was that this wasn't the final test and whether I passed or failed depended on what happened when we returned to the pawnshop and a tall, handsome stranger made me a most unusual offer.

'I get it, *madame*, to sell perfume, you had to look glamorous. You had to be a babe.'

'A *what*?' I ask, not understanding. We move down the long gallery and I'd hoped to make this quick, but I'm wondering what this 'babe' is.

'A sultry siren. A dame with class. You know, *oomph*.' She pushes her breasts together and pouts her lips, making me laugh. And... *uh-oh*... I'm not the only one smiling. I see Ryker in the mirror enjoying the show with a quiet smirk on his lips. Another precedent broken. The man *does* know how to admire a beautiful woman. And it seems Emma forgot we're not alone.

She remembers now.

Her cheeks redden, as if she's intensely aware she's made a dent in his armor but she's under no illusion he's ready to tango.

She doesn't miss a beat.

'Can we go back to the part where you get a new hair color, *madame*?' she muses, then sticks her tongue out at Ryker in the mirror, who shoots her a soul-melty sneer before he disappears.

Oh, my, these two make me feel young again.

If only I were.

17

PARIS, 1940

Tiena – Angéline

Perfume:
No Regrets
Jasmine, Tiare flower, musk

'The bracelet has got to go, *mademoiselle*.'

'No, *I can't*... I won't.' I wrap my fingers around the bronze coins and I swear they vibrate in my hand. Maman's ghost is upset... *very* upset.

'It's the details that count, Tiena. You won't pass for a sophisticate from Lyon wearing that gypsy bracelet. You want to work at the House of Doujan, *n'est-ce pas*? You wouldn't want to disappoint the Count?'

She's well aware I yearn to please the elusive Resistance fighter.

Hands on her hips, she glares at me until I take off the bracelet and hand it to Jarnak. He smiles his approval and puts the bracelet on the counter near the cash register. I have much to learn, she says. How to walk, talk, sip tea... until I'm ready for my 'interview'. Getting this job will prove to *le Comte* I'm capable of joining them in their fight to rid France of the occupiers.

Learning how to sip tea doesn't make sense, but what do I know?

'How long must I train?' I ask.

'Until you don't have to ask me that question.'

The pawnshop is empty except for the three of us, the afternoon sun shooting through the beveled glass door and hitting the cases filled with odd items with a bright sparkle. I sense Yvette is more excited than I am... or she has more confidence in me than I have.

'Monsieur Baptiste is the owner of the perfume company, but Frederic insists on checking out the new girls. He can be a bother with his flirting and roving hands.'

'Who?'

'Monsieur Baptiste's son. I must warn you, he's a Nazi sympathizer and likes to show off to the SS officers at the cabarets. After a few highballs, the Nazi brass become agreeable to his business proposals for the House of Doujan.'

'Does he know many Nazi officers?' I ask. A chilling thought runs down my spine at the idea of running into Major von Risinger.

'A few. They swagger into the shop with their wives or mistresses, demanding our best perfumes.' Her grim expression softens when she takes a step back and looks at me from head to toe, pleased with her work. 'You look beautiful, *mademoiselle*. Wait here while I grab my hat, then we're off to the House of Doujan so you can get a look at the establishment, sample our perfumes, and see how the salesclerks handle themselves with customers.'

'How far is it?'

'About a half-hour walk on the Rue Saint-Honoré.'

She rushes off to grab her hat. I keep tapping my foot. I can't stand still. My nerves shatter my confidence while I wait for Yvette to return. What if I can't learn how to walk and talk like a sophisticated *Parisienne*, what if I *don't* get a job at the perfume shop? I can't go back to my Roma clan. I'll end up on the streets or worse—

The tiny bell on the front door rings.

A tall man enters the shop. Tweed jacket, long overcoat, hat pulled low.

I can't see his face. *What's he hiding?*

The mood in the shop changes, the presence of a customer making me tense with uncertainty. I watch him browse the cases with odds and ends of silverware, tiny clay statues, chatting in English and French with Jarnak about how he's acquainted with Herr Göring and he'd appreciate full cooperation from the shop's owner regarding giving him the best price, then he points to a pair of ancient silver wine vessels.

I can't help but overhear their conversation since I understand English, though I rarely speak the language since I lost Papa. He's asking the price. Jarnak quotes him a ridiculously low sum. He nods, agreeing on the amount, then walks past me, barely giving me a look before browsing the collection of books in the corner. A strange scent hits my nostrils, but with the face powder up my nose, I can't place it, yet there's something familiar about this man with the broad shoulders that makes my heart flutter.

Shaking off the unwanted feelings, I walk away when—

'How much for the bracelet, Monsieur Jarnak?' he asks, dangling the bronze coins.

I double blink. What? That's my bracelet.

'It's not for sale, *monsieur*.' I yank the bracelet out of his hand.

He grabs my wrist; his grip is firm but not painful. 'From what I hear, *mademoiselle*, everything in Paris is for sale... if you're willing to pay the price.'

'Not everything, *monsieur*.' I stand my ground.

'My mistake, *mademoiselle*.' He grins, then lets me go. I'll not allow this arrogant foreigner to confiscate Maman's bracelet.

'*Merci, monsieur*, if you'll excuse me, I have an appointment—'

'I apologize if I was too brash, *mademoiselle*.' He cuts me off, his broad shoulders blocking the door. 'Let me introduce myself. Dr Langston MacBride of the A. J. Seymour Institute of Archaeology and the Arts in Boston at your service.' He tips his hat and I make contact with his smoldering dark eyes watching me from behind round, horn-rimmed glasses. The spectacles make him appear rather odd and I can't grasp what he looks like without them, but the deep tone of his voice sets me on edge. 'My friends call me Lance.'

'Does that include your *Nazi* friends?'

I can't forget his earlier comment about knowing Herr Göring... it leaves a sour taste in my mouth.

'I have no beef with Germany, *mademoiselle*, and I'd advise you to do the same.'

'You're an American, *n'est-ce pas*?' I ask.

'Yes. I arrived in Paris to purchase twelfth-century artifacts before the Germans occupied the city.' He shrugs. 'Fortunately, Herr Göring has allowed me to continue my work.'

'Your work, *monsieur*?'

'I'm an archaeologist and an art critic for the *Boston Star*,' he says, as if that should mean something to me. 'I was in Egypt when I heard about a recent cache of swords, armor, and vessels retrieved from an old castle near the Belgian border. I left Cairo and came to Paris to secure permission to excavate the site. My colleagues in Boston will pay dearly to acquire those artifacts.'

'You're a scientist, *monsieur*,' I challenge him. 'How can you get so cozy with the Nazis?'

He shrugs. 'America is not at war with Germany. It was my lucky day when I ran into Herr Göring at a museum in Amsterdam and he asked my advice regarding acquiring Old Masters paintings for his private art collection.'

'Don't you mean looting?' I blurt out.

'A dangerous statement, *mademoiselle*...' He looks me up and down. 'Even for a beautiful woman like you.'

I pull back. He's toying with me, why?

'However, I imagine Herr Göring would forgive such an indiscretion,' he continues, a warning in his deep voice, '*if* your Roman coin bracelet finds its way into the coffers of the Reich.'

'But *monsieur*—'

'If I may inspect the coins, *mademoiselle*...?'

My inner core rebels at obeying his request with every inch of my being, but my practical self knows the consequences. Besides, I have

Yvette and Jarnak to consider. I'll not do anything to jeopardize their safety.

My hand shakes as I hold up the bracelet and the bronze coins catch the late afternoon sun streaming in through the window panes.

The archaeologist peers over the top of his spectacles to inspect the coins.

'I'd estimate early Roman around the third century... yes, Emperor Constantine... the first emperor to convert to Christianity. See the exquisite detail, *mademoiselle*, the laurel wreath around his head, his profile. These coins will make a wonderful addition to the Führer's upcoming art museum in Linz.' He lifts his gaze to meet my eyes. Even in the dimly lit shop, his eyes pull me into their dark depths. 'I'm curious. Where did you get it?'

'From a gypsy girl,' I say with pride, 'begging in front of Notre-Dame. She traded it for a loaf of bread.'

'Many in Paris are hungry, *mademoiselle*, and do what they must to survive.' He gives me a look that is, at the least, disconcerting. I want to avoid his eyes, but the Roma girl in me won't give him that satisfaction. He keeps staring, waiting for me to say something. I get the jitters again, as if I've already danced this dance. An urge to get under his skin settles in me. I get a closer look at him as he discusses how accommodating Göring's art agent in Paris has been in facilitating his travel documents to dig in Belgium. Scruffy stubble, patrician nose. I can't read the expression in his eyes shaded by dark gray sunglasses. I must be careful. If he has any suspicion the pawnshop is a front for the Underground, he'll bring the Gestapo here and they'll arrest us. Jarnak, Yvette... the Count. I must get rid of him.

Then give him what he wants, no matter how much it hurts.

I rub the Roman coins with my fingers, feeling Maman's magic flow through me for the last time, the musical jangle of her bracelet ringing in my ears and calming me.

Then the moment is gone.

And I know what I have to do, even if I starve.

'Of course, *monsieur,* how could I have been so foolish? Everyone in

Paris knows Herr Göring has excellent taste in art. Take the bracelet. No charge.'

I won't taint my mother's memory by taking his dirty Nazi money.

'We French must do our part to preserve the past...' I continue. *If we want to have a future without you and your Nazi friends,* I finish silently.

He smiles, then pockets the bracelet. *'Merci, mademoiselle, au revoir...* until we meet again.'

Then he's out the door, ringing that insistent bell like a death knell and taking Maman's bracelet with him. I'm shaking so bad, my teeth rattle. I sink down into the blue wingback chair and let go with a good cry, the black shoe polish melting on my lashes and drizzling down my cheeks.

What have I done, Maman? I gave your precious bracelet to a Nazi sympathizer. I had no choice or good people would die.

I pray Maman's ghost will forgive me.

* * *

'Did *mademoiselle* pass the test, Count?'

Test? What test?

I put aside my misery and look up to see Yvette rushing out of the backroom, her right cheek red, her eyelid droopy... as though she's been watching me through the peephole.

'She passed. Barely.'

The Count. He's standing behind me. I shiver when I feel his hot breath on the back of my neck, though his scent is elusive to me. I jump up and spin around, more than curious at this odd turn of events. Dressed in black, a pistol in his belt, the curved handle of my knife protruding from his black overcoat pocket, he's holding my bracelet in his hand.

Mais non, he was the archaeologist. Gone is the tweed jacket, the glasses. The pompous attitude.

And yes, I smile to myself, he's just as appealing when he's not hiding in the shadows. He sneaked back in through the hidden entrance and no doubt had a good laugh when he witnessed my tearful outpouring of despair.

'What games are you playing, *monsieur*?' I blurt out. 'Who are you? And why that silly disguise?'

'Who I am is not important, *mademoiselle*. I had to be certain of your loyalty, see how you'd react when confronted with a life-or-death situation. When you had to put your heart, your emotions into a box and deal with the enemy to avoid suspicion. Whether or not you'd cast doubt on your loyalty to the Reich as a French citizen by openly expressing your hatred of the Germans. Or worse, expose the partisans whose lives depended on you.' He smiles. 'You had me worried when you blurted out your distaste of Göring... a reckless move since he's Hitler's second-in-command, but you bounced back when you gave up the bracelet with a charming smile. I can see how much that hurt you, but you showed grit, fast thinking.'

Then he hands me back my bracelet. Misty-eyed, I clutch it to my chest.

I'll never let it go again, Maman, I promise.

I beam at his praise, something I've wanted since I first met the elusive Count.

He turns to the hunchback. '*Mademoiselle* is perfect for the job I have in mind, Jarnak. A glamor girl. With *mademoiselle's* talent as a *parfumier*, she can gain entrance to the elite Nazi High Command, enter their world and move freely. Become privy to conversations even I can't gain access to.'

'Me?' I ask.

'*Oui, mademoiselle*,' he says, 'while the Nazis prefer to plant a plain gray mouse as an operative, someone who raises no red flags, they're often blindsided by a seductive woman spying on *them*. I must advise you that high-profile activities increase the risk.'

'I'm not afraid, *monsieur*... or should I call you Dr MacBride?'

He grins. 'See, Jarnak, *mademoiselle* is daring, bold.' He circles me, admiring my new look. 'But she also needs a new name, something glamorous.'

'Maman said I reminded her of an angel.'

'*Ah, mais oui, Monsieur le Comte,*' Yvette rushes her words, 'like the heroine in the Sylvie Martone film, Angéline.'

He nods. 'Yes, Angéline suits you. Now for a last name... something that fits your unique personality... ah, I have it. Cadieux. *De Cadieux* to give it elegance and class.'

'What does it mean, de Cadieux?' I want to know.

'I had a French professor back home in Boston by that name. He said it was an honorable moniker from the days of Louis IX and meant *fighter.*' He looks me up and down. 'That is definitely you, *mademoiselle.*'

'Oh...' The simple word escapes my lips before I can stop myself. *A new name.* I can't believe Tiena is gone. Forever. My past is but a silhouette of a gypsy girl fading into the grayness of yesterdays and dissolving before my eyes, like I've put on shoes belonging to someone else. Wherever they take me, I must follow.

Tiena Cordova is no more.

Tears well up in my eyes, but I blink them away. I can't cry over what cards were dealt to me by the winds of time. As Maman would say when she read fortunes, 'Look around the corner... not behind you... you never know what riches await you.'

Now she gives me courage, reminding me that death may separate us from the family we love, but nothing will erase the lost ones in our hearts. I feel like that now. I grieve for the death of the Roma girl I was, but without tears. I will never erase her from my heart, but embrace her wisdom, her passion for scent.

I shall make Maman proud of me.

I imagine her hovering around this man with his raw masculinity and worldly sophistication, questioning *who, what* he is... how he's turned her Tiena into a creature that frightens yet intrigues me. I ask myself: *Can I use my gift of scent to fool the Nazis? Mesmerize them with my perfumes?*

I can't focus on that now.

I barely notice when Yvette nudges Jarnak and they disappear into the back room, leaving us alone. All I can think about is the warmth of the Count's body pressing against mine when he pulls me closer to him, sending me into a swoon. His overwhelming maleness makes me woozy. Feeling breathless and silly, I hold on to his coat as if it's a cloak of invisibility and he'll disappear if I don't hang on tight. His dark eyes hold mystery and romance and something else, too. The promise of a protector. I'd never admit that as strong as I push myself to be, I crave to nestle my head against his shoulder and close my eyes and feel safe in a world gone mad.

He senses my need and holds me tighter.

Then he breathes in my ear, the intimate moment making me shiver as his tone deepens and he says in a husky voice, 'Welcome to the Resistance, Angéline de Cadieux.'

18

PARIS, 2003

Emma

Perfume:
Sunrise
Lime, French marigold, moss

'Is this where the pawnshop stood in 1940, *madame*?'

I strike a pose outside the black and red façade of the shop located in the multi-story building on Rue Saint-Jacques, nothing left of the original dreary gray wooden front with the marble plaque *madame* described to me.

'*Oui, mademoiselle*,' she says, 'I'll never forget that rainy night when I sneaked in the back entrance... meeting the Count... then the days, weeks, months I made my way here, keeping my head down, my business private... and the worst day when the French police and gendarmes pushed me out of the way when they descended on the district and rounded up Jewish merchants, women, and children.'

'When was that, *madame*?' I ask, making notes.

'July 1942... but I'm getting ahead of myself. I came here as a young

Roma girl and here, Mademoiselle Emma, is where I learned to be a spy.'

I take a moment to watch her reliving those years in her mind, her red hair blowing about her face, her long camel coat whipping around her ankles. She doesn't move. I understand. Baring her soul to me when the urge to revisit this place is so strong, when the blood in her veins is so alive, to let her heart run free, brings back every moment to her as it was then, over sixty years ago.

We're both overwhelmed. I can't believe I'm here, the scene so vivid in my mind after hearing *madame* speak about the pawnshop and her amazing transformation from gypsy girl to sophisticated spy. I scope out the street, try to imagine how it looked then. I see it in black and white like in the old war films. Girls with bows in their hair riding bicycles, women with scarves wrapped around their heads struggling to carry their meager groceries, men standing on the corner, smoking those smelly Gauloises that define the era. And German soldiers carousing in cafés or harassing a poor man with a yellow star on his coat.

Now small restaurants line the street, what we call Ma and Pop shops back in the States. Rue Saint-Jacques isn't a wide street; just a single lane of traffic, no street parking. Stone buildings about four, five stories high with tiny wrought-iron balconies... not big enough to hide from anyone – yes, I'm thinking Gestapo – then taller buildings farther down the street, a church, and an abbey.

I scan the shops looking for street numbers – not easy to find. My gut tightens when I locate the number where the pawnshop stood. The shop is gone, but in my mind I see familiar faces in the window panes staring back at me. Yvette, Jarnak... the Count... and a young Angéline de Cadieux.

Her big, wide eyes telling me there's more to the story and to be patient.

Finally, *madame* speaks.

'The Count... Lance, as I called him... welcomed me into his operation, but I could tell by the way he observed me... following me... asking me to repeat my backstory several times... he wasn't convinced I was as innocent as I claimed to be. He admitted to me after the war that he wondered if I was from an impoverished French aristocratic family recruited by the Nazis to gather intelligence for a price or to save my own neck. Especially since I had a fondness for an abandoned château outside Paris. I knew every nook and cranny in the ruined castle since my clan had camped there since I was a child... and Maman is buried nearby in the tiny cemetery in the forest.'

Madame de Cadieux takes a moment, standing across the street from where the pawnshop once was, glancing over her shoulder.

I write fast on my yellow pad crammed with big, crazy writing as I'm wont to do when I'm desperate to get everything down. What's not on the pad is written on my heart, bits of emotional upheaval I add at night on my laptop when the words flow faster than my fingers can type, when I dare to engage the idea of *madame* and Lance... a nerdy archaeologist yet... falling in love. I hope I'm right and he's a good guy. I like my heroes to be strong and brave.

Men who don't keep a girl out of the action just *because* she's a girl.

Speaking of powerful men, especially ones wearing London gray silk suits, where is Ryker anyway?

It doesn't matter. I've decided to ignore the undeniable effect the man has on females. I don't put myself in that category. I'm a reporter. Enough said. I don't respond to his type. Handsome but overbearing. Strong but distant. We have nothing in common except *madame*.

End of story.

I keep writing, trying to catch up with her recollections of her entrée into the Resistance. I'm surprised she doesn't want to go inside the establishment that's now a bar, but she insists on remaining outside, taking my arm as we stroll up the street and she continues her story.

'I sometimes wonder, Emma, how I ever survived the war as a member of the Resistance,' she continues. 'I was so green. I had no knowledge how to operate a wireless or fire a pistol, but I knew the landscape around Paris, where the roads intercepted, where the railroads crossed... when the Nazi sentries changed, how to evade German patrols on hidden paths through the forests.'

I see her eyes light up as she rambles on about those days, promising that next we'll visit the shop of the House of Doujan on the Right Bank so we can 'sniff perfumes till we can't tell the sweetness of rose from the pungent scent of musk'. She doesn't elaborate any further about *le Comte* – Lance's code name – making me believe she's holding back those memories for a more intimate moment. I'm itching to know everything about their affair, but I have something else on my mind.

The more I get to know her, the more I wish I could ask her if she'd take me on as a student of perfume. Sure, I love my job, but a girl's got to follow her bliss sometime. I don't want to grow old and never know if I have the right stuff to become a 'nose'.

The question is: *how to convince her?*

I can see by the powder lines cracking around her eyes, bluish circles, she's tired and exhausted. Nope. Not the time to spring that on her.

We walk down the street toward the old abbey (a convent during the war, she tells me) and the church, musing about whether or not the secret passageway has been sealed up—

When I get the feeling we're being followed.

I can't be sure, but I catch snippets of someone darting in and out of the shoppers, tourists crowding the street. I panic, then let go with a smirk. Ryker, of course. I'm not used to him tailing me and I don't like it.

I'm pondering how to take him down a notch or two, walking arm in arm with *madame* like two Parisian besties, when two punks approach us.

'You want fancy handbags, ladies?' singsongs the first in English in a thick accent. 'We got designer bags for you.'

'*Merci, non.*' I sling my tote bag over my shoulder and hang on tight to *madame* while the second punk tries the same spiel on passers-by on the street.

Madame de Cadieux eyes them warily, then speaks to them in Romani. They laugh and call her crazy when someone brushes up against me and tries to grab my cell phone out of my jacket... *pick-pockets*.

'Hands off!' I yell out, then put my arm around Madame de Cadieux and pull her to safety into a nearby shop before they can grab her purse. 'You okay, *madame*?'

'*Oui, très bien... merci*, Emma.' She's shaken up and requests we put off visiting the perfume shop of the House of Doujan till tomorrow. I agree.

Where the heck is Ryker?

I call Marcel on her cell phone as *madame* requests and, like Aladdin, he shows up minutes later with the black town car and whisks us back to the hotel. I keep looking over my shoulder.

No Ryker.

I insist on accompanying *madame* to her hotel room and request a nurse to come check on her, which she immediately cancels. Only Marie can get her to lie down, showing up in record time with hot tea and the aroma of cinnamon wafting in the air. That calms her down... me, too, when Marie brings me a cup and I head off to my room. I check my tote bag... cell phone, wallet, usual stuff... then I nearly choke when I find a cryptic message written on classy, heavy linen paper. In English.

Chills race through me when I read the message.

Back off, bitch. She's mine.

* * *

Angéline

I had quite a jolt to my emotions today when I visited the site of the old pawnshop on Rue Saint-Jacques. It's a sophisticated cocktail bar now, but the exquisite, beveled glass door is there, gussied up with fancy etched lettering. I peeked through the glass and noted the long counter where Jarnak took up his post remains intact and shines like black lacquer. The storefront is colorful with fresh paint. I wonder if they sealed up the peepholes or replaced them with cameras. In my mind, I saw Yvette waving to me and I swore Lance was standing outside the shop, smiling at me with that grin of his I love so much. Tall, broad-shouldered in his long, black overcoat, mysterious looking with his black Fedora pulled low, looking for me. It was a mirage, of course. Both are gone.

I sigh. My brain knows that; my heart doesn't.

I did my best to choke back the tears and not break down.

There's nothing more pitiful than seeing an old woman cry.

I cry now. When I'm alone, I allow myself the indulgence of putting on my favorite silk kimono and wrap myself up in a muddle of emotions I haven't felt in years. Love, anger, curiosity, even hate. During the war, we kept so much bottled up, we didn't dare show weakness... *God*, never in front of the Nazis... then afterward, we were so happy we were afraid to show anything *but* happiness. It was a carousel ride we never got off.

I was getting comfortable in my old memories this afternoon when we had that awful moment with the young thugs. They weren't Roma – they didn't understand a word I said – but they could have been. So many of my people live in poverty on the outskirts of Paris in Saint-Denis in shacks without running water or *toilettes*. For years, I've given large donations to help them get medical assistance and food, and I won't ever stop. I can't forget where I came from. Or the horrors I saw at Auschwitz in the Roma camp.

Having Emma at my side was what I needed to deal with the situation. *Alors*, I shall miss her when the interview is over and she returns to New York. A funny ache settles in my chest. I can't keep her here in Paris forever, though I'd like to. Oh, I know that's selfish, but there's something about her presence that goes beyond her questions and observations about my life. Like we've formed this bond and she's guiding me through my personal reckoning with my past, helping me walk through it with a clearer eye.

And I swear she understands the gift of smell more than she lets on. I see her sniffing everything from the coffee to the leather in my town car, her brow furrowed, her nose scrunched up like a curious rabbit, as if she's interpreting the scent.

I smile. Is that how *I* look?

Amused, I ponder why she seems reluctant to share her gift with me. I shan't press her, but it would be fun to compare notes – literally – on perfumes. *Alors*, these are the musings of a lonely woman and I won't deny it. I'll not give up trying to find out more about her, but first I must focus on the matter at hand.

After a long nap at Marie's insistence (she's more of a stickler about my health than I am), I order tea and pastries in my hotel room for Emma and me.

As the evening settles in, my curiosity dips its toe into our conversation. Something's not right. I'm concerned about Emma. She fidgets with her teacup, picking it up then putting it down, doodling on her yellow pad, heaving out long sighs. She looks shaken up. I'm relieved she wasn't hurt. She was so busy eyeing the young pickpockets, she didn't notice the phony brunette wearing a wig with the big sunglasses following us.

I did.

The woman didn't try to hide herself from me. If anything, she enjoyed the commotion with the boys. It added to her drama.

Brooke Hansen.

I can't forget the flash of her greedy smile before she slithered off like a deadly cobra, a woman intent on ruining me.

Emma doesn't bring up the incident and I don't wish to discuss it further until I speak with Ryker. I sent him to Dublin overnight, a short flight from Paris, and ordered him to turn off his mobile, making him unreachable. Today is the seventh anniversary of the loss of his wife and daughter. I insisted he go back to Ireland to honor them as he does every year. Of course, he'll be angry with me for sending him and leaving me unprotected, but I don't regret it. I know how important healing is to the soul, even more so to the heart. Except I don't think the man has done one bit of healing, that he still blames himself for the loss of his family. That his enemies took out their revenge on him by destroying what he loved the most. Guilt is a terrible thing to live with, how well I know that after surviving the camps, but I told no one, not even Emma. He depends on me to keep his secrets. It's a pact we have. I don't try to change him. He doesn't try to change me. I let him be, even if I don't approve of him beating himself up and putting his heart in a dark place. I fear the day will come when he'll never find it again. I thought Emma might be the one to break through that darkness.

I still do.

Sipping tea, I seek to regain the repartee I shared with Emma earlier, speaking about my entrée into the perfume business and the cast of characters I met and how the most horrible of circumstances put me where I am today as the owner of the House of Doujan.

But first, I keep my voice steady as I go back to the Paris of October 1940.

My first day as a spy.

What I feared most was that I wouldn't be any good at it.

19

PARIS, 1940

Angéline

Perfume:
Madame D
Yellow rose, raspberry, honey

'Ready, Angéline? Today's the day.'

Yvette kisses me on both cheeks, her breath sweet. Chocolate. Her weakness. The Germans haven't rationed it yet, as they have butter, cheese, and eggs... meat is next. Life in Occupied Paris moves along at a steady, routine pace. We're starting to feel the effects of rationing while the 'green beetles', as we're wont to call the German soldiers under our breath, act like hormone-infused boys, indulging in the 'decadence of Paris' in the cabarets and brothels while the rest of us suffer.

I feel my anxiety worsen.

Three weeks. Four days. That's how long I've jumped out of windows, learned to forge the official Nazi seal... engage in the art of blackmail... how to pick the pocket of an unsuspecting German officer... how to fire a pistol and always aim for the heart... *I know how to pick a lock*, I remind Lance. That evokes a rare smile from him.

From me? The intense training makes me sigh heavily, then fret... then *shake* like Maman's tambourine. I imagine myself in a dangerous situation with a band of Nazis... or God help me, Gestapo... a certain confidence then fear making my imagination run wild. How will I react? What hits me as strange is, before my training I'd strike out in sheer brazenness, get the job done.

Now I have to *think* first and hope I get it right.

Mon Dieu.

Next, the gentle art of persuasion. Lance believes weapons and explosives training is vital to the agent, but more so is feeding disinformation to the enemy and gleaning information without them knowing it. I might hear a Nazi officer mention a Renoir in a shoddy apartment or black-market beef dumped on the side of the road after an accident. *It happened*, he says. The abandoned beef led back to information about a secret Nazi meeting. The large amount of beef was headed to a five-star restaurant in Paris, indicating German officers were meeting there. An agent was put into place as a waiter to gather intelligence and intercepted orders from Berlin to arrest a notable businessman, giving the Underground time to get him out of France.

I take it in, doubting I'll come across information that provocative working in a perfume shop.

Never underestimate the Boches, I hear from Lance every day. Or you're dead. Worse, you'll end up in the hands of the Gestapo.

I nod, clench my fists. Bite my lip. I try so hard not to blurt out, I'm wanted by the Gestapo and if they catch me, the major will have me executed without so much as a blink of an eye. He killed Maman. He can't get away with that... I have to do this job.

I work harder and the stress is killing me. Made more so by my growing attraction to a man who sees me only as an asset, not a woman. Lance is a hard taskmaster, ruling my life from morning till night. *Bonne nuit*, he says and then kisses me on my forehead. Like a child. *We'll start again tomorrow.*

That's it. No holding me in his arms, no passionate kisses. He's keeping his distance and I have the feeling that how it's going to be. So

I'm stuck with it. I can't leave, so I've decided to be the best agent I can. I even have a code name. *Mimosa*.

What if the Boches *never* leave?

I can't believe that, so I don't.

I'm ready for my assignment, I tell Yvette. (Her code name is *Swan*.) Secure a position at the House of Doujan and then report back to Jarnak at the pawnshop on a regular basis with anything I've seen or heard that could be important. The crafty pawnbroker will then transmit that intelligence to Lance. What happens to it afterward, I'm not privy to.

The wind is brisk at our backs, swastika flags flapping in the breeze from the Hôtel Meurice when we head toward the shop on Rue Saint-Honoré, a decent walk from Yvette's apartment on the Left Bank on Rue du Sommerard. I sleep on a rollaway cot which we put in the kitchen during the day. The nosy concierge couldn't barge in fast enough after I moved in. Yvette told her I'm her sister from Lyon here on a visit. She grumbled but seemed satisfied, though we look nothing alike. Yvette is a light brunette contrasting to my dyed, raven-black tresses. Paris is filled with informers and I have no doubt she reported my 'visit' to the local police *and* the Gestapo as she's required to do by law. Yvette says not to worry because she has 'protection'.

Namely, Frederic Antoine Baptiste.

He's the son of Jean-Claude Baptiste, owner of the House of Doujan. Yvette introduces me to Frederic as he's flying out the door after planting a wet kiss on her mouth... then flirting with every sales-clerk in the shop... touting how he's late for luncheon at the Ritz with a Nazi general and *Don't forget, mamselles, sell lots of beautiful perfumes today. Heil Hitler.*

I cringe. That was the last thing I expected to hear in the shop. It gets worse when he slows down long enough to ask me if I'd like a bottle of the latest perfume he's created.

'She's immune to your charms,' Yvette coos, answering for me. I haven't yet found my voice after hearing the dreaded Nazi greeting spoken by a Frenchman. 'She's here to meet with your father for a job. Is he busy?'

'Ester is with him, pouting her red lips and seducing him with his own perfume to entice him to advance her another fifty thousand francs.' He winks at me. 'My soon-to-be stepmother doesn't care there's a war on. She's an expert at getting my father to do her bidding. But *you, mademoiselle*, need only a smile to make a man fall in love with you.' He kisses both my hands, then holds them longer than protocol dictates. I should pull away from him, but there's an underlying command in his grip. That he holds my fate in his hands. I will myself not to show anger in my eyes, but it's not my face he's intent on inspecting when his gaze dips lower. With a smirk, he says, '*Bien*, I approve of your... qualifications. You're hired, *Mademoiselle*...?'

I lift my chin with pride. 'Angéline de Cadieux.'

'Till we meet again, *ma belle* Angéline. *À bientôt*.'

Then he's off. Dismissing me like the wretched coffee we're forced to drink since the Occupation. Why am I not surprised to find him pompous with a royal air and full of himself? Good-looking with dark hair and a trimmed mustache, but he's too neat, too slick. I bet he sleeps with a beret on to keep his hair pomade shiny.

His father, on the other hand, is a gentleman of another era when duchesses and baronesses graced the shop with their presence and their pocketbooks, and the swish of silk and the scent of lavender prevailed.

'What do you need, Yvette? A new sales book, perfume samples?'

Monsieur Baptiste doesn't look up from his desk overflowing with paperwork, perfume bottles, advertising sketches. And an atomizer half-filled with scent. Even from a distance I detect Bulgarian rose and cedarwood lingering in the air from a recent spritz.

Heady, strong.

Ester, of course.

Yvette smiles. 'May I have a word, *monsieur*, it's important.'

'I'm busy; the Nazis are tearing up our flower fields for their damn potatoes, what is it?'

'I would like to introduce Mademoiselle de Cadieux, an old friend from school come to Paris to help me celebrate my birthday—'

'*Mademoiselle...*' he mutters, crossing out numbers and writing new ones on a pad of paper. I notice a smudge of lipstick on his collar. Hmm... where is this mysterious fiancée of his? Powdering her nose?

'Angéline's been living in Grasse and studying perfumery at the House of Fragonard.'

'*Mademoiselle* is a *parfumier*?' He looks up, surprised. 'How bizarre. I've never heard of a woman in that position.'

'Is it, *monsieur*?' I dare to answer. 'Is it not we women who *wear* the perfume? Shouldn't we have a say in creating it?'

I can't keep quiet, though I had no idea Yvette was going to put me on the spot. Yes, I can identify scents. Yes, I made small batches of perfume with Maman and I know my flowers, seeds, roots, leaves, and fruits, even animalic scents, but I don't know much about the distillation process except what I learned in books.

'Well said, *mademoiselle*. I like an outspoken woman, but no man in his right mind would hire a female nose. Then, what do I know?' He crumbles up the piece of paper he was writing on and tosses it into a nearby bin. 'I'm a poor businessman trying to make a living in these difficult times.'

He's being coy.

'I'm an admirer of your perfumes, *monsieur*, and I'd love to work here in your shop—'

'Why don't you call her bluff, *mon petit chou*,' a sultry voice coos the endearment as a tall, sophisticated woman swishes into the office. 'See if she knows a rose from a dead rat.'

I stand there in awe of this beautiful creature, even if she did just insult me, her spun golden hair shimmering with ruby-red highlights and falling over one eye adds to her mystery. High-heeled black suede pumps, tight navy-blue suit with covered buttons emphasize her lithe, elegant figure. Navy leather gloves, pearls and diamonds hanging from her earlobes complete her look.

This must be Ester.

'Anything you wish, *ma chérie*.' Monsieur Baptiste jumps up as she leans over to kiss his cheek. He groans with delight. It's pitiful how she has him eating out of her hand.

I wriggle my nose. 'I think the rat just ate the mouse—'

Yvette shushes me, then cuts me off. 'I heard your nose, Professor Oskar Zunz, is going to Switzerland for his health, Monsieur Baptiste. Poor darling.'

'Yes... poor Uncle Oskar.' Ester prances around the office, her hips swaying like the pendulum of a clock. 'I shall miss him.'

Uncle?

Yvette leans over and whispers in my ear. 'The professor fears what's coming since the Germans occupied Paris, *mademoiselle*.'

I raise a brow.

'He's a Hungarian Jew.'

I nod, understanding. *Then Ester is Jewish, too.* No wonder she's so cozy with an influential man like Monsieur Baptiste. I heard the rumors circulating that Jewish immigrants in France lost their civil rights, their homes... even their jobs when the Nazis took over. Professor Zunz is in danger. I imagine a 'nose' isn't high on their hit list so he's safe for now, but is anyone safe in Paris? Even Ester?

Yvette finishes with, 'Angéline would be *perfect* to fill his shoes.'

'*If* she were a man,' Ester chimes in. She sits on the edge of the desk and crosses her legs. Monsieur Baptiste is coming undone.

'A nose is a nose, *mademoiselle*, no matter whose face it's attached to,' I sputter, but she ignores me. She's too busy adjusting her seams. I don't have to guess *where* she got the silk stockings.

Yvette is undaunted by Ester's game. Her voice is most determined and assured, as if she's rehearsed her lines, my mind translating what that means. Lance, of course. He's behind this. 'Angéline can smell hundreds of scents—'

She gestures toward me and I nod up and down. 'Yes, hundreds, *monsieur*.'

'She can work with the professor in his laboratory, coming up with new ideas,' Yvette insists.

I can? My laboratory was two pots on our tiny stove, cold water, copper tubing... for which I traded bronze coins Papa found... to induce steam distillation of the oils from the plants and flowers.

'*Mademoiselle* has traveled throughout France and Belgium and visited the luxurious flower fields of Provence.'

In a *vardo*, singing ballads and picking flowers and herbs with Maman and Papa.

'She has years of experience choosing smells to evoke emotion.'

I've been blending perfume essences since I could stand on a stool and squash the flowers in the pot.

'Then mixing the scents in different ratios,' Yvette continues nonstop, 'testing them, creating wonderful new perfumes—'

Monsieur Baptiste looks doubtful.

'A female nose? In the House of Doujan?' He mutters an expletive under his breath. 'The idea is sacrilegious. The answer is *no*.'

'*Bien, mon chéri*.' Ester can't keep her mouth shut. 'What would the major say if you hired a female nose?'

I don't care who this major is, I'm not letting this woman ruin my life.

I jump into the conversation with: 'Don't listen to her, Monsieur Baptiste. You're behind the times. Packaging perfumes in fancy Baroque bottles and Oriental spicy scents reeking of Bulgarian rose and cedarwood, ambergris, and cloves doesn't work anymore.' I pick up the fancy atomizer and spray it into the air to make my point. 'Heavy perfumes sold well in the past, *monsieur*, but we're at war and even if no one will say it, things *will* get worse under the occupiers.'

He nods. He's well aware what I've said is true. I take the advantage while I can.

'I've seen how the Nazis can destroy a home, a family,' I continue without taking a breath. 'Murder innocent women for trying to protect their children. And that's just the beginning. They have plans, *monsieur*, big plans and they'll destroy anyone who stands in their way. We have to fight back in the best way we can by giving hope to French-women with a light, airy fragrance. A top note that doesn't overpower, a heart note that soothes, and a base note that endures to sustain that courage no matter what during these difficult times.'

I turn to Ester, my eyes begging her not to interfere. She knows she's on shaky ground being Jewish, and does the smart thing. She agrees with me.

'Well said, *mademoiselle*.' She kisses her fiancé on the forehead. 'I must be off, *chéri*. I'm lunching with the major at the Ritz.' Then she turns to me. 'You may have some talent after all... but be careful. You never know who your friends are these days.'

A whiff of scent and she's gone, but Monsieur Baptiste is still under her spell. His eyes brighten. 'Ester's right. I like your ideas, Mademoiselle de Cadieux, still—'

Yvette picks up the ball. 'The running of the business won't change, Monsieur Baptiste,' she assures him. 'Frederic will remain the official "nose" of the House of Doujan. Who will know? He can be quite convincing extolling the endless possibilities of his *talent* to the German High Command whenever he has the opportunity.'

'I admit my son keeps the Nazis off my back as they seek to Aryanize every business in Paris... but for how long are we safe? I, too, *mademoiselle*, fear what's coming since the Vichy government took over. They're nothing but puppets for Berlin, passing laws that help no one but themselves, sending anyone who gets in their way to forced labor camps... no matter *who* they are... arresting citizens because of their religion, excluding Jews from making a living.' I see a sadness come over his face and Yvette shakes her head, begging me not to ask questions. He clears his throat. 'Tell me, why *are* you in Paris, *mademoiselle*? Yvette's birthday was last month.'

'I find the weather more pleasant here than in Vichy, *monsieur*. Not so stormy.'

'*Ah, bien*. I understand. Well, your business is your own. Whatever you're running from, I don't want to know.'

I nod, shaking more from his honest words about his feelings for the occupiers than his dismissal of my past. He's afraid of the Boches since his fiancée is Jewish, but the less I tell him, the better it is for both of us. Here is a man also hiding secrets in his soul. We both reside in a painful, lonely place.

'*Merci, monsieur.*'

'Well, I hope you know what you're asking me to do, Yvette. I'll be the laughing stock of Paris for hiring a female nose, yet the arrogant Nazis leave me no choice. My son can't smell the difference between a Damask rose and a civet, but I need him to do business with the Boches.' I blink, surprised at his candidness. 'And I need *you, mademoiselle,* to keep my business going if it becomes too dangerous for Professor Zunz and other Jews to remain in Paris.' He exhales, worry furrowing his brows. 'And Ester.'

'I won't let you down, *je vous promets*. I promise.'

'*Bon*. When can you start?'

20

PARIS, 2003

Emma

Perfume:
De Cadieux
Passion fruit, Egyptian jasmine, green tea

'We celebrated the success of my mission at the House of Doujan...
Yvette, Jarnak and her brother Alain... Lance and me. Sitting around
the table in the back of the pawnshop, toasting, planning. At the time, I
didn't know how deep Lance's connections to the Nazis went. I shall tell
you this, Emma, he was a most extraordinary man, brave and clever.'

'You amaze me, *madame*,' I say, inhaling the familiar smell of scrambled eggs as our waiter serves breakfast off a silver platter. The intimate
hotel dining room is buzzing this morning with a full crowd. 'How you
had the guts to face every obstacle thrown at you. And still you found
time to fall in love.'

'Ah, but I was young and assumed that brazen kiss in the shadows
meant Lance was in love with me.'

'Was he, *madame*?'

'He was twenty-nine, a rugged man well-known in his field. Multilingual. English, French, German, Arabic. I was seventeen. A virgin. When months went by and he never kissed me again, touched me, it hurt.' She picks up her knife and fork, but doesn't touch her eggs. 'In short, *mademoiselle*, I made a complete fool of myself.'

Like me.

Going at it with Ryker like I might actually like the man. Okay, he's gorgeous, but it stops there. I have a bigger agenda. Like fulfilling my promise to Mom and if there's even the teeniest time left over, asking *madame* to give me pointers on being a 'nose'.

So here goes... I either make this happen now or I'm toast.

'You've been so honest with me, *madame*, telling me your most intimate thoughts about your *maman* and Lance and I've been, well...' I put down my knife and fork and pat my mouth with the linen napkin. 'I have something I need to tell you—'

Before I can get the words out, the scent of musky lime and a man's sweat hits my nostrils. A man in a hurry.

'Madame de Cadieux,' comes the interruption loud and clear. 'I must have a word with you.'

Ryker.

'Alone. In private.'

'I have no secrets from Emma,' *madame* says. 'Sit down and get on with it. She's writing my story. She may as well know the worst of it.'

He scowls at her request. The nerve of the man. I give him a look of disdain that borders on profanity. I'm angry with him for not being there for her yesterday while *he's* fuming that *madame* included me in their conversation.

We're all on the same team, Ryker. Get used to it.

'I heard what happened on the street with that riffraff.' He looks *madame* square in the eye. She takes it in her stride and smiles.

'Of course. Marcel. He picked you up at the airport.'

'Yes... but I want to hear from you what happened.'

'*I'll* tell you what happened,' I butt in, my eyes narrowing. 'Madame de Cadieux was accosted by pickpockets and nearly killed.'

'*Madame* was... *what*?' His dashing dark eyes shoot over to me with a steely look that shoots daggers and they're pointed straight at me. Sending quivers through me I choose to ignore.

Instead, I go on the offensive. 'Okay, so I exaggerated, but you should have been there protecting her. Where the heck were you?'

Ryker glares at me. 'That is no concern of yours, *mademoiselle*.'

'Isn't it?' I counter.

'No.'

I hold back a few choice phrases that would reset his compass... I don't want to offend *madame*. I bite my lower lip and go at my eggs with a vengeance, counting to ten in whispers, while Ryker rakes his hand through his hair, trying to contain *his* temper. It's then I realize we're a lot alike, each tamping down our deep, raw emotions because we both want the same thing: to keep *madame* safe from such predators.

My gut instinct kicks in and I try to make amends. 'Look, Ryker, I know we got off on the wrong foot—'

He grunts. The primal response spikes the air like wild musk. *Madame* looks as if she wants to shake him.

'I'm sorry,' I continue. 'I got carried away because, well... because I worry about *madame* as much as you do.'

'You hardly know her.'

Cold, flat tone. Is he jealous of my closeness with her?

'I know her better than you think.'

'I bet you do, *mademoiselle*. You have a way of getting under a person's skin that's unsettling.'

I balk. Is he talking about *madame*... or himself?

Which brings up a new dilemma. Am I crazy? Or does Ryker seem different? The way he looks at me when his eyes meet mine, more than curious... challenging yet dangerous. As if he wants to eat me up. I shiver. Hmm... I don't know if I like this new Ryker better, but I'm stuck with him. The sparks between us make my toes tingle. Like someone let go of a live wire in the room. I've touched a raw nerve in him.

What did I say?

Our breakfasts grow cold. Coffee colder. The seconds tick by. Neither of us is speaking to the other. Finally, *madame* takes over the lead in this soap opera. 'Calm down, Ryker, no harm done. I'm fine. Just some ruffians harassing us.'

'We can't be sure, *madame*.' His dark eyes remain on me with an unrestrained heat that's doing more to my libido than I want to admit. 'I never should have left you alone with this reporter.'

'And what's wrong with reporters?' I stand my ground.

'You're all crazy.'

Is it my imagination or does his voice sound huskier than usual? Like he knows I'm in this race to win and coming up on the outside to challenge him as he races toward the finish line.

Then he stomps off with a hasty, 'We'll discuss this further, *madame*.'

To my surprise, she doesn't stop him.

No wonder. He's used to getting his way with the female sex, tossing that masculine charm around like sweet bonbons... the women eat it up. Not me. I can handle him. First, I've got to tell Madame de Cadieux it's not just a story I want. I *tried* to tell her I'm damn well sure I'm a nose like her – well, I *could* be with the right training, but I'm too chicken to chuck my career to give it a try – seriously I did.

It's not as though we're family and she'd be passing the baton to me, but I get a funny tingling when we talk about her past... as if it's mine, too, because we both faced obstacles in our careers.

And we both share a connection to the camps.

God knows what happened to the poor Polish woman who gave birth to my mom under the most horrible circumstances. A woman, my grandpop says, who begged another prisoner to save her baby before she died. I would have asked *madame* about that, too, if that arrogant Irish hunk hadn't shown up. So I backed down. I'm sorry I did. I came so close, but something keeps holding me back.

And it is... *drumroll*.

I'm a coward.

I don't want to lose the camaraderie we built, but I detect a frosty tone in her voice when the waiter refills our coffees and we chat about the hot weather. *The weather?* You're kidding me. What happened to the emotional rollercoaster we were on back in 1940? Seems it stalled at the top and I've got to get it rolling again.

For both our sakes.

'I'm sorry, *madame*, I went off like a wild woman, but I wanted to tell you something and when I saw Ryker—'

'I should have told you, Emma. He was on my orders to leave Paris on a personal assignment for me.'

'No wonder he shut me down.'

Still, that doesn't excuse his rudeness. That snarl. That bad boy swagger that did something to my libido I'd rather forget.

Madame smiles at me, though she's avoiding my eyes. She's upset over my outburst. Very unprofessional on my part, but that man makes me so mad, I end up losing my cool around him.

'What did you wish to tell me, *mademoiselle*?'

'Well, um...' She takes my hesitancy for embarrassment and I let it hang there. I've already made a fool out of myself over Ryker. I apologized to the man in spite of his 'brooding lord' act and he acted more beastly than any beast in a fairytale. Instead I go for the shock treatment to take her mind off me. 'Those pickpockets yesterday weren't after your purse, *madame*... someone stuck a note in my tote bag.'

'*Zut alors*, what did it say?'

'It's too vulgar for me to repeat, *madame*.'

'*Ma chère* Emma, there's isn't anything that could shock me anymore. I saw the worst of humanity during the war, what with the terrible things the Nazis did to me and those I loved. Let me see the note, *s'il vous plâit*.'

I hand her the folded-up piece of paper and she reads it. Funny, she doesn't get upset. Instead, she crumples up the paper and tosses it onto her empty butter plate.

'I'm not surprised, *mademoiselle*. I have a stalker, a woman who blames me for ruining her career.'

'Brooke Hansen,' I blurt out.

'You know her?' Her eyes widen.

'Yes, I saw her at the Waldorf that night when I asked you for an interview. I had no idea she was that desperate for a story. She's here in Paris?'

'I saw her following us yesterday on Rue Saint-Jacques, but I ignored her. We were having so much fun, I didn't want her to spoil it.'

I smack my palm on my forehead. 'So *that's* what Ryker was trying to warn me about and I didn't get it. *Damn*, I owe him an apology but the way he glares at me with those smokin' dark eyes and tries to put me in a box, he makes it so damn difficult. Not that I'm interested in him, *madame*. I'm not.'

Her raised brow tells me she doesn't believe me, but she lets it pass.

'He's too old school in his attitude toward women,' I insist.

'Don't judge him too harshly, Emma. He's like most men. Pigheaded and single-minded when it comes to protecting us. Of course, you and I don't need protecting.' She winks. 'But we'll never tell him that.'

I laugh. '*Madame,* how do you see life so clearly?'

'I didn't always. I was stubborn and determined to do things my way. Until I met a wonderful man who taught me that beauty and goodness win out over evil, *if* you have courage.' She pauses, trembles. 'Lance taught me the tradecraft of espionage, though I often asked myself, *why didn't he warn me being a spy was this hard?* Fight the Nazis outright, *spit, kick, yell...* I could do that. But *smile, cajole, laugh...* pretend you're enjoying yourself with the ripe smell of Boche in your face? I didn't know if I had it in me. I soon found out.'

I can't get my yellow pad out fast enough. I forget about the chill from her I felt earlier. Madame is revved up and so am I.

Or is it because we both feel more comfortable talking about the past... while we ignore the present?

And *I* ignore the future when I ask her to dig deep into her time at Dachau and, if I'm lucky, help my mom learn more about *her* mother before it's too late. *Damn*.

'I'm ready, *madame*.'

She sips her hot coffee, then begins to speak. 'An October chill and rainy days accompanied me everywhere as Paris went *back to routine*, what the newspapers called life under the new regime. The government attempted to persuade French citizens that accepting (they meant collaborating with) the occupiers was to our benefit. Whether it was going back to school, refugees returning to Paris, dining at restaurants... *if* you didn't mind putting up with the German officers or soldiers bellowing and burping at the next table. Otherwise, you'd find yourself isolated from any social life.'

'What about those who resisted?' I ask.

'Not as prevalent as filmmakers would have you believe. After the violent putdown of the student protest at L'Étoile in November 1940, the glory of armed Resistance didn't materialize until around the end of 1942. Lance and his operation in late 1940 were unique in that he saw what happened in Belgium and the Netherlands and knew what to expect from the occupiers. So he gathered together a small operation consisting of Jarnak, Yvette and her brother Alain, and two other men.'

'If the Resistance was spotty at best,' I say, 'how did an American archaeologist get involved with Jarnak and the others?'

'Lance recruited Alain for his operation after he caught him trying to pawn a phony Degas he copied on the black market to buy food for his family. He saw an opportunity to utilize the young man's artistic abilities to forge new identity cards for those in need as the war dragged on. Jarnak was an old friend from Morocco with a dubious past, and the other two men were students from the Sorbonne eager to do more than print anti-Nazi pamphlets.'

'And Yvette?' I ask with a twinkle in my eye.

'You want to know if Lance had an affair with Yvette.' A curious smile forms on her red lips. 'I never knew if they did, *mademoiselle*.'

'Didn't you want to know?' I find her answer indicative of another era when decorum ruled and a dash of mystery about a man's roguish past added to his appeal.

'No.'

Simple. Direct.

Again, I feel the chill. But this is different. Like she's protecting Yvette. I wonder why. What happened to her?

Okay, I overstepped my boundary. I pose my next question with care.

'So here you are, *madame*, new identity, new hair color, armed to the teeth to fight the Nazis, and no assignment yet, *n'est-ce pas*?'

She nods. '*Oui, c'est vrai.* That's true.'

'And while you're pining for Lance, your new job at the House of Doujan takes off and you lay the groundwork for your amazing contributions to perfumery during and after the war.' I blow out a breath. '*Wow*. I'm dying to hear the next chapter.'

Something in my rambling sentences must have amused her. She chuckles, then takes my hand and squeezes it. 'I never back down from a challenge, *mademoiselle*. My journey began when I entered the fantastical world of perfume under the tutelage of an honorable gentleman from Budapest.'

'Who was that, *madame*?'

'Oskar Zunz, the most incredible nose I ever met.'

21

ARGENTEUIL, ON THE OUTSKIRTS OF PARIS, OCTOBER 1940

Angéline

Perfume:
Black Lace Stockings
Chinese star anise, rose, vanilla

'I never thought I'd see the day Monsieur Baptiste would hire a female nose, *mademoiselle*. And such a pretty one.' Professor Zunz chuckles, his big belly bouncing under his white lab coat, his silver-rimmed glasses sliding down his nose. The professor is a bubbly if portly Hungarian *parfumier* and a most innovative creator of scents.

'Then you're not upset?' I dare to ask.

'Upset? I'm overjoyed to have you here in my laboratory... the company is in jeopardy because we have to slow down production, what with the Nazis interfering with our transports from Grasse. We need new ideas, new thinking,' he says, his eyes sad yet hopeful. I can't help but want to join him in the fight.

'Tell me, Professor, where did you learn about perfumery?' I swallow my nervousness, attempting to get him to talk about himself so he doesn't ask me about my perfume experience.

'Perfume has been my life since I was a small boy,' he offers. 'My family owned a perfume shop in Budapest nestled on a cobblestone street between a butcher's shop and a milliner's. My father used to say a housewife could buy her sausage, take home a new hat, and smell like a queen's lady-in-waiting on her morning walk.' He looks off into the distance. 'Glory days I shall never forget. Maman was so excited when we acquired a lipstick-making machine to entice the ladies into the shop until—' He takes a moment, his chest heaving up and down. 'The Nazis smashed it to bits when they ransacked the shop and destroyed our century-old business. My mother died soon after.'

'I'm so sorry, Professor. I know what it's like to lose your *maman*.' I force a smile. I want to share with him my own story, but I dare not. I sense a camaraderie between us, but I've learned to trust no one. Instead, I opt to change the mood. 'How did you become a *parfumier*?'

He wipes his glasses before continuing. 'The shop was founded by my grandfather in the age of corsets, tiaras, and silky face powders. Old wooden shelves filled with ornate bottles fascinated me as a boy. One day I climbed up on the counter to grab a glass bottle shaped like a boat and the whole shelf came crashing down. Bottles cracked open and perfume spilled everywhere.' His jovial laugh makes his ruddy cheeks wiggle. 'Maman said I smelled like a streetwalker, but I discovered I had a talent for identifying the spilled scents.' He looks at me closely. 'And you, *mademoiselle*?'

'When I was a little girl, I'd wrap myself in long daisy chains of flowers and lie in the fields near our... house.' I almost said *vardo*. 'I'd close my eyes and sniff the plants and flowers for hours.'

'*Ah, bien*, we share a lifetime of scent, *mademoiselle*. I wasn't much younger than you when I secured an apprenticeship in a laboratory in Paris. Since then, I've worked for several houses, but the House of Doujan has been good to me. Monsieur Baptiste gives me free rein to create my perfumes without restraint.' He sniffs a vial and sighs. 'Let me show you my latest creation, *Desert Nights,* infused with a subtle jasmine from Casablanca. A floral invitation of pure delight to the nose.'

I sniff the vial, close my eyes. 'Orchid *and* jasmine... rose absolute... powdery vanilla.'

His fuzzy brows shoot up. '*Bien*, how about this one, *mademoiselle*?' He pulls out another vial filled with golden liquid from the wooden rack on his worktable.

'Gardenia, citrus... rose, blackcurrant bud... amber.'

Then another vial. 'And this one.'

'Mandarin, peach...jasmine, rose... honey.'

'*Très bien, mademoiselle.* Your nose is a remarkable instrument, filtering out the strong odors and highlighting the lesser scents, but I'm most impressed how you identify the heart note.'

Almost tentatively, I relax and enjoy the warm glow in my belly from hearing his words spoken in his charming accent. I am, to my surprise, neither apologizing for my knowledge nor boasting to him, but finding a sincere appreciation from this master *parfumier* for what I can do.

And how lovely that is.

'I like to think of the heart note as the *maman* in the perfume family, keeping it together.'

His eyes grow sad again. I sense the gentleman from Budapest thinks often about his *maman* as I do mine. I don't have to ask if the Nazis had anything to do with her death.

Finally, he says, 'You have the true gift of a nose.'

'*Merci, monsieur.*' I smile, relieved.

He lets me sniff several more blends he's working on and he's duly impressed when I identify the elusive scent of ambergris.

'Whale vomit,' I say after getting a good sniff. How could I forget? I was twelve when Maman and I found a shop on the Left Bank in Paris dealing in Oriental artifacts and spices. I was enthralled with the story, how whales excrete the waxy substance into the ocean.

Professor Zunz nods his approval, then asks me about my experience with dissolving flowers and plants in ethyl alcohol to extract their oils, and how much experience do I have with concretes and resinoids?

My stomach sinks. I'm in trouble. The essences for my perfumes came from my simple steam distillation process. Two pots. A stove. Cold water. I don't think the professor would approve.

Instead, I tell him how many tests I do of each new formula. 'Forty... fifty. I started when I was eight with my first batch of rose water simmering on our small stove... it spilled all over Maman's clean kitchen and I had to start all over again.'

He chuckles. 'Here in my laboratory, I choose chemicals with varying evaporation rates to control how the fragrance is experienced by the wearer, which scent she smells first. And you, *mademoiselle*?'

He wipes his glasses again, waiting for me to answer. What can I say? I do so many things by instinct. *And* in small batches. Not the huge copper vats in the factory in Grasse the professor illustrates for me with pen and paper.

'Of course, Professor,' I lie and he nods and I lie again... he nods. Then—

'You've never been inside a perfume factory, *mademoiselle, n'est-ce pas*?'

I attempt a grin. 'Is it that obvious, Professor?'

'Only to me.' He glances at me over his spectacles halfway down his nose. 'You have a natural gift with scents and blends, and from the way you mix herbs and your handling of creating essences from flowers, I'd say a healer taught you the basics of perfume making.'

'*Oui, ma maman*.'

'So you're not the sophisticated young *mademoiselle* from Grasse you pretend to be.'

'No, Professor,' I confess. 'I – I'm Roma.'

He nods, understanding. 'Ah, *mademoiselle*, then you know what it's like to be persecuted. *Alors*, so many things have changed since Hitler marched into Paris but I'm proud to be a Jew. I get letters from cousins in Budapest, urging me to leave France and return home, but after Maman died, I have nothing to go home to.'

'Yvette said you applied for a visa to leave France.'

'Yes, I pray it doesn't come to that. I'm too old to be a refugee without trade or domicile.'

'You said yourself Monsieur Baptiste respects your talent, how important you are to the House of Doujan.'

'For the moment. I don't trust Hitler. Jews have been forced out of jobs in banks, teaching, and public service, and I fear he won't stop there, *mademoiselle*. The Nazis have barred Jews from the legal profession even if they're French citizens. And there's talk of more restrictions by the Jewish holidays. Who knows if he will order his soldiers to do more than harass Jewish shopkeepers?' He sighs. 'I told Monsieur Baptiste I will not renounce my religion, it's who I am, but I won't leave Paris without my niece.'

I wince. 'You mean Monsieur Baptiste's fiancée.'

'I heard you two met.' He chuckles, no further words necessary. 'Oh, the sleepless nights that stalk me since Ester made her way to France.' He shakes his head. 'Wherever she goes, scandal follows her.'

'It can't be that bad, Professor.' I shiver.

What if the *parfumier* knew the girl standing next to him is wanted by the Gestapo?

'Ester is a charming young woman,' continues the Professor, 'but she's vain and loves beautiful things. *And* she has a gambling problem. She's quite adept at finding gentlemen to support her habit, like when she married a minor aristocrat from Budapest then discovered he was still married to his second wife. Without batting an eye, she accepted a settlement from him and an annulment, though she kept the title of Countess Bulgávari, and came to Paris. To my dismay and *her* pleasure, it didn't take her long to cast her spell over Monsieur Baptiste. She convinced him to take her to Monte Carlo to meet high society and try her luck at roulette. She lost heavily at the tables, but that didn't matter to Monsieur Baptiste. He was smitten by her classic beauty and hired her to grace advertisements to sell perfumes from the House of Doujan, then he proposed to her. He's a lonely man, *mademoiselle*, widowed for years and Ester took advantage of that. She's my niece and I won't abandon family. I pray Frederic's influence will be enough to protect her if the Germans further restrict our lives.'

I remain silent, never saying a word about what the major told me about the Führer's plans for Jews and 'gypsies'.

'Ester reveled in the notoriety of seeing her face in newspaper advertisements and on kiosks... until the Occupation,' he continues. 'Frederic pulled the ads before the Abwehr found out she's Jewish.'

A sudden chill fills the room. The woman may be vain and stupid, but I feel a strange kinship with her. We share a common enemy.

'Don't trust the younger Monsieur Baptiste, *mademoiselle*,' he warns me. 'Monsieur Frederic would sell his own blood to keep his Nazi friends in his pocket.'

* * *

For the next several months, I spend my days with my nose in a perfume vial and my heart in winning the fight. Both are like falling in love. Joy then frustration... and the constant ache to get it right. I haven't heard from Lance after I made a fool out of myself swooning over him. *He's off on a secret mission* is all Jarnak will tell me. Still, I can't forget the way Lance looked at me, his hands wrapped tight around my waist. It puts a skip in my step and makes me smile.

And this from the Roma girl who didn't want a man in her life? I chide myself as I go over the paperwork for the new fragrance I created for the House of Doujan. We're ready to launch it next week, the scent Maman and I made on those carefree days when we didn't fill our bellies with pork and rice so we could afford to get the ingredients we needed to make essential oils. Rose, hyacinth, lavender. Ginger, pink pepper, parsley. Then we created an exquisite perfume that seduces with rose absolute, buzzes with pepper, and makes beautiful dreams come true with lavender.

I call it *Naomie's Dream*.

After Maman.

I stretch my neck to ease the pain, my left shoulder cramped from checking the numbers over and over regarding the perfume stock the factory in Grasse shipped to Paris via transport. The manufacturing of our perfumes is centered in the south of France in the Free Zone, but I dare not travel there even with a new *carte d'identité* in the name of Angéline de Cadieux, thanks to Yvette's brother, Alain. I've taken it upon myself not to let anything go wrong. I created the perfume, but my name isn't on the formula. Frederic's name is listed in the press materials as the 'nose'. Fighting against the inner turmoil within me, I take a deep breath, telling myself that was the arrangement, that I'm lucky to have this job when my countrywomen are suffering.

Yet I can't let go of my dream. That someday when the world rights itself and the Boches are driven from France, *my* name will be listed as the nose, but only if I work hard. Which is why I stay late at the lab to test out a new formula, something I haven't told the professor about, a scent that's been knocking around in my head for months. A perfume to lift the spirits of Frenchwomen... to give them courage. I was thrilled to discover the company has oils and essences not yet depleted. I've been experimenting with different scents – peach, white velvet rose, orchid... but I'm not sure of the base note.

I spend my time here in the lab on the outskirts of Paris at Argenteuil and thanks to Frederic's chumminess with the right people, the Nazi officials look the other way and don't bother us. He shows up at the laboratory at odd times since we're ready to launch the new fragrance, bringing his Nazi friends. He struts around, smelling test strips and naming off ingredients I wrote down for him on each strip in light pencil so, when he holds it up to the light, he can read off the paper without anyone the wiser.

I put up with it because I have to. He warns me not to speak up. I'm not that dumb. I can't jeopardize my position here.

A single beam of light from a long hanging lamp overhead shines down on my worktable, making playful shadows as I gather up my notes and invoices, put them in a file, and then straighten the vials, keeping them in precise order. I put aside the test bottles of the new fragrance I'm working on to give my nose a rest, then cuddle up with a sample bottle of *Naomie's Dream* to savor this private moment with my mother, talking to her ghost.

'We packaged your perfume in a square turquoise crystal bottle, Maman, with a white label and gold lettering. The blue reminds me of your eyes.'

I sit in the shadows, my throat tight and a deep sadness creeping over me. Maman didn't like me to be sad so she'd pinch my cheeks to make me smile, remind me we had so much to be thankful for, that the Boche would never beat us, that we were stronger... *and* we'd been here longer. Over a thousand years. Which is why I can't stop my work. I must continue to search for the right formula for the new perfume I *swear* will make the women of France smile again.

The hour grows late, and I'll be here when the professor shows up in the morning with strong coffee and a crusty baguette. Butter. Jam. He'll greet me with kisses on both cheeks and insist I join him *if* I don't ask questions where he got it. I know he barters damaged perfumes – labels missing, cracked bottles – for food items he procures from his weekly trips to the countryside. Trading for food is no secret. It's become part of our lives and even has a name, *le système D*. Like everyone else, I've fallen into a daily routine of survival, but while the city of Paris goes about pretending everything is normal, the Germans invade Russia, a bomb exploded in a Left Bank bookstore, and there are new restrictions on Jews.

Radios are forbidden.

Which is why Professor Zunz keeps his 1934 Philips radio out of sight under his workspace table behind a box of empty vials and flasks. On a clear, crisp night if we move the radio to the right spot and twist the dial, we can get Radio Londres. I listen every night, not only for the news, but to see if Lance has sent me a coded message. Everyone, including the Nazis, knows when you hear the announcer say he has *personal messages before we begin*, phrases, often silly ones, follow. A fanciful notion on my part that Lance would send me a coded message but I'm ever hopeful since agents communicate information that way.

I flip on the radio and twist the dial and hear loud, bombastic music. A Nazi-controlled station. I keep trying until I hear the familiar baritone of the French broadcaster coming from the London-based radio station.

'*Ooh, mais non*,' I sputter when I get a loud burst of static. The Nazis are jamming the signal again.

I turn off the radio and I hear—

Loud laughter and swinging doors banging down the hall. Guests making merry in Frederic's private office. The Nazi officers sound louder than usual, though I'm used to their raucous parties, with Frederic plying them with champagne and offering them complimentary bottles of perfume to take back to Berlin for their wives.

The laughter gets louder, which means they're getting drunker. I feel as though I'm drowning in noise, first from the awful Nazi music on the radio and now the officers whooping it up. Thank God we don't have many visitors to the lab, though last week two men in brown leather trench coats and Fedoras showed up. Gestapo. They spent an hour in the office grilling Blanche, the records bookkeeper. The poor woman was so rattled, she let it spill afterward the Gestapo made her give them the name of every Jewish employee.

I told Professor Zunz and he went pale behind his glasses and then hid his radio.

We don't talk about it, but he checks the foyer every time a car pulls up and leaves the lab at odd hours so no one follows him.

I keep to myself, huddled over my worktable until late at night, mixing blends, sniffing test strips, and making notes to find the right one for a new perfume.

But I'm not against eavesdropping on Frederic's late-night rendezvous.

I've caught bits of conversation about the comings and goings of German officers based on when they procure perfume to take back to Berlin. Information I write in invisible ink and send to Yvette in Paris in code using the names of ingredients in perfumes as code words.

Rose means Paris.

Vanilla means Lisbon.

Lemon means Berlin.

Orange means Lyon.

Clove means weapons.

Patchouli means trains.

Sandalwood means Nazi officer.

Ambergris means Hitler.

I'm proud of my work, both as a spy and a *parfumier*, and determined to make Lance proud of me, even if he never sought me out again for a kiss like we shared that first night.

Which is why I act before I think.

Frustrated after tossing out the last twenty perfume test strips, I grab a vial of perfume as an excuse, then sneak down the hallway toward Frederic's office on the pretext of asking his opinion of the scent, yet hoping to hear something useful I can pass on when—

I recognize the woman carousing with Frederic and the Nazi officer.

Ester.

I'm not surprised. She came up from Paris earlier this evening and I overheard her complaining to her uncle about Frederic, how he told his father to cut off her allowance because she's 'embarrassing' him with her gambling debts at the horse races at Longchamp.

Professor Zunz wiped his glasses, shook his head. It was no secret the Gestapo is gathering names. He begged her to leave Paris, reminding her of the rumors that thousands of Jews were sent from Drancy concentration camp in the suburbs to a labor camp. A place called Auschwitz.

Ester told him not to worry. That she had everything under control.

I lean in. By the heat in her voice, it doesn't sound like she's in control.

Hands on her hips, chin up, she's facing Frederic, her tall slender body wrapped up in red silk, shining strawberry hair hanging in long, loose curls, black pumps. And a silly black pillbox hat tipped forward on her head with the most ridiculous gray feather curling down her back.

'I don't care if Jean-Claude cut my allowance, you can't stop me, Frederic.' Ester sashays over to a Nazi officer seated with his back to me. His cap sits on his desk along with two empty bottles of vodka. 'Major von Risinger has invited me to accompany him to the races tomorrow at Longchamp.'

Major von Risinger? Is that the major she lunches with at the Hôtel Ritz?

I blink, my stomach sinking again.

No, it can't be him. I won't believe it. I won't.

22

ARGENTEUIL, ON THE OUTSKIRTS OF PARIS, OCTOBER 1940

Angéline

Perfume:
Wild Coquette
Indian mango, white royal lily, musk

The major reaches over to kiss her hand, Ester smiles, and the whole thing sickens me.

'It will be my pleasure to have you on my arm, Countess Bulgávari.'

'Please call me Ester,' she coos in his ear, driving Frederic frantic. He may be a pompous jerk, but he's a prude when it comes to his father's fiancée cavorting with the Nazis.

'As you wish, Ester. I'd be honored if you bet on my entry in tomorrow's race. A fine specimen I acquired this summer.'

'Ah, *merci* for the tip, Major. I shall place five thousand francs on —?' She smiles, waits for the name.

'Zeus.'

I freeze. No, what? Impossible.

'I was quite pleased when his owner agreed to sell him to me,' Major von Risinger continues, 'for a reasonable price.'

The price was my mother's life, you bastard!

I have a moment of utter frustration and the deepest pain in my chest that jabs me so hard my arm goes numb and I drop the vial of perfume. It crashes to the floor, small shards of glass splintering. The sudden pungent smell of patchouli and cypress assaults my nostrils. The horror of that day comes back to me, every slow moment of disbelief watching Maman lying on the dirty straw floor flashing before my eyes. I don't have time to grieve, react.

Think. What's my next move?

If I could find some way to make the arrogant Nazi pay for his foul deed I would, but I'm shaking inside so badly I fear what a horrible mess I'll make of everything. The old Tiena would grab her knife and fight him, wound him… make him bleed, suffer, live with that pain. But I'm Angéline now and without knowing how, Lance's deep, steady voice whispers in my ear to keep control… that I'll accomplish nothing if I strike out.

I hiss at the Boche through gritted teeth, then pull back my anger enough so I don't give myself away when the major turns and sees me. I stare back at the ugly, debauched face I prayed I'd never see again. Dark rings under his eyes, deep lines cut around his mouth suggest the war is taking its toll on the trigger-happy major.

'Ah, another beautiful *mamselle*. Won't you join our party, *liebling*?'

'*Pardon, monsieur*,' I keep my eyes down, my hand shaking. *Get out now, quick, while you can.* 'I have lab work to do.'

'At this hour?' he asks, disbelieving. '*Ach*, the Führer has decreed beautiful *fräulein* should never work after midnight.'

'I must clean up the broken glass, *monsieur*. *Pardon*—'

I turn my back to return to the lab for a towel, but he jumps to his feet and grabs my right arm.

'I *insist* you join our party, *mademoiselle*.'

An order, not a request, so typical of the Boches.

A stark moment of sheer terror grips me as he stares back at me, a glint in his eye as if he's trying to figure something out, a point of recognition he can't quite grab onto and frustrating his Teutonic brain.

Adrenaline shoots through me, making me careful to keep my left arm with the scar from his view. I'm wearing a short-sleeved dress printed with lilacs and violets, and a lab coat that covers my arms. My raven-black hair and red lipstick keep his mind confused as I pile on the sweetness, so unlike the Roma girl he tried to kill on that summer day.

'Who am I to disagree with the Führer?' I mumble, attempting a smile, even as his fingers squeeze my flesh. I wince.

I want to avenge you, Maman, but not here. Not now. I will, I promise you.

'I'm delighted you changed your mind, *mademoiselle*.' He lets me go, clicks his heels and bows. I have the feeling he wants to kiss my hand, but I don't have that much courage. What if he insists I take off my lab coat to get more 'comfortable' and he sees the scar on my arm? It might trigger a memory in him. I pretend to be shy, hunching my shoulders and backing away. The major turns to Frederic. 'Why haven't you introduced me to this fascinating creature?'

'She's merely an employee, Major,' Frederic says, smug, enjoying putting me down. He hisses at me. Ester laughs. 'Go back to the lab, Angéline. *Now*.'

I lower my eyes. '*Oui, monsieur*.'

He seems surprised I don't talk back. Do I detect a new curiosity in his eyes? I'll have to be careful. I turn to leave when—

The major grabs me around the waist, muttering in German in my ear in a rough whisper. The implication needs no translation. I don't move, my heart thudding, a new fear hitting my brain.

If he tries anything, I don't know if I can restrain myself from giving him what he deserves.

'Now I have two girls to entertain me,' he boasts. 'A beautiful Hungarian countess and—'

He struggles to find the phrase in his mind, but he can't catch it in thin air. He looks at me closer. 'I *swear* we've met before... Marseilles, perhaps?'

'*Mademoiselle* is from Lyon.' Ester yawns. 'So bourgeois, *n'est-ce pas*?'

I shoot her a dirty look. I don't need her help. I come back with a quick retort before his mind catches up and he remembers my face. 'I'm Professor Zunz's laboratory assistant, *monsieur*. I work with essential oils in helping Monsieur Baptiste create his lovely perfumes.'

It kills me to acquiesce to Frederic grinning like a French feline, but I have more to lose than gain with impudence.

'*Ah*, that's it. You're the *mademoiselle* Frederic hired to replace the Jew when he's no longer useful.'

I sneak a peek at Ester. She's gone pale. Does she have a heart after all? Or is she scared for her own skin?

I opt for the latter.

'The professor is a renowned chemist, *monsieur*,' I say, determined to defend my friend, 'and vital to the House of Doujan.'

'For now.' He strokes my cheek. 'Things change, *mademoiselle*, remember that.'

'Have you forgotten *me*, Major?' Ester coos like a songbird with a glance in my direction telling me she's sharpening her claws. She recovered quickly. *Why look at me? Doesn't she care what happens to her uncle?* 'Am I forgiven for my bad picks on horses?'

'Of course, Countess. I look forward to changing your luck tomorrow.' The hungry look he gives her makes me sick. 'We German officers are very forgiving when it comes to *mesdemoiselles* as lovely as you.'

'*Merci, monsieur*,' she breathes in a sexy whisper, 'you're too kind.'

I can't believe the fiancée of Monsieur Baptiste is kowtowing to this Nazi murderer. I don't like the woman, think her attitude toward the Nazi is despicable, that she'd stoop so low as to cozy up to him to gain his favor, but I also pity her. She can't see the dire consequences of her dalliance with this cruel bastard who doesn't have a decent bone in his body.

With her chin up, Ester bids the major good night, fluttering her mascaraed lashes and blowing him a kiss. She brushes by me without saying a word. She can't wait to make her exit. For the professor's sake, I don't tell her what I think of her.

'I leave for Berlin in a few days, *mademoiselle*,' says the major after she's gone, 'for an important meeting with the Führer. I'm in need of your assistance.'

'Me?' I freeze, afraid to breathe.

'My wife is begging me to bring her silk stockings and perfume.' He leans over me, sniffing. 'What perfume would you suggest?'

'*Naomie's Dream* is set to launch next week.' I spy sample blue bottles of our new perfume sitting on Frederic's bookcase. *Oh, how I'd love to smash them over the major's head. Drown him in her scent till he chokes.* 'It's a lovely fragrance to brighten a woman's spirit while she waits for her handsome husband to return.' I grab a bottle and pull off the stopper, my lower lip trembling. The rose absolute top note hits my nostrils and I'm filled with her warm memory. *Don't let your hand shake; he'll know you're hiding something.* 'Your wife will be the first to try it. A House of Doujan exclusive.'

'*Merci, mademoiselle...* I'm flattered.' He sniffs the scent from the stopper and rolls his eyes. '*Ach, sehr schöen...* beautiful, like you.'

'Glad to accommodate you, Major,' Frederic is quick to chime in. 'By the way, I'd appreciate a word from you to ensure the safety of our transport truck bringing two hundred bottles from our factory in Grasse.'

Leave it to Frederic, always the consummate salesman. This time I enjoy it, knowing Maman's perfume will be safe on her journey to Paris.

Don't be too angry with me, Maman. What better justice than to put one over on this degenerate Nazi major?

'Anything I can do for the House of Doujan and the lovely *mademoiselle*,' says the major, 'just ask.' He turns to me, clicks his heels. 'If things go well, I shall bring you exotic spices and perhaps a surprise or two from the land of the pyramids next time we meet.'

'I can hardly wait.'

I remain calm, but inside I'm processing what he said about his trip. It might mean nothing, but in this war, any detail could make the difference.

He bows and kisses my hand before I can stop him. I want to pull away, but don't. It takes all my resolve not to retch when his cold lips touch my skin. 'I regret, *mademoiselle*, we didn't have more time together.'

I bid him a weak *adieu*, my skin crawling as I turn and hurry back to the lab but not before Frederic follows me, grabbing my arm. 'I need you to be in Paris, Angéline, when that shipment arrives from the factory in Grasse.'

'Why me?' I pull away.

'Who else but the creator of *Naomie's Dream* to make sure everything is in order?'

'Why not go yourself?' A snide answer since we both know he took the credit, but I'm not feeling in a placating mood after my run-in with the disgusting Nazi major.

'*Touché, ma belle* Angéline, but we both know on what side our bread is buttered. I need to remain here and entertain the major till he leaves for Berlin.'

I snicker. 'Only collaborators butter their bread these days.'

'It's better than starving, *mademoiselle*,' Frederic admits freely. The depth of sadness in his voice paints a different picture of a man known for frittering away the profits of the family perfume empire for years.

'Is it?' I make no bones about my disgust with him. I give him a hard look that could melt the stones in his heart. The air is stifling in the narrow corridor, but it's a private place to speak freely without being overheard.

An awareness of how low he's stooped flashes in his eyes. 'Don't look at me like that, Angéline. Believe it or not, I have the welfare of every man and woman who works for the House of Doujan close to my heart. These are dangerous times, *mademoiselle*, and you never know who your friends are.'

Funny. Ester said the same thing.

'I assured the staff we will continue production without interference from the occupiers,' he continues, a desperate hope in his eyes that moves me. *Am I wrong about him?* 'It's the best I can do.'

That night we establish a truce between us. He's a man facing a world he doesn't understand but forced to embrace. We both want the House of Doujan to survive this war, now made more difficult because of Ester's reckless gambling habit. Frederic is remaining here in Argenteuil to keep her out of trouble. The woman is spending his inheritance faster than we can raise flowers. He bids me *bonne nuit* with a brotherly kiss on the cheek, then returns to his Nazi friend with the usual effervescence in his voice and easy compliments falling from his lips.

I can't move.

It takes me ten minutes to stop shaking before I can pen a note to Yvette at the House of Doujan shop in Paris.

'I love this new blend I formulated with lemon and sandalwood and ambergris,' I write in code, meaning, 'A Nazi officer is on his way to Berlin to meet with Hitler.'

Then in invisible ink, I write: *Major Ernst von Risinger. Cairo.*

I send it off in the morning by post and pray I never see the Nazi swine again.

23

PARIS, 2003

Angéline

Perfume:
Mademoiselle Pink No. 47
Pink rose, jasmine, musk

'After my shocking encounter with the Nazi major, I couldn't sleep, eat. Memories of the horror I suffered at his hands made me sweat till the sheets were damp. I had fierce headaches, my mind replaying that moment over and over again like a living nightmare when I heard the loud crack of the gunshot and Maman fell at my feet, wounded. I couldn't stop the bleeding...'

'It must have been horrifying for you,' Emma says in a whisper, eyes fluttering. She's chewing on the end of her pencil, trying to wrap her head around the absurd coincidence that brought me face to face with that monster.

My girlhood love of horses.

And my destiny as a *parfumier*.

'It took me years of therapy to get past that day and not beat myself up because I acted like a coward,' I tell her. 'Oh, how I wanted to smash the perfume bottle over his head, watch *him* bleed.'

'What stopped you, *madame*?' she asks, her voice heated and breathy.

'Getting a whiff of *Naomie's Dream* when I removed the bottle stopper. It hit me not in my heart, but in my brain. Like Maman's ghost nudged me to bide my time, that if I acted out of revenge to take out *one* Nazi, I'd never have the chance to take out a hell of a lot more.'

Emma smiles. 'Oh, *madame*, you make me so proud *and* you surprise me with your colorful language.' Then in a serious tone, she continues, 'I don't know if I'd have the control you did. Ooh, I'd want to wring his neck and kick him where it hurts.' She pauses, embarrassed. '*Pardon, madame*, you hear about such depraved officers committing atrocious crimes that seem so unbelievable, but you can't grasp their cruelty until you hear a personal story that hits close to home.' She attempts a smile. 'I mean, well... you can't help yourself. You want him to bleed.'

Hits close to home? I wrinkle my brow. Odd choice of phrase from the young reporter, but I let it pass. Then again, my English is rusty since Lance passed... and God knows my emotions are running so high I can't go there, relive those painful years after the war when we separated. My therapist says I never got past the anger phrase of grief when he died. Fat chance now, not when I have so much adversity during the war to live through with this young woman.

Gritting my teeth, I yank my heart out of its dark place and continue, 'I couldn't tell anyone what happened with the major without putting their lives in jeopardy. Still, I pined to see Zeus again, so I made inquiries about horses running at Longchamp. I discovered my stallion was scratched from the racing card soon after and conscripted into service in the German Cavalry Corps. I felt far from relieved, but at least he was out of the major's hands.' I smile. 'When Frederic called me into his office the next day, he kissed me on both cheeks and said giving the major an exclusive on our new perfume was a stroke of genius. That the Nazi officer's wife was related to Göring through a fourth cousin and her endorsement of *Naomie's Dream* would help it take off and we could double production if we got the raw materials we need. Wishful thinking, since our flower fields in Grasse were taken over by the Nazis to grow food and it takes sixty thousand roses to make one ounce of rose absolute.'

'Sixty thousand?' she repeats, writing it down on her yellow pad in big numbers.

'Yes. He also gave me a dire warning I didn't take to heart.'

'Warning?' Emma asks, perking up. 'What about?'

'Ester. *Don't get too friendly with her*, he warned. He rolled his eyes, then wiped his face with his handkerchief. Trickles of perspiration beaded on his high forehead and sparkled like dew in his slicked back dark hair. He hinted Ester went too far, embarrassing the House of Doujan and bringing attention to herself. If she didn't control her gambling habit and her debt fell into the wrong hands, meaning the French Gestapo, it could have dire consequences for her. *She's Jewish*, he said, then smirked. I asked him if the major knew. He shook his head. Frederic never brought up the background of the elder Baptiste's fiancée, but he was up to something. Imagine my horror when the Gestapo man showed up at the laboratory and demanded a count of our employees and personal interviews with everyone who worked there, including Jewish employees.'

'Herr Geller.'

'Yes, he kept looking at me, sniffing. Eyes narrowing into slits, furrowing his brows like a bloated beaver sharpening its claws. I was so shocked, he caught me off guard. I wasn't careful about hiding the scar on my arm when he barged into the laboratory and demanded to see everyone's papers. Luckily, Professor Zunz was in the countryside, but I could see the Gestapo man had his name circled on the list.'

'How awful for you, *madame*.'

'When I handed him my forged identity card, he saw the scar but it didn't register with him. Why should it? My papers said I was French

Catholic, born in Lyon. I tightened my gut to keep from shaking. I was still reeling from my encounter with the major. I dreaded the Nazi officer returning to Argenteuil and I suspected Frederic was behind the Gestapo man showing up. The son and heir of the House of Doujan feared he'd be found out as a fraud and was so afraid of me revealing his secret, he sent Herr Geller to keep me in line. A warning to keep my mouth shut if I wanted to keep my job. That no one was immune from the secret police.'

'Wow... unbelievable.' Her eyes are wide, her face pale, her pencil eraser bitten down to the nub. 'Tell me you catch the major with his pants down, *madame*, please. I don't think I can sleep until you do.'

I don't answer her question right away. I get up from my chair and wander over to the tall window. Storm clouds hover over the rooftops of Paris and a chill fills the hotel room. A tempest is coming... a big one.

'When you pick up a book, *mademoiselle*,' I begin, closing the heavily lined curtain, 'do you go straight to the last chapter to see how it ends?'

She laughs. 'Guilty as charged. I love to read books with happy endings and don't want to be disappointed.'

'You know how my story ends. The camps, then losing my daughter. What the rumor mill called my *secret baby*.' I pause. 'But then you knew that, *mademoiselle, n'est-ce pas*?'

She nods. 'Again, guilty as charged, *madame*. But you never gave up hope. There could be a happy ending in your future. I want that for you so much.' She stifles a yawn. 'I need to transcribe my notes. Can we pick this up bright and early tomorrow?'

I look at my watch. It stopped at 1:36 a.m. It doesn't matter. I have a deep fondness for the quaint gold timepiece with an oval face and old-fashioned hand. Lance gave it to me before he went off to Egypt after the war. A bittersweet moment, but I shall never trade it for a blinking digital watch.

'I *will* tell you this much about the major. I will never forget the look on his face when I confronted him later and told him *Naomie's Dream* was named after the woman he murdered.'

'And... and...?' Emma pleads for more.

I wind up my watch, put it up to my ear. I smile. It's ticking.

'When and where that happened, *mademoiselle*, I shall save for another time, *n'est-ce pas?*'

24

PARIS, 2003

Emma

Perfume:
Deception
Peach, cinnamon, amber

Her story detailing Nazi atrocities touched me in a way I'd never felt before. Injustices like this were also committed against *my* family. I couldn't help myself, listening to *madame* relive her encounter with the monster who murdered her mom. A tear falls onto my cheek before I can stop it. I can't forget what turmoil my own mother is going through.

Mom's hair started falling out soon after she started chemo.

No one knows for sure why, how she got sick. She rarely smoked, but there's speculation she was exposed to secondhand smoke as a nurse in combat zones. Everyone smoked in the field tents, she told me, the living *and* the dying. I never forgot going with her to the hospital and watching the attendant push her through the swinging doors in her wheelchair, leaving me outside for what seemed like forever. I got worried, so my reporter's nose took over (my other 'nose' gets overwhelmed in that environment, absorbing the smells of alcohol, astringent, cleaning solvents... and death) and demanded to know what was going on.

The head nurse tracked down the attendant. Guess what? He was on a break. And where was my mom?

Sitting in her wheelchair. Alone. In a corridor. Forgotten.

That crushed my heart. I couldn't hold back the tears. I pushed her out of that hospital so fast, I couldn't see straight. The sad thing was, Mom had no idea what was going on. She was lost in her own world, sedated by drugs and despair. I refuse to let her give up and will never let that happen again. I'm there with her every time she goes for treatment.

Except today.

First time I've missed in weeks. I've got to talk to her. I grab the phone in my hotel room and ask for the overseas operator... tap my foot like an impatient bunny... it's ringing... no one is answering. Oh, God, where is she... where's Dad? He never leaves her side except for getting her hot soup, then rubbing her feet... it's still ringing.

Finally—

'Hello?'

Weak, but it's her.

'Mom... it's Emma, you okay?'

'Emma, sweetheart, where are you?' She sounds upset. 'I didn't see you on the news tonight...' She coughs and my heart tugs. 'They didn't let you go, did they?'

I smile. She's always worried about me losing my job. I'm the black sheep of the Keane family... all my cousins have *real* jobs and don't go off to Europe chasing perfume divas.

'I'm in Paris, Mom. I'm interviewing the fabulous Angéline de Cadieux for the TV station... you know, the famous perfumer... you bought me a bottle of *Angéline* for my fifteenth birthday.'

'Oh... yes, I remember.' She laughs, then I hear that cough again. 'You smelled up the house for two weeks spraying it on everything—'

The line goes dead. Silence. It's killing me. 'Mom... *Mom!*'

Jeez, what the hell is going on? I get panicky, pushing the buttons on the phone up and down a bunch of times, trying to get her back. I break out into a sweat, face clammy, telling myself I can hop on the next plane home, *madame* will understand—

'Emma, it's Dad.'

'Dad! *Whew*, what happened?'

'Sorry, honey, I didn't mean to scare you, but your mother... well, she's been sick from the chemo and she got real nauseous and her dinner didn't agree with her. I wanted to clean her up.' He sighs heavily. 'I reminded her you were in Paris, but she was in pain and it didn't register in her mind.'

'No problem, Dad. I can come home—'

'No, you finish up over there and we'll see you soon. Mom and I know how important your work is to you.'

'Not as important as you guys.'

I hear my father choke back a sob. It's so hard on him taking care of Mom. I worry about him, too.

To ease the tension, I ask him, 'Hey, Dad, do you remember what Grandpop said about how he found the baby in Dachau?'

He chuckles, the familiar memory bringing him a bit of mirth. 'He loves telling that story about a female prisoner who begged him to adopt the baby girl, that her mother was dead but her father was American... he guessed a downed flier... and that the baby girl's mother was a Polish student and a Resistance fighter. He couldn't find out any more since the Nazis destroyed the records.'

'Thanks, Dad, that intel helps a lot.' I remember hearing the story, but I wanted to get it from the source so I can run it by *madame*... if I ever get up the nerve.

I say goodbye to my father, promising to call tomorrow. I'm shaking, my whole being reacting to my call with Mom. I can only imagine what it would mean to *madame* if she found *her* lost daughter. That's why I've got to know everything I can about her, bond with her. Give her a chance to tell her story and why she made the choices she did at Auschwitz and Dachau, where her baby was born.

The downside of my scheme is she may feel like I deceived her because I didn't tell her I'm trying to find out more about my own grandmother. Maybe if I tell her how much it would mean to my mom, she'll understand.

If she *doesn't*, well... then she'll send me home and I'll never know the whole story.

I can't let that happen. I have to prove to *madame* I'm sincere. And whatever the truth is, Angéline de Cadieux's story of the Holocaust and the Roma people will be told.

I fall asleep for a few hours and get some shuteye, then grab my notebook and a pencil with a new eraser and head to *madame's* room. Even before I knock on the door, the heavenly aroma of cinnamon toast, buttery eggs, and hot coffee makes my taste buds sing.

* * *

Angéline

Bracing myself for the next part of the interview, I barely touch the scrambled eggs *à l'américaine* and nibble at the sweet toast. I became too emotional last night, too willing to bare my soul to someone I barely know. That surprised me... and embarrassed me, too. My interviewing skills are rusty, or is it something else? I want to live up to my reputation. When I started on this idea of talking about the war years, I never dreamed I'd become so emotionally involved.

It's because of her. Mademoiselle Emma Keane.

I glance over at the pretty girl making notes as she sips her coffee, her face shiny and clean, scant makeup. Strong cheekbones, high forehead, sparkling blue eyes with a hint of hazel. Like Maman's. *Why does that thought keep popping up in my mind?*

Her long hair hangs around her shoulders, casual T-shirt and navy jeans with stars on the pockets. Soft pink leather ballet shoes. She reminds me of the girl I once was in ruffled skirts and a low-cut white blouse, a trademark of Roma women. I'd say she even looks like me, but that's wishful thinking on my part. What woman of a certain age doesn't wish to see herself in a younger, vibrant woman? Emma seems honest and caring, yet a part of me is skeptical of the media and their motives. Ratings are more important to them than anything and they take no responsibility for anyone getting hurt in the process.

Yet Emma shared with me that despicable note which I have no doubt came from that Hansen woman. I asked Ryker to track down who sent it before we venture out again onto the streets of Paris.

Fidgeting with the damn toast, tapping my fingers on the linen tablecloth embroidered with the hotel logo, I don't deny I have cabin fever. I wanted Emma to walk the boulevards with me, the covered passages, smell the aroma of Paris that doesn't change but only adds new scents as the years go by, but the bottom note... the gritty core of the city's history is always there to fill you up with its olfactory experience *if* you're a nose.

And Emma is. I'm sure of it.

Ryker rang me up before Emma showed up for our breakfast interview and assured me he'll have answers for me sometime today. Where this Hansen woman is staying, what her motive is. (As if I don't know – she wants me to show her my prisoner number tattoo, which I damn well never will.) Then we can deal with her. I've refrained from asking for an official restraining order against her. I have no desire to ruin her life. But she has no right to ruin mine.

To my surprise, Emma swings the interview back to life in 1941 Occupied Paris, asking me what my everyday routine was like. Not that anything during that time was ordinary, I tell her. We queued up for everything with our ration cards, only to discover, when we got to the front of the line, they ran out of butter or coffee hours ago. I can't forget the Germans infiltrated the queues with French citizens paid to act as 'spies' and report anything incriminating to the Gestapo.

Old habits die hard. No wonder I suspect everyone.

I dab my mouth with the napkin and continue, explaining it was late winter 1941 when we feared the village in the south of France in the *Zone libre* (Unoccupied Zone), where the factory was located, between Nice and Avignon would soon be occupied. Only God knew then how we'd survive. Some owners of French houses of perfume had already left for America – out of the question for us. No one but me spoke English and we couldn't import oils from across the Atlantic since America declared war on Germany.

Emma's questions keep me on my toes digging up facts, leaving me no time to dwell on the churning emotions of fear and anger that haunt me to this day.

Did I travel by train back to Paris? Yes.

Where did I get my clothes? From a dressmaker in hiding in exchange for perfume she sold on the black market.

Did I receive a salary at the House of Doujan?

Yes... but less than the male lab assistants. Years later when I made my mark in the industry, I succeeded in getting equal pay for women in the House of Doujan.

Rationing? By 1942, chocolate and vegetables made their way into the ration books. France didn't stop rationing until 1949.

Gas? Heating oil? The Germans stayed warm in winter, but we Parisians didn't. No gasoline for motorcars, which were *verboten*.

Making love? When I tell her the birthrate in France increased in the middle of the war, her brows shoot up.

'*Madame*, did you... I mean, you were young, beautiful... were you in love?'

'You have a most interesting way of leading into the question you've been wanting to ask since we arrived in Paris. After my pining and swooning over the elusive rogue in black, did I have an affair with the mysterious Count?'

'Well, yes... but if you're uncomfortable talking about it, I understand.'

Or is *she* uncomfortable speaking about *l'amour*?

Is a certain handsome bodyguard making her squirm?

Cheeks turning red, Emma shifts her position in her chair. 'Where did you live in Paris during the war, *madame*?'

'A third-floor apartment on the Left Bank on Rue du Sommerard, bath down the hall, no elevator. Yvette made it cozy with soft mauve and gray pillows scattered on the divan and Sylvie Martone movie posters on the wall. I never saw her films growing up, but by 1941 movie theaters had opened up again. We went to the pictures and *oohed* and *aahed* over her grand adventures. I asked Yvette if she missed the theater and she showed me a photo of her dressed as the *Queen of the Black Swan* in a black satin tutu and jeweled feather crown. It was the only performance her mother came to see her in. She never approved of her daughter going on the stage. Sadly, she was struck by a speeding motorcar soon afterward and died instantly.'

'Oh, how horrible for Yvette. To lose her mother so soon after they reconciled.' Emma looks visibly shaken, biting her lip... while staring at her cell phone as if she wants to make a call.

Strange, Emma never speaks about her family, even in passing as reporters do to 'soften you up' so you start believing they're your friend and you tell them everything. I learned that lesson the hard way. That Hansen woman regaled me with her whole life story – made up as she went along, I imagine – which makes me wonder what Emma is hiding. I want to reach out to her and ask her what's on her mind. Would that be too forward?

Or am I merely avoiding digging into the painful place in my heart that's never healed?

The story of Yvette.

'Yvette was a fun, winsome young woman,' I begin, 'but when I returned to Paris to help launch *Naomie's Dream* I noticed she'd lost weight... she looked pale and was suffering from I thought was a lingering cough from a winter cold. She remained cheery and was so happy to see me, I didn't press her. She told me my letters had arrived and she'd passed them along to *le Comte*. (We never referred to him as

Dr MacBride lest we blow his cover.) I must have sounded like a smitten schoolgirl when I asked if he was doing well.'

Yvette smiled. *'You want to know if he's involved with anyone.'*

'Is he?'

'I've seen him with girls from the cabaret, but he doesn't look at them the way he looks at you.'

'And with that lovely thought, *mademoiselle*, I kept him in my heart, praying he'd see me as a woman, not a wild Roma girl. I visited the pawnshop often, hoping Lance would show up. I was worried about him. As the Count, he could move about in the dark without detection, but as an American, he was subject to the Gestapo picking him up as relations between his country and Germany worsened with US warships protecting supply convoys from attacks by Nazi submarines in the Atlantic. I worried about him, but Jarnak indicated to me with a wink 'that nosy archaeologist is on a dig in Egypt', which meant he was safe. But where? I left with a lighter heart, though I was experiencing emotions for him I had no business feeling. I hurt like a woman, but he made it clear I was still a girl in his eyes.' I take a moment to compose myself. 'I sometimes wonder how I ever got through those years when every day was filled with intrigue and longing for a man I barely knew.'

'Sometimes you know he's the one, *madame,* even if he doesn't.' Emma lets out a long sigh and a smirk crosses her lips. Is she thinking about Ryker?

I smile, giving her a moment to dream about him.

'My life took a different turn when we launched *Naomie's Dream,*' I continue. 'Frederic loved to play God, announcing he would personally go to the German High Command for help to step up production if sales were good.'

'And were they, *madame*?'

'We sold out on the first day.' I can't keep the pride out of my voice.

'Oh, my God, how amazing! You were a success... and so young.' Emma waves her pencil in the air, thinking. 'You were... eighteen, *madame*?'

I smile. 'A mature eighteen. War makes you grow up fast. Life in

Paris during the Occupation teetered from learning to survive with no new shoes for four years to running out of soap, to resorting to eating anything you could get your hands on.'

'You look terribly sad, *madame*.'

'I am, *mademoiselle*; bringing up the past makes you face your mistakes. The hard part is that you can't undo them. You're filled with so many "what ifs", that's a penance unto itself.' I fret with my napkin, digging my fingers into the linen, my pulse racing. 'If I hadn't come back to Paris, I wouldn't have made the choices I did... who knows what lives could have been saved.'

'No disrespect, *madame*, but you can't be certain,' Emma says in a firm tone. 'Your account of life under the occupiers has shown me that survival hung by a delicate silk thread and could be cut at any time by a petulant, selfish enemy who discarded human life at a whim. *No one* could predict that. Not even you.'

I stare at this young woman, her wise words soothing me like a lavender balm. My heart slows, my conscience easing a bit. '*Merci, mademoiselle*. There were many unsung heroines in the war deserving of a place in your piece, Emma, so bear with me as I continue with my story.'

'I promise you, *madame*, I will write down every word. They will have their moment.'

Seeing the determination circling in this young woman's eyes, I want to reach out and squeeze her hand. Feel the warmth of connecting with someone who cares as deeply as I do about the brave people I knew... and lost. I feel the need to make that physical connection with her, but I don't. That I'm still an old fool who can't open her heart completely to this young woman hurts.

'When I came back to Paris to oversee the launch of *Naomie's Dream*, Frederic was in a foul mood, dismissing my contribution to the perfume as "insignificant", even though Professor Zunz sang my praises to Monsieur Baptiste. It didn't matter. Frederic went out of his way to address me as a "salesclerk" in front of customers in the shop on Rue Saint-Honoré.'

'He was jealous of you, *madame*,' Emma says, writing. 'Why? He had money, power.'

'His ego. His role as the "premier nose" of the House of Doujan was in jeopardy if I let it slip it was *my* formula we used for our new scent. He'd already tried once to put the fear of the Gestapo in me. To ensure that, I found out after the war he hinted to Major von Risinger he suspected one of his sales staff of "suspicious" anti-Nazi activities. He was bluffing, of course. He didn't dare name me directly because that would make the Gestapo suspicious of *him*. He had nothing to substantiate his claim... *nothing*, but his accusation was enough to set off the alarm at the secret police headquarters on 84 Avenue Foch where the Gestapo was busy following leads from hundreds of sources even if they led nowhere.'

'How did that affect you, *madame*?'

'Things were getting "hot" as you Americans say, with the roundup of French communists and the members of an important Resistance group later executed in 1942. When two men in Lance's operation were arrested near the abbey on Rue Saint-Jacques, he went into deep cover as Dr MacBride, making it too dangerous for him to be seen near the pawnshop. I swore I saw him disappearing through the revolving doors of the Hôtel Ritz with an SS officer a week later. I was confused, unsure what to do next, so I put our backup plan into play.'

'You were a spy, *madame*.'

I chuckle. '*Mais oui*, Emma. If I needed to contact him, I'd attend the pictures at the Gaumont-Palace Theater and sit in the eighth row, third seat from the aisle on the left side of the theater. I did this twice a week for three weeks when on this night, I found a folded-up paper stuck to the bottom of the plush seat with gum. *How American*, I thought. A note telling me he was safe and I was to continue my daily routine to avoid suspicion.'

I get misty-eyed.

'Take a moment, *madame*.' She hands me a tissue, then gives herself one. 'I need one, too, if I'm to keep my head on, get the details right.' She sucks in a breath. 'Okay, I'm ready.'

She's a feeling young woman. Big heart. Honest. Smart. I like that, yet she's secretive about her own life. *Bien*, I'll know more about Emma Keane when I read the background report Henri-Justin secured for me. Till then, I've never told anyone the complete story about that night after I grabbed the note from Lance and left the theater; the night when I escaped from the Gestapo.

It's time I did.

25

PARIS, 1941

Angéline

Perfume:
Y
Bulgarian rose, lily of the valley, amber

The Gestapo man is nipping at my heels, but I don't stop. I can't. The overpowering scent of heavy garlic and cigar smoke turns my stomach along with his foul body odor. Herr Geller, with his dead black, arched brows, prefers the stink of death. Smelling clean and good would taint his reputation. I never thought much about what the Gestapo smells like.

Now my life depends upon it.

I thought I'd seen the last of the secret policeman after he made such a big deal out of checking everyone's papers back at Argenteuil. Now he's poking his nose into my business here in Paris, following me after I left the movie theater.

I walk faster as I round the corner on Rue du Caulaincourt, praying somehow I can shake the man in the overcoat before I hear those dreaded words, '*Vos papiers, mademoiselle.*'

Then he'll look me up and down with that superior sneer I remember so well when he stopped Maman and me, when I foolishly told him we were 'perfume makers'. How did he find me? It makes no sense – unless someone put him on my tail and that someone can only be Frederic. A man forged from cold stone with no heart, no conscience. I noticed him smiling at me earlier at the shop like a bloated fish who ate a little fish. Me.

I let go with a shiver as I cross my arms over my chest, the late fall chill setting in with the misty rain. The smell of cigar smoke gets stronger. Herr Geller is still on my tail, toying with me. I've got to lose him before he makes his play.

I scurry by the *brasserie*... then the pastry shop... up the boulevard... then a sharp left... no one on the streets since it's after nine o'clock. God help anyone stopped by German soldiers looking for a poor soul to torment. Worse yet if the invaders are drunk, having spent the night imbibing absinthe at the *soldatenkaffee*, cafés for German soldiers.

I cross the Pont Caulaincourt... the metal bridge built almost a century ago over the cemetery several feet below street level. I don't dare look around, but I feel certain the Gestapo man started following me when I sneaked out of the Gaumont-Palace Theater earlier, as though he was waiting for me.

Cold, drizzling rain wets my full black coat with the thick braid adorning the collar and cuffs, pasting my skirt to my thighs. I rub the wetness out of my eyes. It's coming down harder now, leaving a sweet taste on my lips, refreshing my dry mouth. I slip off my muddy shoes in spite of the cold, slippery cobblestones as I scurry down the stairs toward the old Montmartre cemetery. Headstones... mausoleums. I keep going... I can't shake the Gestapo man. I'm scared. He wouldn't waste his time with me unless he's after something. The Nazis have long suspected the movie theater is a drop-off site, but its huge, darkened interior with seating for three thousand patrons makes it difficult to observe any nefarious activity. He must have followed me to the theater when I left the perfume shop.

Raindrops dot my cheeks as I slip into a narrow space between a tall, gilded structure honoring a Russian princess and a gray-faced mausoleum. The lopsided stones scattered in the dirt dig into the bottoms of my stockinged feet, my heart pounding, my whole being covered in fear and darkness. I feel inside my skirt pocket... the folded-up note is there. Should I destroy it? No time.

Footsteps... heavy, loud... echo in my ears and I smell sulfur from the strike of a match.

The Gestapo man found me.

A bright light flashes in my face. I hear a sharp intake of breath, then the man curses and the match goes out.

Mon Dieu, did he recognize me?

I grab a rock to toss at him, but luckily for me the stout Nazi gets stuck in the narrow space between the statue and the mausoleum when he tries to grab me. I don't waste another moment. I take the advantage God has given me and jam over the stones and through the cemetery till I get to the street.

And then run for my life.

* * *

'Are you sure the man following you was Gestapo?' Yvette looks panicked, the blood draining from her face. I've never seen her look so pale.

'Yes. Belted black trench coat, black gloves, Fedora hat, smoking a cigar.'

'Did he follow you here?'

'No. I lost him in the cemetery in Montmartre.' I drop my muddy shoes on the wooden floor, collapse on a stool, and rub my burning feet. I ran back here in my cotton stockings, slipping on cobblestones wet with a misty fog.

'Why was he following you?' she asks.

'I don't know, but my gut tells me Frederic is behind this, sending me a message by setting the German secret police on me.' I feel sick to my stomach.

'Why would Frederic invite trouble with the Gestapo?' Yvette paces up and down the small apartment, clutching a handkerchief to her chest. 'The House of Doujan has always been above suspicion.'

'It's his sadistic way of warning me to keep my mouth shut and not expose his dubious claim as a *parfumier*.'

'The *fool*. Doesn't he know once the Gestapo gets wind of the slightest crack in the wall, *everyone* is in their cross hairs?' She's exasperated, worried. Her body shakes uncontrollably, then she coughs into her handkerchief. Something she does more and more often. 'We must inform the Count so he can warn the others. And Monsieur Baptiste. He's worried sick about his fiancée ever since the Nazis rounded up Polish Jews.'

'The Nazis have also started rounding up my people,' I say, my heart leaden. 'Sending Roma to concentration camps. I could be picked up if Herr Geller finds me.'

She can't keep the shock out of her voice. 'You *know* this man?'

I avoid looking her in the eye as I unbutton my coat and toss it along with my hat on the divan. 'Yes. I had a run-in with him before I came to Paris.'

'I'm not surprised. The Gestapo is everywhere... and they don't forget even if they let you go.' She stops pacing, clinging to hope. 'You have new papers, Angéline. Why are you so frightened?'

'They didn't let me go, Yvette... I – I ran away before they could arrest me and...' We stare at each other, two women both fighting for France but one with a secret she must confess. 'I'm wanted by the Gestapo.'

'What?'

'I swear Herr Geller recognized me when he struck a match and the flame lit up my face.' I stand up, ready to bare my shivering soul. 'There's something else I haven't told you.'

Feeling guilty for keeping anything from her, I try to explain but make a mess of it, how Maman and I boarded our horses and Major von Risinger ordered the Gestapo man to find us so he could commandeer my prized stallion for his racing stable. 'I should have let the major have Zeus, but I raised him and I couldn't let the arrogant Nazi mistreat him. I was obstinate and feared the horse would be whipped—'

'What did you do?' The color drains from her face.

'I assaulted the German officer... after he shot my *maman*.' I feel lightheaded, relieved in a strange way to let it go. Maman's lavender scent is so strong in my nostrils, it's as if she's laying a hand on my shoulder to comfort me. 'She died in my arms trying to save me.'

'Oh, dearest God... how horrible for you.'

'I escaped and returned to my caravan, but my stepfather turned me in and I'm wanted by the Gestapo.'

She wraps her arm around my shoulder and doesn't speak for a long moment. I look at her closely. I'm so ashamed I didn't realize how tired she looks and she's lost more weight.

She says, 'We must get word to Lance—'

A loud, insistent knocking chills our bones. Once... twice... *three times*.

I panic. '*Herr Geller*. How did he find me?'

Yvette doesn't seem surprised. 'The German secret police have files on everyone. If Frederic is behind this, it wouldn't have taken them long to go through the list of salesclerks and make his way here.'

'I'll get rid of him,' I tell her. 'You go out the side window and crouch down on the balcony so he doesn't see you.'

'No, let me take care of him.'

'Are you crazy, Yvette? I can't let you get mixed up in this.'

She shrugs, smiles. 'It doesn't matter what happens to me, *ma chère*. I don't have much time left.'

She shows me the handkerchief I've seen clutched in her hand for weeks. I had no idea she's been coughing up blood. Bright red clots. She admits she has tuberculosis.

'I won't let you do this.'

'You don't have a choice, *mademoiselle*. I have a plan.'

'A plan?'

'What if the Gestapo man *didn't* recognize you in the dark? Why should he? Your hair is different, so is your makeup. He won't know the difference if he sees me dressed like you.' She points to my feet. 'Down to your muddy shoes.'

'This is my fault, Yvette. I'll take the consequences.'

'And abandon the women of France?'

'What are you talking about?'

'I know about the perfume you're working on, how you plan to use it to bring up morale in these terrible times when Frenchwomen are desperate to hold on to their dignity, not lower themselves to do the Boches' bidding.'

I nod. 'The professor, of course.'

'You are the soul of the House of Doujan, Angéline de Cadieux. *You* must live to create new perfumes for the women of France, to give them courage.'

Courage. Of course. That's it. The perfume I've racked my brain to create. Emotion wells up inside me. Hope, pride. And anger if my work is destroyed because of one man's ego. But I won't let Yvette sacrifice herself for me.

'I'll give the Gestapo an excuse,' I insist. 'Frederic is trying to frighten me. He wouldn't dare let anything happen to me.'

'We can't take that chance.' She slips on my muddy pumps before I can stop her. 'Hide in the garderobe and don't make a sound.'

'Yvette, no...'

'Go!'

She pushes me toward the garderobe, giving me seconds to hide inside. When she answers the door, I hear Herr Geller barging inside, his gruff, domineering voice echoing in my ears, asking if she's alone, poking around.

'You were out after curfew, *mademoiselle*.'

'You're mistaken, *monsieur*,' I hear Yvette say with that lilt in her voice when she's lying.

'Your coat and hat are wet.' He clears his throat. 'And your shoes are muddy.'

'Are they?' She looks down, then sighs. 'The Third Reich is not against *l'amour, n'est-ce pas*? I was meeting someone.'

'Your lover?'

'Yes.'

'You're lying, *mademoiselle*, my men and I have been keeping an eye on the salesclerks from the House of Doujan for weeks. Tonight I followed a woman dressed in this hat and coat to the cinema. It was you. What were you doing there?'

'My friend never showed,' she says with hurt in her voice.

'Very convenient.'

'It's the truth, *monsieur*.'

I hear a raspy cough. Yvette... then the ugly smell of cigar smoke weans its way through the crack in the garderobe. I hold my breath till my chest hurts so I don't retch.

'I've had enough of your lies, *mademoiselle*. Since you refuse to answer my questions and we've long suspected members of the Underground use the theater as a drop-off, you leave me no choice.' A loud snort follows. 'You're under arrest.'

26

PARIS, 1941

Angéline

Perfume:
Moonlit Passion
White carnation, mimosa, Indian sandalwood

From my hiding place, I see Yvette cough in the Gestapo man's face in defiance. He turns her around and pulls her hands behind her back, cuffs her, and then drags her away. Leaving her black coat and hat behind.

Cramped, my legs asleep, I can't move, but I can cry. I'm so angry with myself for letting her go through with her insane idea. So what if I have a talent for perfume? It doesn't seem fair.

Why her and not me?

I haven't known her long, but we formed a bond. Two French-women, both injured souls, desperate to do our part to bring down the terrible oppression of the Nazis. They're killing Frenchwomen's souls, tempting us with chocolates and wine, enticing us to give lonely German soldiers a smile... a smile that turns us into traitors. Why should we be servants to the occupiers? Why can't we fight, too? Fight by not giving in to their seductive promises of food to fill our bellies. Then we starve. And we do.

Hovering in the cramped garderobe, I can't stop shaking, admitting there's a sense of truth in Yvette's plea for me to continue my work. I'm reminded of the woman I saw outside the pawnshop falling to her knees and clutching her chest, begging God to help her find food so her children wouldn't become afflicted with disease, their bones withering away, becoming thin and broken with rickets. Her eyes puffy from crying, she admitted she nearly gave in and slept with the enemy so they could eat.

I gave her the few francs I had, but what about feeding her soul, too? I believe I *can* give women courage even if it's as simple as a lovely scent to swoop them up to a higher plane. Give them hope so the Nazis can't break us. What this war has taught me is that no woman is immune to temptation. You don't know what you'll do when you're hungry and lonely for a man's arms around you. So many of our men are in the army... or imprisoned... or killed.

I come out of my hiding place and hug that black coat to my chest... Yvette's scent of white rose and jasmine mixed with the rain forever ingrained in the coat's woolen fibers. I'm caught up in the moment, remembering what Yvette said about how important the perfume I'm trying to create is to the war effort.

I can't fail. I owe it to her.

* * *

Angéline

Paris, 2003

'Please, *madame*,' Emma begs me, 'tell me more about how *Le Courage* came to be.'

I nod. I almost forgot where I was, so intense was my memory of that day.

'Did you know your sense of smell affects your mood?' I begin. 'How you associate different smells with intimate moments in your life? That's what I was working on... a fragrance that would evoke happier times in a woman's life, but I didn't have the complete formula then. After that night, all I could think about was Yvette. I didn't know what had happened to her, but I had my suspicions. Beatings... starvation, sleep deprivation. I had to get her out of Gestapo hands. I pleaded with Frederic to intervene and he tried... how hard, I don't know. He was more scared for his own hide and returned with bad news. Yvette didn't tell me she'd been arrested for handing out anti-Nazi pamphlets at the theater where she danced. That she was on the Gestapo's "red list" and she could have been picked up at any time. That was when I understood what Lance meant about putting your emotions into a box to fight this war. I didn't cry, fret... scream. No, instead I made plans.

'I went to the pawnshop to see Jarnak, making sure I wasn't followed. He was devastated when I told him what happened to Yvette. Through his contacts in the Underground, we found out she was put in solitary confinement at Cherche-Midi Prison, held there, interrogated every day and threatened with being shot. She died three weeks later.

'I blame myself for her capture, but I was young and inexperienced, and the daring moves I made weren't enough to save her. She was wise enough to see the bigger picture, that our band of operatives had its part to do and this was her contribution. I believe I could have done more, that she didn't have to spend the time she had left in such horrible conditions, but she was convinced my work with perfume was so important to the morale of Frenchwomen.

'I will always have a picture in my mind of Yvette humming the lovely music from the *Dance of the Black Swan* as she closed her eyes for the final time and saw herself once again as a beautiful prima ballerina... dancing.'

'Oh.' Emma hasn't breathed for the last ten minutes... the look on her face is the same look I imagine was on my face when the Gestapo man bound her wrists and took Yvette away. 'I don't know if I'd have had her courage.'

'You have the same grit, Emma, or I wouldn't have invited you to Paris. Daring, outspoken... and honest with your feelings. Who knows? Maybe you have French DNA in you.'

'Then I could be a nose... like you, *madame*,' she jokes.

True, I believe Emma has a gift, but I pray she isn't sniffing around for dirt in the perfume business because she'll not get it from me. Yes, we have egotistical and arrogant 'noses' who will steal the formula for your latest creation as quick as a rabbit scrambling down a hole, but I find perfumers to be good people. Honest... hardworking.

Embarrassed, she avoids my gaze and writes on her yellow pad. 'Yvette was a true heroine of the Resistance, *madame*, and deserves a proper place in my story so no one ever forgets her.'

'*Merci*. I will always hold her memory close to my heart. After the war I wanted to do more, so I created a perfume named for her.'

Emma smiles. 'Of course. *Y*, with the delicate etching of a ballerina *en pointe* on the crystal bottle.'

I nod, the sorrow in my heart ebbing. It felt good to tell Emma what I endured that night, spilling out what I couldn't say then.

'Shall we take a break?' I ask, getting up from the table. 'Then I have a treat for you, *mademoiselle*, the story you've been waiting for.'

'The good stuff?' Her face glows.

'*Oui*, the stuff romance novels are made of.' I prepare to shift gears. 'For that we need a lovely setting. A place where we can leave behind Paris at war... where we can revel in the quiet of the countryside where no German boot ever entered, no Nazi flag ever flew... and where I became a woman with the man I loved for forty-eight years.'

'Lance,' Emma finishes with a big smile.

'*Oui, mademoiselle*. Pack your bag and your umbrella, too. I detected the smell of rain in the air earlier, then we're off to Le Château de Cadieux outside Paris. There I will tell you the story about how my girlish longings blossomed into love, though I had my doubts about this man who gallivanted about with the Nazi hierarchy from Amsterdam to Belgium to Paris, advising them on their looted art, its value and history. The war raged on in 1942. The Allies bombed a motorcar factory in the Paris suburbs and Jews were ordered to wear the yellow star of David.'

'What about Professor Zunz?'

'He hadn't secured a visa to leave France and knew then he never would. He warned Ester to stop cavorting with Nazi officers, but she continued dancing at the cabarets, drinking and smoking, and insisting *dear Frederic has my back*. I remained skeptical after seeing how *dear Frederic* helped Yvette. No one was safe. Every day, people were being rounded up and sent to camps. Political dissidents, communists... and Jews. Even for riding a bicycle... forbidden for them to own.'

'And Lance wasn't detained by the Gestapo with America in the fight?'

'No.'

'How was he able to move about Paris so freely?'

'I discovered his connection with the Nazi High Command went deeper than I ever imagined.'

'Oh, my God, no... was he a collaborator?'

I stare at her, not sure how she's going to react. '*Mais non*, Emma, he was a double agent working for the British.'

27

PARIS, 2003

Emma

Perfume:
Doujan Princess
Tangerine, ginger, amber

Early the next morning, I go over how I put my foot in my mouth again.

Maybe I can be a nose like you, madame, I said.

Girl, really? Could it be any more obvious you want more than a story? What next? An apple for teacher?

I had the perfect opportunity to tell her about my longstanding talent for interpreting fragrances and scents and I blew it. I lost my nerve. When *madame* talked about bonding with Yvette, I should have said, '*Oh, by the way, wouldn't you call what you and I are doing bonding? And guess what, I think I am a nose.*'

No wonder the skies open up with storm clouds as I check out of the hotel before we leave for the Château de Cadieux, north of Paris. Wagging their finger at me for my cowardice. *Madame* was right about the rain. By late morning, it's coming down in sheets as we gather our luggage and check out of the hotel.

I sniff the air as we wait under the white overhang outside the hotel for Marcel to bring round the town car. Paris in the rain has its own unique perfume. A clean but seductive scent.

'The air smells like white gardenia...' I breathe in, searching for the right scents.

'With a hint of rose and a dash of romance, *n'est-ce pas*?' adds *madame*.

'Yes. And, I might add, a sprinkle of carnation.'

'*Bon*. You have a gift, Emma, for scent. Has anyone ever told you that?'

'My mom... she says I was born with a nose for news *and* perfume. I'd drive her crazy sniffing the bottles on her vanity table and raiding her spice cabinet sampling the smells.' My chest tightens. There. I finally said it, but my mind is somewhere else. I talked to Mom last night and I guess my concern shows on my face because *madame* lays her hand on my arm.

'Your mother... she's not well, Emma?'

'Well, actually, she's... she has lung cancer.'

'Oh...' she breathes out in a heavy sigh. 'I'm so sorry. Is there anything I can do?' She takes my hand and squeezes it, then hugs me. It's a moment I'll never forget. The driving rain seems so appropriate a backdrop to the swirl of emotions filtering through me when she doesn't let me go.

'I called her last night,' I say, keeping my voice even. 'She's doing fine.'

Mom *isn't* doing fine but no one wants to hear that.

Madame breathes out, relieved. '*Bon*, Emma. Keep me posted, please.'

Keep her posted? Why am I suddenly opening up to her like this?

This is nuts. I can tell her Mom is sick, but I can't tell her about my Polish grandmother who died in Dachau? Or my dream to be a nose? And how all this ties together in my story about her? I know why. I'm having a major guilt trip because I should be there for my mom.

God, I miss her.

'*Merci, madame,* for your kind words.'

What else can I say? I have no plans to continue this conversation about Mom and I can't tell Madame de Cadieux why I'm here. She'd think I was using her to enter the world of perfume. I'm not. I don't know if I even have enough talent to go *pro nose.* I just want to find out from the best what I *do* have so I can go on with my life instead of wondering *what could have been.* It's built up in me for years, distressing me.

On the other hand, I could tell her we have something else in common, but I don't mention my grandmother because, well... her baby – my mom – survived. That would devastate *madame.* I can't let anything interfere with the good vibes between us, her telling me her story like the tides, ebbing and flowing. Any stormy interruption will change that flow.

Meanwhile, we postponed our visit to the perfume shop and to avoid any more confrontations with Brooke.

Finally, the town car rolls up and Ryker jumps out with a huge, striped umbrella. I'm sure he'd prefer I get wet. The man is his usual handsome self, which doesn't help my mood. Gray suit, impeccable as always, but it's the way his broad shoulders fill it out that makes me stare as he helps the perfume diva into the car.

I feel his eyes on me.

His sexy gaze sweeps over me and he nods in approval at my navy-blue trench coat, then gives me a disapproving look when he sees my ballet flats.

'Doesn't it ever rain in New York?' he says, talking to me as though I'm a child.

'I swim like a duck.'

'In those shoes?'

'I sprout wings, too.' Why do I get all angry around him? Because he's got this dark, magnificent hero thing going on? That I have to prove I'm as tough as he is. More so after our last encounter. I judged him wrong and jumped to conclusions, but he left in a huff. That's it.

I'm done. I'll work with him, but I'm not going down that Pity Highway again.

You don't need him and his 'tude.

Shoulders back, then walk gracefully from the sidewalk and get into the town car.

Piece of cake.

I've run through the rainy streets of Manhattan in these shoes a hundred times. But there I didn't have a rogue bodyguard unnerving me. I feel exposed under his scrutiny as Ryker holds the umbrella over my head because he *has* to, keeping close to me as I head for the curb. I'm not changing the way I walk for him. I sweep my ponytail over my shoulder and sashay over to the waiting motorcar, grinning.

I've got this.

Or do I?

I take a nosedive when my delicate slippers hit a big rain puddle and my legs go out from under me. I skid over the pavement on wobbly knees, arching my back... *uh-oh!*

Before I go down on my butt, Ryker throws down the umbrella and scoops me up in his strong arms like a reluctant superhero. He sucks in a breath, his eyes flashing, his strong hands digging into my thighs. *Ouch*, that hurts, but he's keeping me secure in his arms. *That* bothers me more. Like I'm his captive and he enjoys the control it gives him over me. Keeping me in my place. Why? Because he's got this vendetta against reporters.

I gather by the whiff of his heady scent spiking and mixing with the rain he's pissed. Big time. Still, the scent is intoxicating... a fresh citrus... and is that a sweet licorice I smell?

'I should have let you fall on your arse, *mademoiselle*,' he says, gritting his teeth, raindrops splattering on that expensive suit.

'Then why didn't you?' I challenge him with a sassy tone.

'Because *madame* will have my head if anything happens to you.'

'As if you care.'

'I don't,' he states flatly. 'But I won't have you accuse me again of slacking on the job.'

'Don't tempt me.' I squirm in his arms; his grip gets tighter. I get wet, my hair plastered to my cheeks. I should apologize to him for being out of line yesterday and wrongly accusing him. If it was any other guy, I would. But Mr Gray Suit's arrogance makes that impossible.

Still, for *madame's* sake, I have to try.

'Madame de Cadieux told me—'

'Told you what?' A dark shadow crosses his eyes and again I sense hurt in them.

'That you were on a business assignment for the House of Doujan yesterday.'

He shoots me an aggravated glance. 'I'm back now. I assure you, it won't happen again.'

Is there no getting through to this man?

He keeps staring at me, those burnished baby blues studying me, curious, probably wondering how I ended up in his arms and what to do with me.

God help me, I know that look.

He wants to kiss me.

He won't. Oh, he'd like to taste the forbidden fruit, compare me to the French girls I bet he keeps in a garret on the Left Bank. Yet I also sense a vulnerable side to him he tries so hard to hide. Like the powerful sorrow I see cross his face when he doesn't know I'm watching him. How he goes off alone and sits in the bright sun, letting the searing heat beat down on his brow. As though he's paying a penance for a deed gone wrong. Is that what makes him act so untamed and defiant?

I swallow, stare back without flinching. Is it my imagination or does he hold me longer than he needs to?

What the heck are you doing? This is your job at stake, your career. Not a reality TV dating show.

And did you forget? *Madame* is watching your every move.

'Don't get your knickers in a twist, *mademoiselle*,' he teases me with as much subtlety as a tiger baring his fangs. 'I'm not going to take advantage of you.'

'It never crossed my mind.' I squirm in his arms. 'Put me down. *Madame* is waiting.'

What is it about this man that makes him dangerous and appealing at the same time?

'If you insist, *mademoiselle,*' he says with a glint in his eye. He makes a grand gesture, swinging me around in a circle before putting me down next to the passenger door of the town car.

I jump into the backseat and catch *madame* smiling, enjoying my embarrassing moment.

She whispers to me, 'Ryker is an interesting opponent, Emma, *n'est-ce pas?*'

'What makes you say that, *madame?*'

'Love is war, *mademoiselle*, and victory tastes the sweetest when you both win.'

Then she chuckles, keeping secrets again from me as I watch the bodyguard grab two thin blankets from the vehicle's storage bin to dry us off, then we're headed north of Paris, speeding up the autoroute to Château de Cadieux. I huddle under the thin white blanket, sneaking peeks at Ryker in the front seat, noting even the back of his head is sexy with his wet, shiny dark hair curling over his white collar. He never turns around once, instead keeping his eyes trained on the side mirror, and I wonder what I would have done if he had kissed me.

Why, I'd have kissed him back.

Keeps us even.

* * *

Angéline

Whenever I'm away on business from Le Château de Cadieux and I return home, I take a moment to stop at Maman's grave: a quiet, hidden piece of ground on the sloping hillside of the Chouffard Forest. I stand before the gray marble marker I added after the war, bow my head and say a few words. Talk about where I've been, leave a vial containing a lovely new scent she'd adore. I enjoy the peace I find here, the rustle of the chestnut trees, the smell of Scots pine... the gurgling stream that leads to the spot where I left her so many years ago. I find joy in tending to the wood violets that have taken root around her grave, finding a deer or even a crafty badger taking up the vigil when I'm away. It's a silly habit of an old woman etching out a bit of privacy in a fast-paced world where she feels comfortable to talk out her feelings.

Not today. We go straight to the seventeenth-century, four-turret castle I've called home since the war.

Maman will understand. I chuckle... besides, her ghost will seek us out. Snooping around, wondering, _who is this American girl I've become so fond of with the amazing nose?_

I continue going over in my mind how Emma opened up to me about her mother and revealed how ill she is. Heart-breaking. I wish she'd tell me more about her _maman_, but I sense she doesn't share her personal troubles easily.

I sent Henri-Justin on ahead of us to make sure the château is ready for our guest. _And_ to print out the background check I requested on Emma in a font big enough so I can read the damn thing. I feel like a sneak going behind her back... old tradecraft never dies... but it's more important than ever I know more about her so I can help her if she needs me.

I heave out a sigh, realizing I'm diving into extremely private information, but something urges me on that I don't understand. Gut instinct. Then again, I resent it when the press does a nosedive into _my_ past. I tell myself my motive is to help the young woman and her family. Of course, as soon as Emma is back in New York and files her story with the TV station, she'll be done with me.

And that _does_ make me sad.

First, we have an interview to complete. And this is such a lovely part of my life when I began a journey with the man who loved and adored me for nearly half a century of ups and downs, sorrow and joy. The first night we made love... I chuckle. I never thought I'd share *that* with anyone. I pray it will lift her spirits.

Having Emma here lifts mine.

* * *

'Where did you get this gorgeous red kimono, *madame*?'

Emma sits on the long blue divan in the upstairs study, her notes spread out around her. Wrapped up in my red geisha satin kimono, her hair damp, pencil in hand, she's ready for me to continue my story. The rain beats against the square windowpanes, not letting up, but inside we've gotten cozy after I made sure my two lovebirds got into dry clothes. I was smitten to see what happened between Emma and Ryker when he swooped her up in his arms, but I zipped my lips and didn't ask questions.

Somehow I shall get these two together. I feel so *maman*-hen-protective toward Emma. She's lonely... too career-driven to let anyone see her heart. And Ryker is my work in progress. A remarkable man so in need of healing. They belong together. I shan't stop trying to make that happen.

'The kimono was a gift from Lance years ago when he went gadding about in the Far East.' I smile. 'I remember his exact words when he showed up after a trip to Kyoto after the war. He'd ventured there to help the team from the US Army assess any damage to the ancient artifacts of the spiritual city.

'Lance was always bringing me back gifts from his travels – a set of cocktail glasses from the bar at the Raffles Hotel in Singapore in 1949, a white alabaster replica of King Tut's sarcophagus in the 1950s. And a blue-beaded and silver wedding necklace a Tuareg noble, lord of the desert, gifted to him when he traveled to the Sahara Desert on a dig in 1970. I'll show it to you later... then you shall have the love story you came for, *mademoiselle*, and why I'd never give up this place.'

I press the buzzer on the desk next to my comfy chair and a young woman enters with a silver tray filled with croissants, raspberry jam, cups, and a pot of hot coffee. I run a small household here at the château... housekeeper, cook, and two girls from the nearby village who help with chores, along with Henri-Justin, Marie, and Marcel.

Emma checks her notes. 'You and Lance married after the war, correct, *madame*?'

I nod. 'Yes, but *mon amour* could never sit still... he'd race off on a new adventure at a moment's notice, which caused more than one rift in our marriage. I loved him anyway. He always came back to me and our home, the château. After the war, we restored the castle – from the roofs to the plaster and the beams in the ceiling to buying up antiques from manor houses that survived the bombings. I'd just become part owner of the House of Doujan, but I wasn't officially recognized as the head nose until the mid-1960s when a new generation turned the world of traditional perfume upside down.'

'You mean the pop culture of mini-skirts and white go-go boots.' Emma spoons jam onto her croissant.

'*Oui, mademoiselle*. But I'm getting ahead of myself. When my Litaro clan first camped here more than two hundred years ago, the *Duc de Parmontagne* owned the château, but family scandals depleted his coffers, forcing them to eke out a living growing vegetables they sold at *Les Halles* in Paris. The last royal died in 1912 and was buried in the tiny cemetery in the forest. During the Great War, French and American troops requisitioned the residence as barracks, then squatters took over, but the last duke had the château declared a historical structure and paid the taxes for years by selling gold he discovered belonging to—'

Emma grins. 'The Roman Emperor Constantine.'

'*Bien*. By the time Maman and Papa and I camped here with our caravan, it was rundown and abandoned. Freezing cold in the winter... sticky and hot in the summer. When Lance and I first made the château our meeting place, we slept on the floor, then on straw pallets until we hauled in an old four poster on a cabbage truck, the mattress stuffed with rifles and pistols and grenades from the British, dropped by parachute. We made wild, crazy love here on that mattress during a spring storm in 1944 and many nights after, a place where we found peace from the war raging around us and where our child was conceived—'

'*Madame!*' Emma gasps so loudly, she spills jam on her hand. 'Oh, dear, I've made a mess. I'll go wash it off.' She's off to her room before I finish my story. I've upset her with something I said... my frank talk about making love? I'm not surprised. Americans are uptight about sex and I shouldn't speak so freely. Or is something else? I get a shiver there's more here than she's telling.

Again, that itchy feeling Emma is hiding something tickles my brain.

I take a hard look at the brown envelope Henri-Justin left for me. Emma's bio. I've been debating whether or not to open it. We're having such a good time, two women sharing, learning from each other, I don't want to ruin it.

But what if—

I've learned during my time upon this earth never to ignore my gut. And it's telling me not to dismiss Henri-Justin's concern when he insisted I read the report 'out of earshot of *la jolie mademoiselle*'. That I'd find it 'eye-opening'.

I rip it open. *Bien*, no time like the present to sneak a peek. I scan the usual rundown of the girl's life. She doesn't come from a stodgy upbringing. *Mais oui*, she was born in Philadelphia to Judy Elizabeth Keane, née O'Flaherty, an army nurse, and Terence Keane, ex-soldier and math professor. Graduated from university with a degree in journalism, worked at odd jobs including a perfume model (no surprise here) while attending college, interned at a New York City TV station, then worked for years in a secondary TV market before getting her big break at WJJR-TV. She's received numerous awards for her in-depth stories, including one on Holocaust survivors a few years ago. *Hmm...* interesting.

I keep reading... she's researched Ravensbrück, Auschwitz, Dachau, interviewing women who survived the camps, telling their stories with heart and depth. One in particular strikes a chord with me.

I can't stop the tears running down my cheeks when I read Emma's piece about the dying German woman in the nursing home... and her remembrances of Dachau. The filth, disease... the awful underground bunkers. The summer heat... the cold winters with snow on the ground. She must have been there a while and yet she survived, God bless her. I squint at the grainy photograph. The woman looks familiar. Thin, bony. I don't see a number on her arm, but prisoners at Dachau didn't get tattooed. I look closer. Nice features and that long braid. Why does that look familiar? Back then we all had short hair.

I start sweating, my chest heavy with grief as I take in the too familiar details of life in the camps. No one old survived for long... they pulled the humiliation deeper into their souls than we younger prisoners did, the horror of stripping naked and racing through a gauntlet of SS men... it killed them faster.

I heave out a deep sigh. Say a silent prayer.

I turn the page. What's this? A photocopy of a document marked 'Declassified': US Army liberation of Dachau. Statement of a female German prisoner taken down by Captain Sean O'Flaherty, May 5, 1945.

Emma's grandfather? The name fits. I keep reading. Usual military jargon, mentioning rules, regulations, then—

Mon Dieu... it can't be true. A postscript from the researcher that Emma's *grandmother* was a prisoner at Dachau. She died before the camp was liberated in 1945 after giving birth to a girl.

I scan it quickly. No name given, very basic information... that she was thought to be Polish and a brief mention of her baby being adopted by the American officer in charge. I know of several Hungarian babies born in the camp, but no Polish. That must be Emma's mother... and now the poor woman is ill, no wonder the girl is so upset. My heart stops and that jittery, jagged set of nerves I haven't felt in years pushes in on my chest. I'm stunned, but not surprised Henri-Justin uncovered this information. He was a secretary to a member of the British Foreign Office before he came to work for me. He must have pulled strings to get a look at declassified Allied documents that traced Emma's grandfather's service during the war.

My stomach clenches. Ever since we started this interview, I imagined Emma was hiding something. Why keep this information from me? Of course, the child. No wonder she's curious about my 'secret baby'. Her mom was one, too.

'I'm back, *madame*.'

Emma smiles at me, tilting her head just so, blue eyes sparkling like...

The strangest emotion comes over me that I can't explain... it gives me chills.

* * *

'When did you move into the château, *madame*?' Emma grabs a croissant *sans* jam and munches on it, her eyes lowered. I can see the wheels turning in her brain. She notices me staring at her, knows something is different. The funny thing is, I, too, know something is different. I just can't tell her what it is.

Clever girl... keep the interview going, but reveal nothing.

'It was the summer of 1942, known as the Roundup of Vél d'Hiv,' I begin, deciding to chew on this new information later when it's settled in my brain. For now, the interview is more important. 'A time of heartache and chaos when the French police, under orders from the Nazis, herded thousands of Jews into the *Vélodrome d'Hiver*, the Winter Velodrome stadium, where sporting events took place.'

'Please explain, *madame*.'

'For two days in July, the police rounded up more than thirteen thousand Jews with foreign citizenship from Paris and the suburbs. Men, women, and children crammed in the covered stadium with few *toilettes* and little food and water. I panicked... wondering if Roma were next. Yes, I had new papers, but I became aware of an undercurrent in our everyday lives that frightened me. French citizens "shadowing" other citizens and then accusing them of wrongdoing to the Gestapo. I couldn't take the chance, especially after Yvette died.

'I stayed on at the apartment on Rue du Sommerard until a new concierge took over. A dowdy woman with long, nervous fingers, poking about, asking questions, rubbing her stubby nose against the windowpane, watching me come and go. I had to move, but where? I couldn't stay at the pawnshop and rooms were hard to get with the Nazis commandeering everything for their generals and officers. So I returned to Argenteuil, took a room in a *pension* and worked on my secret formula for *Le Courage*. Remember, I wasn't a chemist, so I needed Professor Zunz to guide me through the difficult process of adjusting the ratios of the essential oils and absolutes from sweet floral to spicy to woodsy. I could see his mind wandering... wiping his glasses numerous times an hour, looking over his shoulder. He was on edge, expecting the police to burst into the laboratory and take him away. When they didn't, we believed Frederic used his influence with the French police commissioner to look the other way, not out of decency, but because the professor's skills and talent were a key element to keeping the House of Doujan profitable during the war. None of the other chemists had his talent.'

'Thank God, *madame,* I was so worried for him.' Emma heaves a cleansing breath. 'What happened to the professor after the war? And his niece?'

'I was convinced the professor and Ester were safe, however...' I set my coffee cup down, laying my hand on my chest. 'I was wrong.'

'*Madame...* tell me, *please*?' Her notebook slides off her lap and onto the rug. She makes no effort to pick it up.

'The professor found out from an unlikely source – Frederic – that Ester was stepping out on Monsieur Baptiste, that she'd sneak out of the fancy apartment in the *16e arrondissement* in Paris in the wee hours of the morning while her fiancé was asleep.'

'I can't say I like her, *madame*.'

'Neither did I. Especially when I discovered she was involved with a French aristocrat collaborating with the Nazis.'

'How did she get away with it?'

'Her lover had no idea she was a Hungarian Jew. She hid behind her count ex-husband's moniker and a fantastic story she concocted about her connection to a sixteenth-century imperial baron from Budapest.'

'Too bad she didn't use her skills to help the Resistance.'

'I learned from the professor she got mixed up with a vicious gang known to the Nazis as the French Gestapo, criminals who did the jobs the Nazis wouldn't. They were more feared because they *were* French and could infiltrate partisan operations. They were active in the black market back in 1942 and cavorted with wealthy Parisians... including Ester's lover. He couldn't save her from their scrutiny when she couldn't pay her gambling debts... debts she owed to their leader, a man known for his "execution basement".'

'Wasn't that horrible major *what's-his-name* crushed on her?' Emma asks, picking up her notes and scribbling as she speaks. 'Why didn't he help her?'

'Major von Risinger chose to "look the other way" which didn't surprise me. The man had no backbone.'

'You mean the Nazi had no balls.'

Now it's my turn to look shocked.

'Precisely, *mademoiselle*. I couldn't have said it better. The irony is, she wasn't caught because she was Jewish, but the gang member who blew the whistle on her was a former detective.' I sigh. 'His expertise was following unfaithful wives and sweethearts. That was how you did business in Paris, how the Abwehr, German military intelligence, teamed up with French underworld gangs to perform the more vicious jobs the Gestapo didn't want to deal with. It was dirty and sexual and killed your soul if they went after you.'

'Poor Professor Zunz,' she says with genuine feeling. 'What happened next?'

'The professor begged me to secure a new *carte d'identité* for his niece and get her out of Paris. I was shocked. Did he know I was helping the Resistance? Or was this a trap?'

'No, not the professor. I don't believe it.' The tone of her voice is tender yet incredulous.

'Neither did I, so I took a chance. I told him I had "friends" who could help Ester since the professor didn't dare leave Argenteuil for fear of being picked up by French police. Yet I was leery of putting myself in danger after what happened to Yvette. But I couldn't say no. I'd seen how gambling got a hold on my stepfather, making him a desperate man, so desperate he sold me out to the Gestapo. Ester was also addicted, though I didn't know her story, what drove her to seek the high that comes with challenging the unknown... I wondered if she had an abusive father or suffered at the hands of invading soldiers in her country. How well I know the scars of abuse on a woman's soul, but it didn't excuse her in my eyes. If she were arrested and they found out she was Jewish... I tell you, *mademoiselle*, what we knew about conditions in the camps was sketchy back then, but horrific enough that I couldn't turn my back on her. I returned to Paris to warn her.'

'I don't know if I'd be that brave, *madame*.'

I cock an eyebrow, then ask a question hanging on the edge of my brain. 'What if *I* were in trouble, Emma? Would you face danger to help me?'

'*You, madame*?' She jumps to her feet. 'I'd do anything to help you, no matter what the risk.'

'You hardly know me, *mademoiselle*, why would you help me?'

'Well, besides the fact you're amazing,' she says with a huge grin, 'it's the right thing to do.'

I nod, my heart pleased to hear her answer. 'Like I helped Ester.'

'It took courage. I wish I were more like you.'

'You do?'

'Yes. You worked hard to follow your dream under the most horrible conditions... *and* fell in love with a wonderful man who adored you.' Her voice sounds envious, yet also wistful and my heart goes out to her. 'I haven't done so well in that department.'

She looked so longingly at Ryker when he held her in his arms. She's fallen harder than I thought.

'You'll find a man like that, Emma... you're more like me than you think.'

That sent her eyebrows shooting upward. '*Me, madame*... seriously?'

If I thought my words would evoke a reaction, I didn't expect the color to drain from her face. If anything, she looks scared. I pour another cup of coffee and ask myself, *what kind of game are you playing? What is it about this young woman that gets under your skin? Because you want so desperately to see yourself in her?*

Or am I looking for something that isn't there?

I sip my coffee in a slow manner. 'Perhaps I've painted too rosy a picture of myself, *mademoiselle*, as one tends to do in retrospect. That young Roma woman you met earlier filled with so much spirit, the girl who defied the Nazis in a reckless manner, by 1942 she'd retreated into a different world in Occupied Paris. A world where glamorous Parisians resisted the occupiers by not giving up their couture clothes, elaborate hats, exquisite jewelry. And perfume from the House of Doujan.'

'*Your* perfume, *madame*.'

'Yes. These *glamor girls* refused to become *collabos*, as we called collaborators after the war, but carried on as before. When I saw them enter the shop of the House of Doujan in their veiled hats and soft furs, I yearned to be like them. Why not? Yvette had taught me how to dress, act, speak. I never dreamed I'd enter that world, but first I had to save what I considered a selfish, vain woman from the French Gestapo. I was angry with Ester for cavorting with the enemy while Yvette lost her life, but I was certain the former ballerina would approve of my mission.' A beat. 'Losing her took a toll on me. I trusted no one.'

'You saved Ester... I get it, but how?'

'I took the next train to Paris, headed to the pawnshop and told Jarnak I needed to see the Count. That the French Gestapo held the notes on Ester's gambling debts and planned to extort Monsieur

Baptiste to pay up or Ester would be sent to a labor camp. Her life was at stake and I wouldn't take no for an answer.'

'And did he come, *madame*?' Emma pulls her knees up to her chest, eager to hear more. Her eyes sparkle with anticipation and I have the sudden urge to go straight to the 'good stuff' as she'd say, but I must lay the groundwork first.

'I waited for hours for this man who spun words into gold when he spoke, closing my eyes and falling half asleep in the blue wingback chair, dreaming of losing myself in his incredible dark eyes.

'When dawn broke, Lance showed up wearing his horn-rimmed spectacles and English tweed, questioning me why we should get Ester out of Paris. Besides the fact she's Jewish, I told him, she could have information about the movements of German officers the British would be interested in. He agreed, but there was one problem: the Nazis had put extra guards on the trains after the roundup, along with Gestapo men, hoping to snag Jews trying to escape. Ester was a high-profile society girl often seen at Nazi gatherings and would be recognized by SS officers. We couldn't hide her in the pawnshop... and I'd given up my apartment. Besides, I didn't trust her or know where her loyalties lay, especially if she were faced with arrest and detention at a camp. She could try to talk her way out of it by making false accusations against me or anyone in the House of Doujan. Still, we needed to convince her she had to leave Paris or else end up in Gestapo hands.'

'So what did you do, *madame*?'

'We kidnapped her.'

28

ON A ROAD NORTH OF PARIS, 1942

Angéline

Perfume:
Empress
Bergamot, India cinnamon, cedarwood

'Are you sure the gag is tight enough so she can't cry out?' I ask, my heart in my throat.

Lance grips the steering wheel tighter. 'She's as helpless as a prized pig tied up and ready for market.'

Traveling at a fast clip in a 1936 green Peugeot Lance had commandeered, we left Paris after sunset, our eyes on the dark rainclouds rumbling overhead after we waylaid Ester sneaking out of her apartment in the *16e arrondissement*. No doubt she was off to meet her secret lover, but we got her first. Dressed in black with bandanas covering our faces, we hid outside and grabbed her, then rolled her up in a twelfth-century medieval tapestry woven with silk and golden threads, her hands tied and gag in place. Where Lance got the woolen tapestry for our adventure remains 'classified', which I'm guessing means he 'borrowed' it from the cache of items he's helping the Nazis catalog.

She was decked out in a form-fitting evening gown, sandals... diamond bracelet and earrings. And a tiara. I remember thinking as she wailed and kicked her feet, I hope she doesn't lose an earring because she'll need to sell them when she gets to London. I don't worry about her getting on once we get her out of the country. A woman like her always makes do and I imagine her charming the RAF pilot as our motorcar heads for a secret landing field where a single-engine Lysander will pick her up.

We didn't count on three... no, *four* German soldiers standing guard up ahead at a roadblock in the middle of the two-lane highway. Lights flashing, two barriers set up at an angle, they motion for us to stop. A long gray Mercedes touring car is parked on the side of the road.

'Shall we turn around and go back to Paris?' I ask, panicked.

'And let the Boches put a bullet through our heads?' he says. 'Let me handle this, Angéline.' He maintains a steady speed down the highway, not making any rash moves that would warrant them shooting at us. His eyes narrow. 'Follow my lead.'

'Do I have a choice?'

'No.'

'I didn't think so.'

We've been going at each other since the mission began, Lance taking control like he's a rogue masked highwayman and me carrying on like an avenging archangel. He disapproves of me putting myself in danger and I like to believe it's because he cares for me. My determination to prove I'm no longer a young girl but a woman doesn't have an impact on him. If anything, his protective stance toward me has intensified. He keeps mumbling he made a mistake, that I'm too young, too inexperienced to work with his circuit – his cell – a closed unit where we have no contact with other cells so we can't identify members of the Underground if we're captured.

I keep mum, rather than engage in a confrontation with a man who has made it clear to me he has no sympathy for this woman. Not that I blame him. Ester wouldn't simmer down even when he told her the French Gestapo has no qualms about sending her to a concentration camp once they discover she's Jewish. Flying her out of France is something I never expected. Emergency pickups not timed around the full moon are rare because the pilot depends on moonlight to gauge his landing on a grass field, Lance told me, but do happen when an agent has vital information for the British Foreign Office. Or in this case, is the arrogant fiancée of a prominent French businessman who could be useful to the Allies.

I get a familiar feeling of nausea in my stomach when I think about his work as a double agent, but I want this insane plan to work so I can see relief on Professor Zunz's round face, his eyes blinking behind his spectacles. I hope Ester understands how much her uncle cares about her in spite of her wayward lifestyle.

'*Alt!*' comes the shout from the German soldier brandishing the bayonet on his rifle in our faces as we slow down. A Nazi officer flanked by a soldier approaches our motorcar and shines his flashlight on us as he taps his gloved hand on the driver's side window. 'Your papers.'

'*Guten Abend, Herr Oberleutnant,*' Lance says, rolling down his window, 'what's the problem?' He affects a friendly, lazy smile in spite of the light in his face, while I don't dare breathe. I try to focus, keeping my hands in my lap, feeling the rough leather of the seat digging into my back. A humid evening breeze shoots through the window, dragging with it a precise smell of clove and human sweat which makes me wince.

'We're searching for a downed RAF pilot, *monsieur,*' the German officer says in French, peering inside the motorcar, his flashlight making a small arc. 'I must search your vehicle.'

'That won't be necessary, *monsieur.* I'm an American archaeologist and art curator.' Lance pulls out his passport and an official looking letter embossed with a swastika in the left corner. 'Dr Langston MacBride. I have special permission from Herr Göring to deliver this priceless tapestry to his agent for the Führer's museum.'

'But you're driving *away* from Paris, *monsieur.*' The officer glances at the paper, then circles the motorcar, his hands clasped behind his back, stomping on the ground with his jackboots to shake loose dirt off them.

'Do you think Herr Göring is stupid, ordering me to meet his agent in Paris where the tapestry could be stolen?' Lance goes on the offensive. 'I'm meeting him in Amiens.'

'Of course not,' the officer acquiesces, not wanting to offend the Reichsmarschall. Then he shines his light in the backseat. I panic. What if Ester wiggles, the tapestry slips off and he sees her tied up? I can't let that happen.

I dally a moment as a sultry Frenchwoman would, curious and bold, rolling down my window, then asking him, 'You wouldn't keep Herr Göring waiting, *monsieur, n'est-ce pas?*' I smile big, run my fingers through my dyed black hair in a provocative manner, which doesn't go over well with my American companion when the Nazi shines his light in my face and smiles at me with a toothy grin.

Let him simmer. Calling me too young to do the job.

I do it *too* well.

With an approving glance at my full bosom outlined in a tight black sweater, the Boche peers at me like a fox foaming at the mouth. I want to spit in his face.

'Nor would I keep a beautiful woman waiting, *mademoiselle.*' He rests his boot on the big front fender. Wipes his gloves, adjusts his cap, and continues smiling at me.

Lance snorts his discontent, then says in a rush, 'It's urgent, *Herr Oberleutnant,* I must deliver this artifact to Göring's agent waiting for me before the transport leaves for Linz.'

I have no idea if there's a shred of truth in what he's saying, but the Nazi buys it.

The German officer snickers. 'The Führer has excellent taste when it comes to art.' He continues to stare at my chest and I glare back at him, refusing to show fear while my pulse races so fast my cheeks burn. '*And* women. My compliments, *monsieur,* on adding the beautiful *mademoiselle* to the collection.'

I shiver as the wind picks up and a sweet, pungent smell hits my nostrils... rain is coming. How much longer will the dark skies overhead be on our side?

'*Mademoiselle* works for the task force and is assisting me,' Lance says, attempting to keep his tone even, but I detect an edge in his voice. I know what he's thinking. If it rains, the pickup is off. 'Now if you'll excuse us, we'll be on our way—'

The first lieutenant isn't finished.

'I imagine the *mademoiselle* is sympathetic to the hardships we officers endure for our Führer so far from home.' He pokes his nose inside the window and I get a whiff of bad breath smelling like sharp vinegar. 'And she'll join me for a brandy in my motorcar.'

'We're late,' Lance protests, grinding his teeth. 'We must be on our way.'

'I insist.'

'Is that an order?' he asks flatly.

'A request, if you prefer.' The German officer opens the passenger door and clicks his heels. A deliberate gesture of superiority that makes me angry, followed by a cold, hard order. 'Get out, *mademoiselle!*'

I don't move. I'm not about to get into a motorcar with a lonely Nazi officer who considers me ripe for his plucking. 'I'm staying here. I have a job to do.'

'So the beautiful *mademoiselle* wants to play hard to get.' He strokes my cheek with his gloved fingers.

'Take... your hand... *off* me.' I say each syllable as if it's a bullet, meeting the German's agitated gaze and ignoring Lance's disparaging expression as I fight to keep from losing control. The intense memory of another run-in with an arrogant German officer attacks my brain. I've no desire to get myself killed. The fear must show in my eyes because Lance attempts to help me... no, he's... *what*?'

'Get out of the car, *mademoiselle*,' Lance says to me in a smooth voice. 'It's bad manners to turn down the request of a German officer.' Then to the lieutenant: 'She'll be happy to join you in your motorcar, *Herr Oberleutnant*. I'll return later to pick her up after you've enjoyed...' He snickers. 'Your brandy.'

A fierce pang of anger hits me hard. I can't believe I'm hearing this. *He's turning me over to the Nazi... then what? I get drunk with him, let him fondle me?* I can't... I won't. I open my mouth to speak... but nothing comes out.

'*Gut... sehr gut.*'

'I must warn you,' Lance continues with a deep, sexy groan, his eyes shining. 'She's a hellcat with those long nails.' He lets out a low whistle. 'And she likes to bite. Deep. So it breaks the skin.'

What's he doing? Then I think about how the German acted so fastidious, cleaning his gloves, shaking dirt off his boots. A Parisian hellcat isn't his type.

Got it. Brilliant.

Picking up his cue, I snarl at the German officer and brandish my nails which aren't that long, but in the dark he can't tell. He backs off, then pulls at his pristine uniform, tugs his collar.

'Dirty, uncivilized French. Get going... *now!*'

Lance wastes no time and puts the Peugeot in gear and takes off down the road like a jackrabbit with its hind legs singed, muffled sounds coming from Ester in the back seat, but it's over. I let out a deep breath and hold my arms to my chest to stop shaking.

'What were you thinking, Angéline?' Lance scolds me, his words harsh. 'Flirting with that Boche.'

'I was saving the mission until you threw me into the Nazi's bed.'

'It worked, didn't it?'

I snicker. 'Pray tell, what would you have done if he accepted your offer?'

'I'd have shot him.'

* * *

I'm not sure whether to be flattered or insulted by how the scenario played out with the Nazi officer. Offering me up like a bonded servant girl. *Would* Lance have shot the German officer? *And* the three soldiers? I'm shaking, but I'm not sorry for my actions. We're saving a woman's life, her dignity, and I believe in my heart Ester *will* accept what we've done for her. Perhaps she'll change her ways, though I'm grateful she had enough sense not to draw attention to herself when the Nazi officer poked his nose in the backseat. As if she was as terrified as I was. Lance remained cool under pressure. The man is made of steel and I'm convinced he has no heart. I was a fool to think I could ever be in love with him. He was only protecting me because I'm an asset, part of his operation.

Why does that make me feel as lonely as the last poppy in the field?

We continue driving in silence till we get to the secret landing field in a clearing surrounded by tall oaks. Lance parks the motorcar behind the trees and jumps out, scanning the skies as he covers his nose and mouth with his bandana, then motions for me to do the same. 'We haven't much time, *mademoiselle*. The longer we stay here, the more likely it is we'll be spotted.'

I give him a quick nod, fasten the bandana and then look up, but the dark night skies reveal nothing more than a single streak of moonlight scurrying across the sky... oh, wait... the sound of a single-engine aircraft buzzes overhead.

'There he is!'

'*Quick*, let's get the package ready and get her on her way.'

Ester tumbles out like a rag doll, sweaty and bleary-eyed when we unroll the carpet on the ground, the scene illuminated by the motorcar's dimmed headlights. Lance removes the gag and unties her, then helps her to her feet. She staggers, dizzy, muttering to herself in Hungarian as she adjusts the thin straps on her evening dress and then wipes her face with the hem of her long gown.

'I thought that Nazi prig would never let us go.' She spits out her obvious distaste of the Boches, surprising me.

Lance grabs her arm. 'You're leaving France, Countess, and you're not to return. Is that understood?'

She smirks. 'Paris isn't the only place I can ply my trade, *monsieur*. The world is full of men who enjoy my company.' She smiles at him and in the light, I swear I see a tenderness in her eyes toward him that flashes bright for a moment, then disappears. What alarms me is, Lance drops his anger toward her in that same moment. It chills me.

What's going on between these two?

Ester turns to me. '*Merci*, Angéline. You showed you have grit, *mademoiselle*, the way you handled that German swine. In spite of what you think of me, I'm not ungrateful. Thank you for saving my life.'

'You know who I am?' I ask, surprised.

She smiles. 'Your scent gave you away. Unique, intoxicating.' She means the new fragrance I'm working on. 'I've never smelled anything like it...' She observes me under heavy, lowered lashes. 'Except when I visited my uncle in his lab. Tell Uncle Oskar to keep his head down, *mademoiselle*; these are dangerous times and we won't all survive. *Adieu*.'

I've no time to reconcile why she sought me out to thank me. That's not the woman I knew in Paris. I chalk it up to our encounter with the leering Nazi. His domineering personality, not to mention offensive body odor, is enough to turn off anyone to collaborating with them.

The pickup goes off without a hitch even though there's not much moonlight. Lance waves around a small bicycle light attached to a pole and sends out a predetermined Morse code letter; the pilot responds with his light, then we set up two burning torches and the airplane lands.

Without hesitation, Ester climbs up the fixed small ladder on the side of the aircraft and into the cabin as if she's done this before, and the small aircraft takes off. She never looks back. I wonder what will happen to her. Why I should care angers me. She's a selfish woman who uses men. Again, I'm visited by a deep shudder within me that makes this whole scene look as murky as perfume tainted with sugar. Something's not right.

I push my unsettling thoughts to the back of my brain and let my curiosity fizzle. I have to. Otherwise, I won't get past my jealousy of 'that look' Ester passed on to Lance. I say nothing to him as he puts out the torches with me helping him. He'll think me a spoilt child and that won't help my case for him to see me as a woman.

Then we're off, like we were never there.

Thank God. The whole operation takes about three minutes.

Then it starts to rain, making the road muddy and slippery.

'It's too risky to go back to Paris tonight.' Lance drives slowly along the deserted road. 'We'll wait until daylight rather than take a chance of running into another German roadblock.'

I lay my head back on the seat, my heart still beating fast. He's right. It's after curfew.

'We'll have to sleep in the motorcar.' He turns off onto a side road.

'No, we don't.'

'You want to take the chance of getting picked up by a German patrol and spending the night in a Paris police station?'

'Well... no, but—'

'Alain got caught out after curfew last week by a German soldier on a bicycle. Fortunately, he didn't suspect him, but he made him shine his boots before he let him go.'

'I have a better idea, Dr MacBride.' I address him by his title to jiggle his brain, make him think.

'Yes?'

'You once asked me where the bronze coins on my bracelet came from.' My heart swells at the memory of our first meeting and that kiss in the dark in spite of his cold demeanor toward me. He's a wild rogue of an agent who flaunts his authority and treats me like a child but I can't help myself. I still love him.

'I'll show you.'

29

LE CHÂTEAU DE CADIEUX, PARIS, 2003

Emma

Perfume:
Red Tango
Spanish red rose, bergamot, ambrette

'You came here to the château that night, *madame*, didn't you?'

She nods as I sit back, take a breath. The room is bathed in purple shadows as I huddle in my chair, the red kimono wrapped tight around my legs. Ryker popped his head in to check on us, his eyes widening when he saw my long bare legs peeking from under the kimono. With disapproval. He considers me a bad influence on *madame*. I quickly covered them... okay, not so quickly, and I admit I enjoyed torturing him with a peek before he disappeared.

I pray he'll be back so I can continue the game. I'm winning, by the way.

'Yes,' she admits, refilling her coffee cup. 'After an episode so exhausting, I felt lightheaded yet exhilarated. And scared out of my drawers, as Maman would say.' She laughs. 'I had my first real taste of the terror agents faced every day in Occupied France, yet everything went smoothly. Or so I thought. I found out later how dangerous it was for the pilot to land with so little moonlight, that he nearly missed the field and hit a haystack. That the small aircraft was caught in German searchlights near the coast and only by the hand of God they weren't shot down. I never did feel like I measured up to the other agents, but I cut my teeth on that mission, daring to challenge the Nazi lieutenant and learning how pickups in designated zones worked. How Lance had sent a coded letter in a personal message over Radio Londres to request the immediate pickup of an agent.'

'An agent?' I ask, curious. I smell the whiff of female secrets in the wind. 'What do you mean?'

She smiles, lays her hand over mine. It's cold and that saddens me. She's shivering, the memory of that night still affects her. 'How young I was, *ma chère* Emma, and so naïve. Lance was right. Inexperienced didn't begin to describe me. Instinct served me well and would save my life more than once when I ended up in Auschwitz and Dachau.'

She pauses, her eyes darkening like uncut jade, and I suspect she's remembering so many horrific things she witnessed, experienced. Inhuman things. Unseen scars we've yet to tap into in our interview. Then she looks up at me, her eyes once again clear as the moment passes.

How does she do it?

'That night in 1942,' she continues, 'I was fooled by the skills of a professional agent who not only wore my perfume, but flaunted it in the faces of the Nazis. It wasn't until years later Lance spilled the beans about the deception the two of them pulled off.'

A groan escapes my lips. 'You don't mean... *Ester*?'

She nods. 'After the war, I had the pleasure of meeting up with her in London and we spent hours together, talking about those days and how she became a special agent for the SOE... Special Operations Executive, French section.'

I wave my pad in the air, shaking my head. 'I can't believe it...'

'She was Polish, not Hungarian, and had seen her mother and sister murdered by the Nazis in late 1939. She worked in the theater in

Warsaw and blended easily into the hierarchy of French society, using her acting skills to become this fascinating creature the Nazi officers couldn't resist. She was so flamboyant, so outrageous, the Gestapo didn't take her seriously.'

'What about Monsieur Baptiste? He was an okay guy... did he know?'

'Ester admitted the kindly gentleman fostered a real love for her and had no idea she was an SOE agent. She hated deceiving him, but she hated the Nazis more.' *Madame* takes a sip of coffee, her eyes softening. 'And yes, Ester *was* Jewish, but that never stopped her from rushing into danger. Soon after the Paris incident, the British gave her a new assignment and dropped her into Occupied Belgium where she worked for the Underground for the rest of the war.'

'I assume Lance was aware of her identity.'

'Oh, of course. He and Ester worked together before the Germans took France. They met in a flea hole of a cabaret in Montmartre where she was scrounging out a living as an artist's model and Lance was acquiring bohemian art for his Boston institute. I also discovered they had a torrid affair... but Ester broke it off.'

'Amazing...' I can't write fast enough. A secret, high-profile agent unmasked. A beautiful Jewish girl risking everything to avenge her family's murder. Seems *madame* and Ester had more in common than they realized. Who knew?

'*Mais oui*, the entire act of restraining her was for my benefit, to keep her safe should I ever be interrogated by the Gestapo.'

'And Professor Zunz?' I have to ask. 'How was he involved if she wasn't his niece?'

'The professor was one of Lance's most trusted agents. They'd worked together in Cairo in 1937 when he needed a *parfumier* to identify the composition of Egyptian unguent perfumes he unearthed in a pharaoh's tomb.'

I don't hide my surprise. 'The professor sure fooled me.'

'Me, too,' *madame* adds with a chuckle. 'That's why he made those trips to the countryside and why he asked me to help Ester escape. The

French Gestapo had her in their sights, making it impossible for her to contact anyone that would arouse suspicion... except for the professor. He had no other means but me to get a message to Lance without risking his own life... and hers.'

'You've never mentioned these two agents in other interviews you've given over the years, *madame*, why now?'

'It's time I hold nothing back, Emma. Ester died last year and the professor passed away in 1966, his heart giving out. I never would have become a *parfumier* without him. He taught me everything I know about the chemistry of perfume. I found out after the war, he was arrested soon after I was and sent to Drancy, a concentration camp outside Paris where he was held until the liberation of Paris in 1944. Frederic could no longer keep the Gestapo off his back and they whisked the brilliant chemist away and held him with other Jewish dissidents. He escaped being shipped to a death camp by claiming his status as a "nose" could be useful to the Nazis at some point. It worked.'

'What an amazing story.' I can barely breathe. 'I wish I had known the professor.'

'He became quite ill because of his ordeal in the internment camp,' *madame* continues, 'though he professed he never lost his sense of smell and sneaked out at nights to inhale the sweetness of the wild-flowers that grew up around the barbed wire.' Her nose wiggles, her eyes tearful. I have the urge to hug her, but I don't. She pulls up her chest, gets back to business. 'Whether or not it's true, considering the stench of death that surrounded us day and night, I never questioned him. His skill as a "nose" was his pride and I'd never take that from him.' She sounds as sad as I feel, but determined. 'I want to make sure they both get credit for their tremendous work and sacrifice since I'm not getting any younger and I have no family—'

I dig my pencil into the pad so hard it breaks when she hits me with that remark. I never expected to hear her blurt it out like that.

She grabs my hand and squeezes it. I glow. So she also feels this urgent need to reach out for human contact. This from a woman who protects herself from the press with a certain aloofness. Yet with me she *knows* something is different. Or am I reading more into it than there is? I want to tell her about my family ties to the war but I have the God-awful feeling this whole interview will go south if I do.

She's remembering a horrific time in her life and she's had to dig deep into herself to get here. Speaking about the professor and Ester publicly for the first time, her skill as a raconteur is as smooth as it is sad. Telling her I have ties to Dachau would shock her too much. If I take her out of her zone now, it's over.

So I don't.

Once more the stalwart reporter, I grab another pencil from my tote bag and change the subject, focusing again on that amazing night back in 1942 when she and the dashing archaeologist get it on.

With a straight face, I ask her what happened next.

She speaks in a quiet voice that touches me every time she says his name. 'Lance let down his guard... the rain and thunder setting a dramatic backdrop... the exhaustion he felt under the Nazi scrutiny ebbing away... and the scent of my perfume arousing him... a blend of peach, white velvet rose, orchid... and civet stirring his senses with an intensity he couldn't resist. He couldn't deny his feelings any longer and wanted to show me how he felt by...'

'Yes...' I lean forward, chewing on my pencil. 'Tell me, *please*.'

She looks down at her hands, a moment of immense pleasure slithering through her as that night reforms in her mind. 'By making love to me.'

'Oh, *madame*! At last.'

'But first, *chère* Emma, I must rest, gather my strength...' she says, her voice breathless and trailing off. 'We shall continue tomorrow...'

How can she do this to me? She closes her eyes and lays her head back on a soft, rose-red pillow, but I see her peeking at me.

She's teasing me.

'I can't wait till tomorrow, *madame*,' I burst out, playing her game. '*Please*.'

Lightning streaks flash through the long French windows... the small, cozy study... damask-covered chairs... teak desk... bookcase...

then thunder booms overhead. Situated in wooded grounds with the biggest, fluffiest trees and a rose garden, the château is twelfth-century chic with eight bedrooms and six bathrooms and the most amazing, vaulted ceiling in the Grand Hall. Tapestries hang everywhere, reaching down to the herringbone parquet floors. These details are side notes to the real story.

An unforgettable moment in *madame's* life.

It's 1 a.m. My hand is killing me from taking pages of notes. Madame de Cadieux reduces me to a wide-eyed kid when I'm around her, but I love how she doesn't back down from danger. Or going after the man she wants.

I can learn from her.

'Are you ready, Emma?'

'Am I!'

She grins and spreads out her arms in a grand, theatrical gesture. 'It was a dark and stormy night when this lilac lost her bloom...'

30

LE CHÂTEAU DE CADIEUX, PARIS, 1942

Angéline

Perfume:
Bel Amour 67
Chypre, mimosa, musk

'Make a right turn about five meters past the two tall oaks leaning into each other... here... where the stream meets the small cemetery.'

My voice catches as we pass by the place where Maman is buried, but I say nothing. The tall yellow daffodils I planted are bent over, touching the earth and drenched by the rain, but still there. That sets my compass right again. My roguish double agent wouldn't comprehend my deep sentiment for that corner of earth. Though earlier he was curious to know more about my Roma life when we camped here, where my papa found the bronze coins... questions I shall answer in due time.

'You were quite convincing with the German officer, coming up with that story.' I push aside my shaky emotions. 'How do you do it?'

'It's my job, Angéline.'

It turns out the story he told the Nazi officer is true. He cataloged several items from a residence in Saint Germain-en-Laye confiscated from its owner, who barely escaped with his life. Lance then 'borrowed' the tapestry from its new home in the *Jeu de Paume* art gallery in Paris for tonight's escapade, changing the facts to fit his story. A daring move and one that would have ended our mission if the lieutenant had detained us and checked with Göring's office instead of eyeing my bosom in the tight black sweater.

I say what's brewing in my mind.

'How can you play to the ego of the Boches, knowing what they're doing to France?'

I can't keep silent any longer. I adore this man and God knows I've missed him since our intense training sessions before I left for Argenteuil. This brave man who wanders around Paris at night, gathering intelligence at clandestine meetings and arranging for pickups. This same man then takes tea with the Germans during the day in a tweed suit and wearing phony spectacles (I looked through them) and catalogs stolen art. He reminds me of the grand lords of the manor Maman recounted to me in the folktales she told me when I was a little girl. Princes who gadded about the countryside disguised as woodsmen or highwayman, helping the poor, kissing the girls.

Lance has that same lordly aura about him, that his blood is blue. Funny I should think that, but I do. He has a way of turning a phrase that sings like poetry, the way he eats so properly with his fork in his left hand, knife in right, his extraordinary knowledge of art and history that took years to learn. Years a young man who toils the earth or sits at a clerk's desk wouldn't have. A man not in my league. If I'm right, why would such a man risk his freedom to fight an enemy who can destroy him with a flick of the wrist? Send him to prison should he stumble and they unmask this prince who moves about in darkness but dazzles in tweed?

'I've told you too much already, Angéline, the deed is done.' His words are cold. He won't reveal his secrets, something he makes clear. 'Now you must move on, as will I.'

I fail to understand his motivations as we ramble down the muddy ground toward the iron gates of the château.

I take his silence for what it is... a firm reluctance to treat me as an equal in this upside world of tradecraft. I allow myself to inhale the rich, jasmine-infused memory of my girlhood as we approach the château. I wipe the condensation off the window and sigh. Little has changed since we camped here. I see Maman dancing to a tune she hums... Papa digging up bronze coins... me scouring the meadow for violets and hyacinth. An innocent time when my heart was filled with their love, when I had a family—

I miss them so much; I fight back tears that never seem spent.

My mood shifts when Lance makes a sharp right, rain pounding on the windshield. My resolve to keep strong making me dig in and keep going. I hold on to the door lever as we bump over the uneven road. Papa had to push and push to get our *vardo* over the terrain when it rained, but the Peugeot is a sturdy piece of machinery and its big, heavy tires bode well for getting us through the mud. Then I see it. The sight of the stone structure looming ahead of us like a Gothic archangel welcoming us.

I barely have the chance to take in the infusion of smells from the past before Lance opens the passenger door and hustles me inside, keeping us dry with the centuries-old tapestry over our heads. Rain beats down on us and he doesn't ask if the grand double portals are unlocked. I have no doubt he would have shot the lock off if they were. Yes, I spied a pistol earlier on the floor of the Peugeot. I hadn't noticed it before. He wasn't kidding when he said he would have shot the German officer. I'm not sure if I'm comforted or scared by that.

We exchange a few words, grateful for the tapestry keeping us dry, though how Lance is going to explain to the Nazis how it got rain-soaked I don't know, but it saved two souls seeking shelter in an empty château. The musty odor and lacy cobwebs I remember from the last time are replaced with stagnant cooking odors, putting me on the alert. We always cooked outside, preferring the delicious roasting smells of a raucous open fire. *Someone's been here since my clan last took refuge in the château*, I tell him, *someone who isn't Roma*. Someone most likely taking refuge from the Boches.

Lance flips on his blackout torch lamp (ever the archaeologist) when we creak open the door to the study. A charming room with a high bay window. Walls once vibrant with fashionable red bleed a dull rust, wooden beams, star-crossed parquet floor scuffed with boot prints over the centuries, though I bargain to say none of them Boche. Its present state of decay and disrepair would never suit them. Rain beats against the multi-panes framed with iron with a steady beat matching the beating of my heart. Stone fireplace.

Lance moves the flashlight in an arc, both of us amazed to find this room furnished with a blue velvet divan ripped in places, a fraying blue-and-white floral shawl draped over it... and empty wine bottles and cigarette butts strewn about the parquet floor. By the positioning of the butts and bottles, Lance concludes there was only one occupant.

And he's long gone.

I breathe out of a sigh of relief.

Lance searches his pockets and starts a fire with sulfur matches which, thank God, are dry. Tired and still in our damp clothes, we huddle together on the divan... I wish he'd hold me. Instead, he speaks in a slow, steady voice as if he's thought out what he wants to say.

'How can I explain this insane job I've taken on, Angéline?' Lance stokes the fire with a black iron poker. 'A man doesn't wake up one morning and announce to the world, *today I'm going to be a spy*. But when the world he lives in goes mad, he has no choice. He has to do something or he can't live with himself.'

'But you're a scientist.'

'Yes, I'm a man who digs up the past, but the present is now my calling.' He shifts his weight and the divan creaks. I take the opportunity to move closer to him, inhale his manly scent infused with fresh rain. I doubt he notices. 'I must do something to stop this inhumanity toward innocent men, women... and what pains me most... children. This monster has destroyed countless lives and, God help us, I fear countless more as this war drags on. It's true I'm a dreamer. I go where the dream takes me and unlike others in this war, I've not suffered the personal loss of family, though I know what it's like to lose someone dear to you. A beautiful Egyptian art curator working for the cause of freedom... she was a skilled linguist, a wireless operator the Gestapo tortured and murdered.'

I wait, my heart skipping. Guilt floods me for my insensitivity toward him... that I dared not to give him a heart when indeed he has one, but it's broken.

I get up, pace the room. Even as I watch him in profile, I see a different man. A man who hasn't gotten over a great loss. Then we're more alike than I thought. Like me, he isn't ready to share more than what he told me. How can I blame him? I haven't told him everything about Maman and the disgusting major who made me watch as her beautiful soul slowly ebbed away in a pool of blood.

He lets the moment pass before he continues. 'I couldn't bury myself in old tombs when the world was off its axis, so I created my own spy network. I used my contacts in archaeology to secure a position on Hitler's task team, while posing as a disgruntled art critic sacked by the British for imposing art forgeries on them. I remained in Berlin moving priceless artifacts, including the bust of Nefertiti, to secure shelters, observing, watching. I arrived in Paris weeks before the Nazis marched down the Champs-Élysées to set up operations here. I contacted the SOE in London later that summer, but they ignored me. *How can an archaeologist fight Nazis?* they asked. I pushed on, submitting misinformation to the Germans. As a member of Göring's inner circle, I gathered critical details of Nazi troop movements from drunken German officers living the Paris high life, including intelligence regarding details of Rommel's proposed plan to land on Tripoli and join the Italians fighting the British last November.'

'So that's where you were.'

'Yes. The British finally took notice of my work and I joined a secret network in London consisting of a handful of double agents. The Foreign Office likes my style, how I use art mumbo jumbo to confuse the Nazis.'

'And so you became the Count. A Scarlet Pimpernel.'

He grins. 'I liked the idea of a masked man running around Paris at night, saving beautiful damsels.'

'Like me?'

'You're quite a challenge, Angéline... and you looked so beautiful in your ruffled skirt and red petticoat. I didn't know what to do with you, but I couldn't abandon you to life on the streets.' He heaves out a sigh. 'You're an innocent girl and I'd never take advantage of you.'

'I'm not a child any more, Lance.' I stand in front of him, hands on my hips, the heat from the fireplace warming my backside. A gnawing burns in the pit of my belly. An aching that makes me hot then cold with shivers. I lift my chin and pronounce proudly, 'I'm almost nineteen. I'm a woman *and* a nose. I created my first perfume for the House of Doujan. I called it *Naomie's Dream*.'

'So I heard. Professor Zunz says you sold out at the Paris shop.'

He smiles, then gets serious, grabbing me by the shoulders, his dark eyes glowing by the light of the fire. 'I'm worried about you, Angéline.'

'What about you, Lance? America is in the war. You could be arrested at any time. You know how cagey the Gestapo is, using trumped up charges to bring in anyone they suspect of being a spy.'

'The Nazis aren't easily fooled, but so far they're buying my intelligence. London gives me enough accurate material to feed them so they believe whatever false information I give them.' He holds me close, my ear against his chest. I can hear his heart pounding. 'There's something big in the wind, Angéline. I can't speak about it, but it will change the course of the war.'

I pull away slightly. 'A secret weapon?'

He laughs. 'I can't tell you anything more... I'd rather talk about that wild impetuous girl I met that first night who couldn't wait to get revenge on the Boches.'

'And I did.'

'What have you done?' he growls. 'The Gestapo will be breathing down your neck.'

'I gave a Nazi major a bottle of perfume.'

A special perfume so he'll never forget me. Someday, I will see that he pays the ultimate price for murdering my mother. This I swear on Maman's grave.

He breathes out, relieved. 'Is that what you're wearing now?'

'No. I'm testing a new fragrance. White rose, peach... oakmoss. Can you smell it?' I lean in, giving him a whiff of the provocative scent.

'Are you trying to seduce me?' He stares at me undaunted, but I detect an uptick of danger in that look and it fuels the fire in me.

'What if I am?' I ask. 'You're a man who loves a challenge, *n'est-ce pas*?'

'I promise you, it won't work. I'm immune to your charm.'

'Are you?' I rub my body against his and I feel him stiffen. He's breathing harder, clenching his fists, sure signs of a man weighing his options.

* * *

He isn't immune.

I squirm with delight when Lance plants kisses up and down my thighs, tickling me, caressing me.

Ooh... I pray he never stops.

We lie on the divan by the fire, our damp clothes in a shuffle, our bare skin hot and sweaty. Our passion unspoiled, barriers broken down on this rainy night because I longed for him too many nights to go on wondering if, *how*, I'd ever know him as a man. I've seen how fleeting each moment is in this war, how you have to grab onto happiness... *anything* can destroy a life never lived. Or loved. I'm determined not to let that happen to us even if he's too bullheaded to see it. The moment I first heard his commanding voice in the dark, inhaled his musky scent, he took my breath away and instilled a new confidence in me that I don't have to be alone. Something I fear so much, a Roma girl without her clan, her family, her Maman and Papa... I pray my roguish man will love me as a woman.

So I become bolder. It happens so fast, that blistering kiss when I press against his chest and melt into him and he pulls me closer, a hotness erupts in him that excites and frightens me at the same time. We're past flirting, sparring, playful kisses in the dark. I want him like this, hungry for me, but I haven't taken into consideration there's no turning back... and I know nothing about pleasing a man. Oh, I want to, to take him inside me, find that soaring space where you can't think but follow your passion to be as one, infusing your soul with his, your sense of smell springing alive and stinging your nose with the purest silky rose and exotic jasmine... and velvety amber.

Peeling off each layer like night creatures shedding their skin, tossing our clothes aside, I open my eyes to gaze upon his nakedness, his skin bronzed, his body muscular. I never dreamed a man could be so magnificent to look upon... taut, sinewy abdomen, broad chest rippling, shoulders so broad I could snuggle up against him and get lost forever. Nor did I believe such a man could find me pretty enough to gaze at me as he does now. Ebony eyes swirling with secrets I want to know, mesmerizing me into surrendering to him... the tables turned... him seducing me and I don't resist.

How can I?

My body feels heavy, so heavy, his kisses singeing my skin, my excitement spiraling. I close my eyes and the sheer intensity of his love-making makes me writhe wildly about on the ripped blue velvet divan, my need for his caresses blotting out any notion that he doesn't want me.

I moan, struggling to move my arms, my legs. I can't. My thoughts scramble as he runs his hands up and down my body, caressing me and mumbling to himself.

'So beautiful you are. A cruel trick the fates have played upon me.' He lets out a deep sigh, then a moan of anguish. What's he talking about? Is he beginning to regret making love to me? Have I done some-thing wrong wanting to be with him?

Or is there something in his past that gives him such anguish he can't stop hurting... Can I ever soothe that pain? Oh, God, I have to try even if my brain can't focus on anything but this moment. His touch is driving me mad, his words confusing me. I pay them no mind as we become one.

A long sigh comes from deep within me when the last wave of pleasure subsides, then I fall asleep in his arms... and dream.

Do I dare dream that love will last forever?

Dreams no longer innocent, but filled with dark enchantment. And memories of the man who made sweet love to me tonight.

The mysterious double agent, code name 'The Count'.

I'll never love another man.

31

LE CHÂTEAU DE CADIEUX, PARIS, 2003

Emma

Perfume:
My Destiny
Rose absolute, black narcissus, vanilla

'You made love *here*... in *this* room, *madame*.'

'Yes.'

She observes me, waiting for me to say more. I can't. I've never been moved like this before, my heart overflowing with emotion... This was 1942, her baby was born in the camp at the end of the war... which means they spent other nights here... oh, my.

'I lived in awe of this man,' *madame* continues, 'his acute maleness and deep mystery every time we made love exciting me, knowing the risk we were taking, that either of us could be followed by the Gestapo and arrested on the slightest of indiscretions. A careless word about the Führer... whistling a forbidden tune... failing to give way to an officer on the pavements. His eyes betrayed that fear, his words insisting I needed protection, how he could have an agent follow me, but I insisted I didn't need protecting.'

Sound familiar?

'How often did you meet, *madame*?'

'We met at the château once, even twice a week under the cover of darkness *if* he wasn't conning the Nazis with misinformation. Jarnak was our go-between, daring to drive from Paris on a motorbike disguised as a German soldier, sneaking into the lab after everyone had gone, leaving me a "poem" in my lab coat pocket. Red rose poem: no. Blue rose: yes. Then *X marks* for kisses – three marks, Wednesday. Four, Thursday, and so on. Then the word 'Love' followed by dots denoting the time, always after dark. Seven dots: seven o'clock. Anyone finding the note would believe I had a secret lover. Something even the Nazis couldn't ration.'

'How very French, *madame*.'

She nods. 'I rode my bicycle from Argenteuil as twilight crept through the forest and waited for him here. He'd pull up the long driveway in a requisitioned motorcar that changed every time we met, the sound of the engine a distinct music that aroused my senses like a purring tiger. It wasn't the secrecy of our rendezvous that aroused me, but something else. Something primal and bold, like the base note of a perfume that sears your skin when you spray it, branding me with his memory that still excites me.'

'Are you telling me, *madame*,' I have to ask, 'passion doesn't diminish as you age?'

'It changes to something deeper. This fierce longing for my love persists in spite of the insistence of nature that I grow old... A woman enjoys physical changes you come to accept, even welcome. And the urges... *ah, mais oui*, you rely on lovely dreams to release that pleasurable sensation in the pit of your belly, but the heart needs companionship. I've found it in my circle of friends, including those who work for me and, I thank God, that companionship is also fulfilled in lasting memories you replay over and over in your mind whenever you feel lonely.' She smiles at me. 'You wouldn't understand, Emma... not until you reach my age and know the satisfaction of watching romantic love deepening over the years and grow stronger. I pray you do.'

If only.

She sips cold coffee, but her hand is shaking. 'Thanks to you, *mademoiselle*, I felt the sun on my face tonight and I'm not as lonely. *Merci*.'

'Oh, *madame*, if only I could turn back the clock for you—'

'You already have. Telling you my story has brought back my youth, the joy of becoming who I am with a man who loved me, something I've been afraid of remembering in a darkened space at night, or an empty room smelling of the past. Telling my story to you enriches my memories, making them less painful. I've been so caught up in acquiring a fortune and becoming the head of the House of Doujan, and getting old in spite of expensive face creams and hair extensions. You've given me back the one thing I've never been able to hold onto since I was that young Roma girl skipping through the fields with her *maman*.'

'*Madame*?'

'Family.'

Okay, this is the moment. Ask her. It's now or never, girl.

'I have something to tell you, Madame de Cadieux...'

'You're not leaving Paris?' Her mouth droops, her eyes glaze over like a lacy veil slipping down over her face. She looks so frail and hurt that even if I *wanted* to leave, I wouldn't.

'Oh, no, nothing like that,' I joke. 'Do you remember when you said we were alike, that I have a gift for scent?'

'*Mais oui*, an amazing gift. You remind me of myself so long ago, sniffing and exalting in the joy of smell.'

'Well, we also have something else in common... it has to do with—'

A loud *knock* on the study door and it bursts open before I can finish my sentence. I'm miffed.

Ryker.

Again he foils my plans. The man has rotten timing... or the universe is playing games with me. I opt for the latter. He's not *that* good to read my mind... *is he*?

He's drenched to the skin. White button-down shirt open to the waist and sticking to his bare, bronzed chest. I shouldn't look, but I can't help myself. The man is gorgeous in *or* out of a gray silk suit. His hair is in sexy disarray, falling over his forehead, his eyes blazing. He looks as though he's been in a brawl and yes, I take this all in, in under five seconds.

Why now? When I'm about to tell *madame* about my connection to a Dachau prisoner.

Can't it wait?

Seems it can't. My mouth drops when he announces, '*Madame*... we have a situation.' He glares at me as if it's my fault. 'I caught a prowler outside watching you through the window.'

* * *

Angéline

An obnoxious blonde prowler... standing dripping wet in my Grand Hall.

Hands on her hips, complaining nonstop about the mud and the rain and the lousy road leading to the château, designed that way, I add, to keep out interlopers with an agenda like hers.

Brooke Hansen.

Ruining this lovely evening when I feel so connected to Emma as I come to grips with the ups and downs of my past. When I was so brokenhearted and determined to survive no matter what... no man, no regime, *no one* could break me again.

And now this.

My heart sinks. I want to tear up, I'm so disappointed. This woman won't give up. Usually I admire such a trait, but this individual uses her talent to tarnish people's lives for her own gain. My colorful background makes me fodder for the press, yes, but why am *I* being punished? It's unfair, but then what *is* fair? Was the war? Was what the

damn Boches did to my people, to the Jews, fair? It was beyond despicable, but we survived, *I* survived, dammit, and I'll not let that Hansen
woman or anyone else make me into a half-crazed, *gypsy* anti-heroine
with a vendetta, which is why I've avoided scrutiny, even before that
Hansen woman targeted me. Then Emma came along and the air
flowed through my lungs fresh and clean. I see the world again as a
bolt of glorious silk, ready to unroll and start anew. It's almost as if I've
found the kinship missing in my life since the war... and since I lost my
love.

I squeeze my eyes tight. I need a few seconds to reconnect
with him.

Oh, my darling Lance... I wish you could meet Emma. You'd adore
her as I do. She's so much like me as a young woman. Did you see her
eyes light up, her lip quiver when I relived those precious moments
with you? Don't be angry with me for sharing our great love with her...
I want her to write about us so the world will know what we accomplished during the war... so no one will ever forget.

But first I have to deal with this Hansen woman.

'Snooping around my château like a housecat?' I ask her. I owe her
nothing and would give her a dressing down if I wasn't certain she'd
turn *that* into a front-page scandal. 'What are you doing here?'

'*Me*?' she says, indignant. 'Why don't you ask *her* what *she's* doing
here?' She wags her finger at Emma, biting at the bit to give her a piece
of her mind. 'Taking over my turf to make a name for herself—'

'Don't listen to her, *madame*.' Emma sweeps in front of the reporter
in a wild flurry of frustration as if to protect her turf... *me*... which I find
amusing... and is she shaking?

I cast a critical eye in her direction and draw a deep breath, a sad
one. I know she's hiding her grandmother's connection to Dachau,
which disturbs me. Why? Ripples of tension grab me, upsetting me.
Doesn't she trust me?

'She doesn't know what she's talking about,' Emma continues. 'I
have only your best welfare in mind.'

'Do you?' Brooke demands. 'Or is it your own ass that's on the line?'

'You're wrong.'

Brooke narrows her eyes. 'Am I?'

'You're a disgrace to our profession, Brooke,' Emma spews. 'Using every trick in the book to get a story and not just with *madame*. It's no secret you bribe your sources to get dirt on celebrities.'

'That's just talk and you know it.'

'Is it?' Emma shoots back. 'I've got sources of my own who will swear—'

'Stop it!' A shiver rips across my shoulders. I don't like where this is going. 'I don't know what's between you two, *mesdemoiselles*,' I say in a firm voice. 'Professional jealousy, I imagine, but I'll not stand for it in my home. So whatever game you're playing, I'm ashamed of you both.' I take a breath. 'I'll see you in the morning, Emma... and as for you, Mademoiselle Hansen...'

I nod to Ryker who, though always a gentleman, is the muscle I need to end this ridiculous conversation between these two reporters. I sigh. Whatever game she's playing, I don't trust the blonde vixen.

He hustles the woman outside and back to her car after procuring a large umbrella and blanket for her (the thought of her keeping a personal monogrammed item of mine makes my skin crawl). Head down, Emma disappears without a word, taking her yellow pad and her secrets with her.

I swallow hard. That Emma continues to hold back information about her family history upsets me. *Why* she's doing so, I can't imagine. Yet the idea won't fade in my brain and, *mon Dieu*, hits me with a fierce pain in my heart. She *was* on the verge of telling me something... *was it about her Polish grandmother?* The sad part is, I can't ask her. Then she'd know I'd gone snooping deep into her background and *I'd* be the guilty one. She'd never trust anything I tell her again, so I have to remain mum, act surprised if she ever *does* tell me and hope for the best. I feel miserable. I could ruin everything with my fickle curiosity, and after we'd developed a kinship where Emma would ask me anything on her mind about my life and I would tell her. Maybe I'm reading too much into our relationship; maybe I am just a story to her. Even so, I've enjoyed coming out of my self-induced exile, letting her into my life. It won't be easy to return to the shadows and lonely solitude after she's gone. So to assuage this old woman's ego, I shall let things lie. I need her as much as she needs me, though I predict our motivations are quite different.

What worries me is: what if the Hansen woman is right?

What if Emma is planning to do a celebrity trashing number on me to advance her career and is digging for dirt?

I'd be devastated, crushed. My heart broken. Can I take that chance? I'm too old to fight my battles in the press. At times, I get so tired I just want to let go. But I don't. That's not me. Even when I'm in pain, I force myself to block it out and I do the job. That's how I got through the camps, that's what I have to do now. Because I have no choice if I'm reading Emma wrong. Do I really want to torture my soul all over again with loss? It *would* be easier for me to send her home, but the last thing I want to do is terminate our friendship on a sour note. Call it vanity, but am I a bigger fool because I cling to the notion she finds me interesting for myself and not because I make a 'great story'?

I pace up and down the study. I have to prepare myself to go through with this interview to the end. Relive every crushing moment that nearly killed me so Emma can understand how victory has its dark side. That you don't cover up the terrible things they did to you; instead you must find the courage to talk about them. It's taken me more than sixty years to see that.

I pray tomorrow will be bright with the sun shining, the rain tucked away under an umbrella sky for another day. I need hope to live in my heart, that Emma is what I want her to be. For somewhere in my brain, a chilling notion is forming... a notion that has to do with that German woman she wrote about in her Holocaust piece... a memory from Dachau slowly coming back to me so compelling. I shiver.

Mais oui.

I want it badly.

* * *

Emma

I had to stop Brooke Hansen from blowing my cover, making something out of my family's connection to *madame's* story that makes me look cheap, like a gold digger. Especially after that upsetting voice-mail from my dad saying Mom is back in the hospital.

I have this acute ache in my chest from worrying about her that won't go away. I needed to hear my mom's voice, tell her I love her and that I'm working on a big surprise for her, but Dad said she was sleeping when I called a minute ago. I'm scared sick about her, but my dad said there's nothing I can do and she's responding well to the medication.

Meanwhile, I'm a wreck, unsettled.

I can't sleep.

How did everything go so wrong?

My brain is spinning, trying to understand why I felt the urgent need to spill my guts tonight, to beg *madame* to understand why I wanted this interview so bad. She didn't have to buy my story right away, I get that. Tell a famous perfumer you want to pick her brain about prisoners she knew in Dachau because your mom is sick and maybe, just maybe, *madame* knew your grandmother and that would give your mom closure? Come on, it sounds crazy even to me.

So I blew it.

I waited too long to make my play and Madame de Cadieux will never trust me again. I stiffen, totally blaming my bad judgment, or should I call it cowardice? I've always wondered how she lost her baby... rumors fueled by Brooke Hansen abounded she didn't want her, but the Madame de Cadieux I've come to like and respect would never abandon her child. What unspeakable horror happened to her in Dachau that she turned her back on motherhood? I've got to find out, though I imagine she's conflicted about completing the interview with me. She's a pro, so I expect she'll finish her story during the war years as we agreed, then we'll go our separate ways.

I'll write my story, she'll read it and send me a *Thank You* note, and that will be the end of it.

'You're giving up? And you call yourself a reporter, Emma Keane?' I hear Granger in my head, telling me. 'Get back in there and fight. Don't disappoint me... or yourself.'

He's right. But this time it's not my professional ego on the line. I've embraced *madame* like family and I feel responsible for how the public sees her. I have the power to make her human in their eyes. And okay, I'm going to miss sparring with that Irish hunk. If only he didn't act like such a dumbass, a girl could like him.

Ain't gonna happen.

I head down the long corridor to my room, ready to take on Madame de Cadieux bright and early in the a.m. when—

'You're not as tough as you pretend, *mademoiselle*.'

I spin around and Ryker's intense dark eyes bore into me, asking questions, waiting for answers I'm not prepared to give. Arms crossed, tall, muscular frame silhouetted against the dimmed lighting in the corridor leading to the staircase. He's changed into dry clothes... tight T-shirt, black cargo pants, and brown boots. His dark hair is damp and falls lazily over his forehead. God, I can't take this man looking at me like I'm a horrible person. First, I mess up with *madame,* then Robin Hood waylays me in a dark corridor and won't let me go. *Now what?* This entire incident tonight caught me unprepared, something I'm not used to feeling. I *always* have my notes written down, questions on the tip of my tongue. *Damn,* I know the answers to the questions *before* I ask them. But this Irish rogue who makes my heart jump and my libido tango like never before accused me of being a softie. No way.

'You think *I'm* a softie? I wouldn't talk, Ryker.'

Knock him off balance. Play offense. It always works.

'Yeah?' he shoots back, smirking.

'Yeah. I've seen how you are with *madame*, giving her space but you're never more than a breath away if she needs you, how you protect her against everybody, including me.' I suck in a sharp breath. 'She may be your employer, but you care about her like she's family.'

'To me, she is. Madame de Cadieux reminds me of my nana... my grandmother.' He looks at me with unveiled shock, as if no one ever dared to invade his life.

'That's it? C'mon, there's more to it than that.' I prod him to get him talking.

His eyes narrow. 'You *do* dig deep, don't you, *mademoiselle*?'

'Afraid to talk to me, Ryker? Afraid I might find out you have a heart?'

My knees are shaking and I'm wired like a battery-happy bunny, but this moment had to come between us sometime. Now is as good a time as any since I've got him talking.

'My grandmother raised me, a boy of nine orphaned during the Troubles in Belfast when my ma abandoned me. I never knew my da. I lost him to a bomb attack when I was a baby.' He takes a moment, then: 'I grew up wanting revenge, but my nana was a wise and patient woman and encouraged me to channel my passion elsewhere and use my skills in military intelligence. She also gave her blessing when I married my sweetheart, an *au pair* from a small French village, but my beloved nana had passed when I again suffered heartbreak and loss.'

I nod. He just blew the wind out of my sails. 'I get it. You and *madame* share a history of losing family.'

'Yes, not that it's any of your business, but Madame de Cadieux pulled me out of a downward spiral when I was at my lowest point and had no one.' He sucks in a sharp breath, a sadness radiating from him so thick, I can cut it.

'You want to talk about it?' My voice is soft and I hope comforting because it hurts me to see this big lug in so much pain. He hates me, but he's talking to me.

'I lost my wife and daughter in a car accident seven years ago when I was away on assignment. But it was no accident.'

I gasp loudly. I can't help myself.

'Oh, I'm so sorry, Ryker.' I want to reach out, touch his arm, stroke his cheek, but I don't. I'd never let him go if I did. What he shared with me unnerves me, but it explains a lot about the man. His work in the military... undercover, I'm guessing, then his family pays the price in a revenge killing. The horror of what he's going through hits me so hard, it sucks the air from my lungs. I want to ask him for more details, walk him through steps I've learned in my job that help healing, but that hard stare he's giving me tells me he doesn't share easily and he's already regretting it.

His next words confirm it.

'Now's not the time to talk about me. I'm more concerned with what you're holding back. There's something you haven't told Madame de Cadieux, something you're both afraid and excited to share with her.'

'Yes... how did you—?'

'You don't spend a decade in military intelligence and not to recognize the signs of a covert operation. At first, I had you pegged as unscrupulous, out to make a buck off *madame's* sorrow, but I've watched you. I admit, it's taken me a while to accept it, but you're not just a note taker. You feel every sadness in your heart even though you try to hide it behind your tough reporter image. I don't believe you mean to harm Madame de Cadieux. On the contrary, I believe you're trying to help her, but if I'm wrong you'll have me to answer to. Remember that.'

He towers over me, arms crossed, his gaze surveying this poor, stumbling reporter.

He doesn't look away, but instead intensifies his scrutiny on my cold, shivering body like I'm his to do with as he pleases, which I am, but I'm not telling him that. He makes my pulse race faster than a Black Friday sale and shreds my sanity into confetti.

Pull yourself together, girl.

I clear my throat and focus on what I want to say, the truth about my obsession to interview *madame,* but I'm afraid if I look at him I'll lose my nerve. He has a way of turning me into mush as well as bringing out the tigress in me. Right now, I don't want to fight him. I need a friend. 'I have a personal connection with *madame* that goes back to the war.' I pull the kimono over my legs. I feel naked with him watching me. 'I know it sounds crazy, but I think Madame de Cadieux knew my grandmother.'

There. I said it.

'You *think*?' He lets out a low whistle, but those stern black eyes don't soften. He's not on board with this, not yet. 'That's quite a bombshell, Emma, can you prove this connection?'

'Well, no... not exactly.'

'I get it. Another reporter's hunch for publicity.'

'No, I *swear* it's true, but I need to know what happened at Dachau before I lay this on her. Growing up, I heard the story about how a female prisoner insisted my grandfather take a baby girl into his care when the US Seventh Army liberated the camp in 1945. A child born to a Polish woman, a political prisoner who died. That's all my family ever knew.'

'What if you're wrong? You'll feel more guilty about your charming charade.'

'Please try to understand. I came to Paris to find answers to a mystery that's haunted me since I started interviewing Holocaust survivors, making me think I could find out more about my own grandmother, especially now when my mom is battling cancer. It would mean a lot to her to know more about her biological mother. I thought *madame* could help me since she was in Dachau. I have to try, for Mom's sake. I was about to ask her when Brooke showed up with her accusations. How she found out... She must have spies everywhere. Someone at the news station tipped her off or she blackmailed some poor soul into giving me up or—' I blink. 'You *knew* the reporter was following us in the town car.'

'When I noticed someone tailing us, I surmised it had to be her after the incident on Rue Saint-Jacques.' He gives me a hard look. 'I had no idea she was after *your* blood.'

My cheeks tint. 'You waited long enough to grab her. She was soaking wet.'

He grins. 'Exactly. Justice served, *mademoiselle*.'

'No wonder *madame* adores you.'

'I'm not keen on you keeping secrets from her,' he says, 'but I see the logic in your plan. God knows, this interview is important to her. I've never seen Madame de Cadieux so alive as she has been this past week, but I don't want to see her hurt.' He looks at me with such dark smoldering in those eyes, I feel both turned on and guilty at the same time. 'She's scheduled to fly to Grasse for a board meeting next week. You should have the interview wrapped up, then I expect you to tell her the truth about why you're here.'

'I will. I promise.'

'I pray you know what you're doing, Emma.'

'I do, Ryker, trust me, *please*.'

His eyes sear through my kimono with a look both terrifying and seductive. 'I shouldn't, but you have a way of disarming everyone with your boldness and that cockeyed manner of yours that...'

'That what?' I dare to ask, the words catching in my throat.

He takes a long stride toward me, his fists clenched, his breathing labored. There's an intensity in his dark eyes that speaks of walls coming down between us that neither of us can stop. '*Dammit*, that makes a man want to kiss you.'

Did he say kiss?

I have to get my mind to focus, but it's impossible. 'You wouldn't dare. What would *madame* say?'

'I know her damn well, her quirks, how she loves a good game. I'd say she'd approve.'

'Well... then kiss me!'

Before I can think about how I let those words escape my lips without considering the consequences, how I allowed the heat building in me to explode, his mouth is covering mine, pressing against my lips with a steamy passion that melts my willpower... as if I have any when to comes to him... and gives me the sexiest French kiss a woman has no right to enjoy as much as I do.

I grip his broad shoulders and before I know what he's about, he wraps my bare legs around his waist.

How long can this man go on holding a 125-pound female in his arms?

We kiss... and kiss... I'm about to pass out from the lack of oxygen but *who the hell cares*. He pulls away after... ten... *fifteen* minutes? *Whew.* I let out my breath in a big *whoosh*. We're both breathing hard in tandem, him putting me down so my bare feet gently touch the cold stone floor, me wrapping the kimono tight around me.

'Now that we've gotten that out of the way, *mademoiselle*,' he breathes out in a husky whisper, pushing his damp hair out of his eyes, and does he look sexy doing that, 'it will be easier for us to do our jobs. Agreed?'

'So you say.' I can't stop tingling, my lips are swollen, and I'd do it again in a Paris minute. 'I'm not so sure.'

I have the feeling he's up for it, too, but instead his eyes deepen to a low, smoldering vat of melted chocolate when he says, 'I wish we'd met under different circumstances, Emma. You're brilliant, exciting, fascinating. And did I mention beautiful? I don't regret kissing you, not one damn bit, but my loyalty to Madame de Cadieux *must* come before anything else.' The fierce passion in his voice takes me aback and I've no doubt he means it.

'Even love?' I ask.

'Yes.'

Don't let that hot look he's giving you fool you. Now that he's resumed his role as *madame's* personal bodyguard, the intimacy I so loved being in his arms is gone. I let go with a tiny shiver. There it is, plain and simple. I'm an itch he couldn't resist scratching, a sexual moment to appease his Irish manly ego.

What else can I think?

Yet there's something in the way he looks at me, holds my gaze that says otherwise. That the personal hurt he shielded from me is still raw and the man is grieving for his wife and child, but I see a spark... no, I'm imagining things, a dangerous place I'm not going because I'll get hurt. I respect his position, so I'll push aside my crush and go back to doing what I do best. Pretending I don't need a man. Unfortunately, I loved every minute of it, but I'm done. I have my own agenda and I'm not changing course because of one kiss.

I say goodnight without falling apart and head to my room, swaying my hips because I know he's watching, my way of adding a punctuation mark to end this conversation. Full stop. I won't allow this gorgeous man to make me feel guilty because I set out on a quest to find out if Madame de Cadieux ever came into contact with my grandmother. And what she was like.

You bet your damn life I won't.

32

LE CHÂTEAU DE CADIEUX, PARIS, 2003

Emma

Perfume:
Mademoiselle Doujan
Violet, iris, vanilla

I only get two hours' sleep, but I'm not droopy-eyed when I arrive in the study at 8 a.m. sharp. I'm ready to go. *Madame* is neatly settled in, donned in casual silky-gray yoga pants and top, her red hair frolicking about her face in soft waves. She's drinking coffee... her raspberry croissant untouched.

Oh, my, things *have* changed between us.

She's polite and tries to be friendly, but she's trying *too* hard. Like she's mulling over the scene last night. I don't blame her, though I don't believe she takes anything Brooke Hansen says seriously. Still, I'm keeping secrets from her about my family, but I don't want to spill the beans now when we're coming into the home stretch. I'm bracing myself for an emotional ride. I intend to do justice to her time interned at Auschwitz and Dachau and present a unique and newfound understanding of what happened there.

Oh, God, help me make sense of what she – and my grandmother – went through to bring life into this world.

Yet the interview process today isn't going well. We don't banter back and forth like we usually do and I sense an unpleasant undertone that smells like sour milk. Somehow I've got to find a way to ease her mind. I'm glad at least that I told Ryker the truth. I couldn't have him thinking I was a conniving liar like Brooke Hansen. The smug look on her face when she made her exit set off bells in my head. She's planning something, but what?

I can't worry about her. I have to sort things out about my relationship with *madame* that was going places but came to a screeching halt because I wasn't honest about my intentions. That's something I have to deal with, but first I have to get a grip on myself and be the best damned reporter ever to interview this extraordinary woman and impress upon her no one can tell her story like I can.

Instead of her tuning me out like she's doing now.

I take copious notes as I let her talk about the difficulty of running a perfume business as the war progressed in 1943, how the two hundred bottles they made of *Naomie's Dream* turned out to be the entire run of production until after the war. How the House of Doujan apologized to the anxious women of France about the short supply of perfume by taking out advertisements in cinema magazines, imploring their clientele to be patient. That something new and exciting in perfume was on the way that would warm their hearts.

Madame watches me as she speaks and I feel the tension heighten as I try to process the consequences of my harsh words last night, but I'm torn between speaking up for myself or remaining silent and not making things worse. The raising of her brow and her pursed lips tell me she's not ready to forgive me, that she's wrestling with the demons of the past and I made her pain worse by creating a scene.

So I don't say a word. I listen.

'We kept the name of the House of Doujan alive by adding our scents to soaps.' Madame de Cadieux fixes her extraordinary hazel green eyes on me with an intensity I've not seen before. 'Then soap was rationed, but we had access to a few raw materials Monsieur Baptiste kept in a secret location near Argenteuil. A nunnery surrounded by high walls and home to a cloistered order. Then a miracle happened when I was poking around the storage room behind the chapel and discovered a forgotten vat of *La Rózsa 8*.'

I sit up straighter, a lightbulb memory buzzing in my head. '*La Rózsa 8* is a synthetic base, *n'est-ce pas*?' I dare to add a bit of French to my question to ease the tension between us.

She flutters her eyes, but that's all. At least it's a reaction. I'm no chemist, but I remember seeing the base listed in the company history on their website when I spent hours last night studying the chemical carbons used in making perfume. I discovered it's not unusual for perfume houses to employ the use of a blend of quality raw materials, natural oils, *and* an extra, powerful ingredient like *La Rózsa 8*. I'll show her I'm no dummy.

'The base contained what they called aldehyde C14 back then... it smells like peach skin.'

Her eyes dart in my direction, like I scrambled her brains and she can't believe it. At last I have her attention. 'Yes, *mademoiselle*, *La Rózsa 8* was a special base created by the professor in the mid-1930s with a—'

'Floral accord... a blended scent including Hungarian rose imported from the professor's home country.'

I'm on a roll and she nods in approval.

'*Très bon*, Emma, the base was then combined with a woodsy, oakmoss scent resembling a sharp tobacco and leathery smell, a vital element to the composition of *Le Courage*.'

'Let me guess, *madame,* isobutyl quinoline... a pale-yellow liquid with an intense, earthy odor, a subliminal reminder of the man they're waiting for to come home to them.' I inhale the imaginary scent in my nostrils. 'Not too strong a base note, that feels too masculine, but more of a feeling of anticipation of his homecoming, giving them the courage to carry on.'

She cocks a brow. 'You impress me, *mademoiselle*. And you've never studied the art of perfume?'

I shake my head. She's digging, trying to figure me out. Let her dig. I haven't gotten back her trust, but I have a good shot.

'I was determined to use the base in a wild scheme,' she continues. 'I had to keep up Frenchwomen's spirits by creating a perfume that evoked everything they loved about their home, their man, their family.'

'This was autumn 1943?'

'Yes, the year when we saw the outskirts of Paris bombed but we were spared, then a major Resistance leader was arrested and horribly tortured by the Gestapo, and it was against the law for anyone not to have a *carte d'identité*.'

When she speaks about the solemnity of life then, I notice her accent becomes harsher, more pronounced. She's aware of it, too, imbibing more coffee, her shoulders tensing, then taking a few moments to settle in. Relax. 'I was still an apprentice in the art of perfume during the war, my chemistry skills limited, but Professor Zunz insisted my natural talent, my nose, was tantamount to any scientific training. That advice served me well in the lab when I became frustrated with my lack of experience. I don't pretend I was in any way the *parfumier* I am today. It took me years to get here, testing my olfactory skills every day on a variety of scents, smelling, experimenting... understanding how the rose oil gleaned from one field of flowers differed from another because of the composition of the soil.'

I can't write fast enough.

'I spent hours, days... weeks trying to come up with a formula for a fragrance that meant everything to me, a reaffirmation of my love for Lance,' she continues. 'Then something he said reminded me of Yvette before he took off for Lisbon. We lay next to each other in the abandoned castle, a place we made our own with furniture and odds and ends from the pawnshop, a lumpy mattress, but in our most passionate moments, his arms wrapped around me, we didn't notice. He whispered one word into my ear, *Courage*. And then he was gone.'

Her voice catches in her throat and I so want to grab her hand, hold it tight as she relives such a pivotal moment in her life. I don't, then wish I had when she shudders, but the moment has passed.

'After trying over a hundred variations, I completed the formula for the composition of the alluring fragrance burning in my soul. Ah, the joy that surged within me. The scent was even more provocative and piercing to the heart than I imagined. I inhaled the scent again, savoring the moment and anticipating its effect on every female who dared to embrace it.'

She stands up and twirls around like she wants to believe in magic, making me want to twirl around, too.

'Then what happened, *madame*?'

'*Then, mademoiselle*,' she whispers with delight, 'I wiggled the test strip under Professor Zunz's nose and watched his eyes pop out.'

33

PARIS, 1943

Angéline

Perfume:
Glamor Doujan
Black orchid, jasmine, musk

'Courage.'

'*Pardon, mademoiselle?*' Professor Zunz stares at me over the rim of his spectacles. While the professor is a consummate follower of the great noses before him, his daring into innovative scents is curtailed by the war and reality. I, by contrast, work by instinct and have nothing to live up to, so I take chances where the professor won't. Like the bold scheme hatching in my brain to keep the House of Doujan in the public eye during the Occupation.

'The name for the new perfume is *Le Courage*,' I tell him, waving the precious test strip under his nose. *Test number one hundred and sixty-seven... or is it sixty-eight?* In spite of the heat of my passion, I get a shiver. The makeshift laboratory retains a coolness thanks to the towering oak trees sheltering the old stone cottage we've been holed up in with our vials, scales, oodles of blotters, and eye dropper. The girls and women who work in the main building giggle and whisper among themselves when they see me heading to the cottage every morning. The rumor is the professor and I are concocting a provocative, magic scent out of potato peelings and chemicals. Half-true. I've entreated the professor to work with me creating a synthetic chemical compound from a secret ingredient I brought into the lab. He brought it to life using synthesis – breaking it down and identifying the molecular structure so we can duplicate the scent, thereby changing it from a solid state into a vapor.

But the magic will come from *them*. The girls and women.

My noticeable blonde roots have also been a topic of conversation among the staff. I haven't dyed my hair in weeks. I abhor the smell of ammonia and opt instead to keep my 'nose' pure than retain my raven-black look. I cut my long hair to chin length so the roots aren't so obvious while my hair grows out.

I've also lost weight and have taken to wearing wide-legged trousers and a white blouse tucked in along with wedge shoes with ankle straps. I hardly eat. My sense of smell is sharper on an empty stomach. The only thing I have time to worry about is getting the composition for *Le Courage* right.

And I have. Jumping up and down, joyously sniffing the precious vial of perfume holding my formula. The afternoon sun filters inside, wrapping the pristine white laboratory in a warm yellow hue as brilliant as the test vial of yellow liquid sitting on my worktable.

Professor Zunz isn't convinced.

'Monsieur Baptiste prefers we give the fragrances glamorous or sophisticated names, like *Un Bel Amour*.'

'Trust me, Professor. Take a whiff... *please*.'

'*Bien*, I *am* curious.'

The professor's eyes turn a doubtful gray, then he sucks in a deep breath and gets a good sniff of the white test strip I wiggle under his nose. My heart beats in a wild rhythm and I can't stop tapping my sandals on the old stone floor, waiting. Then the flash in his eyes explodes like tiny stars landing... *everywhere*. The glorious smile lighting up his ruddy cheeks tells me what I need to know.

Le Courage is no longer a dream scent, but a reality.

'*Mon Dieu*, Angéline,' he says, his usual calm voice shaking with emotion, 'the scent is like nothing ever created in the House of Doujan.' He takes off his spectacles, closes his eyes, pinches the bridge of his nose, thinking. 'The top note... lemon zest with a late summer, rosy peach... the heart note, pure and smooth... white velvet rose... fragrant blue orchid with green stem... and a rich, earthy oakmoss at the base accented by a touch of civet and...' He sniffs the strip again, puzzled. 'What am I missing?'

I smile. 'Do you remember the chemical compound you helped me create, Professor?'

He removes his eyeglasses, furrows his brow. 'Yes. Quite an extraordinary scent. *Ah*, so *that's* your secret ingredient... and you didn't tell me?' he protests with a chuckle.

I shake my head. 'Then it wouldn't be a secret, Professor.'

'I must be getting old. You fooled me. I've not smelled anything like it, but I *will* figure out where you found this organic material, *mademoiselle*.'

He won't, but I'll not tell him that. It gives the philosophical professor something to ponder during these dark days of the Occupation. I know he worries about being picked up by the Gestapo for the slightest reason. So far, Frederic's influence with the right Nazi connections has kept him safe. After the war... *mais oui,* the professor shall know everything about this elusive ingredient, I promise.

'All I can say, Angéline, is you've created a masterpiece... like a great Impressionist painter mixing the colors of a rainbow, you've mixed the colors of a woman's soul during these trying times. Her life, her loves, but with a name like *Le Courage*, will it sell?'

'It will sell itself.'

'How?'

'When the *mademoiselle* or *madame* opens the bottle, she'll smell the sweetness of a spring day gone by that pings her memory... then comes the heart note three, four hours later and with that, the longing for life to be normal again... and finally when she lays her head on her pillow at night, the perfume lingers with the scent of her man... inducing her not to give up, to fight the Boches, not give in to their demands. *Le Courage* fuels the soul when you say it and makes your heart cry when you smell it because it reminds you of *him*.'

The professor pats his chest. 'Now I understand why you created this perfume, why you speak so passionately... the woman is you, *mademoiselle*. You're in love.'

I raise a brow. 'Is it that obvious?'

'Only to me. I must warn you, Angéline, be careful if you've fallen for the mysterious man in black. He's a rogue and will break your heart.'

'What do you know about him? Tell me, please.'

My heart pounds. I wonder if Yvette mentioned Lance to the professor and if she was in love with him, too, and it broke her heart. That's the only logical explanation I can think of... the professor didn't mention his archaeologist alter-ego, which makes me think I'm right about Yvette.

'Rumors, that's all,' he says, 'but I will be forever grateful for what he did for Ester.'

He knows about my work with the Resistance, but I trust him. He's the only one I *do* trust. I'm not friendly with the male laboratory assistants and the women from the village treat me as an oddity, but they're curious about how I found my way into the man's world of perfumery. I shall use that curiosity to enlist their help in packaging bottles of *Le Courage* once we have enough perfume to fill them and I explain my plan. I've also seen several Roma women coming around the nunnery, begging for food. I gave them extra bread we have from the professor's trips to the country, speaking to them in Romani. I'll need their help, too, if my plan is to work.

The professor closes his notebook, whistling and humming, and leaving me wondering if I'm a fool since I haven't seen Lance for two... three weeks. 'I'm not going to ask you how you know this man, *made-*

moiselle. In these times, it's best to remain in the dark about men such as him.' He wipes his spectacles with his lab coat sleeve. 'Now, shall we go tell Frederic your plan to save the House of Doujan *and* France?'

* * *

My cork-soled wedges make a soft clacking sound on the stone floor as we enter Frederic's office, a utilitarian space with an arched window overlooking chopped-up flower fields once a glorious plum. Fields waiting for the next planting of vegetables. *If* they grow... even the soil hates the Boches he brings to his office. Rich mahogany furniture and a manly oak desk with a white silk, tulip lampshade on his desk lamp. A feminine touch for the *mamselles* he entertains while he induces them to recline on the gold velvet méridienne in the corner.

I prefer to stand when I tell him about the new fragrance. I know what comes next. He'll sniff it, make a comment or two, something he's heard me say like, 'Lovely heart note... jasmine, *n'est-ce pas*?' He's interested only in packaging and selling perfume, especially as sales are down since the Occupation began.

'You like the new perfume, Frederic?' I risk a glance directly at his eyes. He's squinting, his brow furrowing, like he's already made up his mind. He tosses his pen down in frustration and turns over the paper he was doodling on. I wonder what's got him so frustrated. I don't dare ask. I'm an underling, an assistant, and worst of all, a woman. In his mind, I know nothing when it comes to business.

He sniffs the small vial I brought with me, looking from me to the professor standing beside me. The Hungarian *parfumier* takes off his spectacles and wipes them on his lab coat sleeve, avoiding scrutiny as he's wont to do since he's worried about his position, which these days is as fragile as an eggshell.

Frederic sniffs again... deeper... drawing the scent up into his nostrils, then he does something completely out of character for a man who spends his free time complimenting and seducing women. He kisses the professor on both cheeks. *'Ah, mais oui, c'est magnifique...* the most exquisite perfume you've ever created for the House of Doujan, Professor Zunz. *Merci, merci, merci.*'

I'm thrown completely off balance, my cheeks tinting, the professor, too, putting his spectacles on upside down. We stare at each other, trying to process Frederic's enthusiasm while trying to figure out how to tell him the truth about *me* being the perfume's creator. And our marketing plan. No, *my* marketing plan. Professor Zunz thinks I've taken leave of my senses, but I'm not backing down. We need to shake things up, do something innovative to keep our perfumes out there since production is down, a building block for better times. I can't... no, I *won't* believe France will always be occupied, not with the Resistance getting stronger and America in the war. No, we shall take back our country and this perfume is a small but vital part of that.

In a slow and deliberate manner, I step forward and go *nose-to-nose* with the man who is my superior but who knows nothing about perfume.

'*Le Courage* is *my* creation, Frederic,' I state boldly. 'A composition of vibrant florals and earthy base notes.'

He balks. '*Pardon, mademoiselle... your* creation?'

'Yes.'

The professor nods.

Frederic throws back his head and laughs. 'I don't believe it.'

Arms folded over my chest, I purse my lips. 'I don't find it amusing that you refuse to recognize a female nose is as good as a male nose.'

He glares at me, his eyes flashing, expecting me to cringe at his disapproval. I stand my ground, my chest heaving up and down, my lips set in a determined line. 'No, *you* don't understand, *mademoiselle*. If it gets out that a female nose is behind our newest fragrance... this *Courage*... whatever you call it... *I'll* be a laughing stock.'

'You refer to, of course, your Nazi friends. You needn't worry. I'm not after fame. I want to help Frenchwomen survive this war by calling it *Le Courage*... *and* keep the House of Doujan alive.'

Somewhat relieved I'm not after blowing his cover as the official 'nose', Frederic leans in toward me, a different notion spinning around in his head. 'And how you do you intend to produce *our* new fragrance, *mademoiselle*? According to our latest inventory figures, our supply of essences is nearly depleted and receiving shipments from our plant in Grasse is unreliable with the roads being bombed by these damned Resistance fighters.'

My hand is suddenly shaking at the thought of Lance somewhere out there working undercover, taking risks, but I have to overrule my heart's longing with cold, hard facts. If we don't take back France, more lives will be lost, including his.

I clasp the vial tighter, drawing strength from the subtle fragrance wafting up to my nostrils. 'Thanks to Professor Zunz, I located a forgotten vat of *La Rózsa 8* in the nunnery, then I combined other essences and isobutyl quinoline to create *Le Courage*.'

Frederic's face draws a blank... he has no idea what I'm talking about, but the professor is eager to speak up, confirming my statement. 'Back in 1935, we had a surplus of a unique rose absolute I imported from Budapest which I used to make the base. We stored the excess in the nunnery and forgot about it. *Mademoiselle* used it to create this stunning perfume.'

I pick up the ball and keep going before Frederic can stop me. 'If my calculations are correct,' I say, 'using *La Rózsa 8* with the essences we have we can produce eight, nine hundred bottles of *Le Courage*.'

'How? The manufacturer we buy from stopped making their unique perfume bottles.' Frederic points to the letter he was reading dotted with his doodling, 'All we have in stock are crystal bottles of odd shapes and sizes.'

'It doesn't matter if the bottles aren't alike in size, shape, or color,' I gush, my excitement building, 'we've already got a supply of white and gold labels.'

'Who's going to fill the bottles? We have a labor shortage.'

'I'll recruit women from the town and nearby farms and villages,' I interrupt him, 'even the nuns will help us.'

'Then there's the marketing to consider... our sales force is practically non-existent... our accountants went into hiding ... who's going to keep track of sales?' he demands.

'Sales?'

Blood rushes to my cheeks, my pulse goes mad as I take a leap into the unknown. That a new perfume *can* launch during the Occupation. That *Le Courage* will help Frenchwomen rise up and not give up hope for a free France.

'We don't *sell Le Courage,*' I tell him with a smile, 'we *give* it away.'

34

LE CHÂTEAU DE CADIEUX, PARIS, 2003

Angéline

Perfume:
Le Courage
Lemony-peach, white velvet rose, oakmoss

'I chuckle when I think about how Frederic collapsed in his chair and asked for smelling salts.'

I smile at Emma writing this down on her yellow pad with a grin on her lips. Her eyes widened when I told her we gave the perfume away... the wheels turning in her brain, wondering what my strategy was.

In due time, *mademoiselle*. First, we're on a mission.

She looks tired with dark circles under her eyes, but she didn't flinch when I suggested we go hiking this afternoon up and down the hillside near the château after we had lunch. American hamburgers and *pommes frites* in honor of my guest. I want to continue my story here. We're on a pilgrimage to Maman's grave to do something I should have done years ago, but it didn't seem right until now.

We're on a treasure hunt, but I haven't revealed that to Emma.

'I admit, *madame*, you took me by surprise,' she says. 'You *gave* your perfume away? How, why?'

'I shall hold nothing back, *mademoiselle*, but first let's see if you can keep up with me.'

Her eyes twinkle. 'You're on. I'm a New Yorker... I'm used to walking.'

I grin, eager to get started. I have a joy surging in me that even the late summer humidity can't take from me as we set out at a fast pace into the forest. I shall never forget that day in Frederic's office when I believed I could change the world... or at the least, the war. I like to believe I did.

We're a wandering trio on this summer afternoon after the soaking rain last night, me in the lead showing Emma the way, Ryker bringing up the rear. The vibrant green forest has a warm breeze which blows the peppery, earthy scent of a field of blue cornflowers our way as we walk along the winding stream running through the forest. A busy place with rabbits and squirrels washing their wiggly noses and paws in the cool water and keeping company with, according to Emma, 'a prince or two masquerading as frogs'.

I catch the frustrated looks she's giving *her* Irish prince and I shyly admit, I sense more than the usual friction between them. I can only guess it stems from the fiasco with that Hansen woman. I haven't told her I've forgiven her. I want to. Badly. I saw her whispering with Ryker when she thought I wasn't looking. They were arguing. I know that look passing between them. Did they do it? Kiss? Or has something else upset Emma?

I have the distinct feeling it has to do with me.

Bien, I shall make it easier for her, put *my* feelings aside and continue with the interview as if nothing happened. Whatever Emma's reason for spouting off like she did, she put forth a tremendous effort this morning to impress me with her perfume knowledge. Still, I can't help but feel that she wants more than an interview from me and that it has to do with her family history. The years I spent looking over my shoulder are still with me, but I can't afford to get bogged down in the present with silly misgivings when I have so much pain in the past to relive... days, weeks, months I felt imprisoned not by barbed wire and vicious guard dogs, but my own paranoia and intense fear, finding myself alone with no one I could trust.

I want to trust Emma.

Let her tell me *her* story when she's ready.

So I shall give her another chance.

I push ahead until we get to a shady spot on the hillside, stepping carefully around the chipped and decaying grave markers in the tiny cemetery that bear inscriptions dating back to the 1850s. The one I'm looking for is marked only by a piece of gray marble embedded in the earth with the word 'Maman'.

I continue my story as we walk, praying the iron box I buried here over fifty years ago is waiting for me now.

'Frederic couldn't conceive of the idea of giving *anything* away, much less our short supply of perfume,' I continue, slowing my pace. 'Especially in wartime when profiteers were making a fortune.'

'I can't wait another minute, *madame,*' Emma begs, shielding her eyes from the sun with the back of her hand. 'I want to know *everything* about your perfume giveaway.'

Pushing my wispy hair out of my eyes, I motion for Emma to sit with me on a weathered stone bench under a towering oak tree. Ryker stands off to the side, observing. She keeps peeking at him and then at me, which I find amusing. *Alors*, there's something going on with those two. I swear they're hiding it from me, but my curiosity will have to wait.

'We rounded up hundreds of bottles, all sizes, shapes, and colors, from the back supply we had stored at Argenteuil and managed to come up with a hundred more bottles gathering dust in the nunnery storeroom,' I say. 'Then we designed a simple white label trimmed in gold with the word, *Le Courage.*'

'How did you launch the perfume with the labor shortage?' Emma asks.

'I recruited mothers, aunts, sisters, daughters, teenage girls, nuns,

Roma women... even grand-mamas eager to help. I promised them extra bread the professor procured on his trips to the countryside, bless him, and we got to work. Day and night, we filled bottles. We couldn't manufacture *Le Courage* on a large scale, but with my plan we made a splash, as you Americans say, with the female public. Of course, Frederic was unhappy throughout the entire process and swore the House of Doujan was doomed. *Giving away perfume? Telling Frenchwomen to have "courage"?* He did his best to sway our message to have courage to mean *accept the occupiers*. No matter. The Germans laughed at our attempt, satisfied the business was Aryanized with Frederic at the helm, though if profits continued to plummet he was convinced ownership of the factory in Grasse would be turned over to his German friends to do with as they pleased.'

'Oh, God, *no!*'

'An Allied strike put an end to that idea. The factory was temporarily shut down and I will be forever grateful to the RAF pilot who saved the House of Doujan from being turned into a Nazi instrument of war.'

'Keep talking... amazing stuff, *madame*... what happened next?'

I smile, so pleased with her enthusiasm. 'We gave away the bottles of *Le Courage,* with the village women and girls hustling the perfume everywhere – from the weary *mesdames* waiting in queues for bread... to their friends and relatives... curious teachers, caring nurses, giggly shop girls... to the women on the trains, talking it up, giving them my sales spiel as I rode the local from Argenteuil into Paris and walked around the city, handing out bottles of *Le Courage*. After a while, every woman I met thanked me for giving them "courage". They assumed I was the creator since I spoke so passionately about it. At the time, I didn't grasp how my success posed a danger to me.'

'Okay, I get the free publicity, but what was the spark that gave *Le Courage* the notoriety I've read about?' Emma asks with that noodling reporter look in her eye I've come to know so well.

I smile big. 'You mean my *pièce de résistance*?'

'You got it.'

'Simple. Instead of applying *Le Courage* to the skin where it would last around five hours, I asked each woman who received a bottle to dab the scent on a personal item, a handkerchief, gloves, scarf, hair-brush... even her brassiere and slip to create a long-lasting effect.'

'Seriously?'

'Yes. The fibers in cotton and other fabrics retain the perfume scent longer than you imagine... even after washing.'

'Then what?'

'I requested the woman pass the bottle of perfume to a girlfriend, co-worker, their *maman*, sister, daughter... *grand-mère* with the same instructions to apply the fragrance to clothing so the scent of *Le Courage* stayed with them. It worked. Parisians and Frenchwomen in the Occupied Zone spread the word by the exchange of hundreds of perfume bottles from one woman to the next. I couldn't believe the feedback we got. It became a bonding experience, a sisterhood of women supporting each other when their men were gone – in the army, prison, the Resistance.'

'Amazing. I have to ask, *madame*, didn't some women hoard their bottle of perfume? Or fill it with another scent and pass it off as *Le Courage*?'

'I imagine that did happen, *mademoiselle*, but I never heard about it personally. I like to believe the overwhelming majority of women were filled with such wanting to help free France that the idea never crossed their minds. Naïve on my part, yes, but I wanted so to believe in the good of human nature in a time when so much evil existed.'

'Did the Nazi higher-ups or the Gestapo get their noses bent of shape with your success?' Emma grins, enjoying her pun.

'I don't think they took us seriously, *mademoiselle*... especially when Goebbels' wife and other wives of top Nazi officials continued to wear French couture, chain-smoked, and indulged in fancy, hand-made Italian shoes. Besides, Hitler abhorred makeup and perfume on women. *How could a silly perfume win the war?* I imagine him saying to his generals. Like he underestimated the cleverness of the Allies in planning the Normandy invasion.'

'At any time, did you fear your plan wouldn't work, *madame*?'

Stepping back into the past, I grab onto a moment that has never left me. 'What disarmed me most, Emma, and sent me into a panic was when a young Roma mother told me she barely escaped when the Nazis herded my people in the Unoccupied Zone into a broken-down hospital guarded by French police... how her child died from starvation, then her man was sent to a special "gypsy camp" in southern Poland. Only through luck did she escape by climbing out of a second-story window and making her way down the trellis entwined with prickly roses, her heart broken at losing her man and her child. She didn't give up and found a partisan farmer and his family willing to shelter her... in the end, she and others like her were the women I created *Le Courage* for. I encouraged her to keep telling her story *and* the stories she heard whispered... how my people were herded into crowded camps and forced to do mindless labor for meager food rations... the beatings, medical experiments, how female Roma prisoners were forced nude into a communal bath with SS officers watching them, a strict violation of our moral code. Then enduring the pain and despair having the bold ID number tattooed on their left forearm preceded by the letter Z for *Zigeuner*, gypsy. I would soon become one of them.'

Emma's jaw drops as I speak, her eyes wide. She's too stunned to say or write anything down. I warned her there'd be difficult moments, but *damn*, I've yet to scratch the surface. I pray she's up for what's coming... *zut alors*, am *I* ready? I pushed aside the nightmares, the sweats, and the agony after the war and threw myself into my work as a *parfumier*. I had Lance by my side and the professor to ease the pain. I never wanted to revisit that time in Dachau when my baby was born, but an unknown force is driving me and I can't stop it. I feel an unnerving sting behind my eyes, but I refuse to let tears fall.

I shudder, then continue, allowing Emma a moment to take in what I said.

'I survived near rape and the brutal murder of my mother and I didn't scare easily, but what I heard about these camps terrified me.

What the major boasted about *happened*, how that madman Hitler didn't stop at conquering a people, but he intended to exterminate every Jew, Roma, and anyone who dared to disagree with him. I only visited Paris when I had to, the cacophony of noise unpredictable. It could explode with gunshots and then plunge into a deadly silence with the dearth of motorcars on the boulevards, then seesaw back into a pounding in your head with marching hobnail boots straining your nerves to the max.'

'But you survived, *madame*. And most importantly, you became a voice of courage to Frenchwomen the Nazis couldn't suppress.'

'Yes, I did. *Merci*, Emma. You're right. We were able to give away *Le Courage* because we had the bottles and labels on hand to make the fragrance and the local women and nuns helped with the bottling of the perfume and the distribution. The movement continued into 1944 while everyone was waiting for the Allies to land on the coast of France, but *when? Where?* We didn't know.'

Emma taps her pencil on her pad, thinking. 'Did you make more perfume?'

I shake my head. 'We had no ingredients – synthetic or raw materials.'

'Yet the House of Doujan survived.'

'Yes. The Nazis bought out the stock we had over the course of the war. Then we began preparations to launch new fragrances after Paris was liberated. We were that certain the Allies would win. Meanwhile, the lingering scent gave women courage. It saved me when betrayal came in spring 1944. I had a small bottle of *Le Courage* I kept in the lab under wraps as a precaution. I wanted to keep the composition alive in my mind. I doused blue ribbons with the perfume and used them to pull back my hair. Fortunately, I'd tied back my hair with a long blue ribbon doused with the perfume the day when... no, I shall reveal what happened later. All you need to know is I kept that ribbon with me when I was sent to a transit camp outside Paris for political prisoners, then Auschwitz-Birkenau, and later transferred to a sub-camp in Dachau. I'd hold it close to my nostrils when things became unbearable, inhaling it. I swear it *never* lost its scent, though the stench of death that surrounded me at times diffused my ability to smell.'

'You haven't told me what the secret ingredient is in *Le Courage*.'

'Which is why I've brought you here. This place holds a sacred spot in my heart. Come. I'll show you.'

Emma follows me silently along with Ryker as I lead them to Maman's grave, the wood violets in bloom, their sweet scent greeting us... along with Maman's ghost. I swear I hear her laughter when we approach, so joyous she is to have company.

She looks like me, Tiena, *non*?

This *mademoiselle* with eyes the color of mine. Is that why you're drawn to her? Taken her under your wing because you're lonely?

Why you stare at the picture of the German woman in the story Emma wrote?

Desperate to believe she's the same woman you knew so long ago in the camp near Dachau... that would explain everything, *n'est-ce pas*?

Nonsense, I tell myself.

I ignore Maman talking to me. It's my own subconscious daydreaming and wishing for something I cannot have.

35

LE CHÂTEAU DE CADIEUX, PARIS, 2003

Emma

Perfume:
La Roma
Rose scarlet, jasmine, musk

Caked with dirt, I dig my fingers into the soft mud in the tiny cemetery. *Proud of me, Granger?* Who'd have thought when he said 'dig' deeper, I'd end up scooping up mud around a cemetery marker.

I feel a sting behind my eyes when I see one word inscribed on the chipped marble.

Maman.

Madame observes me with a careful look in her eyes, aware she's asked me to disturb the resting place of her *maman* and my reluctance to do so... but encouraging me. Telling me I'll find the answer here, which is a mystery to me. I expected her to be teary-eyed and look away, but her gaze hasn't moved from the specific spot where I'm digging.

Half a meter from the top of marker near a tall oak, she instructed me. About a foot and a half.

I see her smile then tap her fingers on her cheek, tilt her head, nod... then laugh as if she's listening to...?

Of course. Naomie's ghost.

It sounds crazy, but I swear I also hear the Roma woman's gentle whispers, though I know it's the afternoon breeze come to taunt me. I wish *madame* would share her mirth with me, but she doesn't. I keep going, picking out round stones from the soggy earth. I have to get over my guilt for keeping silent, but Ryker convinced me not to tell her about my family here, albeit in a heated exchange out of *madame's* earshot. I want to get this off my chest and beg for her forgiveness so I can move on and finish this interview as an honest journalist in her eyes, but Ryker said this is not the time and to wait until the interview is completed as we agreed. I've waited this long, he pressed on, I can wait a bit longer.

He's right. This is definitely *not* the time. She's reliving those last days of the war, crucial days when her world whirled around her at a dizzying speed and tossed her into a death camp, the loud, excruciating sounds of the suffering and the dying in her head lasting for months... *years* afterward. He wanted to help me dig, but *madame* shooed him away.

'No, I want Emma to experience for herself the emotional turmoil I felt when I buried the iron box here in 1944.'

'Box?' I look up, my heart skipping. 'What's in it?'

She grins. 'You'll see, but first I shall let you discover the secret ingredient in *Le Courage*.'

'Here?' I don't hide my surprise.

'Mais oui, mademoiselle, take a moment and smell the earth, the mud on your hands.'

My pulse racing, shoulders hunched, I sniff the dirt on my fingers. 'I get it. The soil.'

I'm cognizant of a strong, musky odor reminiscent of a deep sandalwood with an orange-rose scent that baffles my nostrils. It's downright sexy... of course, my Irish superman is supervising while I slosh my fingers through the mud, his manly scent reminding me of our glorious kiss last night, our bodies entangled, hot and sticky. Then today, he's back to his brooding self. Men… *who can understand them?*

'What do you think, Emma?' *madame* asks.

'It's an amazing sexy scent, it smells like…' I inhale it again and avoid looking at Ryker lest I give away the compulsion I have to grab him and kiss him. Hair askew, waving muddy hands, I must look a bit crazy, but I'm curious, overwhelmed, excited. 'A gorgeous hunk of a man.'

'Exactly, *mademoiselle*. I noticed it when I came here and sat with Maman on late afternoons when I had to get away from the madness of the war. An unusual blend of minerals from the cache of bronze Roman coins Papa found here and the floral roots entwining around each other in the soil for centuries. As if the bronze coins oxidized the soil. The scent comes from the roots of the violets and wildflowers fertilizing the earth, making it rich and giving a power to the base note that lingers for an unbelievably long time… the key to making *Le Courage* longer lasting.'

'How did you turn the soil into an ingredient for perfume?' I ask.

She smiles. 'I asked Professor Zunz to assist me in designing a synthetic carbon compound duplicating the scent and then blended it with the traditional essential oils we had on hand with the base note.'

'My head is spinning. Carbon *what*?' I blink, embarrassed. 'I should have taken chemistry in high school instead of cheerleading 101.'

She laughs. 'I imagine you were quite charming, *mademoiselle*, but I was a cheerleader for France when I dabbed *Le Courage* behind my earlobes, inhaling the scent I created. I felt like a sensually liberated woman for the first time.' She looks at me straight on, hazel eyes clear and determined I not miss a word. That it's of the utmost importance she not shield her thoughts from me. A funny, warm sensation makes my toes tingle. That what she wants to tell me is important to me, too.

'That I could stand equal with any man,' she continues, 'including the man I loved with all my heart.'

'Lance,' I whisper.

'Yes. I wanted to tell him I'd had a scare in the lab, but what woman in love wants to spoil the moment when *l'amour* is in the air, arousing him, exciting you? We couldn't keep our hands off each other. But on this night, the joy is in the emotional response he arouses in me, lending an intimacy to our kisses, a hunger I can't quench no matter how much I warn myself of the consequences... a primal need to conceive, our bodies so in tune with each other as we move in unison, I give in to my longing to give him a child... and surrender. To him. And for the rest of my life all I ever need... want... is to hold him in my arms. And now, forever in my heart.'

She stops abruptly, shivering. The memory is so real to her, her hands shake.

'*Madame*, are you okay?' I wipe dirt off my hand on my sweatshirt and lay mine over hers. It's cold.

She nods. Barely.

God help me, if I was ever at a loss for words, it's now.

I can't believe she'd share such intimacy with me... a reporter. Or does she feel deep in her soul we're kindred spirits linked by our gift of scent?

'Are you telling me what I *think* you're telling me, *madame*?' I say with a huskiness in my voice that surprises me.

'Yes. I was a young girl and my body was fertile and ripe for motherhood, but more important, I *wanted* to get pregnant. Not sensible, stupid actually, but I thought I was safe from the Nazis in Argenteuil. I was riding on the wave of success with *Le Courage*. I didn't have more than a *sou* to my name, but I had glamor to line my pockets with and when you're young, ah, *mademoiselle*, that's enough to fill you with the hope you can survive anything. I wanted a child I could pass on my perfume skills to, no guarantee it would be a girl, much less a nose since nature has a way of skipping generations...'

Her voice trails off as the wheels turn in her brain. She looks at me funny and I get chills. The curiosity in her eyes turns a dark green as confusion muddles her thoughts. As if she can't grab onto something. An unholy feeling slithers down my spine. I don't speak. Blink my eyes. I must look like a wax dummy in a museum.

She clears her throat, the moment passed. 'I believe that on that night, my dream of motherhood came to be.'

'How exciting for you, *madame*,' I jump in, remarking how someday I'd like to be a mom while I keep writing, making personal notes along with what she's telling me. I'm past the embarrassment stage with her candid talk and, putting myself in her shoes, I discover they fit better than I thought. I'm learning more than I imagined about this woman. She makes me question my own ticking biological clock. Something I keep putting off because I'm waiting for the 'big one', the story that will make me. *Career first*, I always say, *babies someday*. So why does that sound so hollow to me now?

Am I losing out on something way more precious?

I decide to table that discussion with myself... again, and get back to business and ask her the hard questions. 'You must have been overjoyed to find out you were having a child, *madame*... but didn't it make your Resistance work more dangerous?'

For a moment, she remains silent. 'Yes, but I was young and lonely, Emma, no family, and so much in love with Lance I wanted to keep that love with me always. I believed I was conceived from such love between Maman and Papa and in my wild, crazy way, I wanted to keep their spirits alive by having my own child. And I admit, in the midst of chaos, the thought of motherhood aroused warm and comforting sensations in me, that I could do anything. I was tired of war. We all were. I never took into consideration the increasing lack of food in Argenteuil or how I would get medical care if the pregnancy became problematic. I never regretted that night, *mademoiselle,* the night my baby was conceived, though the wisdom of age makes me sigh with frustration, not for myself but for putting others at risk in Auschwitz and Dachau and, of course, what became of my baby.'

I have the nauseous feeling in my stomach I get whenever I get stumped during an interview. Whatever I say, it won't come out right, so I wait for her to continue.

Madame lets go with a heavy sigh, wistful. 'After I lost her, I prayed to every saint Maman taught me that my child was alive and safe and not...'

Again, a quiet moment, but I have no urge to speak, tell her anything. As much as it hurts me, I have to play this out in silence.

'On that special night before my world came crashing down,' *madame* continues, leaving the end of her last sentence unsaid, 'I passed the time in bliss in Lance's arms, thinking about the life I was certain formed within me... until the songbird outside our window chirped the arrival of dawn. I longed to remain in that dreamlike place where the war was far away and our lives didn't depend on the whims of that evil madman and his henchmen, and nothing existed but our love for each other.' She sighs heavily. 'But it wasn't to be.'

'What happened, *madame*?' I ask.

Her voice drops to low pitch and cuts through me like a sharp blade.

'I was betrayed.'

36

LE CHÂTEAU DE CADIEUX, PARIS, 2003

Angéline

Perfume:
Bal de Cadieux
Wild strawberry, pink jasmine, royal ambrette

Anger wells up in me as I clench my fists, fight to compose myself when the words erupt from my mouth while Emma goes pale, eyes big and wide with shock. For years, I repressed the memory of that day into a place so deep and dark inside me it never healed. And now, I've opened the wound and it's festering... and painful.

'How were you betrayed, *madame*,' Emma asks, 'and by who?'

'Frederic.'

'You're kidding!' She can't hide her surprise. 'The man was a pompous cad, but I didn't expect that from him after you struggled so hard to keep the House of Doujan open, while others closed their doors.'

She keeps digging, then faster. Did she find the iron box?

'The *egotistical phony nose*, continued his liaison with the Germans, accepting money, favors. Otherwise, the House of Doujan would not have survived.'

'It's a brave thing to do, *madame*, openly admitting Frederic collaborated with the enemy.'

'It's a vital part of my story I'm ashamed of. He was an arrogant fool eager to please the Boches and I paid the price.'

'How, *madame*?'

'I knew the day would come when my bold ways and determination to be a *parfumier* would entrap me.' She pauses. 'I had to protect myself and my child's future. Keep the formula for *Le Courage* in a safe place. I buried a rectangular iron box containing the formula and Maman's bronze coin bracelet and ring here under the small marker near her grave, along with my Celtic pocket-knife. I told Lance where I buried the formula should anything happen to me.'

'You brought me here to find that box, why, *madame*?'

'Because I want you to understand that for all my success with *Le Courage*, I found out there was a dark side. Call it my Roma instinct, but I knew I must keep my gypsy past secret. In the eyes of the Reich, I was vulnerable to arrest and deportation.'

'What spooked you, *madame*? You were safe in Argenteuil.'

'I let my passion for *Le Courage* overrule my reason. Riding the train into Paris, talking to villagers and Roma women hanging around the nunnery in our own language. No doubt I made enemies, putting myself in danger. I couldn't be certain who was loyal to me and who would sell me out to the Nazis for a loaf of bread and a block of cheese.'

'Were you recognized?'

'I'm not sure, but someone broke into the lab and tore apart my desk, taking the notes I'd made on the launch of *Le Courage*. I have no doubt they were looking for the formula. I hid it in an empty blue crystal bottle, put the stopper in to seal it, and then placed it in an iron box.'

'And the bottle's here? In the box?'

I smile. 'At your fingertips, *mademoiselle*.'

I imagine her legs are cramped, but she keeps digging away at the soggy ground, eager to find the box. It's then the sun's rays slither over her shoulder and catch the glint of something buried in the ground.

Not long now.

I couldn't have asked for a nicer day to come here and dig. A sky clean and blue from the rain. The healing scent of the earth and flowers filling the air thick with humidity. I inhale the familiar aroma that only thickens with time. Like a dewy veil over this sacred ground. A powdery sweetness so alluring I can't help but get a good sniff when a breeze picks up and sends it my way. A divine scent summoned by the gods.

I look over at Emma. She pauses in her digging, then also sniffs the air. A huge smile curves over her lips and she has 'that look', a reverie only a true nose can understand. In that moment, I put together all the clues and open my mind to something so outrageous it stays there only a moment, but it's there nonetheless.

'*Nature has a way of skipping generations,*' I said to her earlier.

I let go with a shudder, my heart racing. Could her grandmother have been a nose and Emma never knew it? She was Polish... or was she? I'm certain the German woman in the nursing home photo is someone I knew back then.

My brain is spinning so fast and yet not fast enough for me to add things up because the emotional side of me has already come to a conclusion.

Emma is my granddaughter.

I have no proof... yet, somehow, my baby daughter survived that horrible day after she was taken from me and her birth was mixed up with another prisoner's child, or God help her, the death of that baby. I stumble, feel faint, but I must go on. What if I'm wrong, then I'll really look like an old fool.

I ramble on, talking, *anything* to keep from blurting it out until I have proof.

'For years there was a rumor I enlisted the help of a British spy to reduce the formula to a microdot and hid it behind the label of a bottle of *Le Courage*,' I begin, relying on my brain to finish the story for me since I can't think any more, can't reason. 'I have no doubt anyone who'd kept the empty bottle ripped off the label to find out if they had it. I have no idea how the rumor started, but it added to the mystique around the perfume.'

'Why didn't you relaunch *Le Courage* after the war?' Emma asks, then gasps when her hands touch something hard. She keeps digging.

'It was a different world. The men had returned home, the women went back to the kitchen and no one wanted to talk about the war lest they be accused of collaborating with the Boches. Better to sweep the whole thing under the rug, as you Americans say, and get on with rebuilding France. Women ached for glamor and, after four years of sacrifice, rationing, and drudgery, Frenchwomen wanted to feel young and free, they wanted something new. *Le Courage* reminded them of rationing and cork-soled shoes and no butter. Paris perfume houses weren't immune to post war struggles. We had more competition than before the war. New York became the place to launch a new fragrance—'

She scraps away the mud from the metal. 'I've found it, *madame*!'

She goes at the soggy earth like an avenging angel rescuing a lost soul. The last bright rays of the sun point a laser bright finger at something metallic. She scraps away the dirt, her breath coming faster when she pulls out the iron box and opens it.

Her jaw drops.

'*Madame*... it's here. The blue crystal bottle... your ring... knife... and oh, my God, your bracelet.'

I mumble words in Romani when I reach inside the box and take out the bracelet, coins jangling, and slide it over my wrist.

'*Mais non,* I can't cry. Not yet.'

'Why, *madame*?'

'Because I remember that cold, frosty early morning when I got down on my hands and knees and buried the box here. And the unspeakable horror that followed. The early months of January and February of 1944 brought snow and clouds, bad weather for flying, keeping German aircraft on the ground. The Americans pushed forward in spite of the danger, bombing industrialist sites. We had such high hopes the war would end soon in spite of the executions and arrests and deportation of Jews. No one felt safe. Professor Zunz stayed on my couch many nights and bunked in a tiny cell in the nunnery.'

'War makes strange bedfellows, *madame*.' Emma smiles. 'You must have felt the change in the air.'

'We had no doubt the Germans were tired of living with the pretense of "happy Parisians", but their roundup of Jews persisted. Neither we nor the Nazis knew the Allied commanders didn't consider Paris a major objective of liberation.'

'Seriously?' She wipes her hands clean on the towel Ryker hands her. 'Leave the Eiffel Tower in the hands of the Boches?'

I nod. 'I'm glad we didn't know, it would have deflated morale to the lowest point. Eventually, the Allies changed their plans but we had no idea the greatest land battle was yet to be fought in Belgium and Luxembourg. As for me, I became alarmed when Frederic brought news that Major von Risinger was back in Paris. The news did more than grab my attention. It cut me deep, a horror rising up in me I couldn't deny. It wasn't just my young self in jeopardy, but a new life, my child... Lance's baby. I felt more vulnerable than ever. The irony was, I had become complacent about my appearance, allowing my hair to grow out to a lighter color and to be cut in a curly bob. I believed I was safe as long as I remained in Argenteuil and the war would be over soon. But I was wrong, so terribly wrong.'

'We're talking early 1944, right?'

'Yes. My life changed forever in April, the cold keeping us in sweaters during the day and I had my lovely black wool coat from Yvette to keep me warm and my spirits up.' I try to keep my voice light, not reveal the still unwinding reel of film in my mind that pushed me to conclude Emma and I are family. 'I took good care of that coat. It became a symbol of her sacrifice, a tangible reminder why I had the chance to create *Le Courage*.'

'Do you still have the coat, *madame*?'

I grab her hand for support, my fingers digging into her palm. She squeezes my hand in a show of understanding. I close my eyes, reliving the moment I haven't allowed into my soul since the terror I felt that day engulfed me.

'I was wearing that coat the day the Gestapo arrested me.'

37

ARGENTEUIL, ON THE OUTSKIRTS OF PARIS, APRIL 1944

Angéline

Perfume:
Luxor
Cinnamon, Egyptian jasmine, ambergris

'Ah, just the *mademoiselle* I'm looking for. The best nose in the business... and the prettiest.'

Frederic bounces into the lab looking as happy as a poodle strutting in the Bois on a Sunday afternoon. He wriggles his nose when he sees my two-toned hair. Dark curly tresses down to my chin... grown-out blonde roots.

'*Mon Dieu*, what have you done with your hair?'

I fuss with the wispy ends. 'I'm going blonde.'

'You look like a raccoon... *bien*, it doesn't matter. I have important news, Angéline, and am in need of your talents.'

I should be flattered, but I'm not. I sense a different energy the moment he bursts in here. Overly confident... forced compliments. He wants something from me, which makes me uncomfortable.

I put down the test strips, my latest attempt to capture the saintly smell of a chapel candle, a sweet amber scent inspired by the sisters' work with *Le Courage*. I need to keep busy. The factory in Grasse is in flux after the Allied bombing, several vats were damaged and our essences depleted, but my nose is a fine instrument I must keep tuned. Experiment with accords to create new formulations, study the chemical breakdown of synthetics, and test myself on every dried-up spice I can find in the supply cabinet. A challenge while I count the days till I see Lance again and pray he has news about the upcoming invasion, a hint... *something* to give me hope this war will end soon.

I'm desperate.

My monthlies are late. Do I dare hope a new life is growing within me?

The sun showers my worktable with a happy 'good morning' glow giving me a false security. I've been hiding in my tiny lab, working, planning... dreaming about a perfect pregnancy, a perfect life with Lance. A *gypsy blessing* as Maman would say when she told fortunes. I wasn't expecting Frederic to drop in on me, requesting my 'talents'.

He's up to something, but what?

'I have news, too, Frederic, about *Le Courage*.'

He smirks. 'You're still torturing me with your crazy scheme? I must have lost my mind letting you talk me into, giving away perfume last year ... it was the dumbest idea I ever heard.'

'Really?' I sniff test strip number 36. Heavenly, smooth vanilla base. 'I'll have you know the sisters at the nunnery participated in our giveaway and several women made a shrine in the chapel with bottles still smelling of perfume, surrounding it with votive candles. When they come to pray, they get a sniff of *Le Courage*. Everyone's talking about it.'

'I'm only interested in what the *Germans* are talking about and it's good news for the House of Doujan.'

I frown. 'What can be good about the Nazis?'

He ignores my comment. 'My services have been requested at a special exhibition at the Jeu de Paume this afternoon as the guest of a German officer.' He smooths back his hair and tugs his pointy sleeve cuffs. 'I'd like you to accompany me.'

'Count me out, Frederic.'

I toss down the test strip, a queasiness rumbling in my belly. This is *not* good. The last thing I need is scrutiny by an ignorant SS man intent on grabbing whatever perfumes we have left. Which aren't many.

'I must *insist* you accompany me to the exhibit, Angéline.'

'Why not bribe one of your *mamselles* with a bottle of your black-market cognac to play parlor games with the Nazis?'

'Because they, *ma chère*, are not a nose.'

'So? What does that have to do with it?'

'Everything. This exhibit highlights unguent perfumes from the days of the Egyptian pharaohs. White alabaster boxes buried in a tomb more than two thousand years ago.' He leans in, tries to work his charm on me by rubbing shoulders. I pull back to stop the assault of rich and greasy pomade on my nostrils. 'The German officer needs an expert opinion to give provenance to the artifacts and impress Göring's agent with their origin and the composition of the scents found in the perfume jars before they can be sold—'

'You mean confiscated.'

He scowls, the fire in his eyes at odds with the charm in his voice. 'To the Reich. Which is where *you* come in, *mademoiselle*.'

I give him a half smile, more like a smirk. 'I get it. We go into our song and dance routine where I sniff the perfume, break down the ingredients for you, and then feed you the list so *you* can take the credit.'

'Exactly, *mademoiselle*.' He can't and won't deny it. 'Think of the prestige if we obtain permission to showcase a two thousand-year-old Egyptian perfume box in our shop.'

I *do* find the idea of being the first nose in centuries to indulge in the mystical scent of the pharaohs intriguing, explore their blends which, according to the professor, the Egyptians wrote on the tomb walls. We often have long discussions about the history of perfume and its link to immortality. Is it possible the ancient perfume jars exude the aroma of myrrh, honey, and almonds?

No... no matter how tempting to my nose, it's wrong. I won't hang out with Nazis.

'The answer is *no*. Besides, I have no experience with Egyptian perfumes. Professor Zunz is the expert.'

'*Ma chère* Angéline, be logical,' he says, his voice smooth as brandy, 'the professor is Jewish *and* a man... not the perfect dance partner for the major. God knows I've taken enough flack for keeping him on staff.'

'Did you say *major*?' I blurt out. An all too clear memory of the arrogant officer boasting about bringing back art works from Egypt floods my brain. A sharp stab of nervous energy hits me hard and I buckle over, hoping I'm not going to throw up.

'Yes,' he continues, undeterred by my freakish fear, my loud gasp. 'Major von Risinger has returned from North Africa and requested I bring you along, which couldn't have worked out better if I planned it.' He claps his hands with glee.

'I haven't changed my mind. I won't go.'

His eyes narrow, his mood darkening. 'You will do as you're told or you'll find yourself on the streets, *mademoiselle*. And the professor in a concentration camp. I will not allow your arrogance to bring down the House of Doujan.'

'And you haven't by collaborating with your Nazi friends?'

I regret the accusation as soon as I say it. It's common knowledge Frederic is cozy with the Boches, but no one on staff dares to label him a Nazi sympathizer.

Except me.

He strikes me hard across the face.

'How dare you, *mademoiselle*!'

The sting of the back of his hand makes me reel, but I don't back down. I stare back at him, touch my cheek. It's burning hot, but it's the look on his face that strikes a new image of him in my brain. Like a hurt animal licking its paws. Biding its time. I have no doubt he'll make good on his threats if I don't do as he asks. I can't let them send the professor to a camp.

'I do what I must, *mademoiselle*,' Frederic insists, 'so my legacy will survive, so *France* will survive.' His tone is crisp, decisive. He isn't backing down. 'My father's an old man and this war has broken him. He doesn't understand how the game is played. I do. I won't allow the Germans to take everything from me, so pretty yourself up and let's get going.'

'I'll accompany you to the art gallery,' I say, my cheek still burning, but my heart cold. 'But only to save the professor.'

I have so much to lose if I don't play this right. I must take control of myself and let *nothing* the major says rattle me enough to make a wrong move.

'*Bon*. And for God's sake, do something with your hair!'

* * *

It's my hair that gives me away.

I know I shouldn't be here the moment I walk into the Jeu de Paume, the smell of high ranking Boches overpowering my scent of rose absolute with their arrogance. It makes me gag, but I have no choice. Frederic is determined the House of Doujan will survive until liberation. I call it collaborating and it makes me sick. He doesn't see it that way and I wonder how many others doing the Nazis' bidding feel the same, that what they're doing is *saving* France. I wonder how they'll be judged after the war because I firmly believe the Allies will drive out the occupiers. I almost feel sorry for him when Frederic lets it slip how much he owes the Nazis. Half a million *francs*. Still, I believe the professor and I helped the fight by keeping our eyes and ears open and God knows, *Le Courage* did its part for the war effort.

Then why do I feel so dirty?

Lowering my head to hide my shame, hating myself for giving in, I follow Frederic down the long hall of the art gallery, glancing at the number of paintings stacked up in rows and leaning against the wall. I hear loud male voices echoing somewhere in the building. Curious, I peek into a room filled with file cabinets and get the door slammed in my face by an arrogant SS officer. Is this where the sins of the Nazi plunderers are cataloged?

My feet tap on the worn carpets gracing each room as we approach a high archway leading into a large display room when—

I see Lance.

My heart stops. He doesn't see me. He's conferring with a man in a stiff, dark suit and two SS officers in German over two large, beautiful landscapes.

'*Vite, mademoiselle*, quick.'

Frederic grabs my hand and pulls me back in the opposite direction, but I can't forget what I saw. *Mon amour* surrounded by German officers. His rich, deep baritone holding them in a trance as he pointed to the paintings, giving orders as the man in the suit pulled out another painting from the stack and they got into a heated discussion. Göring's agent, I assume. Even at a distance, I could see the cold blue ice in his eyes. He's bargaining with them; God knows how it will turn out.

My shoulder aches from Frederic pulling me from one room to the next decorated with sparse furnishings. I feel like a terrified chicken sneaking into the fox's den, rustling my feathers, trying to fly away. I can't. Why Lance is here, I can guess... to catalog the latest works headed off to a castle in Bavaria for safekeeping. *How* he's here makes my skin prickle. The Nazis must trust him implicitly since Frederic let it slip this is a secret operation, even French officials aren't allowed to be present save a quiet young Parisian curator who gives me an odd look when I catch her staring at me, then she disappears behind a closed door.

'If it's so secret, why are *we* here?' I whisper to Frederic, who is leading me into a small antechamber. The room is bare except for a polished, round mahogany table. On top sits an exquisite white alabaster box sculpted like an altarpiece along with a tall diorite vase shimmering with black and white flakes of crystal. I've never seen anything like them. I'm struck by not only their beauty, but by their pristine condition. Like new.

'The major is in a delicate situation, *mademoiselle*. He's needed at the Eastern Front, but he prefers to stay in Paris.'

And you want me to help him? That pains my soul more than you'll ever know.

'He intends to buy his ticket to the high life by impressing Göring's agent with his knowledge of these Egyptian artifacts.'

Which he stole.

'I assure you, *mademoiselle*, no one will ever know we were here. Do your job and the major will be in our debt.'

So he can erase your debt?

Then he's off to find out what's keeping the major. I give a cursory, second glance to the artifacts when—

'*Bonjour, mademoiselle*,' I hear behind me, then a woman with a thick German accent announces herself as Ute Schmidt, a 'friend' of the major and assistant to the Reichsmarschall's wife. 'What a lovely coat you're wearing. Couture, *n'est-ce pas*?'

'*Bonjour*.' I give her a weak smile, nothing more.

Frau Göring is a devotee of French couture as am I,' she adds, her strong cedar scent seeping through her sweat when she wipes her brow. Wearing a metal-gray coat and hat, she gives me the onceover as I study the Egyptian artifacts. I keep my head down, my back turned. I've heard about the German officer's wife and her expensive buying sprees from the clerks at the House of Doujan, how she commands attention, smoking and spraying on every perfume in the shop.

Her assistant, however, is fascinated by the braided collar and cuffs on my black coat, calling it '*so Parisienne*'. I had no time to change and barely had time to tie a black silk scarf around my head like a turban to hide my hair... after I pulled it back with a blue ribbon doused in *Le Courage*. I rubbed red lipstick on my cheeks since I'm out of rouge, then drew dark arched brows with the nub of an eyebrow pencil. I added red lipstick, praying I look different enough so the major's memory of a 'gypsy girl' isn't triggered.

I also look glamorous. Wearing gray trousers and a white blouse, high wedges, the plump German woman sees me as competition for the major's attention.

What sets my heart pumping is her curiosity about *Le Courage*.

'I've heard the House of Doujan is responsible for that giveaway shop girls can't stop talking about,' she baits me. 'A perfume with the ridiculous name of *Le Courage*.'

'I merely work in the lab, *mademoiselle*,' I insist, running my hands over the smooth, tall vase then wiggling the stopper to loosen it. Someone has already broken the seals on both artifacts. 'I create the chemical compounds for our fragrances. I know nothing about the finished products.'

'Oh? I've contributed *my* talents to the German fashion institute for years,' she boasts, 'and if there's one thing I know, *Le Courage* was *not* created by Monsieur Baptiste. Only a woman would have the sensibilities to come up with that name and the marketing behind it.'

'You're mistaken, *mademoiselle*.'

What's she driving at?

I can't help but be annoyed at how she's agitating an already tense situation. I'm suffering from a profound case of nerves, which doesn't help the rolling in my stomach. I struggle not to get sick as I pull harder on the stopper until it pops open. Oh, God, the hot and spicy aroma hits my nostrils with a wild intensity, wrapping around me like a shield. A few minutes exposed to the air and it should settle down so I can dictate the composition to Frederic.

But I can't get rid of this annoying busybody.

'Am I?' she sneers at me. 'Fortunately for you, the Gestapo doesn't have time for such petty schemes to undermine German authority, but they *could* be persuaded to look into the matter if—'

'I assure you, Mademoiselle Schmidt,' I cut her off. 'The House of Doujan complies with the guidelines handed down by the Reich.'

'Except when it comes to keeping Jews on your staff.' She tilts her head like a coquette, waiting for my response.

My hand slips and I nearly drop the priceless vase. I put it down. Slowly. 'What do you want from me, *mademoiselle*?'

'Your coat. It's an exquisite design with such beautiful braiding, so elegant and *so* French,' she coos, biting her lip. She's salivating with a primal look in her eyes, though I doubt the coat fits her wide waist. 'Wool and silk are so hard to come by these days, it would make a lovely gesture if the Reichsmarschall's wife received it as a gift from the House of Doujan.'

I won't make the mistake of thinking she's *asking*. She's a Boche. They take what they want.

Not this time, *Fräulein*.

I fight to keep my voice calm. 'What you mean, *mademoiselle*, is you want the coat for yourself.' It makes me sick to even think of her touching Yvette's coat, the silk lining wrapping the Nazi cow up in the French woman's sacrifice. 'However, it's not your style.'

The sound of heavy boots pounding the carpet announce the arrival of the major, all smiles and salutations. Frederic is right behind him.

'What's this about a coat, Ute?' asks the major, filling his lungs with the scent of females in heat, savoring it by the gleam in his eyes. I dare to look directly at him and have the most terrible feeling I'm about to jump into the abyss. I place my hand over my heart pumping so fast I feel lightheaded.

Run, girl, run!

This time I can't. My feet are leaden. I can't go anywhere lest I raise his suspicions and then I'm done for. That doesn't change how I feel, how I want to see him bleed, the bastard, grovel at the gates of hell, begging to be let in because it's nothing compared to what I'd do to him if I could. Sniveling, pretentious, he hasn't changed since our encounter in Argenteuil. His Nazi strut, phony broad shoulders, his face so clean-shaven his skin shines in the yellow glow from the lighting. Except for the scar on his upper right cheekbone.

The one I gave him.

Fräulein Schmidt smiles sweetly. 'Frau Göring will look beautiful wearing *mademoiselle*'s coat. A gift from the House of Doujan.'

'I never agreed to that,' I butt in, defending myself when Frederic grabs my arm and squeezes hard.

'We'd be delighted to gift the coat to Herr Göring's wife,' Frederic is quick to add in his usual boyish French charm. 'Won't we, Angéline?'

I want to scratch the woman's eyes out, but a sudden lurch in my belly stops me. What if I *am* pregnant? I can't jeopardize my baby. But I won't make it easy for the German.

Fräulein Schmidt's eyes shine. '*Gut*... let me try it on.'

'You'll find the coat too tight around the waist, *mademoiselle*,' I say, goading her.

'She has a point, Ute.' He chuckles, then snaps his baton across her rump, making her eyes bulge. She bites back her anger. 'You've been enjoying too many black-market Parisian chocolates, unlike *mademoiselle* who wears it well.' The major stares at me, noting my slim figure and licking his lips. 'You will join me later for dinner at the Ritz, *mademoiselle*.'

I nod. '*Avec plaisir, monsieur*.' I'm tempted to throw up on his precious Egyptian artifacts to get out of dining with him.

He turns to Fräulein Schmidt. 'Not all the couture houses have closed down, Ute. Make it a priority to find Frau Göring a similar coat.'

'But, Major—'

'Enough. We have more important business to discuss. Make notes of the perfume ingredients. When we're finished, take the list to the curator.'

'Who?' she asks, snippy,

'That silly Frenchwoman in glasses who's always on the phone.'

He dismisses the German girl with a wave of his gloved hand. By her subservient manner, I gather she's *not* his mistress, which affords me the upper hand. She's also not giving up. She's got an obsession with this coat. *Ah, mais oui,* that's it. She *wants* to be his mistress and thinks if she dresses like the Frenchwomen he lusts after, he'll find her more attractive.

Not even a gorgeous coat can turn that German sausage into French pastry.

I make it my business to ignore her as the major continues rambling about how thrilled he is to have the premier nose of the House of Doujan create provenance for the artifacts along with his lovely assistant. I'm seething inside as I pick up the vase, the irony of the situation making me dizzy, that this man has immense power over me. Again, I can do nothing but placate him when all I want to do is make him pay for Maman's death.

I'm tempted to smash the artifact over his head when he comes up behind me, blowing his hot breath on the nape of my bare neck.

'I told you we'd meet again, *mademoiselle*.' He lays his hand on my shoulder and I stiffen. The heat of the moment in the stifling barn when he shot Maman revisits me with such intensity, I smell only the coppery odor of blood. It's so powerful, the memory floods my brain with nothing else but that smell. 'You're just as beautiful.'

And you're an arrogant Boche in a uniform too big for you.

Aloud I say, '*Merci*... Monsieur Baptiste is an excellent teacher.' I take a moment, calming my nerves and sniffing, trying to get back my sense of smell as I put the vase to my nose and breathe in, desperate to remember what scents came to mind before I panicked. 'Cinnamon...' I begin, struggling. 'Raisins... seeped in wine... peppermint.' I add several more ingredients I've learned from the professor, but I can't be sure. Even when I get my nose back, it will take weeks of testing, time I haven't got.

'*Bien, mademoiselle*... perfect. Let's go over the composition of the perfume in the alabaster box.' Frederic grins at the major while the German girl makes a face as she scribbles down the ingredients. 'I've trained her well.'

Zut alors, is there no end to his impertinence?

I sniff the alabaster box, my nose blind to whatever scents remain after two thousand years. I have to say something, so I guess, using ingredients popular centuries ago. Who's going to refute me? Not Frederic. I doubt Göring's agent is a nose or any Nazi within smelling distance. That's like saying a Boche can tell the difference between a Damask rose and a Louis Phillipe. *Impossible.*

'Myrrh, lily, cardamom... saffron—'

'*Sehr gut, mademoiselle.*' He raises his hand, indicating the session is over. 'Now we shall celebrate by dining at the Ritz. *Allons-y*, my motorcar is waiting.' He takes me by the arm and indicates for Frederic to follow us. Fräulein Schmidt nudges in beside me, making the major scowl. 'I gave you an order, *Fräulein*. Take the list to the curator. Do it, *schnell*!'

I breathe out a sigh of relief. The obnoxious woman isn't invited, but I underestimate her desperation to take what she feels is owed her. What she never had in Germany and came to Paris to get. *Glamor*.

She makes her play and it's a good one.

There's a threat in her narrow brown eyes as she looks at me then the SS officer. 'She's a traitor to the Reich, major. You can't trust her.'

'What?' He looks genuinely surprised at her accusation, as if the thought had never crossed his mind.

'*She's* the nose behind that perfume stunt for *Le Courage* that you dismissed when the Gestapo started asking questions. Convincing them Frenchwomen care only about their looks and not politics because you wanted to keep the House of Doujan off their hit list for your own profit.'

The major isn't amused. He turns to Frederic. 'Is that true, *monsieur*?'

Frederic tugs at his collar. 'Why, no, I mean, yes... Angéline came to me with the idea and I saw it as a way of keeping the company name alive so I could regroup and pay back my debts.' He sells me out completely with: 'She showed up one day with no references. I should have known better than to hire her.'

'You disappoint me, *mademoiselle*. A woman of your talents could do well under my guidance. However, I'm not sure where your loyalties lie.'

'I'm a Frenchwoman first, Major, and unlike Fräulein Schmidt, whose only talent is jealousy, I worked hard to perfect my perfume skills. If you'll excuse me, I've done what you wished.'

Pulse racing out of control, I turn to get out of here when that German woman bars me from leaving. Feet spread apart, hands on her ample hips, I fear she's itching for a catfight, a sadistic play to get what she wants.

'How *dare* you insult me, *mademoiselle*.'

'I only told the truth. Leave me alone.' I turn and walk away.

'Not so fast,' she yells, grabbing my coat collar and jerking me backward. I stumble and slide on the rug in my high wedges, landing on my backside. A sharp pain jabs me in the hip, but I instinctively grab my stomach, praying I won't lose the baby. I come undone when the black scarf tied around my hair unravels and falls onto the rug, revealing—

'You're a blonde, *mademoiselle*.' The major gasps. 'You look so different... like...' He curses. '*Gott im Himmel*, you're the gypsy girl who gave me this.' He points to the scar on his cheekbone. 'I always thought you looked familiar, I just couldn't believe it.'

'You're mistaken, *monsieur*. I'm Angéline de Cadieux, from Lyon. I have papers to prove it.'

'Forged, no doubt. You'll pay for your subterfuge, *mademoiselle*. You're under arrest for assaulting a German officer.'

My heart slams against my chest, my breathing ragged and fast as he calls for the guards, sending me into a wild panic, attracting the attention of the SS officers meeting in another room nearby, including Lance, his tall, muscular body leading the pack when they rush in, bellowing and yelling in German. I've never been so happy to see his handsome face, those broad shoulders in his familiar tweed. He whips off his spectacles and the concern on his face is so powerful I force my breathing to slow, the moment so unexpected I will never forget it. I truly love this man. He's taller than the Nazis, stronger, but he's outnumbered and by the way he sizes up the guards, the officers, calculating his moves, he knows it. I have to face the truth.

He can't save me.

The fierceness in his eyes says he'll take that chance. He makes a move toward me, but I shake my head vigorously, silently warning him to stay back. He struggles not to slam his fist into the jaw of the SS guard grabbing my arms, digging into my flesh, his grip strong and tight. Any attempt I make to struggle is quickly countered by more pressure so tight I nearly pass out. There's no point resisting. I've seen men shot for less. But I'm not going down without getting my revenge on the major.

'You can arrest me, but you'll *never* forget me.'

'I already have, *mademoiselle*.'

'Have you? The perfume I gave your wife, *Naomie's Dream*, is named after my mother... the woman you murdered.'

'How dare you!' he yells. 'Get rid of her.'

The SS man yanks my arm, but I dig in my heels. 'Every time you smell the sweet jasmine on your wife, remember what you did to my *maman*.'

'Take her away!'

'Wait!' Fräulein Schmidt snarls at me with a satisfied sneer. 'What about the coat?'

'It's yours. The gypsy girl won't need it where she's going.'

The SS guard rips the precious coat off my back and tosses it to the German woman, who is squealing like a pig. I ignore her ranting and hold my head high, locking eyes with Lance. I wonder if I'll ever see him again as the SS man drags me outside the gallery and into the early spring afternoon. I can't stop shivering, as much from fear as from cold. The Resistance leader would do anything to keep me safe, but this is an impossible situation. Make a move, and his cover is blown. We both know what's at stake. The Germans will question every bit of misinformation he fed them and that will jeopardize the coming Allied invasion.

I'm afraid, more so than on that day when the major shot Maman, knowing the power of life and death the Nazis have over us. The rich color scenes on film they show to the rest of the world are fake. The truth is, there's the underbelly of Gestapo torture on Avenue Foch and the cold, dark military prison in the *6e arrondissement*. I'm headed into that dark place. Alone. I have a child to consider, my changing body giving into the sheer exhaustion of this horrible afternoon. I have no strength left and I'm shaking, but I couldn't let Lance see that. I had to make him believe I won't falter, give up. He won't let anything happen to me. He'll find some way to track me down wherever they take me. I have to believe he'll find me and bring me back home to him where I belong.

I have no other choice if I want to survive.

38

LE CHÂTEAU DE CADIEUX, PARIS, 2003

Emma

Perfume:
Forever Paris
Damascena rose, jasmine, peppery carnation

'I'm dying inside, *madame*, what with that despicable major and that sadistic German woman treating you like that.' I tie back my damp hair into a ponytail, thinking. 'I haven't given much thought to SS women, how they figure into the whole Nazi equation. What a bitch.'

Madame raises a brow, but doesn't deny what I said. 'Fräulein Schmidt wasn't SS, but she was heartless, though there *was* a compassionate SS officer at Auschwitz who warned the Roma about a roundup in 1944 so we could arm ourselves.' A long sigh. 'You shall also meet an SS female guard... as well as a German girl at Dachau I shall never forget. Ah, but that's for the telling when we get there. First, tea.'

Her hand is shaking as she pours me a cup from a silver pot.

'Lance couldn't do *anything* to help you?' I sniff the tea... sweet lavender, coriander.

'He made discreet inquiries, but all he could find out was I'd been arrested and imprisoned.'

'It's beyond horrible, *madame*. Rips me apart inside. Like a festering wound that never heals.'

I shouldn't press her. It's been a long day with us going to her *maman*'s grave, then finding the formula for *Le Courage*. And her bracelet and knife. We're back at the château. *Madame* looks refreshed in lemon and white yoga pants and top; I'm in clean jeans and my favorite blue hoodie. The truth is, I want to pull the hood up over my head and hide. I can't explain it, but after the excitement earlier, a simmering depression is settling in me as we move forward to the next part of the interview. The survival stories we're familiar with, but the horror never goes away, only deepens as my mind absorbs more prickling details that get under my skin each time I go down that road to—

The camps.

Madame spent the rest of the war in more than one... and after all the interviews I've done with Holocaust survivors, I never fail to come away in major depression mode and filled with such anger these disgusting creatures in hobnail boots with those stupid batons destroyed good and loving people. Roma, Jews, political prisoners, LGBT, the disabled.

And nearly killed my mom... but my grandmother wasn't as lucky.

My family.

Oh, God, how am I going to hold up without giving myself away?

No, I tell myself, I'm not going to distance myself. If I feel like crying, I'm damn well going to cry. I'll explain to *madame* later. Because when people stop reacting to what happened in those camps, then we can't call ourselves 'human' any more.

'Emma, are you okay?' She observes me over the rim of her teacup. We're sitting in the study, a cozy setting I've come to enjoy.

'*Très bien, madame*.' I make a show of bravado that makes her smile, then I get serious, yellow pad in hand. 'You mentioned it was springtime in Paris, 1944, when you were arrested... so I can get my bearings.'

'Yes. D-Day was less than two months away and I didn't believe

Lance could rescue me before the Allied landing, so I fortified my mind and my soul not to break down, admit nothing. What happened to me wasn't nearly as important as those boys landing on the beaches of Normandy. We were at war, *mademoiselle*, and if I may be blunt, your generation has no idea at what cost we won that war. I was lucky. I survived, but millions didn't. I've been selfish keeping it bottled up inside me, but no more.'

'Well said, *madame*. So little has been written about the Nazis' persecution of the Roma. It's time.'

She finishes her tea and pushes the cup and saucer away. '*Bon*. Shall we continue? This time of my life is also filled with the sexual yearnings of a young woman madly in love, my hormones on fire as my pregnancy advanced.' *Are my cheeks tinting?* Must be, because then she says, 'I shall omit those feelings if you're uncomfortable, Emma. I don't want to embarrass you.'

'You already have, *madame*.' I chuckle. 'Several times.'

She smiles. 'Then once more won't hurt. How I pulled up strong, sensual emotions that blocked out the mental anguish that washed over me like burning oil when the SS didn't take me to Gestapo head-quarters, but deposited me in Cherche-Midi, the same military prison where Yvette died.'

'No, *madame*... how cruel.'

'When I entered the horrible place through the arched entrance, I could hear Yvette's spirit reminding me the prison was once a convent and I should draw strength from that. I tried, but I could barely get through the humiliation of having to strip naked and then a bored female guard searched me. My pregnancy wouldn't show for months, so my baby was safe. Then I had my photo taken with a number pinned to my chest and my head imprisoned in a metal clamp to keep me from moving. I was booked as Angéline de Cadieux from Lyon. A male guard came to take me to the third floor, the women's quarters, but an official not in uniform... Gestapo... ripped up the paper with my number and ordered him to take me to what they called the "punishment" cell. That if I was lucky where I was going, I'd get a *new* number.'

'Auschwitz.'

'Yes. We walked through the prison and my knees buckled under me, but the guard dragged me. No chance for escape. Sentries stood at their posts, their rifles fixed with bayonets. There was no air, the windows were high up in the cell and as big as the yellow pad you write on. Instead of smelling the perfume of Paris, I smelled urine and mold. When he pushed me inside and slammed the door, I got through the night by remembering Lance's arms tight around me and his lips trailing down my neck and over my bare skin, between my thighs... his hungry kisses arousing me... then his hard, muscular body moving against mine, our passion reaching a feverish pitch. I swear he touched the baby growing inside me and I cried for joy.'

I keep my head down, say nothing... and write down *everything* she says. I can censor it later. A tear trickles down my cheek... *no*, I won't change a word.

'I was certain I'd be shot,' *madame* continues, 'and I wanted my last moments to be with the man I loved, even if he was only in my mind.'

'How long did you stay in this "punishment" cell?' I ask, breathless from her telling.

'Mercifully, only two days. I had nothing but a stone bench to sleep on and a century-old chamber pot for my ablutions. The stench got worse when I threw up. Morning sickness. I had nothing to eat but weak tea sweetened with a chemical I recognized. Saccharine. And soup swimming with a mass of German ingenuity made from whale meat.'

'You are kidding?' I smile. Is she trying to lighten the mood?

She gives me a saucy grin. 'I use animalic scents including amber-gris to formulate my perfumes, *mademoiselle*. I also know whale meat when I smell it.'

I admit her turn of a phrase keeps me on my toes and makes me want to tell her about my personal connection to Dachau, hold her hand, let her cry on my shoulder if she damn well wants to, but I promised Ryker I'd wait. And so I shall, writing down how the major ratted her out to the Gestapo and, surprisingly, why she wasn't executed.

'I found out after the war, Lance and Jarnak "kidnapped" Frederic and threatened him with a gun pointed to his head to intercede for my release from prison, warning him the French Gestapo hired them to take him out. A lie, but Frederic had no spine and agreed to find out where I was being held. He told me later that *crazy man in black I was sleeping with* nearly murdered him.'

'Bravo, Lance!' I cheer. 'What happened next?'

'The major wanted me executed, but Herr Geller believed I had information about the Resistance. I was no good to him dead, so he ordered me sent to a prison holding political dissidents to "re-educate" my mind. An old fort turned into an internment camp for political prisoners as well as hostages picked up to retaliate for missions carried out by the Resistance. My life was spared, but he changed my name back to Tiena Cordova, *Zigeunerin*. Gypsy. The major would never find me there.'

'Amazing.'

'Lance knew the Allied invasion was weeks away and he made plans to get me out of the prison. He also did something special for me,' she teases, then grins. 'But I shall save that for when we finish the interview.'

'Can I have a hint... please?'

She shakes her head and continues her story, making me so frustrated I chew on my pencil eraser. The third today.

'Of course, I knew none of this and was thankful to be alive when I was loaded on a truck headed for Fort de Romainville with other "asocials" and Jewish ladies. All women.'

I hold my breath, waiting. I have never seen such horror on her face.

Finally, she says, 'I feared what unspeakable events awaited me there.'

39

FORT DE ROMAINVILLE, OUTSIDE PARIS,
SPRING 1944

Angéline

Perfume:
  Mamselle Mimi
  Marseilles rose, jasmine, salted vanilla

I shiver from the cold, flapping my arms like a hummingbird's wings. We've been riding in the open vehicle for about an hour, heading east of Paris, wind in our faces, our bellies empty.

And me with no coat.

I'm still shaking inside, no way to fuel my anger with that German woman for confiscating Yvette's coat. A symbol of her sacrifice and courage. I *do* have my blue silk ribbon smelling of *Le Courage* to tie back my hair and that gives me strength. I'm being silly, of course, but thinking of something else keeps the dread from taking over my brain. The unknown facing us. Women crying... others fretful... but one very kind.

'May I, *mademoiselle*?'

A woman in her early fifties opens her plain brown suitcase, the leather straps worn but the brass buckles shiny, and pulls out a blue sweater with a fancy scalloped collar and a yellow star of David stitched onto the left side. With a loving hand, she pulls out the threads one by one then places the star in her pocket. Then, with a smile, she wraps the sweater around my shoulders.

I shiver again, this time from the kindness of a stranger.

'Merci, madame.'

'I am called Sara,' she tells me.

I wonder if the Nazis arrested her while she had bread in the oven. She smells of flour and lard. Kosher salt. A baker's wife from the Marais district. She has a sweet face, apple cheeks, and grave eyes which sparkle as she adjusts the sweater on my shoulders.

'I knitted it a lifetime ago from heavy sheep's wool when the shelves in our shop were filled with braided egg bread and savory onion rolls.' She sighs. 'Now I have only enough flour to bake two loaves a day... one for the Nazi officer who taunts us with his threats... and the other for his mistress.' Her eyes narrow. 'She's not a nice *shiksa* like you, *mademoiselle*. She's mean, with a mouth on her I don't wish on the dogs.'

'I'm Roma, *madame*.'

'Oh...' she mutters, grabbing my hand in a show of sisterhood of those oppressed by the Nazis, whatever our beliefs are. 'And where is your man?' She lowers her eyes. 'They took mine to the trains. I don't know if I'll ever see him again.'

Then she begins to weep quietly and I put my arm around her and feel her shudder. What if she knew I was pregnant and not married? Would it matter that my lover is a Resistance fighter? Does it make it any less of a sin? I see some things are better left unsaid, things I will never speak of... *never*. I won't be judged because I dare to love a good, strong man. Instead, I tell her I make perfumes for the House of Doujan as I fidget with the long sleeves covering my hands, keeping them warm. I weep, too, when she tells me a lady friend let her dab her *Naomie's Dream* behind her ears and how much her husband loved smelling it on her... that was the week before the Nazis took him away.

We finish the journey in silence, each in our own thoughts, and arrive at the prison after dark. Cold stone, colder still under the cover of night. I can't see much, but the smell of indifference reeks. Heavy tobacco. Foul body smells.

It doesn't get any better over the next two weeks. The prison houses mostly women quartered in tiny cells. The guard brings me a bowl of soup and half a loaf of bread for a daily ration. I can barely keep it down. A rolling wave of fear hits me each day when I hear the guards beating the women, their screams bouncing off the watchtower outside my cell. I wonder if I'm next, making me fear a miscarriage. The guards are brutal to female prisoners they identify as operatives or hostages taken in reprisal. Fortunately, they skip my cell, calling me a 'dirty gypsy' and not worth the trouble.

I pray Sara is safe. I haven't seen her since we arrived. If only they'd put us together, I'm so hungry for a kind word, gentle look, anything to remind me I'm still alive, not slowly dying inside from the isolation. Hungry, sick, I hallucinate. I can't see the women being tortured, but I get nightmares. Slapping my brain with visions that swirl around me like wailing ghosts, squeezing through the keyhole in my mind. I hold my hands over my ears to block out the agonized screams, but the mind is a powerful magician that makes the unknown worse than anything I can see. I imagine women restrained, the skin on their backs sliced open from the pounding of the whip over and over, their eyes blank, their once lovely hair matted with their own blood.

Then, one day, the courtyard is quiet. No screams, no guards yelling. I wonder if the Boches have abandoned the prison, but the peace settling within me is short-lived.

'Get up, *mademoiselle*,' yells the guard, swinging open the cell door. 'You're going on a journey.'

'Where?' I demand, pulling my sweater tighter around me as his eyes roll over my body, watching as if he's disappointed I'm to be moved.

'Ravensbrück.'

'Where's that?'

'Germany... it's a women's camp.'

God, no. I crush the bundle of straw in my hands, its prickly ends stinging the flesh on my fingers. The pain in my heart is worse. *Lance will never find me*, I keep thinking over and over, even when Sara rushes over to me and I see her holding her familiar suitcase, her eyes joyful at seeing me as they herd us onto the freight truck. She's gaunt, her chin sagging, circles dark as black moons under her eyes.

Do I look like that?

'You two, *alt!*'

The guard points to us. We cling to each other, our ears ringing when he informs us orders just came down for three Jewish women and the gypsy girl to be reassigned to Auschwitz.

What does it matter? Ravensbrück... Auschwitz. What *does* matter is we're together and I'm again grateful for the company of the baker's wife as we're transferred to another transport truck. Her sweater and soft words of hope keep me warm on the long journey as I struggle to survive by dreaming of Lance, thinking about the future, that someday when we're old and our passion has turned into a gentle rolling wave instead of a tempest, we'll look back at this time and wonder how we ever survived.

I pray we do.

40

LE CHÂTEAU DE CADIEUX, PARIS, 2003

Emma

Perfume:
Riviera Madness
Yellow rose, lemony-orange, warm musk

'Did you ever go back to Auschwitz after the war, *madame*?' I have to ask.

'Yes. In the spring of 1975. Lance and I went together.'

On cue she pulls out a photo she had in her pants pocket. I blink. What a power couple they were. *Madame* posing in the color Polaroid at Auschwitz in a white pantsuit with wide bell bottoms, white boots, and wearing big, dark sunglasses. Platinum hair wound up in a twist. Lance towers over her – I had no idea he was that tall – black leather jacket, jeans, aviator glasses, dark stubble, longish dark hair tied back with a leather strip. A devilishly handsome man at... what was he... mid-sixties? I can't stop looking at them. Seeing them together gives me chills. You never think of anyone's grandparents as being sexy, but they damn well were.

'I never thought I'd return to the camp to try to save my marriage,' she says.

'What do you mean, *madame*?'

'We weren't the same two people we were during the war. The dashing double agent and the wild Roma girl. We searched to find our places in peacetime but as we did so, we drifted apart. Coming back to Auschwitz was something we had to do before we could move on. I had to come to grips with the shadows pulling at me and focus on what kept my spirit strong.'

'And that was, *madame*?'

'*Mon amour*. I didn't have a chance to tell him how much I loved him that day at the Jeu de Paume before the SS took me away. It hurt me so bad, I *swore* I'd be free again to embrace him and never let him go. I was determined to stay strong. For him.' A long sigh escapes her lips. 'That day we faced my demons together. I was too embarrassed before to speak about it. I never thought I'd share the horror of what happened to me with anyone else but Lance.' She grins. 'Then you came along, *mademoiselle*.'

Embarrassed, I force myself to reconnect with my yellow pad and pencil and wait for her to continue.

'We reconciled before he took off for Cairo after we visited Auschwitz,' she says. 'Before he left we talked about the war honestly with each other. Something we didn't do when we were reunited back in 1945. Who wanted to dwell on the past? The filth, the humiliation, the stink of death. It isn't the Roma way. Besides, we were too filled with plans for the future and it wasn't until years after the April day in Paris when I learned Lance had planned an escape for me from the military prison but had to call it off when he discovered Angéline de Cadieux was "dead", though he didn't believe it. He had no idea I was on a truck to the transit camp as the gypsy girl, Tiena Cordova.'

'You must have been devastated to know how close you came to gaining your freedom.'

'I was. Our relationship had its up and downs... the nightmares, not to mention survivors' guilt. I was also embarrassed by the humiliation I suffered at the hands of the Nazis and became ashamed of my body. Lance understood and held me in his arms whenever I had a "bad moment", but the panic attacks I suffered didn't stop. We prayed if I came to grips with my time here at Auschwitz and how I cheated death, we could move forward.'

'You never returned to Dachau?'

'No. It was too painful. I couldn't cry any more... my anguish was beyond tears.'

She means losing her child.

I hate seeing her so low in spirit. Like she's pushed it into the past, but it's sneaking back and she's not sure how to deal with it. I focus on the two people in the photo. 'How did this trip save your marriage?'

'It wasn't just my nightmares and problems with self-esteem causing problems. I headed up the House of Doujan, creating gorgeously different perfumes while Lance sought adventure on his trips to Egypt and the Near East. It didn't help we couldn't have another child and our baby daughter was lost to us. Another reason why I didn't want to go back to Auschwitz, the idea sending bouts of nausea through me, and I had the most terrible shaking, my lips quivering and I couldn't stop. Then a clamminess, wet and cold, hit me, a desperation that cut like a knife... the same fear I felt in the gypsy camp when I washed out my underwear and had to sleep with them on. Wet.' She's reliving the moment, then she glances at me, almost as if she's forgotten I'm here. 'Wrapped up in a bundle, I kept my underwear under my leg till morning so no one could steal it.'

'Stealing was common in the camps?'

For a moment she looks at me as if deciding whether to answer my question.

'Yes... I stole food, *mademoiselle*, bargained for shoes to keep my feet dry, rags to wrap my baby in, then sewed them together to put on her tiny, shivering body. I traded my bread ration for milk to feed her, celebrating each ounce she gained like it was a Nazi defeat. I lied when I had to, *anything* to live another day. I lived by animal instinct, my wits, and my Roma gift to bargain to get what I needed. I was used to upheaval, so that worked in my favor. I was different when I came back and wanted to walk away from that girl, but she shadowed me everywhere until finally I laid her to rest when we returned to Auschwitz. A cleansing that took weeks afterward to complete. I wanted so dearly to save my marriage. This trip healed us, a means to repair the rift caused by the suffering and degradation I'd endured at the hands of the SS. Lance understood me better, why I became more independent.

'He was also facing his own demons. He was a wealthy man. He didn't work for the Boston institute, he *owned* it and a steel mill. His grandfather was a great philanthropist and founded the institute to pay back the city that made him a fortune and give children the education he never had. Lance never had to work a day in his life, but his passion to correct the mistakes of the present by studying the past overwhelmed him. During the war, he bankrolled several Resistance operations long before the British Foreign Office finally believed in him. But his real passion was archaeology, the challenge, the mystery.

In 1975, he was hell-bent on joining an expedition to Egypt of a newly discovered tomb, but he didn't want to leave me. I made him go, knowing what it meant to him. How could I not? I loved him and understood his passion, though it nearly killed him when he was trapped in a cave-in. He was never the same, but he didn't become bedridden until the early eighties. I nursed him till the end.'

'Oh, my God...' I lean back with a sinking heart, close my eyes. It was hard enough to hear about the troubled marriage they had, but to know this was the last time they were together before the accident stuns me.

'That's why I never spoke of our trip to Auschwitz.'

'Why now, *madame*?'

'You, Emma, with your heartfelt curiosity, so different than the other reporters, and a keen desire to understand me. And what happened in the camps.' She sighs deeply. 'You convinced me there comes a time when you have to talk about it so the world never forgets what happened there.'

'*Merci, madame.*' I take the compliment, then move on. 'What helped you survive the camp?'

'Not what, *mademoiselle*, *who*.' She leans forward. 'Her name was Rosela and she was Sintessa... a German gypsy. We couldn't have survived without each other. You needed somebody when things got so bad you didn't know if you *could* survive.'

Her eyes darken and she's back in Auschwitz. This time it's not after the war with Lance in 1975.

It's April 1944.

41

AUSCHWITZ-BIRKENAU, POLAND, APRIL 1944

Angéline

Perfume:
Angéline
Spanish mimosa, tuberose, musk

'*Sei ruhig, Fräulein!* Be still!'

I yank my arm away from the Jewish prisoner with the long needle in his hand. What barbaric act is he about? He yells at me in German... I yell back in French... then an SS guard hits me in the back with the butt of his rifle. Cursing in Romani, I fall to the ground, hugging my belly, biting my lip, determined not to show weakness in front of the Boches, when a husky female voice whispers in my ear, 'You want to die, girl?' she says in Romani. 'You will, if you don't get your number tattooed.'

She tilts my head up to meet her eyes and I see a young woman about my age dressed in a faded blue dress with a tan shawl wrapped around her waist and a bright red and yellow scarf covering her short black hair. Her skin is dark and smooth, her eyes burning like embers of coal. By her dialect, she's Sintessa. A German Sinto woman.

'I want to live,' I whisper back in our language then, looking over my shoulder, I see others waiting for the needle to pierce their skin, eyes wide, mouths open. In shock. Old people sprawled on the clay floor, wailing and praying, children crying. Unlike the Jews arriving on trains, the Roma families aren't separated but follow the SS in a trance. No wonder the Nazis can do what they want with us.

'Then get up.' She shoves me back toward the prisoner with the long needle, his brow furrowed. In a lower voice, she adds, 'I'll help you.'

Her name is Rosela. Teeth clenched, I do what she tells me, her chilling words cutting me to the core. For the first time since that day in Paris when the SS man clamped my hands behind my back so tight my fingers went numb, I fear I'll never be free again.

How can man do this to his fellow man, Maman?

Cunning, cruel, they revel in destroying a woman's self-respect as each domino of humiliation falls one after another... we're herded like cattle in a freight truck or cattle car... ordered to leave our belongings outside in a heap... then branding us like mindless sheep.

I pray her ghost is nowhere close.

In spite of my fear, I can't help but follow the drama, watching the Jewish tattooist dip the needle attached to a penholder into the fire on the stove while Rosela grabs my left wrist and dabs the outer side of my forearm with alcohol from a dirty bottle. Then she holds up a piece of paper with numbers on it while keeping my arm steady.

'Gypsies aren't registered by name,' she whispers, 'only a number.' The tattooist dips the blunt end in ink and pricks holes in my skin with the hot needle. My skin is soft, bleeds. I wince, each dig of the needle stinging me like a buzzing insect and a painful reckoning sealing my fate.

The letter Z... for *Zigeunerin*. Gypsy.

Then four numbers.

Sketched onto my skin, the black ink shimmering on my sweaty arm, each needlepoint cementing in my mind the grueling process that put me here. Standing in a straight column after the armed SS men pushed us off the truck, screaming at us. Shivering, desperate, I took my place in the row, eyes darting everywhere, my sense of smell overloaded from the burning stench and billowing black clouds of smoke. What struck me were the blood-red flames touching the sky. I detected the slightest fruity scent in the air, coming from where, I don't know.

I evaluated a plan for escape. Impossible. Armed guards, howling dogs pulling at their leashes, SS men wielding batons, yelling, screaming for us to stand at attention while they counted us... then again... and again until a railcar rolled up to the end of the tracks with over a hundred people crammed inside, Jews and Roma, the dead lying on top of the living.

Just when I thought I could take a breath, the selection process began.

Selection for what?

All eyes were glued on an imposing SS officer making his decision from a list in his hand, the night air biting my cheeks, the waiting unbearable especially when I realized the frightened prisoners gleaned not even a blink of his heavy eyelids as the line progressed. The Boche pointed left then right... *where were they going*? When he came to the baker's wife, he smirked then pointed left... he smiled at me... pointed right.

I was confused, but didn't protest when Sara shoved her suitcase into my hand, begging me to take it, praying she dies quickly lest anyone desecrate her body, forbidden by the Torah.

She meant the tattooing.

It's done.

I look down at the fresh ink. I'm no longer Tiena or Angéline but a number. The first words I learn in German are from that number. 'Memorize it,' Rosela whispers, 'and tell them when they ask or you'll get a beating.'

I nod. Harsh reality sets into my bones, my mind fighting the indecency inflicted upon us... these innocent women, their men... even children. I can't ignore the whisperings... hushed voices, the wailing as we march out of the barracks, down a broad road, going... *where*?

If they're going to murder us, I convince myself, they wouldn't bother with the registration... which means Sara is dead. *How?* I heard no gunfire... but the smell of smoke taints my nostrils with a powerful odor that turns my stomach. My acute sense of smell picks up what I detect as meat roasting...

What? No, no... it's not true.

My ears ring with denial, my insides twisting into knots so tight, I'm short of breath but I keep walking, clutching the worn leather handle on the suitcase with my sweaty palm. My nerves deaden to the stinging pain on my arm smeared with ink, bleeding from the pricks on my skin, but my heart feels so heavy in my chest. I'm desperate to know what's going on, command my brain to remain alert... focus on the heap of clothes, suitcases, shoes bundled together near the large brick building with the billowing smoke coming from the chimney stack.

Including a pair of red shoes with cotton stockings stuffed inside, sitting under the accusing spotlight. Waiting for their owner to return.

It's then I know she's never coming back.

* * *

'Strip, *Fräulein*, now!'

I fumble with the buttons on my sweater, steeling myself to lose the last of my dignity. I suck in a deep breath, holding in my stomach, still flat. I wonder if they'd have compassion for a pregnant woman. By the sneer on the guard's face, I ignore that foolish idea and remove my shoes, stockings – hiding my blue ribbon in my left shoe – then my trousers, blouse... turning my back to him when I slip my brassiere straps off my shoulders, my skin prickling from a sudden coolness, as though someone opened the door.

A stiff, short, bespectacled SS officer swaggers down the rows of confused women and girls in various state of undress and starts hitting hard with his cat o' nine tails, urging us to hurry, how we're behind schedule... and announcing in a gleeful tone that the showers are next. '*Macht schnell!*'

It's early morning and this living hell is worse in daylight. I see wave after wave of human flesh in every form evolving into one nameless mass... the final humiliation. During the longest night, after I received the mark of the Teutonic devil, the SS guards herded another railcar of Sinto and Roma men, women, and children into wooden barracks for tattooing, then prisoners in striped shirts and trousers fumbled about like busy mice, sewing inverted black triangles onto our clothes along with our number. Then a big X in red oil on the back. We're told they'll be cleaned and scoured for vermin, then we'll get them back because we're going to the *Zigeunerlager,* gypsy camp, in Birkenau about two and half kilometers from the main camp at Auschwitz.

I don't know whether to laugh or cry.

I'm back with our people, Maman.

But never have I seen us Roma in such shock, horror, these proud wanderers disjointed and fearful. I feel for the older women forced to disrobe in front of their family members. I'm mesmerized by the chaos around me until there's the sound of heavy boots behind me and an SS man rips my brassiere off me, then twirls it around on the end of his bayonet, laughing.

Laughing.

I've seen monsters before... and will again, but never have I been filled with such hate for *all* Boches like I am now. Disgusting pigs with no decency. I'm scared out of my wits I'm going to die right here and *he's* laughing. I manage to keep my tongue from sealing my fate, but barely. Goose bumps prickle my skin. I've felt the heavy hand of the enemy before, and I know striking back means death... but I won't let him degrade me. A moment later, when he reaches for my drawers, I disappear into the shadows, then wiggle out of my underwear and toss it in his face, half expecting to the feel the blade of his bayonet between my shoulder blades. My defiance sets off a rousing shout from the short commander for the hysterical women to form a line and they run the lot of us... a hundred... two hundred... through a gauntlet of his men jeering and shouting at us in German, their guttural grunts evoking a hatred in me so heated, I don't feel the morning chill.

Running us like four-legged animals onward to the sauna where the same sadistic officer turns the water temperature from cold to hot... then cold. Drenched and shivering, we line up again, each taking our turn with stoic prisoners armed with scissors and razor blades. A stone-faced female prisoner with broad hips and a rag around her head cuts my hair off and forever lost are the remnants of my dyed black hair I so dutifully showed off that day at the Hôtel Ritz. I can't believe there ever was such a day, standing here in this menagerie of humanity, men and women... children... stripped of our dignity like skinned hares.

By her hand gestures, she's ordering me to get up on the stool... I hesitate and the strike of a guard's baton across the back of my legs startles me into obeying so quickly I stumble and rock the stool back and forth. Then, to my horror, she shaves off my pubic hair. *Indecent, bold*... That's the moment I break down, slump my shoulders and hold my hands, palms down, over my slightly protruding belly. She keeps pushing them down to my side, grumbling in Polish, then a moment of understanding strikes her. She glares up at me, her eyes fierce and questioning. I stiffen, then twitch, desperate to keep my fear tamped down.

But she knows. *She knows.*

To my surprise, her deep brown eyes soften, then she puts her forefinger to her lips, warning me to be silent. With quick, even strokes of the razor, she lowers her head and finishes the job with care before moving on to the next woman. Her compassion gives me courage.

I stand motionless on the small stool.

Naked.

My skin smooth. Shaved everywhere. It's quite surprising how much of a breeze I feel between my legs, tickling my smooth mound, even in this hot room. I should be embarrassed, but I often bathe nude in the streams surrounding the château... *mon amour* splashing me with cool water, a necklace of wildflowers strung around my neck announcing my claim to be fairy queen. I have to think of *something* to hold myself together or I'll go mad surrounded by evil and inhumane men when—

'*Raus*! Out!' shouts an SS guard.

He draws close enough to see the determination in my eyes as he raises his baton to strike me again but I don't back down this time, unleashing my 'gypsy spirit' on him, goading him with confidence with the sway of my body, warning him with a look not to damage the goods... I'm no fool. Rape... sex... they're as much a part of war as guns firing and soldiers marching. This soldier has never tried to humiliate a Roma girl before. If anything, I take the advantage while I have it before I lose my female curves that mystify him, lose my sex appeal from lack of food, from the filth... before, God help me, if the worst happens, the fire in me dies. If the cruelty I've witnessed here indicates the subhuman treatment afforded to us... Roma and Jewish alike... then I face my greatest challenge.

I slide my bare feet off the stool and join the others. I learned one thing. Show courage and find their weaknesses. Then use it against them, exploit them, because no matter what they do to me.

I will survive.

*　＊　＊　＊*

Two weeks Later

'They call him the Angel of Death.'

'Who, Rosela?' I ask, taking note of the SS officers hovering around the hospital barracks, laughing, smoking. Reading numbers off a long list. Counting prisoners... always counting. Morning... evening roll call. Anytime it strikes them. It drives me crazy.

'That one... with the dark good looks. He's as evil as Lucifer himself.'

We hug the side of the wooden barracks, our square scarves tied in neat bundles and filled with herbs we picked around the perimeter for the camp soup. Ginger. Rosemary. Basil. And wild garlic that grows in the forest. I can't eat too much garlic since it causes bleeding. A fall, a blow from a guard... I could miscarry and bleed to death.

Fortunately, no one pays attention to us. As Roma women, we're subject to different rules than the other female prisoners, but that doesn't make our lives better. *You don't come to Auschwitz to live*, I've heard too many times, *but to die*.

Still, I'm curious. I lean forward and peek around the corner—

Rosela pulls me back. '*Don't look at him...* he's cunning and can't be trusted. Above all, don't tell him you're pregnant.'

'Why?'

'It's a death sentence for your child.'

Yes, she knows about my condition. It was a chance I had to take. We stand next to each other at roll call every morning and night, eat together, monitor the children at the 'kindergarten'. We watch each other's backs. She's alone here, too, after losing her husband in a fight during a roundup, then separated from the rest of her family. She has no idea what happened to them.

'And don't fall for his tricks,' she finishes, pushing me along and away from this horrible man before he notices us. 'Or you'll end up in the crematorium burned alive.'

'I can't hide my pregnancy forever.'

She leans closer to me. 'I know a doctor, a woman prisoner, who can take care of that for you.' Harsh words, violent words that pierce a mother's soul with the devil's fork, but her eyes tell a different story. Dark circles underneath with so much pain swirling within them I have to ask—

'Did you—?'

'Yes.'

I'm shocked.

'I lost two children to starvation,' Rosela says, 'four and seven, their cheeks eaten away with big holes in their flesh, their mouths inflamed with sores... infection wasting their bodies... none of my poultices healed them and they died.' She shudders, hunching her shoulders and grabbing her knees. 'Then my Nicolas was born, a strong boy with curly dark hair... they took him, that Nazi doctor with ice in his heart, to his laboratory.'

'Laboratory?' A word I never thought to hear in this place.

'Yes, in the sauna barracks... they infected my child with typhus as an experiment. He died a week later.' She beats her fist on her chest. 'When I got pregnant again, I swore I'd not let another baby suffer like that. I will *die* first.'

Her words haunt me that night as we huddle together in the bunk... four of us... a quiet girl of about fourteen and her mother along with Rosela and me. I swear I feel tiny things crawling over me. I struggle to keep clean, nearly impossible. No running water, clay floor in what were horse stables, a breeding ground for disease.

The days fall into each other, sucking up the day before, with us never knowing if there is a tomorrow. What terrifies me is I'm losing who I am. *Angeline de Cadieux, parfumier.* I've managed to keep my blue ribbon I so lovingly doused in perfume, but some days I can't smell the invigorating scent of *Le Courage* the surrounding smell is so bad, wrapped up in the bodily odor of the three women as well as my own.

Courage... such a brave word. I didn't know what the word meant before.

I do now.

Sara had courage... and helped me survive. I say a prayer every morning for her. When I opened her suitcase, I found two loaves of stale bread covered with eerie green mold, which I crumbled up so no one would eat it and get sick. Bread destined for the Nazi and his mistress? I imagine she derived a bit of pleasure depriving them of their ill-gotten bread. I also found cotton stockings, lace-up brown shoes, drawers, a slip, a pair of amber round sunglasses... and a gold wedding ring hanging on a string from the glasses. I slipped it on my finger and, though it's tight, it keeps the Roma men at a distance. They respect family and the honor of another man's wife and believe my story about my husband being a political prisoner at a different camp in spite of his military service to France.

I've also taken to wearing the amber sunglasses since it's not uncommon to see Roma men with their wide hats, smoking their cut-off pipes, the women wearing shawls and scarves. Each day the stench of unclean bodies and men with foul breath reeking of tobacco and decayed teeth sets me up for headaches so blinding, I cover my nose with my scarf. I keep my head down, my shoulders hunched... anything to keep out of the way of the SS men.

Most worrisome is the fear of losing my baby. By my guess, I'm eight weeks pregnant and due in December.

Then one morning the SS man in charge of our block marches up and down the row of women at roll call, offering expectant mothers extra milk rations if they come forward. My eyes brighten. I'm losing weight, my baby needs more food, but I heed Rosela's warning. She's right. The women enjoy their milk, then they disappear. Gone to the crematorium.

We don't talk about it... we can't.

Speaking in Romani and teaching me enough German to survive, Rosela fills my head with camp rules – how to bargain for extra food with the trinkets I found in Sara's suitcase, to cozy up to the *kapo,* the supervisor who is a prisoner himself, to get a job in the kitchen so she and I can work together gathering herbs.

I wouldn't have survived without her. She shows me how to shun unwanted attention from SS men by scratching my crotch, then under my arms when they come round looking for 'volunteers' for the brothel in the main camp.

Then, one day in May 1944, the SS men stop coming.

The gypsy camp director – a Nazi – orders everyone to remain in the barracks. He received a notice from the Angel of Death... the filthy conditions in the camp dictated something must be done.

The kitchen closes... SS guards leave their posts... the gate remains closed and the men don't leave on the wagons to gather stones, sand, dirt to build the roads inside the camp.

The whispering among Roma and Sinti prisoners begins. Word is... the order to remain in the barracks was sent as a warning.

The Kommandant has decreed the gypsy camp and everyone in it be exterminated.

42

LE CHÂTEAU DE CADIEUX, PARIS, 2003

Angéline

Perfume:
Sintessa
Muscat grape, lily of the valley, cedarwood

'I armed myself with a knife and a long stick, stones in my pocket, then dug in with the others in the gypsy camp, waiting... *daring* the Nazis to make us come out.'

Emma stops writing, squeezes her hands together. 'The Roma uprising, *madame*?'

'Yes. On May 16, 1944, a horde of SS men armed with machine guns surrounded the barracks, yelling "*Los, los!*" for every gypsy to come out, show themselves.'

'And did you?' she asks.

'So we could be gassed? No, we swore, we wouldn't give up so easily. We kept strong in silence... men carrying crowbars and shovels, many with military backgrounds, waited to lead the charge. I took my place with Rosela... armed like the men and ready to fight. Hours passed.

Complete silence in the barracks. Twilight deepened into night... and no gypsy came out of the barracks. The SS men were stunned, these soldiers so used to giving orders dumbfounded by our courage.'

'I'm so proud of you... of your people.'

'Finally, we heard a whistle,' I continue. 'Loud. Then the sound of hobnail boots retreating and it was over. Oh, the elation we felt, the power, the strength. We'd beaten back the Boches by barricading ourselves in the barracks, showed them we were capable of organized resistance. We felt certain they'd have to let us go.'

I sigh.

'They didn't, of course, and life continued... dirtier, uglier... less food. And I got bigger... my stomach more rounded, my breasts fuller, though we suffered so much malnutrition in the camp, bloating wasn't uncommon. I played that card, knowing that as long as I could work, stand up for roll call every morning and evening, I'd survive another day. It helped that I made myself indispensable in the kitchen with my skills for mixing herbs. To my joy, the *kapo* turned his back when I stole margarine, sausage, marmalade from the Nazi coffers and shared it with Rosela. In the end, it paid off. We weren't dying a slow death of starvation... not yet.'

I lean back, grateful to have finally voiced the horror of those first weeks at Auschwitz. *Getting it off your chest*, Emma says. She's visibly shaken, asking me if she can take a break. I see the tears welling up in her eyes. Me, too.

'I need to go cry,' she says. 'A hurt cry.'

I nod. I understand.

Ryker appears out of the shadows and approaches me with a question in his eyes and worry wrinkling his brow. 'If I may be excused, *madame*... she needs me.'

'Yes, go to her! I'm fine.'

I'm not, but I've had more than fifty years to mull over these horrible events and have learned to cope. Emma has not. In the middle of talking about so much pain and horror, it does my heart good to feel the closeness between these two growing and I will do anything I can to foster it. It's only later that evening after we have a light repast of cheese, fruit, fresh baguettes and coffee that I continue my story.

43

AUSCHWITZ-BIRKENAU, LATE SUMMER 1944

Angéline

Perfume:
Gypsy Fleur
Passion rose, Casablanca jasmine, sandalwood

I'll go mad if I don't rid myself of the stench in this place.

My nose is so sensitive to smell, I suffer a physical torture that pierces my brain, makes my nose swell up and I find it hard to breathe. I've got to do *something* to heal myself. Wrapping my sweater over my head, I make my way along the broad road leading to the men's infirmary. I almost passed out during evening roll call when the SS guard discovered someone missing and we had to stand for two hours until they found her. I missed my dinner ration, and now I'm desperate enough to beg the kindly doctor I've befriended to allow me a drop of peppermint oil from the medical supplies. Prisoners are only allowed a short amount of free time to socialize in the barracks, but I took a chance and sneaked out. The doctor won't report me to the *kapo*. He knows me from my kitchen work with herbs, knows I'm from Paris. Hillel Platt is also a prisoner, a Jewish doctor from Poland, but he studied in Paris and speaks French... a delight to my ears even when my nose is suffering.

I wipe my face with my skirt, the humidity making my skin hot and sticky, my blue *Le Courage* ribbon tied around my wrist, the black smoke especially heavy today. I almost turn back, then I hear coughing... not a raspy sound but a violent burst of frustration coming from someone in distress.

Curious, I peek through the half-opened door and see Dr Platt pounding on the back of an SS officer coughing his guts out, trying to dislodge something in the man's throat. My breath catches, pulse races, I recognize the block commander. I almost feel joyful watching the Nazi suffer... why shouldn't he? How many women has he killed, raped?

Still... I can't tear myself away.

The intensity of watching him suffer, it's doing something to me I never imagined.

It's reminding me I'm human, even if he is not.

'You could kill him, *docteur*, doing that,' I say in French. 'I've seen it happen.'

The doctor stares at me, his fist pounding the man's back. Then recognition flashes in his eyes. 'What are you saying, *mademoiselle*?'

'If what's choking him moves, it will block his breathing completely.'

'I have to take that chance, *mademoiselle*. Help me.'

I again hesitate, my anger, desperation and pure hate for everything the SS man stands for pounding in my head, yet I also hear Maman's voice begging me not to let her down and become one of *them* when I know how to help. Papa showed me what to do when someone in our caravan was choking, a trick he learned from a sword swallower in the circus. A man too often in a life-or-death choking situation.

'Put your leg between his legs, *monsieur*,' I begin, gesturing for the doctor to stand behind him. 'Find his navel with your finger... then make a fist with your hand, placing it with your thumb against his stomach.'

'I can't get his jacket open.'

'You must.'

The SS man is coughing more violently and though it turns my stomach, I get so close to him I can smell the greasy chicken on his breath. He must have swallowed a bone. My hand tightens around his belt, unfastening it, then the buttons on his jacket, the fearsome SS emblem staring me in the face. Every medal, stripe, symbol representing lives destroyed. *I hate him... all of them.* Yet I can't stop. I fling open his jacket, allowing the doctor access to his abdomen, his hands in position as I instructed, then—

'Stay below his ribcage, then grab your fist with your other hand and thrust inward and upward again and again...'

The Jewish prisoner isn't a tall man, but he's sturdy, strong arms, big chest. He keeps thrusting inwardly and upwardly with force without stopping... the doctor grunting, the SS officer choking with such violence the walls shake when—

'*Aaargh... mein Gott!*' yells the SS man when the offending chicken bone is expelled, his hands going around his throat, eyes bulging as if he can't believe it. I clench my fists, waiting. The doctor assures the SS man in German he'll recover, then he turns to me.

'Where did you learn this, *mademoiselle*?'

'From my Papa.' I stare down the officer and add proudly in German, '*A gypsy.*'

The SS man observes me with no change in his expression, neither thanks nor hate. It's then I see him... *them* for what they are. Arrogant, disrespectful bastards incapable of feeling or emotion.

Licking his lips, he slicks back his clipped blond hair, adjusts his jacket and races out, not even a *Heil Hitler*. I don't know whether to be insulted or grateful. I don't care. I did what's right. I close my eyes, breathe out, listening. Around me hangs an amazing aura.

The Polish doctor, muttering.

Me. Wondering if I'll regret saving the SS man.

An odd thought, but a real one. That someday this same man may send me to my death.

* * *

'You're pregnant, *mademoiselle*.'

I panic, grabbing the doctor's sleeve. '*Please* don't report me. They'll kill my baby.'

'Has it come to that, *mademoiselle*?' Dr Platt says, rubbing his forehead. He's a young physician... no more than early thirties... but his face drags downward from the horrors he's seen. 'That I've forgotten my oath, what I swore to do? To save lives, not take them?' He grabs me by the shoulders and the pain in his deep, dark eyes swirls like the sheaves of rain that turn this camp into rivers of mud.

Two weeks have passed since I helped him save the SS man's life. We've become close, him sneaking me extra rations, medicine for the sick in my barracks. I remember how he looked at me that day we saved the SS man, the off-white of his lab coat a beacon of goodness against the drab olive of the German's uniform, his eyes showing me respect. Something I've not experienced since I've been here.

We speak in French in low tones, my pulse racing. I wonder if I can trust him. My child is in danger as each day passes. I'm not showing... yet, but if the Nazi doctor finds out, I can't bear to imagine what will happen to me. My child.

'I'll be safe in the gypsy camp.' I begin pacing, forgetting the ginger I came for to quell my stomach pains. 'The Nazis leave us alone there—'

'You *must* listen, *mademoiselle*, another order has come down,' he says, his eyes pleading with such intensity, I'm both angered and confused. 'The May uprising was only a delay.'

'A delay? What do you mean?'

'Tonight... the trucks are coming to take everyone in the gypsy camp away ... I can't help them, but I can save you, *mademoiselle*. I'll hide you in the camp hospital where they won't find you.'

Jaw clenched, my brain can't catch up to what he's trying to tell me... that horror is a living, breathing fire you can't put out. I foolishly believed I could deal with the ongoing ordeal of surviving, the gut-

tearing hunger pangs that plague me during the day and the bloodcur-
dling fear that keeps me awake at night. I've learned to say nothing,
pray whatever task the SS officer has in mind is something I can do,
keep my eyes lowered. 'Survive.... another day,' I repeat to myself, the
heat unbearable, especially at night when we're huddled together in
the bunk. Human sweat mixed with raw desire so overpowering, I bury
my head in my hands and nearly stop breathing to keep the stench
from invading my brain. The sounds of raw sex between desperate
men and women huddled in the lavatory, their souls screaming not just
for physical release, but the power of a loving human touch... I don't
blame them. I yearn for the touch of *mon amour* but find comfort in
rubbing my belly, knowing his love lives within me.

During the day, I gather my herbs, help Rosela with the children—

'Rosela!' I blurt out, panicked. 'I've got to warn her.'

How could I have been so stupid not to see this day coming? The
signs were there. Gypsy men fit for labor transferred to other camps,
allowing them to say goodbye to their families, promising them they'll
soon join them. It was a farce. The Nazis have a plan, they *always* have
a plan.

'I must go back to the barracks before the trucks come, grab her...
we'll hide together, we'll—'

Dr Platt... Hillel... grabs me around the waist. The smell of that
disgusting disinfectant the Germans use is strong upon his clothes, but
his embrace is warm, protective. Whispering to me in hot breaths, he
pleads, 'You can't, *mademoiselle*.' His voice turns tender, betraying his
feelings for me. I never expected this. I've heard him speak of a fiancée,
a Polish teacher working in the Underground. God knows if she's still
alive.

'I can't stay here, Doctor. I can't.'

'If you try to save her, you'll both be gassed, *mademoiselle*.' A pause.
'Think about your baby.'

His words hit me hard. I can no longer sleep in an endless dream
where I'm safe, the baby's safe. With those words, everything I know
about life in Auschwitz ceases to exist.

The trucks are coming tonight, he said, to take every gypsy and murder them.

With his help, I go into hiding in the camp hospital, moving from room to room... spending two hours lying still under a dead body before hiding underneath a cot in the doctor's office when night falls and the room is pitch black.

Then I hear the roar of the trucks, tires squealing... shouts from the SS guards, dogs barking... shots fired, the screams from the prisoners confined to their barracks in the gypsy camp. Dragging out the women and children, the sick and few men remaining onto trucks and taking them to the gas chamber where their bodies are burned in pits next to the crematorium.

I shall never forget tonight. It's August 2, 1944.

The gypsy camp is completely annihilated, then readied for a new shipment of Hungarian Jewish prisoners.

My ears don't stop ringing for days, my pulse racing every time I hear the sound of hobnail boots stomping down the hospital hallway. *I can't stay here, it's not safe. If I'm caught, both the doctor and I will be tortured and hung on a meat hook.*

I hide in the large kitchen cupboard during morning and evening roll call... squashed between sacks of potatoes, then the doctor keeps me hidden in his office, sometimes under his desk, other times wearing a nurse's smock with a yellow star that covers my forearm so no one sees my 'gypsy' number. I become so confused I hallucinate, dreaming I'm back in Paris, not knowing what day it is, but I'm thankful for the time to rest, no hard labor... keep my baby safe. Two... three weeks later, I'm not certain, I'm still numb when Dr Platt rushes to grab me from the cupboard, his voice curt but reassuring.

It's time, he says, adding my number to the list of female prisoners being transferred out of Auschwitz... adding two numerals and omitting the 'Z' for gypsy so it coincides with the other numbers on the list. Then he matches the number on my arm with a black pen, praying it will stay, and tries to bleach the 'Z'. No telling if it will work. To make the transformation complete, he instructs me to put on a woman's prison dress with a red triangle sewn on it. A political prisoner. *They need workers where I'm going*, he whispers, and chills fill me. Ravensbrück? Word spreads quickly in camp how the female prisoners there are forced into prostitution... am I next?

Yet I can't believe the Polish doctor would send me to my death. He's a good man. He never asked for sexual favors from me for more rations as is so common here. I meet his gaze squarely when he cups my chin, wishing me God speed with a husky voice, warm and tender like we're not here in the camp hospital, but standing under a canopy, saying vows.

He's in love with me.

I keep that thought with me, praying he doesn't get caught when later that night I find myself standing in the rain in the railroad installation, drenched, SS men running around like roosters on the wrong side of daylight, eager to get their job done and be rid of us. Women considered fit enough to work for the Führer.

Not in a brothel.

But in a Messerschmitt factory.

* * *

'You're not a Jew, why are you here?' is the first thing I hear when I arrive at the Augsburg concentration camp. The SS man in the wire rim spectacles refers to the red triangle sewn on my dress.

'I'm French,' I answer in a calm voice. 'A political prisoner.'

'*Ah, ja*, I see it here... one French female prisoner,' he reads from a list from the Kommandant's office at Auschwitz. Somehow Dr Platt switched the original list with the one where he added my name. He studies my arm, adjusting his spectacles as sunlight bounces off the glass. 'Your number isn't clear...'

Before he can look closer, I rattle off my new number in German, then French, trying to confuse him but not challenging his authority. I know how the game is played. The selection process rolls out the same at every camp, like clockwork. The Nazis follow established procedure like mindless ants performing endless drills, but never knowing why they're doing them. Someday, I pray a giant wielding a big foot will stomp on them all.

Another SS officer shouts: what's holding up the line?

The SS man grumbles then snarls, frustration overtaking him. He marks me off the list then waves me on to the showers. He has no desire to explain to his superior that out of three hundred Hungarian Jewish female prisoners, he's wasting time questioning a fair-haired Frenchwoman with Aryan looks. I follow the other women to the factory building to shower, but I don't feel the horror that ravaged me at Auschwitz. We're here to aid the German war machine as forced labor, working in the armaments factory, not murdered. The Allies are getting closer, the Nazis need planes, but that's not on my mind when I wiggle out of my damp, dirty clothes, shoes – as always I hide my blue ribbon, fraying and nicked, in my shoe – then shower without fear of rape. The cold water washes over me, erases all traces of Auschwitz... the black ink running down my arm. The deed is done. If I can stay out of the crossfire, my baby and I have a chance to survive.

I grab soap, smell with pleasure the fatty solids emitting a tart lemon scent, then dry off and pick up a clean dress. Socks, shoes. I say a prayer of thanks to the brave Polish doctor who risked his life to get me here and saved me and my baby from a horrible fate.

I soon discover my short blonde hair, eyes hazel blazing with green on this autumn September day, get me special work deemed worthy of my 'superior intelligence'.

It saves my life. For a while.

As a Roma girl growing up, Maman and Papa insisted I attend parochial school wherever we camped. Sometimes we'd stay a whole season in one town and the nuns taught me beautiful cursive writing, which added an elegant touch to the labels we fastened onto our perfume bottles.

Now I copy charts in German about armament components, which are then mass produced on a big machine. I have no choice but to do as I'm told. Any act of sabotage means instant death.

I sit behind a desk during my twelve-hour shift, my expanding stomach hidden from view. Except from that of the German supervisor, an older man with big, chapped hands and a grumpy snort.

I catch him watching me with compassion and I often find extra food wrapped up in muslin in my desk drawer... cooked potatoes, boiled carrots.

I remain diligent to keep out of sight as my belly expands and summer passes.

Fall is shedding her cloak in waves of rusty red, yellow, orange. I shall start counting down the days soon. I'm seven months pregnant and due in December. I keep my head down, my hands busy, my mouth shut. I have a desk job on the second floor, so I don't report to roll call. I hide my belly on these cold days by wearing my supervisor's overcoat, traveling between the women's barracks and the factory.

I find a strange peace here in my daily ritual until my world crashes in early November.

I'm late getting today's assignment printed out, stacked, and delivered to the SS officer in charge. The grinding of the mimeograph grates on my ears as it spits out today's work, but the gears are sticking. Loud, screeching high-pitched tones and... oh, no, blue-inked sheets spew out of the machine and go flying everywhere. *Everywhere.*

On the floor, under my desk.

My face is pasty, clammy. Sweat crawling down the middle of my back. I can't bend over to gather them. If I get on my hands and knees, I'll never get up.

And the damn phone won't stop ringing.

I panic when, minutes later, the SS Kommandant in charge bursts into the office and strikes his baton against the mimeograph, then kicks the papers scattered on the floor, demanding to know *why* today's charts aren't on his desk. Himmler needs them... *schnell.*

My heart pounds in my chest, instinct pushing me to cross my arms over my protruding belly to protect my baby. The arrogant officer yells with a thunderous voice *you will pay*... then he makes a move to strike me with his baton when my German supervisor races into the office and takes the blow, blood pouring down his arm, begging for mercy toward me.

A pregnant woman.

The SS officer blinks, this new information setting him on a deadly course. Smug, indignant, he fires the German, then he turns to me, snarling.

My punishment?

'Back to Auschwitz, *Fräulein*.'

44

DACHAU, GERMANY, 2003

Angéline

Perfume:
Ma Capri
Pink sugar roses, pink grapefruit, benzoin

'You didn't return to Auschwitz, *madame*, what happened?'

Emma digs her fingers into the leather upholstery of the rental Mercedes speeding along the country road toward the site of the Dachau concentration camp, disbelieving. Her questioning eyes deepen to a darker blue and there's an intensity there today, a drive to understand how my story went into a tailspin after I was sentenced to certain death at Auschwitz in the gas chamber.

'Two SS men accompanied me to the train station,' I begin, rolling down the passenger window and drawing the sweetest fragrance of florals into my lungs, letting my eyes soak up the beauty that has returned here since those unbearable times. The coming of spring breathes new life into the fields of dandelions flanking the road, then past dense woods. 'You shall know everything soon, I promise.'

'You never cease to amaze me with your story, *madame*,' Emma says.

I admit drawing out my account because I don't want the interview to end. If ever I needed her, it's now. Coming here to Germany is my feeble attempt to keep it going. The flight from Paris to Munich was an hour and a half, unlike the train ride I took back then, flanked by two SS guards. Then the march from the train station to the sub-camp at Dachau at night, never knowing if I was going to be raped, but mercifully the SS soldiers left me alone.

I smelled no flowers then... how grateful I am to smell them now.

We hired a motorcar in Munich to drive us here. Emma beside me, Ryker in the front with the driver who speaks English and some French. I notice a new closeness between Emma and Ryker and that pleases me. She'll need his strength to get through this. And me? I have both of them and, for the first time, I feel ready to relive those months at Kaufering I, and my daring escape. It wasn't until after the war I realized how fortunate I was to be housed with the most extraordinary women and one brilliant Jewish physician.

We fly past open fields and, as we get closer to the site, the driver points out where different camp buildings once stood. I see them in my mind, though now the forest trees stand guard around the open clearings where the barracks were, filled with suffering and misery, prisoners dying from starvation, beatings.

Nothing remains.

'*Madame*, we are here.'

Simple words. *We are here.* I heard the same words when the train stopped and the SS men brought me here on that freezing cold day in November 1944.

I pull back the curtain to my past, my heart pounding. 'I never thought the memory would be so clear to me, Emma.'

'What of, *madame*?'

'I see the spotlights from the watchtowers, hear the vicious, barking dogs... smell the stink of suffering that's worse than dying. A human misery that must *never* be repeated. But there was also kindness and female bonding and my daughter was born here. And for that reason, I embrace what I'm about to relive. And lost.' *My baby,* I whisper to myself, struggling to keep from bursting into tears. 'And with all my heart, I'm afraid, Emma... my God, I'm afraid.'

'*Madame*... I'm here. I'll *always* be here.'

She grabs my hand without hesitation and while I ponder what she means and how that warms me, she holds onto me tight. And I'm not afraid.

'It started with that train ride, *mademoiselle*,' I say in a steady voice. 'And an apple.'

45

ON A TRAIN SOMEWHERE IN GERMANY, NOVEMBER 1944

Angéline

Perfume:
Red Apple
Apple blossom, cinnamon, amber

'Why is your hair so short, *Fräulein*? Are you ill?'

I shake my head at this young mother with a basket of fruit in her lap. I can't take my eyes off the glistening red skin of the apple, speckled with golden swirls. Two SS men dumped me next to this German woman on a passenger train, then took off for a smoke in the next railcar, promising me a surprise when they return.

Are they going to throw me off a running train?

The smell of tobacco, the odor of people on the move, and the sweetness of a fresh apple contribute to the surreal feeling whirling in my head. I have a vague recollection of asking why we changed trains earlier, but the SS men ignored me. I ponder my fate, not caring if the woman keeps staring at the red triangle on my dress, her young daughter pointing to my short hair curling up at the back of my neck. I covered it with a drab gray scarf, but I dozed off and it slipped down. I pull it back up, my big belly straining against the thin cotton of my washed-out blue dress, no buttons left on my black sweater to cover myself.

'I work in a labor camp,' I say, eyeing the apple. The blank look on her face tells me she has no idea what that is. In that moment, I want to cry. An impending darkness is descending upon my soul. Why should she move about freely and do as she wishes, have a kind child, fresh, beautiful apples? While I sit here in fear of my life, my baby's life... and the man of my heart has no idea where I am, or even that I carry his child. What cruel twist of fate has brought me to this point? I miss Lance so much, the way things were, my lovely perfumes, and when my time comes, I'll be alone. Without his compelling presence that makes the earth move beneath me when he touches me, kisses me. He's tall and magnificent and exciting, but he's also sympathetic to my needs, my fears... and God knows, he puts up with my brazenness. But he won't be with me when my baby's cry breaks the silence of the womb and that makes me incredibly sad... and angry.

I observe this young woman staring at me, but I don't see hatred in her eyes, only curiosity. I hear Maman's voice telling me not to judge her, but focus... *survive*.

I lie back on the seat, rest my head. I must be going mad. No wonder... I've had no food, no water since we left Augsburg. The SS men don't care. I'm another prisoner for the gas chamber. My stomach grumbles and my baby kicks, as if to say, *I'm hungry*. Surely God won't mind if I bargain for an apple?

'I can tell your fortune, *meine Frau*.' I feel confident speaking German to this young woman, grateful for the hours Rosela spent teaching me. The deepest shadow, black and hollow, descends upon me when I remember her name. She'd want me to survive. And the baby.

'Are you a gypsy?' Her eyes widen.

'Yes.' I hold my hand over my forearm to hide my number. If the SS men catch me talking to her, they won't hesitate to beat me. 'I'm descended from a gypsy queen... her name was Naomie and she taught me how to read palms.'

'Oh, yes, *please*! Tell my fortune.' She lowers her eyes. 'I don't have much money.'

'An apple, *meine Frau*. That's all I ask.'

'*Ja, gut.*' She giggles, then shows me her palm. I don't know how to read fortunes, that was Maman's talent. Instead, she encouraged me to dazzle with my perfumes, but that doesn't stop me. 'Your husband is handsome, strong... he's away at the Eastern Front.'

'Yes, how did you know?'

I smile. The Germans were pushing hard to make advances in Russia before I was sent to Auschwitz. An easy guess.

'He's cold, *so cold*,' I continue, rolling my tongue for dramatic effect. 'But his heart warms when he thinks of you and...'

'Else.'

'*Ja*, Else.' I circle her palm with my fingers, 'Ah, he's writing you a letter... *victory will come soon—*'

A commotion in the railcar grabs my attention as unhappy passengers make way for the two SS men rambling down the aisle, laughing and harassing them with *Heil Hitler*.

No, I've *got* to get that apple.

'He'll be home soon, I promise.' I reach out to snatch the apple from her basket, but the SS guard yells at me to stand up as the train comes to a stop. *What, so soon?* He grabs my arm and drags me down the aisle toward the exit.

'You forgot your apple, *Fräulein!*'

The young woman tosses the apple to me, but the SS man catches it in mid-air, then sneers. He takes a bite out of the precious fruit before dragging me off the train. I nearly fall to my knees, but I refuse to beg. Scowling, he's not finished with me. He tosses the apple onto the wooden platform. I make a grab for it, my knees wobbling, and collapse. I don't care. I hold the half-eaten apple to my chest and eat it hungrily while the two German soldiers make disgusting comments.

Swine. Dirty French whore.

I don't care. The mushy texture coats my dry mouth, soothing my lips. It's delicious, the sweet, juicy scent filling my nostrils.

'*Steh auf, Fräulein!* Get up!'

My joy is short-lived when they pull me to my feet. It's then I see the placard hanging from the station depot. A city I've never heard of.

Dachau.

46

DACHAU – KAUFERING I, 2003

Angéline

Perfume:
Dancing Princess
Wild marigold, peach, oakmoss

'I never forgot the succulent taste of that apple, *mademoiselle*... the sugary smell, its smooth texture on my tongue... the fullness settling in my belly. After the war, I created a perfume that evoked the light feeling of apple blossoms in the spring,' I tell Emma, her mouth open in shock after hearing my train story. 'My way of taking a dark moment and soothing my soul.'

'Crawling on your *knees* to grab a dirty apple? An apple with SS spit on it?' She meets my gaze head on. 'I'd have smashed the apple into his—'

'Then you'd be dead, Emma, your hands slick with your own blood when they shot you.' I look out the side window when the motorcar stops. We're here where underground cement bunkers once stood and thousands of Jewish prisoners worked and died. 'It's simple to fight back with words when you're safe in your own skin, *mademoiselle*. But when your gut is twisting because you've seen what a bullet, a knife can do to the human body, when you gag on the stench of rotting flesh, then you can talk. For too long survivors have been criticized for choices we made. Which is why I want you to *feel, smell, taste* what surviving means.'

She simmers down. 'Forgive me, *madame*, I was wrong.'

My directness sobers her up, her mouth twitching. I hear her mumbling as Ryker opens the passenger door, helping me out of the motorcar, then Emma. *He heard every word*, his eyes tell me, but he remains silent. He's not one to sugarcoat things, even for her.

We follow the stone path in silence around the open area which was once Kaufering I, one of eleven sub-camps of Dachau. There are a few markers, a stone fence with a Jewish memorial gate... but nothing else left. We'll tour the main camp of Dachau later, pay our respects, visit the museum, and listen to the audio tour. The driver told us the barracks have been rebuilt, that everything is cleaned up, which is why we've come here first so Emma can absorb what I saw, lived through. I'd get on my hands and knees if I thought I could find the wooden hut where my child was born, so aware I am of the power this place has over me.

I point out where I believe it was... then the dark basement cell where I was first brought, the kitchen where I worked – guesses on my part, but my heart-breaking moment is having a potent effect on Emma, forcing her to see how desperate you get when you want to live. That it's easy to spout words of defiance. It's a lot different to do it. *Bon*. I've shaken up her world. Now she'll put it down in her story in a way that's dark and powerful and strong.

She keeps looking at me with wary eyes, their familiar blue sending me off again on a whisper of recognition that spikes my blood pressure. I'm a foolish old woman, reading something into her presence because I want to. I need her. I've folded her under my wing because I have no one to bond with like other survivors, family who experienced the horror of the camps. *Mon amour* understood, but he's gone. I thought

I'd put the camps behind me, but it never goes away... I never cut the cord that bound me to this place.

Dachau. Today I shall.

'I wanted to... *needed* to survive, *mademoiselle*. For my baby.'

Emma remains quiet, her eyes focused on recording in her mind what she sees, smells. No flowers... dirt getting up our noses. She sniffs, sneezes. She's as uncomfortable as I am. My nerves are unraveling. I told her the apple story because it set the stage for what happened to me here. Hope then fear... then pain and having the courage to do whatever it took to survive. Crawl when I had to. By then I was numb to everything except... my baby kicking.

'I'm beyond words, *madame*. Your determination and courage and frank words put me off on a different course for this part of your story.' She thinks a moment. 'Weren't you in more danger, *madame,* with the baby coming? You were... eight months?'

'Yes. I couldn't imagine why I'd been sent here to this sub-camp and didn't find out until after the liberation that the Red Army was moving in on Auschwitz and would liberate the camp early in 1945, that a shift in thinking was taking place in the Nazi High Command. They needed bargaining chips for what looked like defeat... I was one of those chips.'

Emma lets out a low whistle. 'Talk about dropping a bombshell, *madame*. I'm all ears.'

'I've never told anyone this part of my story, *mademoiselle*. When a reporter asked me about the camps, I always admitted to being imprisoned at Dachau. I never mentioned Kaufering.'

'Which is why that Hansen woman accused you of lying. She couldn't find you on the prisoner list for Dachau because thousands of prisoners were never registered, *n'est-ce pas?*'

I smile. She *does* take copious notes.

'That's why she wants to see your number,' she continues, 'so she can track you down.'

We look at each other with a moment of fear. I don't believe we've seen the end of that reporter, especially after I make my special announcement about my plans for the House of Doujan when we return to Paris. I shan't worry Emma about that now.

'The number of French imprisoned at Dachau were a handful,' I say. 'I never did find out if any were women. The SS guards dropped me off at the sub-camp, hustling me into a basement prison cell holding pregnant women. A single light bulb hanging from the ceiling burned hot night and day. One by one they came, until we were eight. Hungarian Jewish women and me. Oh, *mademoiselle*, I can't tell you the endless flow of tears we enjoyed every time a new woman came down those steps into our world.'

'How long were you held underground in the basement?'

I close my eyes. 'A week... maybe two. I remember the terrifying fear we suffered when SS guards bolted into the basement and ordered us *Raus!* We held onto each other, determined not to let them separate us. They moved us to a wooden hut. No heat, windows covered with tarp. We thought that was the end, but it became our birthing place.'

'Did you work in the camp? You were in your last trimester... you couldn't lift and carry stones, bricks.'

I open my eyes and wiggle my nose. 'We washed prisoners' clothing in the laundry, ridding them of the stink and vermin with brown soap, the smell reminding me of mothballs. A brave prisoner, the *kapo* in charge of the kitchen, risked his life to bring us enough food to keep us *and* our unborn babies healthy. And I'll never forget the valiant young girl from Latvia, also a prisoner, who suffered a beating at the hands of the SS to get us a stove and then rags for our babies.'

'The Nazis sanctioned your efforts to have your children?' Emma asks, writing on her pad. 'What made them change their minds after they'd gone to great length to murder pregnant prisoners?'

'With the limited Hungarian I picked up at Augsburg, I pieced together the facts from the other prisoners. The Nazis were aware their days were numbered, they were evacuating prisoners, erasing their horrible deeds with mass murder. Most likely they wanted to save their own skins, so they decided to show "compassion" for us in our last stages of pregnancy.'

'Eight pregnant moms... please tell me eight healthy babies were delivered?' Emma asks, hopeful.

I smile at her, ever the optimist pushing for a happy ending. 'You have a way, Mademoiselle Keane, of disarming me.'

'Guilty as charged, *madame*.' She grins.

What am I going to do without her?

* * *

Emma

Madame is a rebel with an amazing cause.

Outspoken, opinioned, righteous... and spot on calling me out like she did. I write the stories, I don't live them. I have no business sticking my opinion into the piece, even if it *is* my family we're talking about. I can't wait to tell her that, though we had tense moments when she relived the apple scene and my rant made her flinch. I got caught up in the moment but she's right, I *don't* know what it's like to stare down two SS men when you're half-starved and pregnant. Yet it's up to me to make my readers and my viewers feel like *they're* living in *her* skin.

Wow, did I get a lesson today. Ryker gave me that 'You can't fool *madame*' look while remaining vigilant but supportive. What also hit home is how much I've come to rely upon him. His smarts, his skills... his good looks don't hurt either. But today, it's his compassion that comforts me, whispering to me it's 'okay to mess up' and 'she admires your passion'.

Which brings me back to doing my job. Getting down the facts on the *Schwanger Kommando* – Pregnancy Unit – and bringing alive the emotional journey of *madame* and these women and their miracle babies.

Ryker brings us bottled water from the cooler and the three of us sit down on a stone bench under overhanging trees, a place to contemplate, meditate. And perfect to continue our interview, the spirit of every woman who walked here more than fifty years ago listening, nodding. And, I hope, smiling that *madame* is telling their story.

'December winds howled and shook our wooden hut at night, snow covering the ground in the morning,' *madame* says, sipping her water. 'I got bigger by the day; my back ached and I developed a constant sniffle, my overworked nose hurting so much from the acrid smells, it bled. The kitchen *kapo* told me he'd stored dried herbs from the Nazis' garden at Dachau in a makeshift root cellar. I went mad crushing dried basil leaves on my bread, hoping to induce labor, and consumed peppermint tea to calm me. I used my herbal knowledge to help the other mothers, Maman's hand on my shoulder guiding me, but I wouldn't have survived if it hadn't been for the Jewish doctor who never gave up on us.'

'You had a *doctor* to deliver the babies... amazing.'

'Yes, the SS officer in charge found a Hungarian Jewish gynecologist, also a prisoner. He suffered from malnutrition and couldn't stand without help, but we all pulled together each time one of us went into labor.'

'And you, *madame?*' I ask, my voice becoming thoughtful but excited. 'When was your time?'

Her eyes grow bright and the way she's clasping her hands to her chest tells me this is a moment she's waited for years to relive. 'I shall never forget the day, *mademoiselle*, when I held my baby daughter for the first time. It was December 28, 1944.'

* * *

Angéline

"'Push, *Fräulein*, push! I won't let you die... or your baby," the doctor assured me, his warm, deep voice bringing me something I so desperately needed. *Faith*. That I wasn't alone in my struggle, that my baby had a chance to give me that first smile,' I say to Emma, the words echoing in my ears from long ago.

'How long were you in labor?' Emma asks.

'Hours... a day... longer.'

Lance, mon amour, *do you hear me? It's time...* I called out then as I do now.

I want to share with you that moment when our little girl was born, how our journey culminated on this night in the birth of our child... and yes, my love, this young woman also belongs to us, the blush burning her cheeks telling me Emma feels the connection, too, but doesn't know what to make of it. That our story has a new ending.

'Outside, a howling snowstorm raged, shaking the wooden rafters,' I continue, 'the old stove pumping out whatever heat it could. Someone threw a blanket over my shoulders as I paced the floor of the hut, holding my back with one hand, clutching what was left of my blue ribbon with the other, the contractions getting closer together... a Hungarian mother wiping my brow, another holding my arm to keep me steady... then my water broke. The doctor assured me the baby was in the right position and ready to... how do you say... pop?'

Emma laughs. 'Oh, *madame*, only you could make that work.'

I sigh, grateful for the lighter moment between us. I feel comfortable sharing everything with her. After a lifetime of not trusting, always being suspicious, I'm not used to having support, someone I can rely on... yes, I have Ryker, but a woman's ear is so essential to sharing the trials of birth. The pain, the first cry. We hold that sacred, the sentimental smell of a newborn infant. It can't be duplicated.

Or ever forgotten.

Like the memory of chubby cheeks and the cutest bow mouth. No, not ever... not even decades later. I never let anyone close enough before. And it feels good. Grateful tears spring to my eyes as I continue, 'I shall never forget the fear, the gut-wrenching pain as if I was being torn apart, *mademoiselle*, but the pain was welcome. It meant new life, not death. I wasn't giving up, even though the doctor had no instruments... a few rags and a bucket of hot water.'

'Anesthetic?' she breathes, incredulous.

'None. I lay on a wooden bench, the doctor urging me to push and keep pushing, ready to grab the infant with his bare hands,' I tell Emma with a forward thrust of my clenched fists, then heave out a big breath. 'The skies rumbled overhead... thunder? Or Allied bombers? We knew they were coming... American, British, Russian... *when*? Then, with one last push, Naomie Fleurine came into this world, sweetness and joy, chubby cheeks and a loud cry. Then I had a strange thought. My baby would never know the humiliation of having a prisoner number tattooed on her thigh. My baby was born free. Then I sobbed my eyes out.'

We sit together in silence, holding hands, the trees fluttering overhead, their rustling sound like the wings of angels sweeping away the past so I can embrace the future. I had my say. I'm done. Time to move on.

Finally, Emma asks, 'Were the births documented, *madame*?'

'Yes, the doctor recorded seven live births at Kaufering I, four girls and three boys, but because I was Roma and should have been exterminated as per Himmler's orders, he omitted my name. I never appeared in the camp diary.'

'Ah, ha, another roadblock to keep that Hansen woman out of your family business. And mine.'

She keeps writing her notes, making me smile, not realizing she confirmed what's been sitting on the edge of my brain since this interview started. Somehow, this charming young *mademoiselle* is related to me. How, I don't know, but I can't stop tears from forming in my eyes. The signs are there... the unique blue color of her eyes, her incredible ability as a nose... her obstinance so like mine. I'm overjoyed, but we're not finished yet. There's one more dark character in my story who made her appearance in Kaufering.

'So far, I've only told you the "good parts", as you like to say, about our bonding as pregnant mothers, *mademoiselle*... Emma.' I like saying her name. 'There's also a sinister, underlying element that choked my soul... a human being who epitomized the cruelty of the Nazi doctrine.'

'A German officer, *madame*?'

'Yes... an SS woman.'

She turns to me, shocked. 'A woman?'

'Berta was an SS guard assigned to the laundry, a yellowish-blonde with hair that never looked combed, thick black brows. She strutted around with a gun in her holster, her whip in her right hand, ready to strike any female prisoner who slacked even for a minute.' I heave out a sigh. 'I felt her wrath more than once when she came close to striking my belly. My baby kicked wildly every time that woman came near me. I could see a hatred in her eyes for me, the other pregnant women, as if we had something she wanted. Wanted badly.'

I slump down, lower my head. I'm exhausted.

Emma hugs me. 'I'm here, *madame*, she can't hurt you now.'

I smile at her. '*Merci, mon enfant*, but it's important you understand this woman. Berta loved perfume and sprayed herself with scent. She found the smells in the laundry unbearable, bragging how her "lover" brought her expensive perfumes from Paris. She also bragged about how she knew what was in each perfume by sniffing it. My nose was overwhelmed by so many smells, but even with my hands in hot water I'd rattle off the composition of the perfume she wore *and* the name if I recognized the fragrance from the House of Doujan. She hated me because I made a fool out of her in front of the other prisoners and they laughed at her.'

'Then what happened, *madame*?'

'She became incensed when I said she knew nothing about perfume or how to wear it.'

'Did she retaliate against you?'

'She threatened to beat me, but a young SS female guard reminded her it was against orders to harm a pregnant prisoner and she'd report her. That gave me hope my baby had a chance to be born safe and healthy.'

'You mean the SS women weren't all horrible?'

'No, this girl worked in a dress shop before she was conscripted into the SS. She was fascinated by my stories about Paris and that I was a real *parfumier*. She'd smuggle extra food to me in her wide jacket pockets.'

'Do you remember her name?'

'Luise.'

Emma's hand goes to her throat. 'Are you sure, *madame*?'

'Yes. She wore her dark hair wrapped around her head in a long braid and she was thin and flat-chested, something Berta never let her forget. That she wasn't the robust German ideal and couldn't bear many children for the Führer.'

Emma's gone pale, her face is sweaty and she's stopped writing.

'Are you okay, *mademoiselle*?'

'I understand now. No one would believe an SS woman helped you after Dachau was liberated. The horror, the shame, the townspeople ordered by US Army soldiers to bury the dead, the naked prisoners. The fear of imprisonment. But she followed her heart and did what was right.'

'Did what, *mademoiselle*?'

'Saved your baby.'

Now it's my turn to feel a rush of excitement like I've never known. 'What *are* you talking about, *mademoiselle*?' Yes, I recognized Luise in the photo in the piece Emma wrote, but I can't see how she saved my child.

I must have been sitting in the sun too long. I feel faint.

'I can't tell you more than that, *madame*, until I get more details about what happened after your baby was born... then I will. I promise.'

She clams up, puts down her yellow pad. I know Emma well enough she meant what she said. She's a reporter and she wants to get her facts straight before opening up to me.

It's time for us to go, leave this place with more questions than when we came here. I intended to close the final chapter here... but that's not to be. Our day at Kaufering ends on an unbelievable note, that Emma is telling me Luise saved my child? *How?* I've never forgotten that day, every minute, every wild moment of pain and agony when I never saw my baby daughter again.

Ryker helps me stand, but I'm shaking so badly I collapse in his arms. This new revelation is too much for me. He picks me up and carries me back to the motorcar and I'm reminded I *am* a woman of a certain age, but I'll be damned if I'm going to let that stop me. I have big plans for the House of Doujan... for Emma.

We drive to our hotel in Dachau in silence. Emma checking over her notes, mumbling to herself, *Of course, it makes sense, why didn't I see it?*

Then, over strong tea spiked with lemon and raspberry leaves, I tell Emma the rest of my story, the Nazis' desperation to cover their murderous tracks, how Berta's hatred of me escalated, and the unbelievable horror that followed when in April 1945, I and the seven Hungarian mothers and our babies were put on a train taking us to the main camp at Dachau. We had no idea an order had come down weeks earlier to send us to Bergen-Belsen.

To be executed.

But the order wasn't carried out. Until now.

We were we on our way to our deaths.

47

DACHAU – KAUFERING I, 26 APRIL 1945

Angéline

Perfume:
Fleurine
Angelica, honeysuckle, lavender

I watch the SS woman with dogged focus, her strong scent of jasmine and civet making me retch as Nazi guards load several hundred prisoners onto the open train wagons. Berta revels in seeing me wait my turn, clutching my baby to my chest, bundled in rags to keep out the cold, her tiny face peeking out from under the cloth. I thank God she's healthy. The *kapo* kept us mothers supplied with milk and food, though our backs were breaking from carrying dead bodies, the Nazis insisting we keep working. I have a desperate need to keep us both alive and lay my hand across my baby's tiny chest to feel her heartbeat, not wanting to believe it can be stilled by what awaits us.

It's late in the day with an inevitable twilight casting an eerie glow on the guard's face. She won't stop staring. I cradle my baby, swaying her back and forth. My child is hungry, waving her arms about, what's left of my blue ribbon circling her wrist. I can't open my bodice to feed her. The way that SS woman leers at me taking my baby to my breast is obscene.

It sends shudders through me.

My gaze is fixed on her, so I don't see the SS guard until he pushes me into the railcar with fifty, sixty prisoners. I'm crushed between two women, the smell of dried-up urine lingering on the straw covering the floor of the railcar makes me gag. I shield Fleurine's tiny nose from the stink, but she won't stop crying. It's been three, four hours since I fed her. They evacuated us from the camp at Kaufering, made us march to the train in the snow, some with no shoes, SS men flanking us, dogs barking. I couldn't believe my luck when Luise showed up, smiling when she found me and helped carry Fleurine. Then she said something I'll never forget... that she's ashamed she didn't do more to help me... and she was sorry... so very sorry.

When we arrived at the train installation, eighteen... nineteen empty wagon cars waited for us.

Where are we going? I asked her.

To Dachau, she whispered, then disappeared.

I almost lost hope then. They're sending us to Dachau to murder us.

Berta knew, smiling a slow smile so sadistic it twisted her face, leaving me feeling helpless against the Nazis, my sense of happiness and joy at being a mother replaced by a rapid fear.

Huddled in the shadows of the wagon car, her words are a brutal reminder of how cruel the Nazis can be, sending us to another camp when the Allies are so close. They crossed the Rhine weeks ago, according to the rumors going around camp, and the Russians are bombing Berlin.

The train rambles down the track, the *clickety-clack* grating on my nerves, the pungent smell of fear, the insufferable wailing... When the train screeches to a halt, its big, heavy wheels spark on the tracks... the sizzling tracers hissing in my ears. We can't be at Dachau yet, then I hear *zug steckt fest*, train stuck. I pray it's not for long. Fleurine is sleeping, thank God, when the unthinkable rattles my soul.

Loud buzzing overhead fills my ears with a thunderous roar. I lean forward, desperate to see—

Allied bombers, flying low.

Shrieking prisoners hang out the open wagon car, mouths open... amazement, joy... then horror when the bombers strafe the train. The *rat-a-tat-tat* sends everyone into panic, pushing, shoving... jumping off the stopped train.

Why? We're prisoners... civilians.

Then I'm drawn into a horrific conclusion that sinks my heart.

They don't know... they don't know.

Fleurine won't stop crying, waving her tiny hands, her body shaking. I have to make a decision.

Stay or jump.

I turn to a man dressed in a prison striped uniform, begging him to hold my baby. He nods. I kick off my wooden clogs and my feet barely hit the ground when SS guards start shooting at prisoners running in every direction with a madness that chills me. The prisoner leans down, hands me Fleurine, then jumps and runs off. Darkness is descending, but I can't let that stop me, nor can I let the screaming of prisoners hit by bullets deter me.

I can run... *run free.*

'Not so fast, *Fräulein.*'

I spin around. It's Berta, her pistol drawn, aimed at Fleurine's head.

'Let me go,' I shout, anger replacing my fear. 'Those are American bombers. The war's over. You and your Nazi friends are finished.'

She snarls. 'Give... me... the baby.'

'No, *never.*' I hold her tighter to my chest.

'Give her to me *now* or I'll shoot you *and* her.'

'You wouldn't.'

'Try me, *Fräulein.*' She bares her teeth, an expression I can only describe as like a bitch in heat flashes across her face. 'Who's going to notice two more dead prisoners?'

I swallow, but my throat is so dry I spit the words at her. 'Why can't you leave us alone? My child means nothing to you.'

'She's *everything* to me, *Fräulein*. Perfect and fair-haired.'

She looks at my daughter, her hand shaking, but the grief in her eyes tells me what I didn't see before. She flaunts her body as though she's the Aryan ideal, but she can't have children. She's failed the Führer, so she wants Fleurine. Then why is she threatening my baby, holding the barrel of the gun against her head?

Because I'm dealing with a woman who revels in the joy of killing like some people do making love. She seeks the only way she knows how to regain her place in the Third Reich. Take the child, claim her as her own. She can't see the Nazi regime crumbling around her. Or she won't. She's desperate. And that makes her dangerous. To me. To my baby. She *will* kill Fleurine if I don't do what she asks.

I make a decision I will have to live with.

Give her what she wants... for now.

I die for a long moment, my heart breaking, tears stinging my cheeks, but I slowly open my arms and hand over my daughter. I pay no attention to the screaming around me, gunfire from the SS, the planes diving overhead, strafing the train and creating chaos.

All I see is my baby reaching for me, arms outstretched, eyes wide, tiny mouth quivering.

A loud sob escapes my lips. I *have* to let her go or lose her forever.

'Now run, *Fräulein*. Run for your life!'

'You won't get away with this... I *will* find you.'

'You'll never find her and that will be your hell, *Fräulein*, I won't kill you. I'd rather see you suffer knowing she's alive, but never knowing *where* she is. Now run, before I change my mind and shoot you both.'

She fires off a shot that rips through my billowing dress and barely misses my leg. *What choice do I have?* If she wounds me, I'll bleed to death in the snow. *No*, I have to take the chance she's so insanely needy for a child of her own, she'll keep to her word, not harm my baby and someday, somehow, I *will* find Fleurine.

I'll never stop looking for you, *ma petite*. I promise you.

With a kiss and a prayer to my baby, I race off into the dark, bullets whizzing by my head. Escaping prisoners dropping around me, dead bodies everywhere. I can't die here. *I won't.* I pull off the boots of a dead SS man killed by the strafing bullets to keep my feet warm. Mercifully, I'm not hit before I reach the dense forest.

I seek shelter under a large, hanging branch touching the ground, keeping out the chill, the wind. Another prisoner joins me... a Czech... then a German Jewish woman... we huddle together, holding on to each other, our body heat keeping us from freezing, hiding in the forest until light, then walking east. Toward Dachau by the position of the sun... stumbling, getting up, but I keep going. I have to find my child... then wild, crazy emotions roll over me when we hear the roar of motorcar engines racing over the terrain... two open vehicles with huge tires and large white stars painted on the hoods coming straight toward us, half a dozen soldiers armed with rifles inside.

The motorcars stop and a soldier jumps out. 'Raise your hands above your heads!'

My heart stops. *Americans.*

I fall to the ground. 'Help us, please!' I shout in English. 'We're prisoners from Dachau.'

'Prisoners? Dachau?'

The soldier pushes his helmet off his forehead. He has no idea what I'm talking about. I want to cry but my tears are long spent for the dead, but not for the prisoners still alive. I pray it's not too late. If there's justice in men's hearts, these soldiers will discover the horror at Dachau and every camp the Nazis so carefully orchestrated to keep hidden from the world. They will save lives and bury the dead.

And then tell the world what they saw here.

The soldier approaches me, sees my torn clothes, short hair... the number tattooed on my arm. 'My God, what have those bastards done to you?' He chokes up, then yells, 'Medic, I need help here.' Then he takes off his jacket and wraps it around me. I collapse in the American soldier's arms, delirious.

'My baby... please find my baby.'

48

PARIS, 2003

Emma

Perfume:
Velvet Nights
Blue Himalayan poppy, jasmine, ambergris

The story is far from over.

I can only guess what happened when the transport train arrived in Dachau. Luise somehow wrestled *madame's* baby away from that SS woman Berta, but where it goes from there I'm still working on. I need to hear my grandpa's version of the story again. Also, Granger wants a bio of Madame de Cadieux pronto. *Interest in her story is building around the world*, he said, and he wants to expand the interview to more than a fluff piece.

His words, not mine.

Which brings me to this moment. We're back in Paris. The three of us. Ryker is at *madame's* side as we prepare for today's press conference at the House of Doujan, but his eyes are on me. We haven't had much time to talk since we returned from Dachau, but we've forged a new bond between us. Seems we're both too pigheaded for our own good and needed a wise woman like *madame* to bring us together.

Now to help her. Today is the day I tell *madame* about my personal connection to Dachau. That somehow I believe what Luise told my grandpop was a lie, a way to protect *madame's* baby from that SS woman ever finding her.

That I believe I'm her granddaughter.

I'm teetering between hope and despair, courage and fear. There's something else.

It's Mom.

She needs me. I'm having a major guilt trip I'm not on a plane back to Philly. When I called my dad last night to check on her, he started sobbing. The news isn't good. Mom is drifting in and out of consciousness and her body is losing the fight. The cancer spread. My blood chills every time I think of my beautiful mother lying in a hospital bed, her body ravaged by an enemy she can't fight.

Still, I've got to see this through. As soon as we wrap up the press conference, I'll fly home and pray I can convince *madame* to come with me. I can't prove my theory, but *madame* needs to know before it's too late.

Until then, I can't let on the insanity tearing me apart inside. *Madame* is as excited as a little girl at her first ballet recital, promising me a 'major news event' and the perfect 'tag' to my story (did she pick that up from me?). I wander around the famous perfume shop with ivory, ribbed-silk walls, plush red carpet, and a raised Art Deco medallion on the ceiling. Two large picture windows face Rue St Honoré with natural light to showcase the gorgeous displays of *madame's* perfumes.

Naomie's Dream.

Angéline.

Y.

The décor is so luxurious. Naomie-blue velvet méridienne, Louis XIV white velvet chairs... and a round Napoleonic table in the center. *Madame* flits around the shop, waving away the salesgirls dying to peek under the silk tent hiding the special display, a secret she'll reveal at today's news conference.

She won't even tell me what it is. I can't wait.

'We did it, Emma, thanks to you,' *madame* says, straightening her silver lamé gown, a single Hungarian red rose pinned to her shoulder, white gloves. Her red hair pulled back with feathery bangs. No one does glam like *madame*, but I still see that fiery Roma girl in the rustling skirts and red petticoat jangling her bracelet. Then the Paris sophisticate in Yvette's black braided coat. I often wonder if that coat made it through the war.

'*We* did it?' I ask, not understanding. 'What do you mean, *madame*?'

'I can let go of my past and embrace what I spent a lifetime building.' She turns to me, eyes shining. 'I almost lost it because I let an old woman's loneliness take over my life instead of opening myself up to new ventures.' She gives me the V sign. 'Which is why we're here today. *To shake things up*, as you Americans say.'

'Before you set the world on fire, as we Americans *also* like to say,' I tease, 'I have one more question.' I grab my yellow pad for the last time, my fingers tingling. Am I already getting nostalgic and we're not finished yet? 'Tell me how you rose to such heights as a *parfumier* after the war. I want to hear it from you, not take it from a press kit.'

'You do?'

'Yes. Please.'

She pulls in a deep breath. 'I worked hard after the war, *mademoiselle*, reading... studying every book the professor gave me... taking classes in chemistry and always... *always* challenging my nose with new scents, expanding my range of smell. I learned how to sniff out the nuances of innumerable ingredients that make up perfume... then used my imagination to think outside the box to create the magic.' She pauses. 'By the 1970s, I was riding high at the House of Doujan. I was in my early fifties and the horror of the concentration camps was behind me. I was a sophisticate with a loving husband and a perfume empire to run. I had it all.' She holds her hand over her heart, going misty-eyed on me. 'If you'll allow a sentimental old fool to recount a moment I've

358   JINA BACARR

never buried, a moment I think about often... when Lance and I were reunited after the war.'

'Yes, *madame*, please!'

'Paris was lit up again with the heart of France shining on the boulevards, in the cafés, stars sprinkled overhead when my train pulled into Gare de l'Est. Lance was waiting for me with roses and a motorcar and a place in his arms *for always*, he told me. He'd wanted to come and get me at the US Army processing office in Munich, but the truth was I needed time to decompress, find my way back home again in my mind, deal with the loss of my baby... and make myself pretty for him.' She runs her hand through her hair. 'My hair was still short, my skin baked a golden tan by the sun... my body thin but my breasts full, though my milk soon dried up from the trauma. None of that mattered when Lance swept me into his muscular arms, holding me by the waist, our bodies radiating heat as we melted into one. And we stayed that way... as one for nearly fifty years.'

'The world was yours, *madame*.'

'We were more successful than ever with the evolution of the British and French pop scene and the youth market in the sixties, then the world of disco in the seventies, and the return of padded shoulders and power dressing in the eighties. My marketing schemes included asking women to take quizzes to find out which perfume suited them, cute young models in mini-skirts and go-go boots handing out free samples in the Galeries Lafayette department store. I discovered I had a knack for reading our customers' needs and the House of Doujan filled them. We made price changes to fit with the younger crowd and I couldn't have asked for a better staff...' Her voice catches. 'Though I lost the professor years earlier.'

'What about Monsieur Baptiste? How did you take over running the company?'

'Frederic was in and out of treatment for an alcohol problem, but he redeemed himself with the press by writing his memoir, wording it so *he* was the victim of Nazi oppression.'

'And you didn't object?'

'He was a dying man, *mademoiselle*, and didn't baulk when his father, Jean-Claude, left me the controlling interest in the company. He saw it as a way of asking for my forgiveness.'

'And did you... forgive him?'

'After the misery of humanity I'd seen in the camps, I didn't want any more suffering.' She sighs. 'And we're at a crossroads again.'

'We are?'

'We've reached the end of the interview. You know everything about me, the war, the camps, *mon amour*. I'd like to know more about you, *mademoiselle*.'

'It's true I've been keeping something from you. Ryker and I figured out one is a lonely number and we want to continue seeing each other.'

She laughs. 'Why am I not surprised?' She squeezes my hand, winks. 'He's a good man, Emma.'

'There's something else, too. I planned to wait, but Mom's taken a turn for the worse and I need to be there, back to Philly...' I stumble over the words. I force my gaze away from the shocked look on her face. What would she say if I tell her I'm sure *madame* is my grandmother? It fits. Luise stumbling over her story... changing facts, then recanting. My crazy scent obsession... it skips generations, *madame* said. We *have* to be family... I feel it in my nose... and yes, that's silly pun, but it's true. I want to tell her... should tell her... I'll wait till after the press conference.

'Madame de Cadieux, the press is getting jumpy,' Henri-Justin interrupts, nodding toward the throng of reporters craning their necks to get a good angle and snap our photos. I see Brooke Hansen's shaggy mop among them. I swing a look over to Ryker, my eyes questioning. He nods, moves in toward her.

That's my man.

'I'll be right there.' *Madame* turns to me. She looks visibly shaken; I've never seen her so pale. She flutters her eyelashes, then recovers her poise and draws me into a warm embrace, the exquisite, top lemony-peach note of her perfume capturing me with one whiff. 'Of course, Emma, you must leave right after the press conference.' *How can I convince her to come with me?* 'I'll have Henri-Justin make the flight arrangements, but first I have a surprise for *you*.'

'You do?'

'We're relaunching *Le Courage* with the original 1943 formula. Perfume, cologne, lotions... even bath soap.'

'Oh, *madame*, what can I say?'

She takes my hand, tears misting her eyes. 'Let's announce the news together. Make it a family affair.'

* * *

Angéline

'*Mesdames and messieurs*, ladies and gentleman of the press,' I announce in both French and English, 'welcome to the House of Doujan. I'm Angéline de Cadieux, *parfumier*. Or, as I'm known around the lab, head nose.'

Laughter.

'I've called this press conference to announce an exciting new venture... *bien*, a fragrance I had the privilege of launching during the war when the women of Paris needed a perfume to heal their spirits, give them hope.' I pause for effect, catch Emma's eye. She's attempting to smile, but her lower lip is quivering. She looked shocked when I revealed my connection to her. *I'm* still reeling over the news about her *maman*. It hit me like a punch in the gut. *My baby daughter*, I'm certain of it. She needs me. *How* this came about is what I don't understand. I clear my throat. 'We're relaunching *Le Courage*, a perfume I created during the dark days of 1943.'

Applause, cheers.

'I, like many women, found myself mired in questioning whether or not I was valued at my age, whether I had the courage to keep going during my own dark days. Then this charming young *mademoiselle* came into my life at a time when I needed her most. I owe my newfound spirit to the courage and investigative skills of my grand-daughter, Mademoiselle Emma Keane, from New York.'

The amazed look on Emma's face is priceless.

Murmuring... flashbulbs going off. Questions from the crowd.

I turn to the reporters, their jaws dropping, then the onslaught of flashbulbs going off in our faces. '*Merci, mes amis* for coming today and I look forward to seeing you at the relaunch of *Le Courage*. Until then, *à bientôt*. My granddaughter and I have a plane to catch.'

I smile, promise them a press release explaining everything, then someone pops the champagne, calling the interview to an end.

Brooke Hansen gulps down a flute of champagne, then plants her big feet in my space. 'She's a fake, Madame de Cadieux,' she insists in her usual obnoxious manner. 'She's lying, telling you a cock and bull story to get your trust.'

I lift my chin, defiant. 'I don't believe you.'

'Then believe this.' Brooke is on a roll. 'She interviewed a woman who claimed to know you from Dachau... pumped her for information so she could get close to you and get an exclusive about your time in the camps during the war.'

I turn to Emma. 'Is this true, *mademoiselle*?' I *know* she did the inter-view, but I want to hear her side.

'Yes, I *did* speak with a woman in a nursing home for a story about Holocaust survivors... she was suffering from dementia, her memory lapsing into the past with moments so vivid and clear, as if it were yesterday, calling herself Luise. When I asked her if she knew a Polish prisoner who had a baby, she panicked and rambled on about a Frenchwoman and *her* child. A *parfumier*. I couldn't corroborate her story so I didn't pursue it, though I wanted to. I kept looking for a survivor from the camps who might have known my grandmother... which is why I sought you out, *madame,* because you were at Dachau at the same time. Anything you could tell me would help my mom find closure. I never dreamed *you* were my grandmother until you told me the real story about Luise. I believe she told the lie to my grandpop to protect your child.'

I feel a moment of hope what she said is true, but we'll never know the whole story.

'I was desperate to find my baby when the American soldiers rescued me,' I add. 'I told them an SS woman had stolen my child so they had no reason to question prisoners. They kept me in a medical unit until I was strong enough to travel, then I made my way to Dachau and searched for Luise, but she'd disappeared. After what you told me, I believe she saved herself *and* my baby by donning a prison dress. Why not? The women at Dachau weren't tattooed, she was thin... drawn... and when she chopped off her hair, *who would know*? She kept a low profile, praying someone didn't recognize her as an SS woman, then escaped dressed as a prisoner.'

'What amazes me, *madame*,' Emma adds, 'is I had the answer and I never knew it. When you came to New York, I thought I'd try one more time to find out if you were that Frenchwoman and had crossed paths with my grandmother, but I had to get close to you, find out everything about you. If I'm guilty of anything, *madame*, it's wanting to know the truth.'

'*Mon Dieu*. Of course, you had no idea who Luise was.'

'Not until I made the connection when you told me at Kaufering about the SS woman with that name. Then I was absolutely sure of the connection between us.' Emma turns to the female reporter. 'Satisfied, Mademoiselle Hansen?'

'No,' Brooke is stewing. 'You don't have definitive proof you're related to Madame de Cadieux.'

'What more do you need?' Emma challenges her.

'Get a DNA sample.'

'That won't be necessary, *mademoiselle*.' I feel my lips curve, in a moment I may even bare my teeth I'm so angry. The woman's insistent prying into my life has to stop *now*. 'I have no doubt Mademoiselle Emma Keane is my granddaughter,' I say in a firm tone, 'and I *don't* need DNA to prove it.'

'How can you be so sure?' Brooke scowls.

'Emma Keane is a nose, *mademoiselle*, and a brilliant connoisseur of scent like I am. *Nothing* is more conclusive in my mind than that.'

Making a face, she turns on her heel and stomps off. *Good riddance.*

Oh, my, I've stirred the pot and there's no telling where this will lead. When I see Emma's grateful smile, I'm damn glad I did.

49

PHILADELPHIA, 2003

Angéline

Perfume:
Le Bel Ange
Jasmine, rose, cedarwood

A mob of reporters bombards me with questions, surrounding me in a tight circle when I arrive at the University Hospital. My head is swimming. Panic squeezes my heart. I never dreamed my story would garner this much attention in the States. I'm all over the evening news with glamorous photos of me in Paris, intercut with black and white stills from concentration camps and newscasters reporting on my amazing reunion with my granddaughter.

Emma.

She's been on her cell phone in constant communication with her dad and the hospital. It's touch and go. She's holding onto me, keeping my spirits up with her engaging smile, with Ryker clearing the path ahead of us, ever vigilant should there be trouble. I don't intend to back down from any controversy, but I'll be damned if *anyone* will keep me from seeing my daughter.

The Concorde flight from Paris was uneventful with a lot of hand-holding, whispering, then prayers and hot coffee. So many times, I felt Lance's presence, his strength and daring reminding me I'm stronger than I think, that age has nothing to do with what Emma calls 'moxie' and I'm one hell of an old broad.

Did you hear that, *mon amour*? If only you were here with me to meet your daughter.

We were escorted by local police to a waiting limousine when we landed, the heavy traffic heightening the tension. I can't believe the avid interest of the American media to track down a French *parfumier* racing to see her dying daughter. I've asked for privacy, but I'm big news here and the hoopla won't go away.

Emma assures me her people at WJJR are praying for us and will remain at a respectful distance here at the hospital, checking in with her for updates. I've promised them an exclusive when I'm ready.

For now, I want to see my child. Naomie Fleurine.

Judy to her family. My baby all grown up. I can't stop the tears from flowing as we're ushered to her private room. I wish Lance were here with me to meet his daughter. I miss him more than ever, his strong, quiet assurance giving me courage. My long journey isn't over... the hardest part is about to begin.

I know you're here, Maman.

Don't go. I need you.

* * *

Emma

'*Maman est ici, ma petite...* Mama's here,' *madame* whispers, taking Mom's hand in hers. Eyes closed, machines hooked up to her, *beeping*, the smell of antiseptic and a fake lemon-bleach scent permeates the piped-in air. My mother doesn't move, not even her little finger. A heavy sigh escapes *madame*'s lips. My heart breaks in two, a lasting pain these two women have to meet like this stabs my chest.

The nurses were in awe when we entered the private room, making way for *madame* as though she's visiting royalty. I smile. She is. She's the bravest woman I've ever known, along with my mom who tended to wounded soldiers under battlefield conditions... two strong women finally getting to know each other.

Madame embraced my dad, kissing him on both cheeks, then she stood tall and straight with reverence when she met my grandfather, the US Army captain who saved her baby and brought her to the States. She conveyed her gratitude with a big hug and it was the first time I saw this military man wipe away a tear.

He was eager to tell his story, how he was writing up a report about the babies born in Dachau... Unbelievably, he found four more besides the Hungarian babies when a young woman dressed in a tattered prison uniform demanded to see the officer in charge, that she had saved a baby from the SS when the mother was shot.

And the baby's father was American.

The only identification on the baby was a frayed blue ribbon tied around her chubby wrist.

My grandfather never told me because it didn't seem important.

While I digest this newest information, he recounts how the prisoner kept insisting the child's mother was Polish, muttering a name my grandfather couldn't understand, and confirming the American father. The Nazis had destroyed so many records in the camps, it was impossible to verify her story. Since the mother was dead, the army brass didn't follow up but, in good faith, they decided it was better to err on the side of caution – and avoid bad publicity – and granted my grandfather permission to adopt the child.

These two have a lot more catching up to do, but for now, *madame* wants to spend every moment with her daughter.

Watching the stubborn look on her face furrow her brow, knowing how vulnerable she is, I have to say something, *anything*, to give her hope.

'She hears you, *madame*.'

Madame de Cadieux looks up at me. 'How can you be sure?'

'She's crying.' I tilt my head, rub my mother's shoulders like I used to do when she came home from her shift at the VA hospital, exhausted but content to help the vets she adored. She'd close her eyes and tears would run down her cheeks, lost in memories of war and suffering.

I understand that now.

I fight back my own tears, my strong feelings escalating. We've been sitting at her bedside, *madame* speaking to Mom in her lovely French accent, telling her who she is... what happened to her in the camps... Auschwitz and Dachau... the night of her birth in a wooden hut, how she was forced to give up her baby by a cruel female SS guard when the Allies bombed their train... then how she escaped, fleeing into the forest with bullets whizzing around her head... then searching for her when the American soldiers took her to the Dachau main camp for processing. There was no trace of an SS woman with a baby... the pain it's caused her all these years. Then how I found her and she discovered I'm her granddaughter and the journey we've taken together that led us back here to her.

A light perspiration covers my mother's brow and her lips move. *Madame* leans in closer and the most beautiful smile lights up her face. 'Yes, I'm your *maman*.' A beat. Her lips move again. 'No, *ma petite,* I'm staying right here.'

Mom looks so peaceful... her eyes are closed, her lovely features soft and unlined, her beauty evident... her light hair grown out... she's wearing the pink-quilted satin bed jacket I gave her. Dad said she told her nurses she wasn't taking it off... that was before she lapsed into a final semi-conscious state.

We sit by her bedside every day for two weeks... nurses come and go... vitals checked... meds adjusted... Mom regains consciousness twice, then she drifts off. *Madame* tells her more stories about Paris... her perfumes... and always, how much she loves her.

Then, on a drizzly morning when a damp chill fills the room, Mom takes her last breath. Everything is still. The smell of bleach and anti-septic wiped away by our salty tears. The only scent lingering in the air is a soft lavender-vanilla. An essential oil I rubbed on my mother's hands.

Madame shudders uncontrollably when the nurse confirms her passing, but she doesn't let go of her daughter's hand. She wipes my mother's brow, her eyes solemn and shrinking to pinpoints, their hazel color darkening, her chin trembling, but it's her words I shall never forget.

'My daughter is with you now, Maman... the circle is complete. I held my baby when she came into this world in the camp and took her first breath. I thank God I'm here when she takes her last.'

50

LE CHÂTEAU DE CADIEUX, PARIS, 2004

Angéline

Perfume:
Emma Everlasting
Tangerine, Louis Phillipe rose, musk

'Go on, Madame de Cadieux, tell us about the war years and how you chased Nazis.'

I raise a brow. 'I didn't chase Nazis, *monsieur*, they chased *me*.' My TV interview isn't going well. Oh, Maman, why did I ever agree to allow the American film company into my château? Emma assured me it wouldn't take more than three days. It's day five. With the pouring rain outside, the crew brings more mud indoors than I've seen in fifty years.

My heart pounds as I smooth down the wool on my black coat. Yes, *that* coat. Lance hunted down Fräulein Schmidt and 'convinced' her to give it up. 'I was wearing this coat when the Gestapo cornered me in a cemetery in Montmartre. I barely escaped. My friend Yvette did not. She died in a Nazi prison.'

'*Whew*... that's quite a story, *madame*.' The director wipes his face. 'Not what I expected.'

'And what *did* you expect, *monsieur*?'

'You know... wild car chases though the streets of Paris with the Nazis racing after you. Intrigue. Romance. *Casablanca* with French fries.'

I heave out a deep breath. 'We had no motorcars in Paris during the war, *monsieur*. The Germans took the petrol.'

'Sit tight, *madame*. I've got an idea.' Frustrated, the director yells, 'Where's that history expert?'

'Here, sir.' A crisp British accent and cologne overload. A citrusy musk infused with too much sweet vanilla. I don't like this guy.

P R Kendall, Esquire, joins me and discusses the origins of Nazi Socialism, Hitler's master plan, and how the Nazi High Command requisitioned residences like my château – which it did not – but I dare not say so and ruin the take. The entire crew is watching: lighting, sound, makeup girl, costume people. They look bored. I'd be, too, if I were listening to this drivel.

What makes me sit through this interview is knowing the director will intercut it with scenes of the relaunch of *Le Courage* and World War II footage of Paris. The campaign was a huge success. Women from all over the world wrote to us about how much *Le Courage* inspires them to be who they are. How they love the idea of sharing and passing it on like we did in 1943. Emma insists the public wants to see more of me so here I am, but I don't like this stuffed shirt historian. He doesn't scratch the surface of the pain and suffering of the war years. I understand that doesn't sell soap, to quote my granddaughter, but we need something inspiring, strong... heartfelt, not his bland history lesson.

By the way, where is Emma? And Ryker?

Those two are rarely apart and I couldn't have been more pleased when Emma and Ryker made the official announcement of their plans to be married. Of course, I insisted we have the ceremony here at the château. I'm not too old to be a great-grandmama, I remind them. My heart pings, and I can't help but remember my lovely daughter, Naomie Fleurine. *Judy* to her family. For so many years I had an empty ache in my heart, but everything fell into place when I held her hand. I have Emma and her wild, crazy scheme to thank for that. If she hadn't been so bullheaded, I never would have found my baby daughter.

I thank God every day I had the chance to be with her. I hope Emma will come visit me often after she's married to my handsome bodyguard. They intend to divide their time between Paris and New York. Ryker promised me the best security detail in the business when he's not here... ex-MI6 agents who report directly to him.

Before I can start planning a wedding, I've got to get this interview over with. I grab the bottle of *Le Courage* sitting on the nearby table as the historian continues his lecture.

'Life in the concentration camp was difficult,' he says into camera. 'Prisoners were issued ill-fitting uniforms, endured food rationing... and had no toilet paper.' He smirks. I'd like to see *his* bare ass sitting on an open toilet hole next to grumbling prisoners on the other ninety-nine. 'The SS guards trained dogs to discipline the prisoners and beatings were not uncommon.'

He rambles on like a human textbook with me shaking my head until I can't take it anymore. 'Stop, please. This is wrong, *terribly* wrong.'

'I assure you, *madame*,' he says, indignant, 'my facts are accurate.'

'You sound like a robot.'

'Madame de Cadieux,' the director interrupts. 'Mr Kendall is an expert on Second World War European history in the camps.'

'Is he?' I raise my brows. 'I was there. He wasn't.' I turn to the historian, his puffy face red. 'I respect your knowledge, *monsieur*, but you don't know diddly squat about life in the camps. If you did, you'd be sobbing your eyes out.' I suck up the moment, figuring I'm sacked after my outburst.

Can they do that?

Now that I've started, I can't stop. 'For years when I remember my imprisonment in Auschwitz and Dachau, I believed it happened to someone else. It couldn't have been me who lived it because it was too unbelievably cruel and painful to remember. Sniffing dirty pots for a lick of stew or a tossed-away jar of raspberry jam so your tongue wouldn't forget the taste. Digging through the garbage in the SS kitchen for potato peelings to eat. The open toilets, the dead piled up. The stench, the filth... in the end, you adapted or you didn't survive.'

'Wow... I was wrong, *madame,* forgive me,' I hear the director muttering. 'Go on, please. Our viewers need to hear the incredible true story of what happened to you in the camps. Keep the camera rolling, Mac.'

I nod, then clear my throat. 'I'll never forget the humiliation. You no longer have a name. You're a number. Then there's the little things... the details that define life in the camps that you never forget... how the SS select you for work or death. If they send you left, you die. Right, you live. For a while. At Auschwitz, you get your number tattooed on your left arm, the ink mixing with your blood when they prick your skin with the long needle.'

I roll up my coat sleeve and show the viewers my number. With a Z. First time anywhere. I feel confident enough to expose my number with my family's support.

'Then come the showers where SS men stare at you naked, gauging your worth by whether or not your breasts sag, while a prisoner shaves every hair from your body. The thin uniform that hangs on you with your identification number sewn on it. Your yellow star or triangle, denoting your status. How your feet are always stuck in the mud, the scramble in total darkness trying to find a place to sleep in the barracks, fighting to get a bunk on the third tier because you have more air up there to breathe. Stealing a rag to cover your head because, after they cut off your hair, you don't realize how cold your head gets. As the weeks, months, go by with little to eat, you fight not to give up. You learn to bargain with your daily ration of bread and still, the selection process continues. Who will live, who will die. What hurts me most is seeing the children sent to die in the gas chamber without their parents. Alone. Frightened, crying, and calling for their *mamans*. It broke my heart.'

I pause a moment. *Silence*. No one moves. But I'm not finished.

'You never turn off the fear of dying in the camps. Praying you don't become one of *them*, those who lose their desire to live. You see the signs, the vacant expression on their faces, the way they shuffle along, then one day they don't turn up at roll call. And you know. Even if you *do* survive, you can never get back what you had. You give thanks and do your best to move forward. Because no matter how terrible things get, you want to live another day. And so I have. I'm one of the lucky ones. I have my family, my perfumes, and my garden, a place where I feel the sun on my face and the scent is sweet and pure. I made it home. Life is good... I'm safe. We must never forget the Holocaust, *mes amis*, but we must also never let it happen again.'

The crew breaks out into spontaneous applause that lasts for several minutes. I nod my thanks, tears welling up inside me, my heart singing that I'm finally free. Not of the memories, they'll always be with me and rightly so, but the fear, the frustration that no one would listen to me. No one would believe me.

They did. *Merci*.

I see Emma and Ryker standing off to the side, his arm around her, my granddaughter crying as I speak. They're like us, Lance. Crazy in love. I pray they have as many happy years as we did... and a hundred more.

I dab perfume on my wrists and sniff the lovely scent.

Lemony-peach, white velvet rose, oakmoss.

'I kept a blue ribbon doused with *Le Courage* with me at the camps. It made me remember how the art of perfume parallels life. The top note is the present... fleeting. The heart note is the past... your memories enriching your soul. And the base note is the future... ever enduring,' I say into camera. 'And so now I shall go hug my granddaughter and make plans for her wedding while we sit in my garden and smell the beautiful roses filling the air with their scent. *La vie est bon, n'est-ce pas?*' I smile into the camera. 'I'm Angéline de Cadieux... head *nose* for the House of Doujan,' I emphasize. '*Bonne nuit, mes amis.* Goodnight.'

'Cut! That's a print,' yells the director, wiping his brow.

Emma races to my side and hugs me, then whispers in my ear, her sweet breath smelling of peppermint and kisses. 'You were amazing, *madame.*'

Ryker nods. 'I'm proud to work for you, *madame.*' He turns to my granddaughter. 'You're also part of my job, Emma, seeing how you're family.'

'Does this mean I get to order you around?' she teases.

He grins. 'It means you'll never get rid of me.'

'I can live with that.' She wraps her arms around his neck and gives him a big kiss. The simple joy of seeing them together, the wonderful closeness they enjoy warms me.

I swoon. 'You two make this old woman feel young again.'

I lean back, close my eyes and I see Maman and Lance. Yvette and Professor Zunz. And my baby daughter, smiling at me.

I'll be here for a while. For as long as my family needs me.

ACKNOWLEDGMENTS

War is hell.

But what does it smell like? The acrid smoke pouring out of bombed-out buildings comes to mind, gritty soldiers on the move... the copper-tinged odor of blood... burnt gunpowder. The deep stench of death that seeps into your pores like invisible maggots.

We rarely think of the lush scent of a red rose or the freshness of a white gardenia blowing in the breeze.

Yet they co-exist, even in war...

I wanted to bring the two together in a story about the Paris Occupation.

What if a young Frenchwoman with a unique gift for scent created a beautiful perfume that gave women courage during the war? Then she's sent to a concentration camp where she endures the foulest smells of human despair that test her *own* courage.

Enter Angéline de Cadieux.

Once I had my heroine, I delved into the art of perfume and what it takes to be a 'nose'. I worked as a perfume model once upon a time and had the opportunity then to be introduced to the industry. I've used that knowledge and experience to shape her story.

My biggest challenge was writing about the Holocaust. Where do I begin? There are numerous books on the subject, but I found the truest source to be the survivors themselves. Thank you to each of them, who over the years with the help of Holocaust organizations, recorded their stories for future generations.

I listened to hours and hours of testimony of what they endured in the camps, not only Jewish survivors, but also Roma. Angéline is Roma and I wanted to bring the amazing story of the Romani people into the fold of the Holocaust experience. I also relied on books, newspaper articles, and letters published from those who survived and those who didn't.

And lastly, yes, there were seven Hungarian babies born to Jewish mothers in Kaufering I at Dachau in late 1944–early 1945. I thought, why not eight? So I added Angéline and her child to tell their story.

Shaping the story and bringing that research to life falls to the writer... but we all need a guiding hand to make it sparkle. Thank you to my editor, Nia Beynon, for her patience and understanding and her special gift to see into this writer's heart and know the story I wanted to tell.

Also, thank you to Cecily Blench, my copy editor, and Candida Bradford, my proofreader, for their expertise and diligence in their work.

And to everyone at Team Boldwood, an amazing group of professional women who work tirelessly to give their authors support, guidance... and most of all, a sense of family. Thank you!

Jina Bacarr

MORE FROM JINA BACARR

We hope you enjoyed reading *The Lost Girl in Paris*. If you did, please leave a review.

If you'd like to gift a copy, this book is also available as an ebook, digital audio download and audiobook CD.

Sign up to Jina Bacarr's mailing list for news, competitions and updates on future books.

http://bit.ly/JinaBacarrNewsletter

The Resistance Girl, another sweeping World War 2 novel from Jina Bacarr, is available to order now.

ABOUT THE AUTHOR

Jina Bacarr is a US-based historical romance author of over 10 previous books. She has been a screenwriter, journalist and news reporter, but now writes full-time and lives in LA. Jina's novels have been translated into 9 languages.

Visit Jina's website: https://jinabacarr.wordpress.com/

Follow Jina on social media:

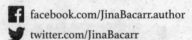 facebook.com/JinaBacarr.author
twitter.com/JinaBacarr
 instagram.com/jinabacarr
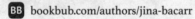 bookbub.com/authors/jina-bacarr

Boldw∞d

Boldwood Books is an award-winning fiction publishing company seeking out the best stories from around the world.

Find out more at www.boldwoodbooks.com

Join our reader community for brilliant books, competitions and offers!

Follow us
@BoldwoodBooks
@BookandTonic

Sign up to our weekly deals newsletter

https://bit.ly/BoldwoodBNewsletter